FROM GREY

BOOK 1 OF THE **OUTPOST WAR**

BY LISA ARCONA

ISBN: 979-8-9917630-3-5

Cover design by: Lisa Langenhop Designs, llc.

Made in the United States of America

BOOK 1 OF THE **OUTPOST WAR**

BY LISA ARCONA

I DEDICATE THIS BOOK,
WITH LOVE AND APPRECIATION,
TO ALL THOSE HUMANS
OF THE PAST AND PRESENT
WHO HAVE SACRIFIED OF THEMSELVES
IN ORDER TO END THE SUFFERING
OF ANOTHER HUMAN.

IF I AM NOT
WHAT YOU SAY I AM,
THEN YOU ARE NOT
WHO YOU THINK YOU ARE.

JAMES BALDWIN

RECORD HAC-3859385738*

IntraCache (Universal) – Historical Archive Designation :

This document is intended for public usage and publication as requested.
Direct reproduction and attribution only.

*Archivists' Note :

This document was received 140.123.414 (*Lūnar Date : December 1, 3011 / Pictor Date : 6.32.191*) into the official archives and was reviewed and accepted for public access. It documents firsthand experiences during the Outpost War of the Pictor Star System and several individuals with influential roles in the outcome, including Hettie Thurgood and First Statesman Nolin Hodgins 7, both considered heroes of the Outpost War (OW). Readers Note: The events of the OW occurred in the remote Pictor System over fifty megas before the submission of this account. Many of the dates, events, and characters can be corroborated by other records and documents within the Historical Archive, but the personal narrative, while highly compelling, cannot be decisively substantiated.

Letter of Intent *(Included with original submission on 140.123.414)* :

To the Archivists,

I lived during a time of greatness. I bore witness to bravery and sacrifice, love and loss, compassion and forgiveness. Now I choose to record some of that greatness which was demonstrated by my friends and chosen family, particularly the histories of my friend Hettie Thurgood, who, before and during the ugly Outpost War, changed the lives of hundreds both directly, in the form of salvation, and indirectly, in the form of inspiration. Her adventures and stalwart personality should never be forgotten or left to the interpretation of later generations. I, who first met her in my youth, already see the collective memories atrophying during these times of peace.

Our stories, along with the personal stories Hettie related to me during our friendship, are recorded here exactly as I remember them. The greatness of Hettie and many others rose into requirement because of astounding injustice, brutal inhumanities, and blatant misuse of Earthens living in the early Outposts. For too long, the Earthens suffered at the hands of those who had the power to make them suffer.

I write now so that we never forget the darkness of which humans are capable, to humble us to power's influence, and to inspire everyone to prevent the future affliction of any and every human being.

Our work is not done.

With sincerity,
Araminta (Minty) Bradford 8 of Shamong, Attis, Pictor System, known by some as Agent Grey

CHAPTER 1 :
ALWAYS BACK TO THE FARM

BE STRONG…BE SMART…WHATEVER happens, choose well.

Those were the last words my mother spoke to me. She said them with both hands pressed against the wall of her quarantine room. Through the thick glass, she stared at me with tawny-brown eyes. Her eyes were all that I still recognized of my loving mother; the rest of her body had changed too much. Just like my father, she was being slowly destroyed by her illness.

She wanted to say more, but the coughs and wheezing that had plagued her for cycles did not allow it. Instead she fell back into her chair and fought for breath. I stayed with her as long as the ABEs allowed it.

Later that night, I fell asleep alone, in my parents' bed, clinging to the memory of their presence as cold fear consumed me. Urgent noises from my Aide woke me before dawn, and the ping told me that my mother was gone. I cried in their bed for two days. Only Linah tended to me. *Stars,* I was just 14 megas old then.

Sometimes I liked to imagine what else my mother wanted to say: maybe anecdotes about the Farm, or happy memories that we had shared, or all the wisdom contained in the mind of a mother for her daughter. Whatever script I wrote for her in my imagination, it ended with a simple 'love you, Minty-girl.'

Be strong. Be smart. Whatever happens, choose well.

Choose well. Her profound words often came to mind at trivial times. *Choose well, Minty,* I thought as I scanned the flavor options at the street vendor in front of me. The crunchy algae sticks could be dusted with flavor powders like Sweet and Tart, Savory Vegetable, Simply Salted, or Fruitiest Fruit.

I was actually ordering my second algae stick since I completed my deliveries. Despite my embarrassment, the vendor ushered me to the front of the line after he noticed the glowing dots on my inner wrist. All eight of them.

I blushed at the special treatment and because of my multiple snack purchases. But the awkwardness was not enough to stop me. During the last few cycles, food tasted good again.

And it had been a while. Since my parents' reentering, I ran the Farm. Just me. In a frantic sort of trial-by-error process, I learned the quotas, the processes, the timing, the execution. I figured it out, but it took everything. With the stress, and grief, I lost weight. I lost friends. I lost my place in the world.

Two difficult megas later, I operated the Farm in perfectly composed cycles. I labored all day and finished work around sunsdown, dead tired, and prepared to do it all again the next day. Every day, the same. Every cycle, the same. That way, I never had time to think too hard about anything.

The Fruitiest Fruit stick crunched between my teeth as I sat on a smooth bench that faced the main street of my settlement, Shamong City. The second stick tasted as good as the first. Should I get a third? I imagined the snack dissipating in my body and coating my ribs with a soft, warm layer where there had once been only been a pattern of protruding bones.

A farmer should like food, I told myself. *I should be exceptionally pro-food.*

I had done it. I kept the Farm functioning, and suddenly food tasted really good. Maybe things might be okay. My heart clenched in betrayal, not wanting to forget my parents and my loss. I could not let myself feel too much. Things were stable, and I could not let it all fall apart. The Farm was all I had now.

The passersby offered a distraction to my unwelcome inner thoughts. The Attisians of my settlement seemed busy that day; they traveled down the road in their neutral work clothes, their dark tan skin completely covered, always combating the suns' damaging radiation. I knew that under their hoods, various shades and textures of brunette hair framed tawny-brown eyes just like my mother's.

I blinked rapidly, self-consciously, remembering the light grey color of my own eyes that was so different from my fellow settlers.

The settlers around me shopped, worked, bustled, and interacted with one another as I watched them: speaking, laughing, gesturing. They had quite a lot to say to one another. I only spoke to Linah anymore, and even then it was just about the Farm. Before the thought could make me feel too sorry for myself, I tossed the empty snack wrapper in a reentering bin and grabbed my trackbasket.

It was time to head back to the Farm. Always back to the Farm.

CHAPTER 2 :
NOT TO LAST

I MANEUVERED MY EMPTY BASKET onto the transport track that ran through the middle of the street. I rode a familiar pattern of splits and turns, until my basket and I reached the outskirts of town and found my unobtrusive, disregarded track that ascended up the hillside.

Only Linah and I used that tiny track. It led to unfinished ecosystems, risk of extra radiation exposure, my Farm, and, at the very end, the outer Boundary of Shamong City proper. So no one but us had any reason to ride it.

I trudged beside my track basket as the pitched ground beneath my feet went from the organized glass and bamboo grids of the city to prairie grasses, then sparsely spaced shrubs, then unedited rocks and boulders. The pale, grey light from the descending suns touched the peaks of the mountain range that wound around my growing settlement.

A familiar beep from my Aide reminded me to pull the hood of my dark grey radiation jacket over my head. The radiation risk grew outside of town—nothing like beyond the Boundary, where there was no artificial atmosphere at all—but my Aide sensed the increased levels and warned me to protect myself.

Though potentially destructive, the sunslight acted very prettily as it flashed on the smooth glass structure of my Farm in the distance. Other Farms sparkled across the dull landscape far to my left and right. Those glass Farms, all identical to mine, functioned far above the deep and shadowed valley I had just left, harnessing whatever growing power they could from the high elevations.

Finally at the end of the track, I trekked the remaining distance to my front door and hauled the trackbasket to its regular, convenient place. It would rest there until the morning after next, when I would refill it with a fresh harvest and repeat my trip to town.

All was quiet at the Farm, as usual. Except for the brief brush with my emotions that I had allowed myself in town, that day was just like all the others.

But it was not to last. The normalcy I had so carefully crafted was about to come crashing down. No, to implode. In a big way. Because close by, something truly horrible was happening. Something that went against the very principals of my Society and my own conscience. Something that was about to change my life forever.

That night, as I made my way inside the Farm, I only had one thing on my mind. Dinner. Despite the double snack in town, I was still hungry.

CHAPTER 3 :

BEYOND MY PREVIOUS EXPERIENCE

AGAIN, I HEARD HER. GROANING grouchily, I rolled over and attempted to return to my dreamless sleep.

Linah's efforts to leave me undisturbed in the early morning hours while she snuck in and out were commendable but unsuccessful. I slept lightly in that generous space designed for a whole family and woke to any irregular noise. Even the soft brush of Linah's feet on the glass floor tiles or the running of the faucet could wake me.

Something heavy bumped the wall, and I scrunched my nose in apprehension. It was not necessarily fear that made me vigilant at night: it was responsibility. A quick response from me meant the difference between a lost crop or a salvaged one. At 16-megas-old, I was technically still too young for formal emancipation, but because of my family legacy and influence, I was allowed to stay on the Farm. Besides, very few people had the right to tell an 8 what to do, even an unconventional 8 like me.

So it came down to me. It was a heavy responsibility, but I had willingly chosen it. After my parents died, the alternative was housing, advanced education, grooming, and social obligations under the supervision of my elitist uncle. No, I preferred my quiet but taxing life on the Farm to that.

Linah, my Earthen Bonder, lived and worked on my Farm under my direction and she often disappeared in the night when I did not require her. But she was typically quiet about it. Sneaky. That night, Linah was downright noisy: shuffling, the occasional muted clink or bump, running water.

Instead of settling back into sleep, my senses activated one by one, and before long, I felt regrettably alert. I gruffly disentangled myself from bed and peered into the hall, where I could see Linah's cracked door. The sounds of her distress bounced around the sterile glass hallway. The noises were punctuated by another sound: sobs. Linah was crying. Stoic Linah was crying hard.

My eyes widened as my brow furrowed. I pressed a hand to my heart as it beat faster.

Nervously, I crossed the hall to Linah's private room, feeling my adrenaline mount and ready to tackle whatever was afflicting Linah. But as I pushed open the door and scanned her modest quarters, I realized the situation was far beyond any of my previous experience.

Linah's typically organized bedroom, now disarrayed, harbored two bodies.

One was Linah. She frantically wrapped strips of her woven bed sheets around the second body's torso–a boy I had never seen before but instantly knew to be Earthen. He, around age nine or ten, was shirtless and bleeding. Bleeding everywhere. Long red lines slashed through the blue and black of his numerous tattoos, disrupting the skin of each limb and muscle, and even his face. He appeared unconscious but for the occasional opening and rolling of his overly large, pale eyes, and the involuntary twitches of his lean muscles. Around one wrist, a hot red band of ripped skin and blisters marked where his SubAide should have been. It looked as though it had been hacked away in clumsy desperation.

The horror of his injuries immobilized me for a long moment. I knew of no machine or chemical that could make such consistent, ferocious marks, but I kept hoping to recall one. No. Another human had done that. Another human had done that to a child, and I choked on the sting of bile in my throat.

"Leave." Linah broke my dismayed trance with a voice both stricken and resolute. Her sobs and administrations began again so quickly that I doubted she had spoken at all, but it set me in motion again. I dropped to my knees beside her, coercing another strip of bedclothes into a bandage for a large laceration on the boy's leg.

"No! Leave," Linah ordered. She squared up to me, her face barely inches from my shoulder, but I did not take the time to understand her expression. I only had attention for the atrocity in front of us.

"I'll get the big wounds wrapped," I calculated. "Then while you disinfect, I'll call Health. They can be here within a few millis for something like this, I think. Maybe sooner if–"

I stopped speaking when Linah grabbed my wrists and forcefully threw them away from the boy. Undoubtedly, my surprise showed. To my recollection, Linah and I had never once touched before. Her pallid skin was blazing hot.

"Let me get the disinfectant," I pressed on, confused.

"Mx. Bradford, no! No!" Linah screeched. She saw my growing disbelief and added, "Don't be involved. Do not call anyone. If you truly want to help, do not tell anyone. Ever. You don't understand what you are doing." Abruptly she returned to wrapping the boy's wounds and sobbing. Her assertive tone shocked me. Bonders never addressed their Taskers that way, especially a Tasker who was also an 8.

"But this boy— just look at him! He needs more than you can give him!" As I said this, I reached again for the cloth bandages. What followed can only be described as a tussle between two determined young people, both convinced that they are doing right. I considered myself fit, spry, and capable, but Linah's quickness and Earthen strength outmaneuvered me. I tried to grab the bandages and Linah forced me away each time. Soon both of my wrists were held tightly in front of me while Linah demanded my gaze. I gave up in shock.

"Mx. Bradford. Araminta. Please. Please." She emphasized each word one at a time. "Please forget all of this. Leave. If you tell anyone, they will take him away from me. They will send him back!"

"Back where?"

"Back to his quarry. Back to the people who did this." Her voice almost vanished in horror by the end of her statement. My eyes darted between Linah and the boy. He was Earthen. He probably labored at one of the many silicone quarries nearby, and he had been dreadfully abused. Could anyone but his Tasker have the power to perpetrate such an act? Revulsion twisted my stomach upside and downside and back again.

I sputtered, "S-surely no one would send him back after this."

"Of course they will, Mx. Bradford 8." Linah's eyes pleaded for my understanding through her cascading tears. I knew our Law, or parts of it, but Linah's claims were outrageous. Our creed even said "abhor acts of violence." Surely such overt cruelty forfeited ownership. No one would send this boy back to be treated this way again, even though he was Earthen, and even if it was his Tasker who hurt him. We did not condone violence on Attis. Never.

There were other alternatives for this boy, there had to be. But with my next breath, I was too afraid to act against Linah's impassioned opinion. Our Laws were for Outposters. Were they applied the same way to Earthens? Doubt kept me quiet for the time.

"Yes. Yes, all right," I resolved as the boy moaned. "I won't call. But we'd better work fast. No more shoving me away." A sob of relief escaped her, and we started methodically working together to save the boy. "What is his name?"

"This is my brother, Vesey."

CHAPTER 4 :
HELLO THERE, LAW-BREAKER

A LONG TIME PASSED BEFORE I stood again, joints cracking. We had done it, or at least we had done it as well as we could in the deep of the night, with torn bamboo cloth and no Health training. The Earthen boy still sweated, swelled, twitched, and groaned, but at least his wounds were covered. Instead of a boy made of leaking red welts, he was a boy made of fabric swaths.

Linah coaxed pain medication down her brother's throat as she tenderly stroked the uninjured portions of his forehead. I heard the tones of a lullaby between her rushed breaths. The song must have been ancient or Earthen because the words held no meaning for me: rain, wind, spring.

As I watched the two of them, the brother and sister, my adrenaline leaked away and left me in a cold shock and a darkening mood. This beaten Earthen boy. In my house. My thoughts swirled in a frenzy so blurred and complex that I could hardly identify them, let alone make them useful to me.

So far, the only witnesses to our misconduct were the innumerable stars above, casting mild shadows on the smooth tiles of the floor and walls. The silent stars offered only false security, because as the suns rose and the day arrived, the boy would still be in my house. A secret. A dangerous secret. *Oh, shek.*

I stumbled to Linah's washing sink. In the flow of warm water, I rinsed my bloodied hands, shaking, shaking. The ashy glass of the washbasin turned red and pink as the boy's blood sluiced from my skin and drained away. I wanted to throw up. My hands. His blood. *Don't panic, Minty,* I told myself. *Solve the problem. Plan. Treat it like any other day on the Farm. Choose well.* But my heartbeats kept pummeling my chest and lungs, and I could not think.

Above Linah's faucet hung a simple mirror, and the movement of my reflection startled me into looking. My silver eyes–Lūnar eyes from my father–

peered back at me, distorted slightly by the sweat still clinging to my eyelashes. My hair that was always unruly now curled and frizzed in every direction. A faint smear of blood crossed my broad nose and faded into my bronze cheek. My features all remained in the correct places and with correct colors, but I hardly recognized myself. I was looking at a memory of a different girl – a girl who did not break the Law and hide brutalized Earthens in her bedrooms. *Hello there, Law-Breaker.* I tried to swallow down a mass of sticky guilt in my throat that was mixing unpleasantly with the panic.

"We just need a plan." I watched the lips of the strange girl in the mirror form my words and preach to me in my voice. The disconnect made me feel more agitated. Linah's meaningless lullaby, along with the boy's horrible cries and groans, chipped away at my faculties. I turned and darted toward the door, more like a crazy person than the rational and capable almost-adult I tried so hard to be.

My hand reached the textured glass handle that would lead me out of the room just as Linah called my name, "Mx. Bradford. 8." I stilled at the sound of her, tightening my grip on the handle, my body telegraphing how badly and immediately I wanted to escape.

Linah's abundant tears cut two rivers through the dirt and blood smeared on her cheeks. Even on normal days, I sometimes found Linah quite unnerving. Her light yellow hair, pale cerulean eyes, and shy expressions gave her a luminous appearance. She was the flesh-and-bone phantom that haunted my Farm, not unwelcome, but not knowable either. That night, the raw emotions carved into her incandescent features almost prevented me from being able to meet her gaze.

"Please, Mx. Bradford 8." Her eyes were ice and blue flame all at once. "Please, please don't tell anyone." We stared at one another for a moment, her gaze intense and purposeful, mine conflicted, both of us nearly crushed by the possible consequences of our recent actions.

With my mind so tumultuous, my heart took over without formal permission. I knew what I was going to say just a moment before the words spilled out. "Fine. I won't tell anyone tonight. But we need to figure something out. This is bad, Linah. What were you thinking?! We've got to make a plan."

In a startlingly nimble movement, Linah rose and clasped my hand gently with hers, smearing more of Vesey's blood onto my freshly cleaned skin, and squeezed slightly. She brought our hands toward her heart in gratitude. That amiable gesture, out of everything that had happened that night, coaxed a sob to my chest. Her touch felt like electricity. No one had touched me with affection or kindness in a long time, and it shook me. I blinked at her through watery eyes.

"He's my brother. I would do anything for him." Linah whispered. "Thank you. Your silence might save him. I know how much I am asking. I know. Thank you."

And just as deftly, she returned her attention to her brother. My hand felt colder than the rest of me without her fingers covering it. I thought our conversation was done, but when most of my body was out of the room, Linah spoke again.

"Mx. Bradford 8..." Her tone sounded hesitant, and her eyes flashed in my direction. "People know that Vesey is my baby brother. I think...Well, I think it's possible that, if they look for him, they will look for me. Here."

I froze as a new wave of dread passed through my fatigued muscles and left them tingling.

Linah went on, certainty returning to her words. "I hope I'm wrong, but it's fair to tell you. We, both of us, need to decide what we are willing to do."

I finally left that room of violence and unknowns. In the open space of my Day Room, I paced, unable at first to hold still. My nerves flared at every noise. My heart sprinted at each turn of my mind.

Eventually, when my feet ached, I lay down, right across the threshold of my front door, like the guard animals at the quarries and factories. I did not know what else to do. My body ached for sleep, and that location, though uncomfortable, would at least give me the earliest warning of danger. Danger. It was not a word I was accustomed to using.

As sleep came and went, came and went, in my comfortless position, Linah's last words replayed like a loop in my mind.

What was I willing to do?

CHAPTER 5 :

TWO CUPS OF HOT KEFF

THE SUNS ROSE TOO SOON on that next desperate and bewildering day. Despite my intermittent fits of sleep, I could not bridle my distress. The mounting daylight glinted through the perfect glass tiles of the walls around me, and made the day look far more cheerful than it was. My Aide pinged incessantly and demanded that I begin my typical morning routine. Apparently, as advanced as Aide technology was, it remained unaware that my day was far from typical.

Perfectly projected alerts shone from the eight golden, glowing dots on the inside of my wrist.

ALERT : Greens harvest with minimum measurement 4cm, Bins 15–21

07:45 : Rotate Farm Level Two 90 degrees for optimal growth

ALERT : Seed trays three, five, and six are below moisture optimum

08:30 : Store dried Chia and harvest replacements in Bin 28

I cleared the alerts one by one with a practiced swipe of my finger. I knew them by heart and routine anyway. I groaned as I stumbled toward the kitchen on the far side of the Day Room. All its colorless surfaces were cool and smooth and were as familiar to me as my own skin. I wanted to take comfort in this constancy, but nothing felt right. I felt dirty, guilty, drained, jittery, tired. I felt everything.

From a high shelf, I grabbed a vial of Keff powder, popped off the top unceremoniously, and poured the contents directly into my mouth, not even bothering to mix it with my favorite oat cream. With a well-practiced motion, I mindlessly tossed the empty vial into the reentering bin. The powder coated the inside of my mouth, bitter and delicious. I guzzled some fresh water right out of the faucet and waited for the chemicals in the Keff to give me a jolt of alertness. When it did not come immediately, I repeated the process.

Just as the powder entered my mouth, the Earthen boy wailed. Startled into an intake of breath, I had to cough out clumps of barely-moistened Keff as I hustled to Linah's room. The boy, Vesey, was too loud. Way too loud. If anyone stood at the door, or in the Day Room, or anywhere in the Farm for that matter, there would be no keeping our secret.

"Linah! He has got to be quiet!" I burst into Linah's small bedroom for the second time in just a few hours, wiping brownish Keff dust from my chin. The boy, so helpless and small, lay in the bed, unconscious, sweat darkening his bright hair, but Linah was not beside him.

"Sheking stars," I murmured to myself. "Linah!" I shouted. I turned abruptly back toward the hall, where I proceeded to crash right into her. Once again, her strength surpassed mine, and I stumbled a few steps back into her room. The circles under Linah's eyes looked almost purple now, muting the icy color of her eyes. There was soil on her fingers.

"Linah! Where were you?" I rubbed the shoulder that had taken the force our of impact.

She eyed me, exhausted and suspicious. "Working," was her simple reply, devoid of any Earthen accent. Linah spoke Common better than most Earthens.

"Working?" I flipped my wrist upward in the manner that activated my Aide to display the date, time, and recent notifications, and I confirmed the early hour. "Did you sleep at all?"

"To keep Vesey a secret, we have to look like nothing has happened. We can't be late, we can't miss anything. So, working."

Linah surprised me again. I resented her for introducing the problem of her brother, for breaking our perfect routine, and for the distress of the last hours, but it did soothe me that she understood the gravity of the situation enough to exert herself to mitigate the damage. I could not help but admire her lucidity amid such an ordeal. I always believed that Linah was smart for an Earthen, but perhaps she was just plain smart.

I eyed her, considering. Linah and I had become a strong team on the Farm. She seemed to share my appreciation for clear expectations and meticulous planning. Back at the beginning, Linah was the only one to bring me food when I had forgotten to eat. Linah insisted that I get out of bed. Linah let me cry as I worked without saying a thing. Everything she did was quiet, but firm.

Though we were similar in age, our differences were too great for much connection beyond the Farm. She was Bound to me, and she was, of course, Earthen. Earthens and Outposters never had much to say to one another.

Outposters had built a sustainable Society, a noble one, that was just at the dawn of its success. But long ago Earthens had destroyed their Society, and it had crumbled into a bleak nonexistence. Since their last wars, nothing good came from the planet of Earth. Nothing except the Bonders that did difficult jobs in the Outposts. But Linah...

"That's...um, that's a very good idea. Thanks," I managed. A better Tasker might have issued a reprimand or list of demands for Linah next, but I fostered a growing suspicion that Linah had the stronger mind for our current predicament. I watched her blink slowly at my expression of appreciation. She looked truly wretched. "You must feel terrible right now, Linah. Of course, you do. How else are you supposed to feel after last night? Hold on."

I shuffled back into the kitchen and made two cups of Keff, correctly this time with hot oat cream, and returned to hand one to Linah. She reached up from her seat beside her brother to grab it. Her bony fingers seemed impossibly grungy against the smooth curves of the opaque glass cup.

"So where do we go from here, Linah?" I queried while I stood awkwardly nearby and blew the steam off my Keff.

Again, she only blinked at me. In strained silence, we considered each other and our developing arrangement. I certainly saw Linah differently than yesterday: a girl so full of love that she argued with her Tasker and stayed up all night to save her brother: a girl that possibly possessed a brain and body strong enough to find a way through her mess. Linah's eyes flickered as her thoughts rearranged about me as well: a Tasker who allowed her brother to stay, who fought to save his life, and who just made her a cup of hot Keff.

I rubbed my eyes with the heels of my hands. Our situation was absurd. Linah's insistence that I avoid Health and any evidence whatsoever of her brother's presence made me wonder what she feared so fiercely. She did not want her brother sent back to whoever had hurt him, which I understood well enough. But would Linah be in trouble with the Law as well?

I wondered what might await them both if I alerted the Law to their presence. Possibly extra labor, debt, or even deportation to the Mid-Lats, but these were just guesses on my part. And surely the Law would do nothing, at least to Linah, without my permission anyway, not with my status as an 8.

I wracked my brain to remember the few rumors I had heard long ago about rogue Bonders. The memories were buried deep, from a time when all I cared about was finding my own way through the world. I knew there was likely a Lawful punishment or consequence, but I never heard what kind. I never cared about the consequences before I was hoping to avoid them.

Just as our silence grew long enough to feel embarrassing, another moan from the boy reminded me of my initial concern. "Linah, he's too loud."

Linah nodded as she swilled a sip of the hot liquid around her tongue. I could not tell if she liked it, until she upended the cup into her open mouth and guzzled half the mug. "I like the way this makes me feel," she explained.

With my eyes wide to their maximum, I could not help but smile a tiny bit. "Yeah. Me too."

"Do you still have the key to Mx. Alan Bradford 1's room?" she blurted, a bit too abruptly.

My expression fell quickly into a glare. Linah noticed my darkened aura and tried to hide the apprehension she felt at speaking my father's name, but those crystalline eyes of hers gave everything away.

It hurt me to hear his name aloud. I had not spoken his name, or my mother's, during those long megas. I buried my eyes with my fists and attempted to focus on the plan that Linah's question implied: Linah wanted to house her brother in my father's old laboratory.

My father built his laboratory before I was old enough to remember it. Under the amused supervision of my mother, he used native rocks and repurposed furniture from our living spaces so that no record of the room existed. My father designed it for concealment. The experiments he did there were not Society-sanctioned, not exactly.

"I'm sorry to bring it up..." Linah began, but I held up a hand to stop her.

"Another good idea," I mumbled and tried to mean it. The problem was that I did not want to go in there. Surely if spirits existed, my father would be in that room, hunched over his worktable, his silver-grey eyes glittering with the joy of growing things. It seemed poetic, or possibly ironic, to hide my biggest secret within the walls of his biggest secret.

I motioned for Linah to follow me back into the kitchen. Reluctantly, I opened one of the smoky grey drawers. Behind some rarely used flatware, my fingers discovered the key exactly where he had abandoned it. I examined the key under the sunslight and frowned; it seemed smaller than it should be in my hand.

"I still have the key." I blew out a long breath. "Let's get this over with."

CHAPTER 6 :
EFFICIENT, PURPOSEFUL, CONTROLLED

LINAH FOLLOWED ME LIKE AN inverted shadow as I passed through the short hallway that opened into my growing spaces. My crops grew in a vast cylindrical enclosure with two floors underground, where mushrooms and herbs received minimal UV from the solar light core, and five floors above ground that rotated to best absorb the natural light of our suns. We walked along a thin path between spiraled planting beds that allowed Linah and I to harvest, treat, and maintain the food crops. Unlike most of our planet at this stage of manipulation, all was bright and green and alive in my Farm.

I admired my potato plants, the tops all perfectly spaced from one another and growing at identical rates. Efficient, purposeful, controlled. In an Outpost, every input and output was monitored, recorded, and improved upon.

The wet and musky smell of the Farm made my fingers eager to tend my plants, but we had to handle the boy first. I led Linah through my supply room of chemicals, tools, and a cycle's supply of freshly manufactured soil. The back wall of the supply room should have been the end of the structure, but instead, on one glass wall panel, an unobtrusive cloth handle hid the small apparatus of the lock. I pressed the key to the lock and roughly slid the panel aside.

We ducked inside, and I gasped despite my best efforts: my father's secret laboratory.

My Lūnar father, though he found some solace in the life of an Attisian farmer, could never quite tame his enthusiasm for plants of all kinds. It was a quirky obsession according to our Society standards, but during his youth on Lūn, he intended to study the biology of plants. There was a fancy name for it that I could not remember. Unfortunately for him, his family's business required interstellar travel far too often to commit to a university. Megas later, after partnering with my mother on her Attisian Outpost, he experimented the best he could in his secret, homemade room.

When he lived, small sprouts covered every shelf, stacks of notations covered every counter. Once he even managed to grow some bright pink blossoms, a jarring color for Attis, for my mother. She wore them in her hair until they wilted to mushy brown. Soil on Attis was always in short supply, and the water was carefully metered by the ABEs. I did not understand how he managed any of it.

As I entered with Linah, the room was neglected and eerily unmoving. Because of the pristine, synthetic atmosphere of the planet, nothing in the room had changed except where something had decayed or desiccated. Everything was brown and grey, like the rest of our planet. Except one thing.

I smelled it, before I saw it. It infused the air of the narrow space with a uniquely spicy, lively scent. I would know that scent anywhere: tomato leaves. Tucked behind the door, in a patch of sunslight, a single wild and gangly tomato plant shot its fronds left and right and mostly downward, spilling over its trough, weighted by an abundance of strangely misshapen fruits. Old fruits cracked and rotted on the floor beneath it.

But these were not the perfect red tomato fruits I grew on the Farm. The interloper presented totally unlike the nutritious, predictable, and productive plants that grew several levels up in my Farm.

These tomatoes were orange but streaked through with hot red. Never had I seen an orange tomato before. Some ancient gene expressed itself, unbidden.

I forgot everything but that remnant of my father's work. I marveled that the plant had survived in that empty space, alone, for more than two megas. Upon examination, I found a single hose gently dripping water into the trough that supported the plant. Realization came in an instant; my father had pirated our irrigation system. Through the megas, I had been unknowingly watering this unruly plant.

I rolled one of the small, streaked tomatoes between my fingers before picking it off the vine.

"Mx. Bradford 8?" I startled and dropped the freakish fruit. Linah asked as she shoved several partially decomposed containers to the far wall, "can Vesey stay here?"

I shrugged my approval. There was enough space. There was enough secrecy. There was even water. I felt a vague satisfaction at finding a safer place to hide Vesey, but it was one problem of a thousand for the day.

My Aide pinged loudly in the undersized room. This time the notification flashed red: unusual moisture levels in some of the lower bins.

I tried to get my feelings back under my control, to somehow remember and trust in the regular, regimented plans for each day. I turned away from the tomato plant and shivered, my body physically trying to shake the shock and grief away. I had to. I did not know what else to do.

"Let's get back to work, Linah."

She nodded resolutely but with what might have passed as compassion in her eyes.

15 MEGAS AGO

Supplemental excerpt from : Making a Way ; the Life and Stories,
Record HAC-3859385738

The eight-mega-old child knew that the tiny, shiny, red tomatoes piled in a huge bowl on the pristine counter were not for her.

Being an Earthie, bound to the greedy Tasker of a massive bamboo homestead, she ate only inexpensive algae products. Algae bars. Algae soup. Algae mash. Brownish, greenish, tasteless algae. She survived all right on algae, as did the other Earthen Bonders on the homestead; she had even developed muscles that rivaled boys her age, but always she felt hungry. Always.

The rumblings echoing in her stomach made her jealous and so very curious. She had never tasted a tomato. No one was there in the room with her. Her Tasker would never miss just one...

The tomato popped open under the pressure of her teeth. She had no idea there was juice inside those little spheres. The juice! Sweet and sharp and amazing. She stopped moving. She maybe stopped breathing. She closed her eyes and tried to savor every last molecule.

Until the spoon whacked her in the cheek, she didn't know that her Tasker had caught her. The woman threw the girl against the nearest wall so that she fell to her knees, exposing her neck and back to the very angry, very strict, very ugly mistress.

"Since you already helped yourself to my food, you and your family will be excluded from tonight's meal, you ungrateful 'log. You do not steal from me."

The fluffy, puffy, enraged woman struck her again and again on the back. The girl cried with pain and anger. It was unfair. She was the hungry one. The Tasker was large and flabby and didn't even grow or pick or wash the tomatoes.

The surprising flavor and texture of the tomato stayed with her forevermore. She lay awake that night remembering it. Other than the loss of her family's meal that night, she didn't regret taking it.

What other amazing things did her Earthen blood prevent her from tasting?

CHAPTER 7 :

DEPENDABILITY MAKES GOOD CITIZENSHIP

ORDERS, PLACED. CROPS, HARVESTED. DELIVERIES, packed. Vesey, relocated. Only an untidy mess remained of our harried day. Spare packaging, smears of dirt, and used Keff mugs attempted to bother me, but I ignored them for the time. Fatigue muddled my senses, and Linah seemed as though she might collapse where she stood.

"That's enough," I said and tried to offer her a weak smile. "We need rest. We have a little bit to catch up on still tomorrow, but first sleep."

Linah nodded. "Mx. Bradford 8..." she began as I turned toward my bedroom. I held up a weary hand to interrupt her.

"Not anymore, Linah. Don't call me that. We're beyond that now, right? Just call me Minty like..." I intended to say "like everyone else," but who was there to call me that anymore? Not my friends, not my mom and dad. A lump of tears threatened to rise in my throat. I must have been so tired. "Just call me Minty, please."

"Minty..." she began, trying out the sound of it. Though the familiarity felt odd, I liked hearing my old nickname again, even from my Bonder. "What will you do? Tomorrow, when you make the deliveries."

"What do you mean? I'll make the deliveries I always make. Why? Did the ABEs change something?"

"I mean, will you keep Vesey's secret? Just tell me now if you plan to reveal us. At least give us that chance to get away." She paused with tension. "Will you keep him secret?"

Ah. This again. "Yes." It was a short answer to a complicated question, but it was all I had. The next day, during deliveries, I did plan to keep the boy a secret. Beyond that, why or how or when, I did not know.

"Then, goodnight."

I pulled my mattress out from my room to the doorway again, where I slept, but not peacefully. My mind battled itself in dreams and semi-conscious debates, but my overly fatigued body kept me from waking. Despite all the chaos on my little Farm, the suns rose, and the planet continued its life around us. Another day.

The pings of my Aide once again pulled me upright. Joints stretching and brain reactivating, I lumbered through the Day Room and beyond. I poked my head into the tomato room where Linah and her brother still slept. I decided to let them.

After leaving a packet of Keff and a mug on the counter for Linah, and drinking one myself, I blearily loaded the basket, again full of fresh produce, on to the transport track. Vendors awaited the tomatoes, chia, carefully bundled greens, and mushrooms that we harvested the day before.

The basket glided smoothly beside me as I hiked down the steep hillside that hugged my Farm on all sides. Though the hour was early, the city was already awake. The retailers, repair shops, and restaurants glowed with bright advertisements that tinged the settlers with colorful light. The smells and sounds of Shamong were comfortable companions; I discovered that I could forget Linah and Vesey somewhat amongst regular people doing regular things.

I pulled the trackbasket off the rails and rolled it to the quiet back alleys behind each Food location on my route. Each time, I unloaded the allotment of produce and then waited for the Tasker to acknowledge my delivery with a touch of their Aide to mine. Most of them tried to offer me a friendly smile or chat, but I was not very good at casual conversations.

"Where are my extra mushrooms? The oysters?" The Tasker at my last stop, Pitta's Food Pit, snapped at me as her Earthen unloaded the last items from my basket. Her question caught me off guard, I had been distracted by her giant Earthen. Muscular, even by Earthen standards, and towering, he displayed dark blue tattoos that stretched from his collar bone to his knuckles and so much wiry brown hair that I could hardly see his facial features.

"What, Mx. Pitta 6?" I refocused on the Tasker.

"I ordered extra oyster mushrooms this cycle. I don't see them here."

"Oh. Was it approved by the ABEs?"

"Of course, Araminta. So, you don't have them. Sounds like you didn't even know about them." Her Aide projected a communique addressed to me between us. I scanned the directives.

Shek. I had missed it. I likely dismissed the alert along with everything else during our scramble to keep up the day before.

"Oh, no. I didn't see it. I'm sorry, Mx. Pitta 6. My Bonder or I will bring the rest this afternoon." Pitta's eyes flashed in consternation, but as she looked hard at me, her gaze shifted to something else. It looked a little bit like pity, and I hated it.

"I know it must be difficult up there, Araminta, without your parents. Look, normally you are very reliable. Just remember that a solid civilization is built upon solid citizens. Dependability is good citizenship. We all need one another to survive out here."

I suppressed an eye roll at her prepackaged words. The same refrains had been drilled into us through school and our various training modules. Society requires superb citizenship. Survival requires superb citizenship. I agreed with the sentiment fundamentally, just not the delivery by Pitta, nor did I appreciate her mention of my parents. I had been an excellent citizen the last megas, almost perfect.

Until today. I nodded curtly and pushed my empty basket back toward the main street. I was annoyed at Pitta but mostly at myself. I had made a mistake.

CHAPTER 8 :
DESPERATE EXPRESSIONS

FATIGUE STRUCK ME HARD AGAIN after my final delivery. Emotional, physical. Both?

I deflated onto a city bench to gather my strength before the hike home and to shake off my nerves from the encounter with Pitta. It was only a small mistake, but the timing was just awful. A mistake meant...well, I had no idea. Linah's earlier words rang in my mind again.

What was I willing to do?

In the urgency of the emergency, I promised not to tell anyone about the boy, but the realities of my adrenaline-soaked promise started to sink in. No matter my promises, the fact remained: an Earthen, a fugitive Earthen, hid and bled at my Farm. That was bad. Possibly, that was really bad. The Farm was my whole life; I should not be risking it for nefarious purposes.

My conscience shouted that brutalizing a young boy was far more nefarious than hiding him, but I did not even know what the boy had done to anger his Tasker. What if he was a thief? Or worse? Earthens were lawless, destructive, poor of ethics; they had ruined their home planet, after all. They had no leader, no capacity for hierarchy or order. They had no higher thinking. The boy might have done anything.

A picture of Linah, steadily austere through the megas, even when I was grieving and reserved at best, popped into my mind. Linah was neither lawless nor destructive. She was purposeful and reliable, nothing like how we described Earthens. Linah was smart, probably smarter than me. Picturing Linah made me doubt that her brother could be all that heinous. How many of the Earthens were more like Linah and less like the assumptions I had always accepted?

I simply could not decide anything until I knew more. That was my fundamental problem. I knew so very little about Earthen policies and Laws. What would happen to them, and me, if we were caught? Maybe, with more information, I could find a way to help the boy without risking the wrath of the Law and upending my whole life. Maybe I could facilitate his sale to a gentler Tasker, pass him off to a merchant headed to another Outpost, or even have him work at my Farm.

Whatever happens, choose well. My mother's words inspired my next move.

It was time to learn. My uncle, the last of my biological family, probably had a solid understanding of Earthen Law, but he also had critical opinions and prideful mannerisms that prevented any closeness between us. His general awfulness included an unwavering disdain for the Lūnar ancestry of my father, and so I avoided his presence at all costs. Apart from visiting an Office of the Law or requesting a data surge from the IntraLibrary or Information outlets–which would give me a digital trail of interest and likely raise suspicion– I only had one idea for some anonymous research.

Resolved, and with a touch of optimism finally coloring my outlook, I rose and marched a few blocks further down Founders Way, Shamong's main thoroughfare.

The windowless Exchange building loomed on the last corner before Settlers' Plaza. Its dark form sucked the light from the buildings around it. A glowing sign, projected in a maroon color that reminded me too much of Vesey's dripping bandages, distinguished the front door. Inside the Exchange, the business of buying and selling Bonders commenced daily. I knew this to be true, but before that morning, I had never gone inside. My parents bought Linah so many megas ago, and she easily fulfilled any labor gaps on the Farm. Since my unplanned independence began, I had no reason to buy or sell any Bonders.

A new curiosity fluttered inside me. The Bonder industry boomed due to the brutally high cost of raw materials in an Outpost. The extreme rarity of metals and the taxes on plastics made products like robots and other automated machines astronomically expensive; every Outposter learned these economics in school. Bonders, in comparison, from the embattled and poor planet Earth, were cheap. When Lūn began trading in Earthen labor, the Outposts grew steadily and easily for the first time since settlement. It seemed functional. It all certainly worked well on my Farm.

I remembered occasional rumblings about Earthen mistreatment in school. They were troubling but had felt far beyond my ability to process or influence. By the time it became my business to know, I had been quite busy obsessively nursing my own private problems for a long time. At the time, I doubted them, but now there was a half–dead Earthen in my home, and that changed things.

At the imposing Exchange building, two Lawmen scanned the streets from small alcoves on either side of the entryway. The sight of them caused a tingling in my fingers. Lawmen: they would not be happy with me and my recent choices.

With my eyes cast downward, I passed through the heavy rotary doors. Surprisingly, two more Lawmen stood right inside the entrance. The gleam of their reflective, charcoal-colored uniforms danced in the dim interior. I could not remember ever seeing so many Lawmen in a single day, let alone at one building.

I heard the chatter of a busy marketplace as my eyes adjusted. Shoppers scuttled to complete their business. Through the prattle, I caught words like "strong," "trained," and something that sounded like "breeding age." A voice, mechanically amplified, boomed intermittently from the far corner. I could see the owner of the voice, raised slightly on a platform, over the heads of many shoppers. Behind him towered a sectional glass wall with transparent panels.

A hush suddenly surrounded me; the citizens nearby held their breath, and it took me only a single glance around the space to see why. Walking toward the door, walking toward me, was an ABE. I quaked. Flashes of the last time I had encountered one flooded my mind. Quarantine. Sickness. Sadness. I froze in its path. Another citizen had to pull me out of the ABE's way by my arm, but the ABE did not notice. They never did.

The ABEs, or Astroterrestrial Biodroid Engineers, were the first to arrive on our planet. Before Attis became habitable, they were sent by the Lūnar Settlement Force to an unedited planet. Their brains, part human and part computer, and their bodies, part human and part robot, made them effective at their only job: make the Outpost survivable.

The ABEs adjusted the planet for megas to prepare it for the first Starships of settlers. And still the ABEs continued the work of creating habitable land, eradicating disease, and sustainably building biodiversity. They did not get involved with elections, education, or anything social unless it affected the survival of the settlement. Math and statistics were their tools, their language, and their culture. ABEs were necessary but mysterious. We feared and revered them. Attisians understood that an ABE would always act for the survival of the Outpost, which was comforting, but the ABE had no regard for the happiness and well-being of individuals, which was unsettling.

After the ABE exited the Exchange, the normal sounds of shopping returned quickly, but my heart pounded, and I struggled to focus. The ABE sent my nerves scrambling; it stole any relief that I expected in pursuing a Lawful resolution to my problem. Instead, something unexpected beat in my chest, something more like dread. I reminded myself that I belonged at the Exchange as much as anyone. I wanted to follow the rules more, not less. The shoppers jostled me, my irregular pace mismatched to their energetic pursuits.

With a shake of my whole body, I took several purposeful steps forward, rallying myself. I wandered, looking for a friendly vendor to question. I hoped it might be as easy as finding the right upload to read at my leisure back at the Farm. My movements eventually brought me closer to the platform and the unusual glass panels. A shrill weeping cut through the buzzing crowd, and, concerned, I looked around for the crier, but no one else seemed surprised or even curious at the distressing sound.

The dread that I had been trying to suppress swept over me like a wave. My adrenaline pumped, my eyes narrowed, and my posture tightened. Without a cause I could identify, my body had gone back into emergency mode.

I tuned in to the other sounds around me, some incongruous to the unconcerned attitudes of the patrons nearby: whimpers, shouts, jeers. I maneuvered toward the stage, just barely more determined to go forward than to turn back.

But I did go forward.

I squeezed to the front of those gathered around the podium, and, in a frightening rush, the reality of the scene revealed itself. The wall of glass towered upward, divided into two-meter boxes...no, cages. Because inside the boxes were people. Earthens.

Is this how the Exchange operated? How Bonders entered our settlement? In cages? I had never considered how Bonders exchanged hands en masse, when they first arrived on the planet or in Shamong from the Mid-Lats; I had only witnessed the occasional, interpersonal sale or trade of Bonders amongst friends. But the scene in front of me was sinister, uncaring, cruel.

Most of the Earthens were cheaply clothed, dirty or ill-fitted. Their wrists were bare; none of them wore SubAides, the bracelets permanently attached to Bonders and linked to their Taskers' Aides. The various colors of their skin blurred to similarity because of the grime smeared over their muscles. They looked wild and frightening. One woman sat on her knees with tears rolling down her cheeks, looking up toward the sky. The short phrases she repeated shook her unevenly cropped hair.

A large male stood in the box next to her, muscles full of friction, eyes full of fury, teeth bared. He glared with crackling green eyes toward the crowd. At intervals, he wrenched the bamboo rope that bound his wrists and did not flinch when blood dripped around his chafed skin. He looked right at me, and I blushed with shame. For him. For me, too, just standing there watching him.

The activity at the Exchange continued to swirl around me, completely uncaring of my growing disgust. I had always known the business of the Exchange: Bonders bought and sold. But this...the cages, the unconcern, the obvious neglect of their health. I had not known. Or perhaps I had not chosen to know.

I blinked and saw Linah there in one of those exposing cages, her brother in the one next to her, both awaiting their fates, bound and afraid, unsure of anything on a new planet, with Outposters leering at them. I blinked again and my imagination subsided. Instead, there stood a group of Earthens that must have been a family, with their shared red–brown skin, black tattoos, and smooth, pure black hair. The father clung to the mother, who clung to the daughter. The girl, strikingly composed, stared determinedly at her parents and paid no attention to anything else. She looked even younger than me, but ferocity radiated from her.

The Attisan man with the amplified voice called out features and prices with gusto. He dramatically gestured toward the distressed family. The mother reacted to something that he boomed at the crowd. It took me a moment to realize that he had just offered different prices for each of them. He intended to sell them to different Taskers.

The desperate expressions of the family choked out my breath. The girl did not cry or wail like her mother, but just held the eyes of her parents, trying to be so strong. The mother and father held the girl's face in their hands as the bidding proceeded around them. They looked. They touched. They knew. They were in their last moments together.

All the feelings from my last moments with my own parents burst open inside me once again. My quickly placed hands were not enough to keep sudden sobs from escaping my lips. I turned and ran out of that place, pushing through the startled onlookers.

I could not watch a family be torn from one another.

CHAPTER 9 :

AN INCOMPREHENSIBLE TORRENT OF WORDS

SHEK, SHEK, SHEK.

I stumbled into an alley behind the Exchange and gagged on my own wet and messy sobs. Air refused to enter my lungs, and I slumped to the ground, trying to pull my cloak further away from my neck.

That girl. She was my age when I said goodbye to my parents. I saw her and thought of myself. I knew some portion of the pain ahead of her, but not all; she was being forced away from her parents. To work. Just to work. No other reason.

Shek everyone in there. It was not right. Families should be together, when they can. A deep conviction in my gut told me this, but every 'Poster in there seemed so unaffected. At ease, even. Because they were Earthens? Because they were only Bonders? Could they not see the feelings painted all over the faces of that wretched family? I grew lightheaded in the barrage of so many emotions.

Had my Linah been torn from her family, too? Is that why Linah, and only Linah, had let me be morose and mechanical for megas after I lost my parents?

Eventually I managed to lift my head. Awareness returned to me, and with it came a familiar itch for action. I wanted to do something that would help me forget; anything would be better than sitting here, confused, with something painful and surprisingly personal swirling and burning inside. I pushed the sweaty frizz of hair from my forehead and tried to think.

There was nothing I could do for the girl inside. Not that moment anyway. Perhaps I could find her and purchase her. Maybe her parents too. I shook the thought away though. What would I do with three unnecessary Bonders? What could I, me, Araminta Bradford 8, possibly do?

Things were actually more troubling after my detour to the Bond Exchange. I tried to refocus my brain on another Earthen, the one hidden in my house at that very moment. My immediate problem had to be Vesey.

"Mx. Br'df'rd 8?" My name, in an urgent whisper, interrupted my thoughts. The shadows of the alley blurred the figure at the corner of the building, but the voice was not one I knew anyway: deep and gravelly with a strange slur on the end of the spoken words. I debated whether to listen or run, and whether I was capable of a choice, anyway?

"Yes? Who is it?" I sniffed and wiped snot from my nose. An enormous form blocked the rest of the light from the street as the speaker moved toward me. An Earthen. Too broad to be anything else. I stood up and tried to present myself like the imperturbable and professional 8 I wished to be. It was not easy to do while cowering in a deserted alley with red-rimmed eyes.

A man's voice, deep and thick like his mouth was full of butter, came out of the hulking figure. "Mx. Br'df'rd 8? I re'qest a wor'."

I knew this Earthen after all. By sight at least. Before me stood the Bonder with blue tattoos from Pitta's Food Pit. I had observed him just the other day as Pitta all but lectured me. The man's tattoos flowed and morphed as his muscles flexed to move him closer and closer. Despite his polite words, his posture was tense and irresolute. When he noticed the recognition in my expression, he let flow an incomprehensible torrent of words.

"Dey no 't. O dey mi no 't. B'ot Linah n de 'oi. De Lawman. Lawman he der. He se de late food. Mx. Luysa sa n't t' de Lawman."

Like many recently imported Earthens, the man spoke Common Language very poorly, and his urgency made the words slur and slide. But finally, after several repetitions, I recognized a few: Lawman. Linah. Late Food.

Shek. Double shek. Triple, maybe.

"What are you telling me?" I croaked, unable to suppress my growing dread. The giant put a hand to his bearded mouth, pointed toward the Aide in my wrist, and finally gestured upward to my ear.

Comprehension hit me in a flash. "Yes, of course, yes." I agreed and used shaking fingers to find a translation operation on my Aide. After it loaded, I held the Aide out toward the Earthen. It glowed in the shadowed alley.

The Earthen flinched at the sight of the eight golden dots of light in my skin. He swallowed and began again. His words became fluid and strong in his native family tongue, but then he returned to rough and almost unintelligible Common Language for his last statement.

"...take up naw, and do'n't delay." We waited in a charged silence, until the translated text projected outward in the space between us.

Translation Operation>> From : Earth Ancient Language #13 *(Russian)* There is danger for Leenah *(Translation unknown, possible pronoun)*, maybe for you. After you left today, a Lawman arrived. He asked many questions. He asked Mx. Pitta 6 why you missed deliveries. They were strange questions. It means danger. The Lawman is hunting. Curse him. He is ugly like his purpose. He is a *(grotesque colloquial insult {select for more information})*. You must tell her. Tell Leenah exactly this, exactly this: take up now and don't delay. *(Transition to Common Language)* take up now, and don't delay.

The Earthen's earnest eyes followed mine as I read his words. How much had he risked to deliver this warning? Detection could mean any number of possible consequences, but he had dared it, nonetheless.

The words sunk in, and like the corona of a star, adrenaline boiled up and down inside me.

Perceptive Linah suspected that they would search for her brother; she had predicted it just hours ago, but this was too soon. Way too much, way too soon. I wanted to be strong. I wanted to be capable. But I suddenly did not recognize my own life. Everything from the last hours felt incomprehensible, impossible, and much too heavy for me.

My Earthen informant gestured with his tattooed fist and barked so feelingly that I stumbled backward. "Go! Ta' Linah! You say, 'Take up naw, and do'n't delay!'"

The huge Earthen knew my business. I was in it now, whatever it was. I did not know how far in, but despite my honorable efforts, I kept getting deeper. As I raced back up the hill toward home, a part of me felt truly awake for the first time since I had been on my own.

But most of me felt, well, terrified.

10 MEGAS AGO

*Supplemental excerpt from : Making a Way ; the Life and Stories,
Record HAC-3859385738*

Her mother's desperation filled the small structure. Could it even be called a structure? Uneven bamboo posts supported a tent of patched and worn fabric. A hundred similar tents surrounded it, most full of sleeping Bonders.

Yes, it was home, but right now it swelled with difficult feelings, and the girl yearned to escape to the quiet of the dark bamboo forests. She had lots of her own feelings to feel, but the needs of her family choked out every other priority.

Soph was gone. Soph. Disappeared.

Two days ago, Stalkers had lifted Soph, her hands bound in bamboo rope, into a rickety transport with seven other stunned Bonders. Soph screamed and thrashed in panic. Her frantic eyes moved everywhere, seeking some hope and unable to find it. The girl had never seen her big sister so wild, so feral.

Her mother, restrained by other Bonders who were less affected by their attachments, shouted her betrayal to the Stalkers, shouted instructions to Soph, shouted to The First Maker for help.

The girl wanted to chase the transport as it slid away. What people tended to call "her pluckiness" grew into something more solid and grim. Determination boiled inside her. Maybe she could rescue Soph if she was tough enough, sneaky enough, brave enough.

But as she drew a breath to run, her eyes found her tiny brother in the dirt. No one else was there to mind him, not while her mother was in such a frenzy.

With rolling tears and deep fear, the girl hugged her brother urgently until Soph's transport was out of sight. Since that moment, she had tended to her brother's needs while their mother wailed, completely incapacitated.

Everyone knew Soph would never be seen again. Once a Bonder was sold deeper into the Mid-Lats, they disappeared. Soph had become Disappeared. She was gone somewhere, alone, where conditions were more unbearable, and the Taskers were more cruel.

Suddenly, the girl felt silence in their threadbare shelter. Her baby brother finally slept. Her mother finally slept. She knew that she should sleep along with them, and forget, but her young mind raced faster in the eerie stillness.

She missed her sister, very much. But mostly she felt afraid. She thought about becoming Disappeared. Would it happen to her brother? Would it happen to her?

CHAPTER 10 :
A SORT OF CODE

"LINAH...LINAH!" THE DOOR BANGED as I barged through it. When Linah failed to appear before me in the Day Room, I kept yelling for her. I knew she had to be close; the Law forbade Earthens from owning or operating Aides like the one in my wrist. Instead they wore SubAides, and when I tracked Linah's SubAide, it showed me that she was on the Farm. But SubAides had no messaging or projection capabilities, so the only way to communicate with Linah was directly. Or so I thought at the time.

"Linah, where are you!? We've got a problem! Linah?"

Linah was not in the kitchen or the spirals of the Farm, so I bounded through to the tomato room. Linah was not there either, but of course, the boy still lay on his makeshift cot. The helpless sight of him pulled at my heart. He slept, sweaty and fitful, twitching occasionally. Some of his bandages leaked, and fresh blood dripped to the floor. I studied him – hands like mine, feet like mine, features like mine, but nonetheless disdained by the people of the Outposts. I felt nothing like disdain for the boy. He just looked innocent. And damaged.

I crouched closer, curiosity and confusion mixing inside of me, and I brushed the tattoos on his arm lightly with my fingers. Skin just like mine, albeit a different color.

I envisioned him inside a glass cage, Attisians judging his face, his strength, his health as he was sold to labor in the bamboo Farms of the Mid-Lats. I imagined Linah's face as he was taken from her. New compassion for Earthens bloomed in me, wild and unpredictable, like the flowers of the tomato fruits that brushed my shoulders in the tight space.

The boy startled and grasped my hand instinctively. He fell back into unconsciousness, but his fingers remained locked around mine.

"Mx. Bradford 8, what are you doing?" Linah finally appeared behind me in the doorway. I wondered how long she had watched me from the open door. Her face was clean and her second-hand tunic fresh, but her posture remained gaunt and tense.

"Oh, sorry," I said and attempted to gently untangle Vesey's hand from mine. He tightened his fingers and made the process clumsy. "Sorry. I just couldn't find you. I promise he grabbed me. I didn't grab him. Um, sorry."

Linah watched me warily. We performed an uneasy circle around each other until she blocked Vesey from my view, and I stood near the room's door instead. Slowly, she corralled me back into the Day Room, one arm wrapped behind her, and her precise and inaudible movements made the sound of my own feet scraping against the tiles that much more deafening.

"You took longer than normal," she accused. Her clear voice rang like a bell through the room. "Where were you?"

I found myself annoyed at her distrust. True, I had no idea what to do about our situation, but so far, I had been very helpful. Then again, if I did not yet know what I was going to do, Linah certainly did not know what I was going to do either.

I could betray them in an instant. She and Vesey were not safe, and she knew it.

"Right. Okay. I get it. But it's okay. I went to the Exchange. But we need to talk. There's a Lawman asking questions already. He made inquiries at the Food locations after I left."

Linah's features blanched to a shade of transparency. "The Exchange? What did you do? Are they coming for us? Which Lawman? Did you talk to him?"

"Hold on, hold on. No, I didn't talk to the Lawman. An Earthen warned me about the Lawman on the way back up the hill. He was this big Earthen. Huge, really. Dark, bushy hair and a galaxy of tattoos. My Aide told me that he's old-world Russian."

"Why did he talk to you?"

"He asked me to warn you about the danger. I think he must know you have Vesey. Is that possible? He also called the Lawman an ancient swear word, which I appreciated. Remind me to look that up later. He wanted me to tell you something word for word. He got all cranky about it." I pulled up the translation hologram on my Aide to be sure I repeated his words accurately. "Take up now, and don't delay."

A new kind of friction exploded in the room. Linah's sharp breath whistled as her head came around faster than a whip. With heat in her eyes and labored politeness, she asked to read the translation for herself, still keeping her distance and one hand wrapped around her back. She did so several times. When she was done, it seemed as though relief rolled off of her in palpable waves; it was a relief I did not understand or share.

"Linah, what does that mean? 'Take up now, and don't delay'? It just sounds like a poorly translated sentence to me."
Her eyes softened toward me, and hints of appreciation or excitement shimmered there intermittently. But still she hesitated before admitting, "It's a sort of code."

"A code?!" I scoffed, almost expecting her to laugh. Stars, this was not a time to laugh, though. When she nodded confirmation, I could not believe it. I really could not; it was so clandestine. "A code for what exactly?"

"I–I can't tell you," she replied, and I could see the conflict in her eyes. Believing that she wanted to tell me eased my annoyance a little. But just a little. Her lips parted slightly to say more–

Buzz, Buzz. Ping!

My Aide pinged the arrival of a guest, and the door alert buzzed. We both startled violently. Whatever connection Linah and I almost made became instantly irrelevant with the arrival of an unexpected visitor to the Farm. I could not believe there would be even more to this day.

My eyes met Linah's for a fraction of a milli, then simultaneously, we got to work. She scrambled to conceal the path to Vesey, while I raced through the Day Room. In short order, I straightened up the space, my frizzing hair, and my nerves.

What do I do, what do I do, what do I do? Something new for the Earthens grew inside me–understanding, maybe sympathy–but that did not change the Law. It did not make me innocent of breaking the Law.

A shockingly composed Linah reappeared in the Day Room. Her demure appearance contrasted sharply with the resolve in her eyes as she focused on me. Linah stretched out the arm that she had been hiding behind her and pointed it toward my chest. In her pale hand, a short knife glinted. She walked purposefully toward me, closer, closer. I froze, exposed in the large space, halfway between my unknown visitor at the door and a knife-wielding Linah.

"Linah," I breathed out, "what the shek are you doing?"

To answer, she uncovered a set of additional knives organized snuggly under her tunic, pressed to her ribs in a tightly-wrapped fabric belt with black hand stitching. Her voice shook, and her veneer of composure cracked a bit. "I don't know who's behind that door. I need your help, Minty. Please. Help us."

"Or you will knife me?!" I squeaked.

Linah gulped. "No, no, I won't hurt you. I don't want to hurt you. But I will fight to save Vesey. I'll do anything to save Vesey."

"Linah! No knives. We'll figure this out." I used my hands in a peaceful gesture. "No knives."

"We'll see," Linah said. In all Outposts, knives were completely and absolutely illegal. Weapons of all kinds were considered useless items in our cultivated and controlled Society, relics from our barbaric past. Up until that moment, I had no idea that weapon-like knives even existed on Attis outside of the Ancient Past Museum on one of the StarStations. If Earthens were smuggling deadly weapons into our cities, perhaps that might explain some of the fear and disgust Outposters felt toward them.

"Do you even know how to use those things?" I asked as the door buzzed impatiently once again. Linah tossed the knife lithely behind her, caught it as it flipped over her shoulder, twirled it on her palm, and shoved it in place on her belt.

At my shocked face, she managed a very partial, very tight smile. "I practice a lot."

I stared for a moment. "Stars, Linah! No knives!"

"I don't want to hurt you…" Linah trailed.

But you would, wouldn't you? I thought as I pushed my hair off my sweating forehead. There was danger outside my Farm and inside now too. I slapped my cheeks lightly in nervous preparation. *Buzz. Buzz. Ping.*

What was I willing to do? Lie? Get shipped to a quarry? Lose the Farm? A decision was upon me: enlist the help of this strange visitor, secure my future, end this bizarre plot twist, and potentially start a battle of knives. Or continue to conceal Vesey and risk everything left in my life. *Choose well, choose well, choose well.*

Linah draped her tunic over her belt of knives once more and took the posture of an obedient little Bonder. I shook my head at her in disbelief. She just kept surprising me.

With a deep breath and forced nonchalance, I turned to the door and opened it reluctantly…and the stars were against us.

It was even worse than I could have imagined.

CHAPTER 11 :
THE TWO WRONG PEOPLE

OUTSIDE STOOD MY LEAST FAVORITE person on all of Attis, which was saying something. The blustering, pompous, but bewilderingly influential Lawman Mudsil scrutinized me condescendingly from my doorstep. Lawman Mudsil ranked highly in the organization dedicated to enforcing the many laws of our Society. As he progressed in his career through the megas, his intense prejudice against my parents, principally my Lūnar father, gave him a permanent black mark in my book, and that morning, an extra something cruel and eager gleamed in his eyes.

Unfortunately, he was not my only visitor. Slightly behind the Lawman stood my second least favorite person in all of Attis – the ever-popular and roguish Harkless Stille 8, who was an unpleasant acquaintance from my school days.

My surprise and distaste overcame my fears, and I beat them to the first word.

"What can the two of you possibly be doing here together?" The reactions of the two unwelcome men varied as significantly as their attractiveness. Harkless broke into a jaunty grin handsome enough to steal the breath of most girls old enough to care about those things. Good thing I knew better. Lawman Mudsil, with his double chin and bluish skin, however, took offense.

"Rude!" he bellowed. "Young one, have some respect, please. For the Law, please. Respect." Perhaps I made a mistake in my abruptness. Handling these visitors might include mollifying the Lawman, even though I loathed him. I reconsidered my tactics.

"Excuse me," I softened with effort. "I very seldom have visitors. You two...very esteemed guests startled me. I am curious, to what do I owe this visit?" Harkless Stille 8 smirked and saw through my overt politeness, but the Lawman seemed partially pacified.

"I'm here on official business, Mx. Bradford 8. It's the job, please. There's been an incident. Another missing Earthie. Goes by Vesey. From a quarry. On the west." He fired off facts like they were strikes with an ax. Perhaps he expected each one to cut me down a little more. After the onslaught, he waited. I waited too. It was so hard to be compliant with someone I disliked so much. "He's the brother of your Bound. He's been missing for two days." Another pause. Mudsil sighed, annoyed by my silence, but Harkless' amusement only grew with my belligerence.

"Mx. Araminta Bradford 8. What do you know about this boy?" The Lawman finally asked me an actual question, and I decided I should finally answer him. To my surprise, I lied. Easily. I could not let the biased, small-minded Lawman Mudsil touch little, broken Vesey.

"This is the first time I've heard of him, Lawman. Why are you asking me? I'm always busy out here at the Farm. I have very, very little time to get out, let alone to a quarry. There's no way I've ever even met him." Before he could respond, I pointed to Harkless and continued. "And you. I'm not sure how any of this concerns you." If the Law wanted to find Vesey, they had sent the wrong two people to make me pliable. My aversion made me feel all the less guilty at deceiving them.

"Can't I come to visit my old friend?" Harkless nonchalantly queried, dropping his perpetual smirk in mock indignation.

"He's observing me," Lawman Mudsil inserted, obviously feeling that this fact made him all the more superior. "He's considering my profession, please." That surprised me enough to show a genuine reaction. Harkless Stille 8 was the youngest son of the enterprising Ad. Calhoun Stille 7, a baron in the starshipping and transport industry and a seat-holder in the Advocacy. Harkless Stille 8 could inherit whatever lifestyle he desired, and Lawman seemed an extremely unlikely pursuit for such a privileged Attisian.

"It's true, it's true. I'm here to learn if I'd make a good Lawman. I've recently renounced the starshipping life, you see..." Harkless chimed while glancing inside and noticing Linah. He contemplated her for a long moment. "And more importantly, it's renounced me! So I'm on a path of discovery." I took this to mean that Harkless' father was imposing a form of discipline on the more reckless of his two sons.

"Not much has changed then," I chided. "Perhaps I haven't changed." He laughed. "But you certainly have." That grin again. I did not trust a word out of Harkless Stille 8's mouth, but I still felt a blush threaten my cheeks. I had to pull it together.

"Onward with business!" the Lawman barked. "We need to see your Bondgirl." I knew Harkless had spotted her earlier, so pretending her absence, which was my first instinct, would not succeed. A glance behind me revealed Linah nodding with relief. She saw that I was going to play along, even though I could hardly believe it myself.

"Her name is Linah." I begrudgingly allowed them into the Day Room and tried to breathe through my distress.

The two large men filled the space. The Lawman inhabited a broad and excessively hairy body, but Harkless stood tall and possessed a confidence that made him appear even larger than his actual form. Between them, they made a significant barrier to the door, and I felt claustrophobic in my own home.

"Can we make this quick, please? I have your food to grow and other productive things to do."

Lawman Mudsil ignored me and instead pointed aggressively at Linah. "Is your brother named Vesey?" She acknowledged his question with a nod. "Then where is he?"

"He is working at a quarry," Linah spoke in her perfect Common.

"Not anymore, Earthie. He broke the Law. In a big way. He's in trouble."

"Is he...all right?" Linah successfully feigned concern and surprise.

"Do not speak to me, 'log, unless I ask you a question." Linah inhaled and placed a hand over her mouth submissively. I bristled at Mudsil's rudeness to my Bonder, but then grinned to myself when I remembered that Linah could probably toss a knife into his accusing finger before he knew what was happening. The violence of my thoughts scared me.

"You will be in trouble if we find you are helping your brother. The worst kind of trouble," the Lawman charged. He slashed his hand back and forth toward Linah. "If you know anywhere he might be, tell me immediately. And! We noticed some strange things around here, please. A vendor noted an incorrect delivery. Your previous record is nearly spotless. Is it your habit to leave an empty transport basket sitting on Founders' Way? Normally on the eighth day of a cycle, you order fertilizer, seeds, and water, and you submitted that order at the end of the day instead of the beginning as is your habit. Very odd, please. I think you are helping the boy. I think you are a criminal."

The trackbasket. I had left it by the Exchange in my haste to deliver the message from the giant Earthen. The numerous, incriminating, and accurate facts brought me into a state of cold sweat. Too many mistakes! He directed his accusations at Linah, but I noticed his eyes darting at me regularly. I had to speak.

"There's been no Earthen boy on this Farm, Lawman," I declared. "It's a small Farm, as you know. It's run efficiently, and I see everything that goes on here."

"Then explain yourselves!" the Lawman hacked. He looked at me but slashed again with his hand in Linah's direction.

"I was ill," Linah softly declared. "Araminta is being delicate. I felt unwell for several days, and it has caused delays for the Farm."

"You will address her as Mx. Bradford 8, 'log," the Lawman aggressively corrected her, and she cast her eyes to the ground, accepting the fault.

I noticed both of my old not-friends take an unconscious step backward at Linah's admission of sickness. Illness frightened Attisians horribly. After megas and megas of genetic study, controlled environments, and disease eradication, our immune systems were unpracticed at fighting diseases. A small mutation of a bacteria or a dormant disease introduced by the more native biomes of the Earthens might be deadly to us Outposters. If it were not for the excellent technologies of the ABEs, many 'Posters would have died since the Lūnars began importing Earthen Bonders. That is, many more.

Illness was a good cover, especially in my house, which had already been ravaged by a mysterious disease. I watched their suspicions fade proportionately to their growing fear.

"Why didn't you call Health? We have no record of a visit from Health," the Lawman asked.

I continued to build Linah's story, the lies flowing like hot Keff in the morning. "That is naive of you, Lawman. Health doesn't serve Earthens. And the medical Bonder couldn't make the long trip up here. Linah quarantined herself before I had any contact and took all the recommended supplements, as did I. We gas cleaned. We did it all. Her bio readings were always safe. No foreign bodies of any kind. Probably just food sickness. We'll be on schedule again next cycle..."

Lawman Mudsil blustered for a while. "Well, this still needs to be reported to Health. See to it. And, stars, it seems to me, Araminta Bradford 8, that you are getting too friendly with your Bonder. Spend more time in town, with your own people. Though you had a Lūnar for a father, you remain an 8, even so."

My 8 designation signified that I was the eighth generation living in our Outpost. It was also the highest generation designator possible and carried with it significant social expectations. Most 8s possessed considerable wealth and ensconced themselves in their importance. Typically, people did not stray far from their designations; 8s married other 8s, 7s married other 7s, and so on. But exceptions existed, like my family. My father, a Lūnar expatriate, was a 1. That made me an 8 from my mother, and a 2 from my father, but we expressed only the highest generational marker conventionally. Which made me Mx. Araminta Bradford 8.

"I mean it, Mx. Bradford 8. Everyone who knows your uncle has spoken of it with him. People think your behavior is very odd. Hardly anyone has seen you since your parents' Reentering celebration," Lawman Mudsil reminded me with a slightly less aggressive tone.

"Yes, of course. Of course, you are right. I certainly do hope to see more of you soon." I may have overdone the sarcasm slightly with that. "But we clearly can't help you, and as Linah explained, we are behind around here. If you'll excuse us…"

"I'm not done!" said the Lawman, but the atypically quiet Harkless finally opened his handsome mouth.

"Lawman, Lawman. I know you want to figure this out, and of course, you will. But I'm sure you've considered our transport up here. You told me that their transport track wasn't used that night. How in the stars would either of these lovely but small individuals carry a male Earthen up the mountain? Especially if one of them has been incapacitated for the last few days? The girl surely wants her brother safe as much as you do. I'm sure, now that you have generously made them aware of the situation, they will contact you if they hear anything about the boy. What do you think, Araminta and…Linah, was it?" During his protracted ramble, he guided the Lawman, who had very evidently not considered the hike up the mountain, to the door. I nodded compliantly, not daring to take anything away from Harkless' line of reason.

"See to it you do! This is a serious and costly matter," Lawman Mudsil managed to shout as a parting statement. "Serious and costly, please!"

Harkless paused at the door after the Lawman had passed through. "Feel free to transport back to the city, Lawman, and continue the good work. I'm going to catch up with Araminta for a milli and convince her to come to a Gathering." He turned back to us.

"Absolutely not," I said, but he rolled his eyes and leaned against the wall. His breezy attitude frustrated me, likely because it contrasted sharply with the panic I fought so hard to control inside myself.

"Really, Araminta. You should try to get out more. There is lots to do and lots to see." Harkless, as an unadulterated 8 whose ancestry ran as deep and long as possible for an Attisian, looked the part. He had inherited the medium skin, medium hair, and medium eyes that perfectly portrayed the purest of 'Posters. Our ideal look derived from representatives of all the Earth's original races slowly breeding together over eight generations into a perfect compromise of coloration. Add a good build, unfairly attractive features, and imperturbably good humor, and the summation was the self-assured Harkless who stood unwelcome in my doorway.

"I've seen plenty of what 8s like to do," I countered.

"Hm. Fair enough. What about what everyone else does?"

"Oh! You're aware there're others?"

He laughed again. He was nothing if not ready to laugh. "I think you've become a bit fascinating, Araminta. All right, I just wanted to make sure everything is truly okay here. The Lawman is a jag, but he can do a lot of damage." Harkless talked as though he came up to the Farm, with the tiresome Lawman, to help us. Unlikely. "I'm going to head out, so he doesn't get suspicious. But hey, try to be a little more careful." As he said this, he looked meaningfully at Linah, who returned his gaze calmly until he walked out the door.

Their connection seemed almost familiar. I scrutinized Linah even as I heard Harkless shout that he would escort me to the next Gathering.

"Linah," I said after giving Harkless plenty of time to distance himself from the Farm. "If you didn't use the transport track, how did you get Vesey up the hillside?"

"I had...help," she whispered, but she glanced furtively to where Harkless and Lawman Mudsil had stood just a moment before.

I sighed. Even after everything, Linah was going to keep her secrets.

CHAPTER 12 :

THERE ARE SECRET WAYS

IN THE MIDDLE OF THE Day Room, a circular space sunk one step lower than the rest of the glass floor. Within the circle, an array of cushions and mats made of various bamboo fibers served as seating. On these cushions, I collapsed, trying to encourage my hands to stop shaking. Linah remained fixed in her position by the kitchen.

"You didn't tell them." Linah mused as though she still did not believe it. "That makes me feel bad that I...you know. With the knives." My mind could not select a response based on all that had just occurred, so I only leaned further back into the cushions and groaned. I rubbed my eyes thoroughly, and when I looked around the room again, Linah had gone.

I checked the records on my Aide. Linah worked all her normal roles, and some of my own during my extended visit to town. The Farm was tended. The Farm was safe.

Suddenly all I had to do was sit anxiously in the Day Room and eat dinner. Alone. I always ate alone, but that moment, it felt strange, like a statement I did not want to make.

My stomach growled. Even the chaos of the day had not stolen my newfound appetite.

I unpackaged and heated two bowls of vegetable soup, added some malformed mushrooms that I could not sell to Food, sprinkled on some extra algae protein powder in my favorite Pepper Punch flavor, and took them to Linah and Vesey in the tomato room.

"Linah." I held out a steaming bowls. "I come peacefully. Tell me about the knives. What was that about?"

Linah, who sat near Vesey's head, considered me in her ethereal way, before taking one of the bowls. "Please understand," she said as she stirred the hot soup. "I thought you had told them. I thought someone had come for Vesey."

"But I didn't," I said.

"No, you didn't."

"I don't want anyone to get hurt, Linah. I truly don't. I just don't understand what's going on here. This is so…so dangerous all of a sudden."

"It's always been dangerous. For me. For Ves. As long as I can remember," she whispered. I raised my eyes to hers, expecting to see an accusation there, but instead, they were gentle. Earnest, urging me to understand.

For a while, we ate as silently as soup allowed. I snuck glances at her and Vesey, and I realized how little I knew of their lives. Their lives. Their history. I came up with a hundred questions for Linah, but they were not the questions that mattered. Not at that moment. A Lawman just invaded my Farm. We were suspects; not just Linah, but me too. Linah and I had to figure something out. Together.

"So, Linah." I set my soup down. "What are we doing to do? Let's start with that code from the Bonder with blue tattoos. Tell me what it means."

Linah tipped the remaining soup into her mouth and tried to hide the glance she took at my half-finished bowl. I pushed it to her across the floor, and she grabbed it with a "thank you." She drank slowly, buying herself time to answer, but I waited, unwaveringly. Linah's mind grappled with something far away from the room in which we sat. I could see her thinking, deciding, thinking again, and changing her mind several times. Her features hid nothing.

"Come on, Linah. Meet me halfway at least."

She finally nodded, unhappy but resigned. "It could mean I can save Ves, Araminta." She gazed toward the murky sky above. "But first, I'll need some information."

"You'll need some information?" I cracked. My patience stretched to the point of snapping. "Linah, stars, I'm the one that needs some information. For the last two days, I've been confused and scared. Not to mention exhausted. I could go supernova any second. I don't want Vesey to be hurt again, but if there's anything that affects me, you, or Vesey and our ability to keep him away from his Taskers, I need to know it. I can't help you if I don't know anything!" By the end of my monologue, I had gone from composed negotiator to frantic interrogator.

"I know, Araminta, I know," Linah responded so genuinely that my pulse slowed a bit. "There are secrets Earthens use to survive. There are secret ways. But I can't tell them to you. Not now. The stakes are very, very high."

I got up and walked out of the room. I knew it was petulant, but I felt angry, discounted after all my efforts. I heard her call me, "Minty!" using my nickname for once, but I did not turn around. Too tired. Too frustrated.

The night was deep and dark in the Day Room, so I pulled my bamboo fiber mattress and luscious comforter out from my bedroom and over to the front door landing. Linah had moved it back to its normal location earlier in the day. But I still needed to keep watch. I curled up all the way underneath my bedding, the covers trapping me inside and preventing the starlight from reaching me. I wanted a small bubble of peace and comfort.

Linah's soft steps approached, but I did not acknowledge her, even when her muted voice crept through my covers. "I'm going out to get that information, Araminta. About the code. About Ves. I'm leaving for a little while. I won't be gone long. I gave Ves some extra medicine. I–" She paused for a breath. "I'm very grateful. For what you have done."

After I heard the door close behind her, I emerged from my fluffy enclosure. Still angry, still confused, and still at a loss for what to do next.

I sighed and activated my Aide, intending to watch some entertainment while I waited for Linah to return, but before long, my stamina failed, and I slept. I never heard Linah come home.

CHAPTER 13 :
DON'T TOUCH ME

I WOKE VIOLENTLY ENOUGH TO pull a muscle in my neck. A nightmare. I rubbed away the goosebumps down my arms. "Just a bad nightmare," I told myself, "Not real, not real." Talking out loud anchored me again to my actual surroundings and pushed the lingering, dream-twisted images away.

My Aide flashed an alert about my elevated heart rate and a query about whether or not Health was required. I dismissed the alert and tried to breathe steadily; a Health inquiry was the last thing we needed.

Even in sleep, I could not shake the anxiety that Vesey's presence caused. And it was not only anxiety; it was guilt, and even more so, doubt. Doubt as to whether I should report Vesey immediately. Doubt as to how much to believe Linah. Doubt as to the right thing, the good thing, in such an unusual circumstance. My parents taught me to be good, to consider those around me, to contribute, to choose well. But what did that mean about Vesey?

I twisted around for a comfortable position, but an unusual sound interrupted my efforts. I had not frightened myself awake after all; something had woken me. What was it? My heart beat thundered as I tried to breath quietly enough to hear the Farm around me.

For a while, only silence. As one only does in the depths of the night, I imagined a million possibilities: a cracked pipe in the upper spiral of the Farm, Lawmen preparing to ambush the house, an escaped creature from the Menagerie. But then I heard it again, and I knew it originated from inside my house. My blood pumped. It seemed almost human. Oh, stars.

"Vesey!" I sprang up and raced into the tomato room, where a fully conscious Vesey stared up at me from the bed. The sight of me, agitated and determined, noisily bursting into the room, sent Vesey, already distressed, into a panic.

"Get away!" he screeched. His Earthen frame appeared robust for his age, but his eyes, expressive like his sister's and awash with confusion and helplessness, proclaimed his youth. Every evasive move Vesey attempted wracked him with pain as his skin stretched and pulled his wounds. "Ouch, ouch, oh God, God, ouch." While he struggled to rise, I stood very still, suspicious that any move on my part might make him more alarmed. Two of his bandages dripped with new blood before he gave up and collapsed back onto the bed. He begged, "Don't touch me."

I squatted low and let him cry for a few moments before I ventured a cautious word. "Vesey?" I displayed my open hands toward him in a peaceful gesture. At the sound of his name, astonishment mixed with his fear. "I'm not going to hurt you. You are safe right now." I read the flashes of hope, mistrust, fear, and anger in his expression as easily as if he had spoken his feelings aloud.

"You are a 'Poster…" He squinted toward me, which squeezed out fresh tears.

"Yes, I'm Attisian, and this is my home. It's a Farm on the hill near the Boundary. I'm Linah's Tasker. My name is Araminta. Linah brought you here. It's okay, Vesey. You will be okay." I paused to gauge his reaction. His breathing accelerated, but his muscles unwound. "Will you let me fix your bandages?"

"But you are a 'Poster. You're an 8." My assurances were short of sufficient to make us instant friends. I pulled my sleeve down to cover the eighty dots of my Aide. "Do…do you know the code?" he stammered.

I shook my head, tired of hearing about codes, and upset that Linah had not thought to give me any useful instructions while she was away gathering her information, even though neither of us thought Vesey would regain consciousness that soon. "I'm sorry. Unless it's 'take up now, and don't delay,' I don't know it. I will help you if you let me. You just arrived a couple nights ago, and I'm still new at this."

"Don't touch me." He tilted his head toward the wall, away from me, and refused to say another word, even after more inquiries from me. Sweat darkened the bright hair around his temples. His chest heaved; his body betrayed his pain.

"Well, aren't you all fire and energy. Fine." I shook my head. "We just need to wait for Linah. You are bleeding through your bandages in several places, so, even if you won't let me help you, just don't move anymore."

His head turned to watch me retreat, and we made eye contact briefly before a blur of yellow hair and grey bamboo fabric rushed past me into the room.

7 MEGAS AGO

Supplemental excerpt from : Making a Way ; the Life and Stories,
Record HAC-3859385738

The young woman liked the young man that worked at the local Supply. He was handsome, at least to her. She tried to smooth her tight crimps of hair. She failed, so in frustration, she ruffled them into a wild disarray. Oh well.

She had a special assignment from her Tasker, and she rejoiced in the reprieve from the prickly, pokey, backbreaking work on the bamboo homestead. As she walked the distance to town, she practiced smiling in an alluring way and talking in flirtatious mysteries. She knew she was ridiculous. By the time she mounted the front steps of the Supply, she had herself laughing so hard that her side ached.

To her great disappointment, the handsome boy was not behind the counter that day. She went ahead with her assignment anyway, dawdling only slightly.

Inside the store, an Earthen, a man with a ratty hat pulled low over his eyes, loitered near the exit. The girl had seen his type before. Destitute Earthens, too proud or scared to ask for help, sometimes waited humbly for a kind gift from a sympathetic shopper. At the last milli, she added an algae stick to her purchase and passed it to him quietly when she headed back out the door.

Suddenly the Tasker behind the counter shouted toward the poorly man. "You there! You 'log! Your face is right here. You're a fugitive!" he accused. A greenish alert shone brightly from the Aide on the Tasker's wrist. It projected a portrait and several headings. Even from the doorway, the girl could read the boldest one: Fugitive.

A fugitive! The girl had heard tales of daring Bonders attempting to escape to other lands through the wilderness of the middle latitudes. Her heart pounded. Was this man one of them? Was he on his way to freedom?

The bedraggled man scrambled to escape the store as the Tasker threatened pursuit. The girl ached for him to get away; she couldn't bear to witness the end of his journey, where only death or torture awaited him if he was caught. She shifted her weight slightly to encumber the Tasker as he passed by, and he stumbled. He held a heavy tool ready to attack the fugitive, but, at the girl's interference, he swung it at her instead.

What a strange sound, she thought. It did not occur to her that it was the sound of her own skull cracking. She fell, and when her body didn't respond to her commands anymore, she silently panicked.

It was there, on the floor, before blackness finally swallowed her up, that she heard the Voice for the first time.

"I will show you the way," it promised. "I will show you the way."

CHAPTER 14 :

PREPARE, IF YOU DARE

"LINAH!" ALL THE STRENGTH AND resolve left Vesey's voice at the sign of his sister. Linah embraced Vesey as fiercely as his prone position and sensitive wounds allowed. She smelled of the night's chill, fresh and clean, in the room's close air.

"Linah," Vesey gulped as Linah brushed damp hair away from his forehead. A streak of semi-dry blood made some of it stand up at conflicting angles. "Oh God, Linah, I messed up. I'm stupid."

Linah urgently provided him with yet another dose of pain medication from the safety kit required by the ABEs and diligently maintained in every Attisian home. The medication was nearly depleted after Vesey's heavy usage. I made a mental note to buy replacements on my next trip to town, if I could do it discretely.

"Hush, hush," Linah coaxed. "No one knows you are here. Try to rest. I'm here, I'm here."

As the medicine slowly relieved Vesey's discomfort, a weight lifted from my chest. Had I been worried about his pain? I watched them as unobtrusively as possible until Vesey noticed me again. He looked up at his sister. "Linah, I didn't tell that 'Poster anything. Just like you taught me," he boasted. He wiped his nose and fought back the cry of pain the movement caused.

"This is Mx. Araminta Bradford 8. She's the Tasker here. She is..." Linah glanced back at me to give me a fleeting smile. "She is also a... a sort of friend for now, Ves. But I am proud of you for following the rules." I felt a little warm at being named a friend, even if it was by an Earthen bound to me, and even if I had to barter for the friendship with secrecy and danger and extreme levels of stress. Perhaps she was attempting to build a bridge after the knives and, well, everything.

Vesey's eyes glazed slightly as the medicine took a deeper hold. Such expressive eyes, just like Linah. Vesey returned his stare to me, his gaze puckish. "But she doesn't know the code."

"I know. But I'm telling you, you are safe here for now. You can thank Mx. Bradford 8. She's helped you, and she's helped me." Linah continued to stroke his head lovingly and to adjust the various bandages that got disheveled when he was asleep.

"Hmm, yeah right. 'Poster.'" He said it with the venom of an insult.

"Vesey!" Linah admonished. He frowned in my direction. I raised and lowered my eyebrows conspiratorially, and Vesey's features melted into a combination of surprise and amusement. His blue eyes changed so quickly. Where hostility had been just a moment before, now there was liquid innocence. Something about him made me feel childlike myself. And truthfully, I did feel relieved that he was awake and lucid. Relief was one of the few positive emotions I had experienced recently, and I relished it, even if Vesey was not talking to me the way a Bonder should.

"No, Linah, it's okay. I'm not offended. Free pass until he can sit up on his own. House rules. But after that, he must be a perfect citizen." I got another almost-smile from Vesey, and the tension in the room lessened.

"Vesey tells me there's more than one code?" I prodded; Linah nodded without meeting my gaze. "And exactly how many codes are there?" My exasperated question produced a muffled guffaw from Vesey.

"Lots," he replied deviously with narrowed eyes and a partial smile, daring my curiosity to rise. Vesey was turning out to be an interesting kid. One who I was instantly tempted to like.

"Okay, lots of codes." I rolled my eyes. "Linah, did the Bonder's code pay off? Did you create a plan on your little adventure off the Farm?"

Linah broke into a genuine smile, this time letting me see it fully. An unhindered smile on Linah felt almost as unnerving as her tears. The emotion took over her entire face, and had I not been a rational person, I would have claimed that she glowed. "Yes, I think so." She looked meaningfully back toward Vesey. "We are going to get you out of here, Ves."

Vesey's eyes found hers. "You mean I don't have to go back to the quarry?"

"No more quarry!" Linah reflected Vesey's enthusiasm, and the brightness they created together shone like a bulb in the dim room. "And guess how? The Waymaker is going to take you." Vesey's mouth gaped open, and his eyes widened.

"The Waymaker?" he whispered in utter reverence. "We will travel with The Waymaker?" Linah's eyes flash toward me, but it happened so fast that I could not read the expression.

"Yes," she replied to her brother. "The Waymaker will show you the way."

Vesey laughed gleefully, and Linah joined him. They babbled to each other so quickly that I could not follow most of what they said. Likely they used words in a language other than Common.

"Excuse me. Are you saying, 'way-maker'? Who is The Waymaker? Is that a job of some kind?" I queried.

Linah ignored my questions, but Vesey opened his mouth in shock. "No way. You don't know about The Waymaker?!" Though he slurred a bit, his Common was nearly as crisp as Linah's. As the fresh medication continued to erase his pain, he became progressively more animated. His coloration mimicked his sister's, but where Linah looked ethereal, Vesey looked spritely. His eyes danced and some softness still clung to his cheeks.

"The Waymaker is the most amazing person ever. She's sugar! No one knows her real name. And she always gets through. She always makes it. Every time," Vesey babbled worshipfully.

"Always makes it? Where?" I asked, confused.

"To anywhere where you aren't Bound. To the poles or to the moons! No more quarries!" The joy in Vesey's voice was contagious even if I did not understand. "Beecher says that The Waymaker has freed hundreds of Bonders! Oh God, there are so many stories. She pulled out her own tooth. She carries weapons! People say that The First Maker speaks right to her! She always makes it. She's amazing. She is the sugar."

"Well, stars..." I looked to Linah for a more linear explanation. To my surprise, Linah was almost as reverent, though less exuberant, as Vesey.

"Ves is right. The Waymaker is an escort, a rescuer. She passes through the lands of Attis and gathers those who are willing to risk the journey. She takes them, anyone who joins her, all the way out. That code the Russian gave you... that's a song that Earthens sing to each other when The Waymaker is coming. It's a sign to prepare, if you dare. She frees Bondspeople, and she has never been caught." For a moment the three of us sat quietly, all considering The Waymaker and her daring endeavors.

"And this Waymaker is coming here? You know this because of a song?" It seemed like superstitious nonsense. I had a hard time believing a whole world of secrecy existed on my planet.

"Yes, and I confirmed it tonight. My friends have heard the song as well and know she is coming." Linah brought her hands together at her chest and clasped her own fingers, almost prayerfully.

"Sing her the song!" Ves insisted.

"I shouldn't," Linah said, avoiding my gaze.

"Linah..." My curiosity raced. I wanted to hear the siren call of this

Waymaker to whom Linah would entrust her brother. "Please."

Linah, analyzing me for a time, finally shrugged and began a melodious song. Her voice was sweet and spooky.

Away, away.
Take up now,
do not delay.
Much may befall,
Fear shan't allay—

"It's an ancient song." Linah's spoken words broke the spell of her song after she had repeated the verse several times. Vesey, lulled by the tune and the needs of his healing body, had fallen asleep once more. "Who knows where it's from, originally. But now. Now The Waymaker uses it. 'Take up now, do not delay.' The code. We sing it when she will be near. If you can wait, Araminta, just a few days, I can send Ves with The Waymaker. Everything can go back to normal after that." Linah pleaded with her overlarge, crystal eyes.

I waved my hand. "Of course," and I realized I had already resolved myself to participate. I could get through a few days. And besides, surely the worst was over.

CHAPTER 15 :
SOMETHING VERY STRANGE

I MADE NO MORE MISTAKES. I worked on the Farm, and Linah tended to Vesey. Then sometimes Linah farmed, and I sat with Vesey. It required some creativity, as Vesey's pain ebbed and flowed or his wounds needed attention, but Linah and I worked well together, and our megas of practice on the Farm showed. No more visitors surprised us. No more secret codes.

Questions still swirled inside of me, but the only time I spent with Linah was also shared with Vesey, and I did not know what was proper to discuss around him. Linah possibly arranged it to avoid the questions she knew I wanted to ask.

During my rare hours alone with Vesey, I tied back the wild boughs of the tomato plant, harvested seeds from the deformed fruits, and prepared piecemeal sprouting beds using the materials left behind from my father's work. The activity eased the restlessness of my hands in the times when Vesey slept. As new sprouts poked out of the soil, and as the old plant grew upward and shot out new vines, Vesey's wounds knit together slowly, and the frequency of his inconsolable nightmares ebbed. We used medicine to help him sleep and to bring his awareness back to him when he was awake.

I often smiled as I remembered my father working in that room, as I worked now. Tending, feeding, caretaking. But the fond memories faltered when I compared the consequences of our different rebellions. My father, already discriminated against, might have incurred steep fines if his laboratory had been discovered. The Law would make him destroy the room and pay reparations for the water, soil, and assets used without permission. The ostracism my family already experienced would increase with the label of 'thief.'

But if Vesey was discovered…I shuddered at the possibilities. I fretted about what they might do to him. Beat him again. Take him away from Linah. And what would they do to me? As a minor, would the Law be lenient with me? Or would they strip me of the Farm altogether? Would I lose my wealth, my status, my whole life? I had to stop myself from thinking about it. For the moment, we were safe, plants and humans alike.

Vesey, while medicated, proved himself to be intelligent, excessively eager, and full of admiration for Linah. I sensed his affection for me growing in fits and starts. He enjoyed stumping me with riddles and puzzles, although I was often at a disadvantage because his riddles referenced Earthen customs or histories.

Vesey smiled at me, his eyes drifting lazily from the painkillers. "Minty, what is harder to catch the faster you run?" I enjoyed his squinty grin when I did not know the answer immediately, so I gave up willingly.

"Your breath!" He smiled. "What is as big as an elephant but weighs nothing at all?"

"What's an elephant? Sounds familiar," I ask him.

Vesey's jaw dropped in mocking indignation. "Huge mammals! Greyish with flexible, long noses. They say that they just walk all over Earth. Don't you 'Posters learn anything about Earth? I didn't even get to go to school, and I know about elephants. Oh well, the answer is, 'an elephant's shadow'!"

I projected an image of an Earthen elephant on my Aide and could not contain my surprise at the sight of the fantastical creature. Together we scrolled through images of elephants and discussed their unique qualities, before I noticed Vesey tiring again.

"Well, Vesey. You know what? That joke works with anything. What is as big as Vesey, but weighs nothing at all?"

"Vesey's shadow," he sighed with a tiny smile and drifted off. After a satisfying hour of preparing fresh soil for more wild tomato seeds while Vesey slept, my stomach made a whining noise and twisted in discomfort. I gazed down at it in surprise. My body's protests informed me it was late in the day, nighttime, likely. I missed a midday meal, and my rekindled appetite did not approve. I picked a handful of orange tomatoes and asked aloud if Vesey wanted any. His complete lack of response informed me that his sleep was deep.

Confident that his medicine would allow him to rest for a long while, I headed to the Day Room to find something to accompany my tomato snack. Instead of the normal smell of soil and chilled air, an amazing scent enveloped me. Rich, thick, warm fumes wafted through the whole space. I stopped to breathe it in.

"Linah?" Clanks and shuffles from the kitchen answered me. I followed my senses and found her, swiping vegetables from a board into a pot of simmering broth. She moved confidently. She noticed me watching and smiled, genuinely and a bit shyly. "You cook things?!"

"Well, I suppose you'll have to be the judge of that, but I do like to cook. Very much." She offered me a spoonful of broth. The liquid coated my tongue with luscious flavor. The whiteish broth tasted rich and fatty, like churned cream, but then bright hints of onion and leek overtook my palate. Familiar chunks of manufactured protein bobbed in the pot with the vegetables. By the shape of them, ovular with two pointed ends, I knew Linah chose the "Ocean Meats" proteins. I never liked Ocean Meats growing up, but the sight of the calorie dense protein soaking in such a delectable bath caused my stomach to growl so loudly that I heard it over the bubbling of the soup.

"Oh, stars. It's amazing." I took another spoonful, this time making sure I got chunks of the vegetables too. To my surprise, I felt the prickle of tears as I savored the bite. The soup tasted so much better than my standard fare of various nutrition packs and dehydrated meals. More than that, it felt better too, as though my body, or maybe my heart, had been waiting for it.

Linah made food for me, when I had not even made food for myself in megas. Not real food, not like the soup. Food was just a necessity, but then why had Linah's soup brought me to tears? To redirect myself from an untimely spiral of difficult thoughts, I picked up jars of spices from the counter, where Linah had discarded them. Most labels displayed unfamiliar names. "Where did all this come from?"

"From the Market."

"The Market? Please tell me that's not another code."

"No, no. It's a Market, a true market, for shopping. In the Sideways. Lots of stuff sells there that is unavailable at Foods or Supplys. Even some traditional foods are grown or smuggled in."

I knew about the Sideways. A small community of unbound Earthens, or bound Earthens that did not live in with their Taskers, lived on the northern hillside of the city. Outposters nicknamed it the Sideways because no transport tracks ran to or from it. I gaped at her. "Traditional? As in Ancient Earthen? Smuggling? How? Is it monitored? What about the ABEs?"

She laughed briefly and held her hands up in a calming gesture. "Not ancient. Just Earthen. And no, it's not monitored the same way as Algae or Protein or Farms," she continued. "I don't think it could be. The Earthens just make what they want with whatever supplies they can manage to gather. Most of the 'Posters stay away. I have no idea what the ABEs think of it."

"You mean people grow things? Outside of a Farm?" I emphasized every word slowly and held my breath for her response. Food growing wild on the hillside, and no monitoring? Impossible. My Farm had ten thousand regulations and production requirements enforced by the ABEs, and all our supplies, including water and soil, came in purposeful rations. And it worked that way! My Farm and all others like it supported the growth of our Outpost, safely and efficiently. A market in the Sideways, unmonitored and unhindered, seemed like a tall tale. I had to see it for myself. "Linah, take me."

Linah hesitated.

"Sorry. I didn't mean; I demand you to take me. I meant; please, take me. I really, really, really want to see the market."

Linah allowed her eyes to dance at my interest. "I think you would like it there, Araminta. Maybe someday…" I stared at her expectantly, long enough that we both smiled timidly, experimenting with our new alliance. "Okay! Yes, someday, maybe I will take you. Some 'Posters shop for things there, from time to time. It wouldn't be too unusual to have you there. But not today. It's too late in the day anyway. Most of the vendors will be packed up. This is Ves' favorite soup; it's an old family recipe that we make for celebrations or Entering Days, when we can afford to, though I haven't been able to use fresh protein like this in a long time. My mom called it 'fiskesuppe.' I thought it might do him some good. And then you have a big day tomorrow too."

My daydreams had filled with visions of Earthen gardens open to the air and suns, but then Linah's last words interrupted me.

"What? A big day?"

Linah grimaced. "Yes. Check your Aide." I did.

2.19.175 at 09:15 : Meeting with Chi Legree 7, Legree Estates

I released a long and disgruntled sigh. "Well, sheking shek." Just the name made me shiver: Chi Legree 7, my uncle. In all the commotion caused by Vesey, I had forgotten my regular meeting with Uncle Chi.

"It could be your last one though!" Linah encouraged. Linah, I discovered, had an exceptional gift for remembering things about my life that even I forgot. Before the end of the next cycle, my Entering Day, my seventeenth mega of life, would allow my official adulthood and emancipation to begin.

I forced a pathetic smile, full of too many teeth, and Linah laughed at my obvious sarcasm. I felt startled, and a little pleased, at being able to make Linah laugh.

We heard a distant voice, "Minty?" Vesey had woken and called for me. For me. My heart thumped once, and I frowned at the feeling. I noticed Linah watching me, her head cocked slightly to the side, pondering, definitely not smiling. What did she see in my expression?

We took the creamy soup into Ves' room, propped him up on some pillows, and swung open the large glass panel of the outer wall so that the room was exposed to the upward slant of the mountainside. At this elevation, there was very little manufactured soil, and in certain patches, the irrigation grid peaked through and glinted in the suns. ABEs came through to deposit more newly produced soil, minerals, and microbes on the hillside at regular intervals, but otherwise this area had received very little attention. Terraforming took megacycles and megacycles.

From our vantage point, we could see the end of the edited ground. Past it, only rocks. Brown to grey.

It was the Boundary. Beyond the Boundary, there was no terraforming at all. A similar Boundary encircled every settlement outside of the livable atmospheres of the Mid-Lats. Boundaries encased the pockets of terraformed ground and manufactured atmosphere that allowed Attisians to settle inside them.

Outside of the Mid-Lats and Boundaries, the planet remained in its native state—rocky, bare, and intimidating. Well, not truly in its native state. The ABEs had slowed planetary rotation rates, concentrated the liquid water, and mined for raw materials, among other things. I would say instead that, beyond the Boundary, Attis remained in its original state of lifelessness.

We ate Linah's delicious soup, watched the cool suns descend toward the mountain peaks, and grinned at the unending noises of appreciation from Ves. Afterward, we helped Ves roll into a more comfortable position, and Linah pulled out her throwing knives.

"She's the best!" Ves beamed from his lounging spot. "I'm pretty good too, you know. When I'm all better, you can watch me."

"Do all you Earthens go around throwing knives?" I inquired, half amused, half terrified at the idea of Earthens with hidden knives and secret abilities.

Linah answered, "No, these knives were a gift from my grandmother's Tasker, long ago, passed down to me. I think they were an heirloom even to that Attisian family. I don't know any other sets like this."

If her grandmother had been a Bonder on Attis, Linah's generational designation was a 3, larger than my father's. Earthens never expressed their generation, and for the first time, I wondered why. Linah was more Attisian than my father.

Linah propped an unopened bale of soil nutrients upright on a nearby rock and demonstrated her skill. *Thunk. Thunk. Thunk. Thunk.* The knives sank into the tangled strands in a nearly vertical line.

My mouth fell open. My Linah looked like a goddess but threw knives like a villain.

"Want to try it?" Linah offered.

"Absolutely I do."

Linah coached me how to grasp the knife's blade and flick my wrist to spin it. The metal of the knife chilled my fingertips, and I forced down a shudder. I failed, again and again, to hit the target, much to Ves' amusement. At first, he clucked his tongue or stifled a noise, but before long, he laughed openly whenever my throw went wide. Or short. Or long. And especially when I let go too late and almost stabbed my own foot.

Something very strange happened, something that had not happened to me in a long time, something almost as unexpected as all the rest of that bizarre cycle. I had fun. I felt like a traitor to my normal stoniness, but it happened anyway.

Linah slapped another knife into my hand. "That target," she gestured toward the mutilated hulk of nutrients, "is your uncle's face." Her eyes glittered, and when I let out a strangled snort, we all giggled. Giggled. Really. I had not known I was still capable of giggling.

I must have surprised us all, because a moment of quiet stillness followed. Linah eventually gestured to the target with overt formally. "Please, your uncle awaits."

I turned toward "my uncle." I recalled the sharp features of his face. The same features that made my mother gorgeous made him look conniving. I hated that I still saw my mother in the turn of his jaw and the outward slant of his nose; he polluted them with his snarky comments and superiority.

Long ago, at the direction of my grandparents, he shunned my mother and father because of their relationship. My father, as a 1 and as a Lūnar, did not live up to their ideas of a suitable partner for my mother. Mother, as the oldest of the two, was meant to inherit the greatest portion of her family's status and wealth. But her whole family did everything socially and financially possible to cut her off. The hatred survived the cycles and was eventually thrust upon me, the result of my parents' unacceptable relationship.

Now, as my only living family, my uncle handled my finances, investments, and community responsibilities until I could be emancipated. It had proved to be a burdensome arrangement for us both.

I breathed in the smell of the mountainside and the sunsets and the wild tomatoes. My muscles calmed and my focus narrowed. Linah's instructions finally made it from my brain to my fingers, and I tossed the knife. Thunk. So satisfying. The knife sunk deep into the bale, fairly close to the center.

"Ooof," Ves exclaimed from behind me. "Right in the chin. Poor uncle."

"No." I sighed. "He's really not

CHAPTER 16 :
SOLID AND SIMPLE

THE MORNING ARRIVED, DESPITE THE time I spent the night before daydreaming a reason to cancel my meeting with Uncle Chi. I eventually resolved myself to just getting it over with, but I did think of a way to partially redeem the day: the Earthen Market.

I begged and bartered with Linah. I asked her one hundred times to take me to the Market after I met with Chi. But every time I brought it up, Linah insisted that it was too soon to take unnecessary trips and too dangerous to leave Ves alone. She was right, annoyingly, but I kept asking. I kept asking right up until something else preoccupied our minds.

Ves developed a fever. His eyes glossed over and his boyish sparkle faded. Then fatigue weighed him down so much that he forgot all his aches and itches. Linah and I watched anxiously, dampened a cloth on his forehead, helped him drink water, but we both knew: he needed different medicine. Our basic painkillers could do nothing for infection. Health would not treat him without also registering his identity.

"There is someone," Linah admitted finally as Ves sunk deeper into his fever around midday. "A Medical Bonder. She's an old friend. She would come."

"Oh! That's sugar!" Over the last few days, Ves' colloquialisms colored my language. "Let's get her up here as soon as possible."

Linah thoughtfully replied, "she will not want you to know who she is. She won't risk it."

I took only mild offense as I acknowledged the reason for the distrust: megas of other Attisians, particularly 8s, acting in distrustful ways – devaluing, manipulating, controlling. An Earthen stranger had no reason to trust me.

These were all new thoughts, new ideas, that came to mind sometimes at a slow crawl, sometimes in a burst of realization.

"Stars, all right. In that case, I'll leave early for my meeting with Chi. You can have the extra time here with the Bonder you know. I'll spend some time in town with friends."

"...What friends?"

I glanced at Linah. A tiny smile played at her lips. She was teasing me. I raised my eyebrows high. Wry humor out of Linah was an interesting development.

She had a point, though. I did not connect with the friends of my childhood anymore.

"I'll spend some time in town...eating. Stretching. Walking?" Linah nodded gratefully and gave me a good natured roll of her eyes along with it.

Barely a quarter day later, after rushing through harvesting and entering Farm data, I left Linah and Ves alone under the pretense of shopping for a new Gathering outfit. Harkless constantly messaged my Aide, reminding me about the upcoming Gathering and expounding on the virtues of his company, so the shopping excuse was plausible. In my absence, the Medical Bonder would arrive, tend to Ves, and then leave again without my ever setting eyes upon her. Secret identity intact. And, at the proper time, I would be in town for the dreaded meeting with my uncle.

The plan was solid and simple, my favorite kind. Down the mountainside in Shamong, I leisurely bought a snack, a fiber cone filled with fried chunks of some kind of tuber, and watched the Attisians around me doing Attisian things. They glided by on the transport, met with friends, conducted business. If they knew about what I had done, I thought, would they hate me? Suddenly, instead of diligent members of my home Society, they seemed like barely tamed animals with predators' eyes.

The city felt lonely and dangerous compared to the new camaraderie and relative anonymity at home. That word: home. The Farm felt like home again, and Ves must have been the catalyst. Every day, I talked to Ves and Linah. Every day, we learned a little more about each other. Every day we took care of each other. We had become a team.

I liked it, mostly, but it also made me deeply afraid. Afraid enough to shut the whole thing down. Though our rhythm at home was pleasant now, there were still so many possible outcomes. The majority of them were grim, and some of them were deadly grim.

Overwhelmed, I stopped to stare into a Clothing named Galaxy Dreamer. Tunics of grey and green and other muted colors hung on the racks inside. A hologram in the window boasted reduced prices on anti-radiation leggings. A dimensional projection activated in the glass right in my line of sight. The projection perfectly mimicked my size and shape and duplicated my movements exactly. The reproduction cycled through different outfits, boots, and hairstyles, with the price of each item displayed beside it. None of the very personal advertising did anything to entice me to buy. More than anything, it made me more indecisive. *Grey? Blue? Simple? Ornate? Do I try to dress like an 8, or spend a modest amount of money and not care that I look more like a 5?*

Those thoughts felt more draining than the hard labor at the farm ever did. I turned away in frustration just as my Aide pinged ungraciously to inform me that the time had come. I abandoned the Clothing and tried to gather my courage for a meeting with Uncle Chi.

I only visited Uncle Chi about the business of his guardianship. In a pretense of familial loyalty, Chi habitually set up such meetings to discuss the technical details of my inheritance: documentation, accounts, or other Lawful things. Every time, he tried to convince me to step back into Society for the sake of the family image. The truth was that I embarrassed him. I was a blotch on the perfect image he cultivated, and he made sure that I knew it. In the beginning of our arrangement, I felt confused and upset by his unfeeling treatment, but as I understood him more through the megas, only anger remained.

The stunning and towering gate doors of the Palisade loomed above the bustling streets and delineated the elite neighborhood from the rest of the city. I pulled up my sleeve to display the eight glowing dots of my Aide, and the Lawman stationed at the gate motioned me through without any questions. She did not even bother to look at my face.

Inside the Palisade, the structures were larger and more intricate, with angled facets that reflected the sunslight. The benches had spiraled legs and the glass tiles had decorative sculptures. Glass had the greyish tint of the native silicon in most of Shamong, but not in the Palisade. There was color and clarity. Tints of red, yellow, orange.

Projections on the windows advertised luxuries, travel destinations, and various political candidates for an upcoming election, many of which supported the reelection of our current First Statesman and her team of experts. Many others supported a new candidate, an entirely unattractive male, named Nolin Hodgins 7. Under his face and name shone a single word: Reform. Stars. Interesting strategy. Collectively, people on Attis were proud and did not like to be criticized. Reform smacked of criticism.

Being in the Palisade gave me a familiar feeling of discomfort. In my youth, I spent hours playing with schoolmates in the sparkling Palisade. We ate at lush restaurants open only to residents and chased each other through manicured parks. But I had difficulty fitting in there as a farmer's daughter—a Lūnar farmer's daughter at that. My outfit was too utilitarian. My nails were permanently discolored from the dark soil. Instead of a household full of Bonders, we had only one...

How did the other families of the Palisade treat their Bonders? My parents had been kind to Linah; they were never violent or harsh. They gave her my mother's old clothes and offered her the same deformed produce that we often ate. Nothing in their actions suggested that Linah was second-rate or deficient. I assumed all Bonders were treated similarly enough, but now I doubted it. I had proof in fact, in Ves. How many Taskers were cruel to their Bonders?

An uncomfortable thought settled in my chest as I trudged onward through the Palisade. Just like other Taskers, my parents had the power to hurt Linah, even though they did not use it. On Attis, all Bonders lived under the threat of that power.

I passed restaurants, shops for pampering, smokehouses, and pubs, all decorated with glassworks of the highest caliber, until I found the woven bamboo door of my uncle's office. The door unsurprisingly displayed his support of the current Statesman: no reform for Uncle Chi. He was wealthy and ensconced and could not imagine changing anything that might change his own life too.

I heard him already ranting inside. "The captain must be stopped. The Captain is a thief. The Captain must be found," the muffled words seeped around the edges of the fiber door. I pictured Chi, red-faced, yelling into his Aide or at some underling.

During a break in the volume of his voice, I braced myself and knocked. I entered at his call. The space contradicted itself: few furnishings and limited decoration acknowledged the supposedly vital minimalism of survival in an Outpost, but the opulent finishes, Lūnar technologies, and an ostentatious ancestry projection clearly announced the wealth and indulgence of the occupant.

I wanted to conclude the meeting as quickly as possible, but my uncle had other plans. I knew it the moment I walked inside. At my entrance, not only did Chi stand to greet me, so did everyone else in the room.

CHAPTER 17 :
A MODEL OF OUTPOST PERFECTION

I FROZE, UTTERLY UNSURE WHY anyone but my uncle was present, and attempted to control my surprise.

Crammed into the office, drinking golden Jui, a bamboo liquor, in faceted glass goblets and looking very self-important, stood a collection of Shamong's richest men and women and their heirs apparent. All of them wore clothes that outshone my utilitarian Farm attire stolen from my parents' closet. The tunics and saris worn in this room, while retaining the same fundamental forms as standard Attisian clothing, conformed to their bodies perfectly with expert tailoring. The fabric, rich and thick, held its form when they moved and displayed their personal styles and preferences with subtle textures, unusual collars and cuffs, and for the most brazen, embroidery and fringe.

Harkless smirked at me from a corner next to his older brother, Rankin, who was slightly less handsome but even more frightening. With one arm draped possessively on Rankin's shoulder, Sarai Olmstead 8, my cousin through marriage, and therefore the current heir to my uncle's legacy and his algae factory, lounged smugly. She did not choose to stand in greeting like some of the others. Her night-black tunic almost disappeared underneath additional items of clothing all made of fabrics that could not possibly be bamboo. While still black, they varied in shine and texture and ornamentation. The oversize jacket was fluffy; the tight hood and vest gleamed brighter than polished glass. Her leggings might as well have been nothing but glittering beads glued right to her body. All of it had to have been imported from Lūn. As usual, she was overdressed for the situation. But what was the situation?

Perceiving my mounting alarm, and possibly fearing I might just run right out the door again, which was a valid concern, my uncle spoke rapidly. "Araminta.

Thank you for taking time out of your busy schedule to come to me today." My uncle had never, ever been polite about my work at the Farm before. But he had an audience.

"Please join us. I believe you already know everyone in this room." His formality and friendliness added to my confusion, and no words willingly came out of my mouth. The group stared at me, calculating, smirking, sizing me up. I felt hunted by this pack of rich people, not welcomed. I held my hands tightly together to keep them from smoothing down my hair or adjusting the open pockets on my tunic.

"What a surprise," I finally stammered.

"I'm sure it is," acknowledged my uncle with more of his standard, caustic tone. His ecru tunic hung loosely on his bony frame, which looked all the more rickety because of his overlarge head and twisting pouf of hair coiffed atop it. I often wondered how he stayed upright. His buoyant hair, whiter every time I visited, had been dyed a jarring dark brown. Uncle Chi's eyes flared below his bouffant, commanding me to control myself. "Since you haven't seen most of them in megas." There it was: the barely veiled criticism. His capacity for politeness exhausted itself quickly.

"It's such a delight to see you, Minty," Sarai chimed sweetly but with an unreadable smile. She wore her lush brunette hair in a pattern of many braids that hung below her hood around her neck and chest, which I assumed were the forward fashion at the time. I remembered Sarai at twelve megas old, striking even then, who somehow commanded equal parts adoration and fear from the other girls in school. She held all of us in a subversive competition to stay in her good graces. My Lūnar blood meant I had to work the hardest for her continual approval. That was, until I stopped caring.

"Sarai," I acknowledged. Uncle Chi pursed his lips at my curt and impolitic reply, but at least he got down to business instead of giving me more chances to embarrass him.

"Araminta. As we've tried to discuss many times, after the untimely reentering of your parents, I became your guardian, financial and otherwise. I've handled the management of your mother's inheritance in the fashion that she requested. Even though she forfeited many of her prospects by partnering with your father and disavowing the family duty, the amount you'll receive is still significant, as is the amount of influence you may choose to wield. It is an honor and privilege to be an 8 in our Society, one that I, as a 7, understand fully. You will be watched and admired. People will look at you to understand our Outpost way of life, the way of life your ancestors worked and sacrificed to create. You, and other 8s, will design the future."

Since I had not even spoken to another 8 for several megas, except for Harkless' recent visit, Uncle Chi's statement sounded small-minded at best, self-righteous at worst. I confidently assumed that Linah and thousands like her never admired my uncle as a model of Outpost perfection.

"I have granted you significant leeway since your parents' Reentering. I assumed your misanthropic response to be based in grief–in grief, and not rebellion or idiocy–and I still assume as such. But the time has come to prove my assumptions founded and allay any misgivings your behaviors have raised amongst your community. Educate yourself, step into your duties."

Chi used more three-syllable words than normal. He must have practiced his speech in preparation for my visit. Dramatically, he lifted both palms toward the occupants of the room.

"These fine citizens, who I invited here today, and who run the very industries our city survives upon, along with myself, form an alliance for prosperity. We work together to survive. To thrive. We have assembled a recommendation for the wealth that passes to your control at your emancipation." He tapped his Aide and my wrist vibrated at the arrival of a new message. "Please review our recommendations and advise me on your intentions and questions. All in this room agree to the appropriateness of this document." Though he spoke of their service to me, there was no kindness in his face. He failed to completely mask the sharp eagerness in his expression.

I strained to keep my expression neutral as frustration boiled under a layer of confusion and helplessness. I could not process his words while everyone stared at me.

"We've had to do this because, as far as I can tell, you are ill-informed and out of touch. I hope to see your interest grow after the generous efforts of this group. I hope you will be the wise young citizen I believe you can be, and that your side of the family will no longer show the imprudence and whimsy that undid your mother." Some of the crowd smirked, some shifted their weight, some frowned, but all of them reacted to the reminder of my mother's choices. To her credit, Sarai rolled her highlighted brown eyes behind Chi's back.

Only the judging gaze of twenty very important people kept me from exploding at my unfeeling uncle. Through gritted teeth, I managed, "You know as well as I, my mother was never undone."

"Well." My uncle licked his lips like he saw me as a Gathering feast. "We hope you'll join us at our next meeting, Araminta. But for now, please excuse us. We have a final issue to address before we adjourn. Candidates-elect have announced their intentions for the upcoming election; it is a heavy matter. Next time, I will expect your contribution to this complex discussion. You, on the other hand, have some important reading and studying to complete. I greatly desire your input and participation once you have proven worthy."

With a motion of fingers too long and spindly to be anything but menacing, Uncle Chi waved me away. I was dismissed. Meeting over. I had said only a single sentence in a meeting about my future.

Forgetting all decorum and forfeiting any of my remaining dignity, I scrambled out of that awful room and back to the open street of the Palisade. Though the temperature outside was the same pleasant coolness as it always was, my cheeks flushed and sweat dripped down my spine.

I collapsed onto a bench across the street while unexpected sobs climbed up my throat and threatened to get loose into the world. I battled to keep them inside. The new message from Chi pinged my Aide again. I looked long enough to see it contained a huge data file entitled: DON'T BE A FOOL, ARAMINTA.

My head dropped to my knees and my tears gently splattered onto the grey glass tiles beneath my boots. I debated whether the unwelcome tears came from fear or anger. Both?

My life, in summary, had abruptly become very uncomfortable. I hid a sick Earthen boy illegally on my Farm. I ran that Farm all by myself. I was becoming increasingly disillusioned by parts of my Outpost, and a few of the most powerful elites just tried to bully me into a future designed by them. And my parents were still gone.

Loneliness. My tears might have been from loneliness.

CHAPTER 18 :
MUCH TO CONSIDER

"MEETING FINALLY ADJOURNED!" A CHEERFUL voice boomed above the ambient clatter of the street. "Stars, I hate those things. Though I don't mind the liquor." Harkless, again.

The biting and sweet smell of Jui settled around me when he moved closer. "It's surprising that I still get an invite. My dad's as delusional as your uncle that way." His joke did not impress me, but my blistering glare did not impress him either.

He loitered casually beside me, running a hand through his impressive hair. "He's trying to intimidate you, you know. That's the purpose of the group meeting back there. He wants you to believe all those people can control you and your wealth. That they know best."

I tried to muster my normal verve. "You always have something to say, Harkless."

"Perhaps. But 99 percent of the time, it's true." When I eyed him skeptically, he amended, "Fine. 99 percent of the time it is something that I want to say." He sat on the bench beside me and leaned back, legs wide, always confident. Though I wished he would leave me alone, his presence distracted me enough to dispel my tears. I thought back to the lanky Harkless from school whose underdeveloped charm came across as pure nuisance. Now he was so much larger and sturdier beside me. And maybe the tiniest bit less annoying.

"But really, I am right about this one." Another hair rake. "That was an ambush, wasn't it? I somehow convinced myself that you knew what you were stepping into. But, then again, your uncle and most of the folks in there are manipulative 'as hell,' as the Earthens so nicely put it. Not all 7 and 8s are like that bunch of jagwads."

"Jagwads? That's your own father and brother in there, Harkless."

He nodded with exasperation. "Disgusting creatures. I'm sure I didn't biologically come from that family."

"Except you look exactly like them."

"Coincidence! So, Araminta Bradford 8, what do you plan to do with your inheritance?" Harkless lightly tapped my forehead between my eyebrows. "You. Not your uncle. Not their little organization in there. You."

"I haven't even thought about it! I know that I should have." I sighed. "But I've been thinking about too many other things. There's no way that Chi and I agree on that entire document, right?" I managed a weak smile. "So, I just don't know."

"Hm. Well, there's much to contemplate when disposing of a moderate fortune. There are investments to consider, travel to experience, partners to attract..." I gaped at him but then observed the amusement in his eyes. I let it pass, hoping to rob him of the satisfaction of a big reaction from me. "And..." he continued, "quite a few causes to support. Particularly of the humanitarian sort."

I stared down at my clenched hands and examined his point. His words struck me in a way he could not guess. My fortune, my choice. I could purchase off-world passage for Ves if I had full access to my own money. I could bribe for secrecy. I could even give Ves enough money to start him well in one of the bond-free settlements. My imagination accelerated as I envisioned using my fortune to help Ves and even others like him. The possibilities were interesting.

Suddenly sensing my prolonged silence, I snapped my attention back to Harkless, who studied me thoughtfully. He stood and offered his hand to help me rise.

"Whatever it is you choose to do, I suggest you play along with your uncle for this last cycle until your birthday. It's the best way to guarantee an easy transfer of your inheritance."

"What do you mean?" I ignored his hand and remained seated. "It's my money when I turn 17."

"True, in a perfect world, which the ABEs have yet to produce. You clearly hadn't noticed, but a few cycles back, your uncle presented a law to the Advocacy adjusting the age of emancipation to 18. It was denied, but he's still campaigning for it. Minty, he's trying to change an entire Outpost law to delay his loss of your assets and your Advocacy seat. And now a Lawman, along with yours truly, made a call to your Farm under suspicion of aid to an Earthen. He may try to portray you as incompetent. It won't hurt to mollify him here and there. Come to the Gathering. Show an interest in life as usual in Shamong. Maybe fake a smile in public. Or actually, any time."

"I do smile," I defended myself, scowling. The family's Advocacy seat. I had completely forgotten about it. I felt weary and sorry for myself all over again.

"When did this all get so difficult?"

Harkless laughed. "It's always been difficult. You've just been hiding from it for a while. Not that I blame you after you lost your parents. You're like a wounded, naive, pretty, little Lūnar-blooded groundhog. Welcome back to the world, little groundhog. It's going to be an...experience."

"Harks!" a musical voice called. Sarai sauntered toward us. "I'm going to take a stroll around Circle Park. I need to shake off that imperious 7 energy. So much formality, endless posturing, unscrupulous manipulation. Stars, get me out of here. Escort me?" She wound her arm into Harkless' with a look that might have been a smile but contained too many layers of meaning for me to dissect.

"Always." Harkless pulled her closer as she draped a perfect hand over his shoulder. "You know I'll get my hands on you any way I can."

"Charming as you have ever been, Harks. I invited Ran, but your father already has him headed back to the Port. Poor repressed soul. Oh, hello again, Minty. Want to take a stroll?" Sarai turned to me only partially. Her offhanded invitation made her expectations quite clear. I bit back an impulsive response because, if what Harkless revealed to me about Chi's motivations was true, his suggestion was smart; I needed to play his social game. But an afternoon in the company of a handsy Harkless Stille 8 and an overt Sarai Olmstead 8 was way too much, way too fast. And, on top of that, I had Ves and Linah back at home.

"No, thanks. I have to work. But...another time, yes." The last phrase practically hurt me to say, but I managed it. Sarai looked startled and amused, but then flashed me a wary glance before turning away and pressing close to Harkless. She led him down the street, away from me.

"Until another time then!" Sarai sung.

Harkless unknowingly had given me just what I needed. Ideas. A little bit of control. The desire to decide for myself. I sat straighter as he walked away.

"Harkless!" I called. He turned his head. "Thanks for the advice."

He winked and kept walking.

CHAPTER 19 :
I SHOULD SHARE THEM

I STAYED RIGHT THERE ON the bench in the Palisade and tried to apply my newfound ideas. I opened the download that my uncle and his team of elites had oh-so-thoughtfully provided. The text went on for paragraphs and paragraphs. Legal jargon and formal language complicated my ability to understand it.

What I did manage to decipher made me angry.

The document suggested a healthy monthly stipend for my living expenses then divided my remaining inheritance into donations, investments, and management, all at the direction of my uncle. Fundamentally, they intended that I have the freedom to live comfortably, and all the excess would be gifted to my uncle, or at least to the causes and companies my uncle supported. The plan left very little flexibility for me to step further into the management of the funds–now, in the future, or at any time I might change my mind. It resigned me to my quiet Farm life forever. A few cycles ago, perhaps that would have suited me just fine, but I had become–different. I had no other words to describe it yet.

The document also clearly instructed me to waive my Advocacy seat. During his time as my guardian, my uncle served in the family seat, as I was too young and had not taken my Oath. I suspected he thrived on the attention and status it afforded him. He likely loved to campaign for the causes and Laws that he saw to be most valuable to his purposes, which were money and power for himself. Though the Advocates should be only motivated by the good of the Outpost, I could imagine Uncle Chi cozying up to the First Statesman and her cabinet without much subtlety.

The original ninety-three families that survived the travel to Attis and began settlement were each awarded a single Advocacy seat. The seats represented wisdom, perspective, and an utter commitment to the Outpost. It was our Society's highest honor. Nothing but death or willful abdication stripped the seat from the first born of each generation.

Advocates endlessly, and sometimes aggressively, argued points to the government and ABEs in their areas of expertise and strongest opinions. I never seemed fit for an Advocacy seat, but now that I had been asked to abandon it, the idea chafed. That seat belonged to my mother. And to her father. And on back through the seven generations on Attis. My mother clung to the seat even when most Attisians stopped listening to her.

"Money is power," my mother said to me when I wished she would not attend an Advocacy session. She always seemed nervous beforehand and depressed afterward. "But wisdom is also power. Truth is also power. Love is also power." She sighed and hugged me or pulled a strand of hair behind my ear. "I don't have much money anymore, but perhaps I have the other things. I should share them, don't you think? With what I have, I can still choose well."

The warmth of the buried memories flowed through me. I told myself that I could do it; reject the plan Uncle Chi crafted and build my life the way I wanted. For a long while I allowed my budding determination to do battle with my doubts and uncertainty. Time passed, until a figure moved in close enough to block the light of the suns and cover me in shadow.

I tilted my face up to a grey, cloaked figure, taller than me, with a hood pulled over a blaze of pale hair.

"Linah!" I said, enthusiastically. "What are you doing here?" I searched her face for fear or urgency, but I saw only a small smile and a mischievous sparkle in her blue eyes.

She gestured for me to follow her, and we ducked into a quiet alley away from the crowds. "Good news!" she almost whispered when she felt confident no one listened. "The Medical Bonder says Ves should be fine! The fever is from an infection in one of his cuts. It hasn't reached his blood. She says there is nothing to fear now that he has the right medicine. She's going to stay with him until the fever breaks, to make sure she's got the right dose..." Though her words were optimistic, Linah's expression still showed deep fatigue. "He's so young and has so many injuries. She gave us some special cream to help the cuts heal faster."

"Whew." That eased one tiny part of the anxiety that boiled in my chest. "That is wonderful news. But you left the Farm to let me know?" Concern about the two Earthens at home without me or Linah crept into my throat, despite my best efforts. I felt protective of the Farm. I felt protective of Ves. I felt protective of myself. What if the Lawman came by again? What if an accident happened on the Farm and they did not know how to fix it?

"Well, yes. Ves has an excellent babysitter for a while: a friend and a

Medical – the best kind. And she still doesn't want you to know who she is. If she is there, she'd like you to stay away. So, I had this idea." Linah's eyes practically projected light as they widened with enthusiastic anticipation "Do you still want to go to the Market?"

CHAPTER 20 :

GRAVE CONSEQUENCES

"OF COURSE I DO," I exclaimed. "You really think we could?"

She motioned onward with a graceful twist of her neck. "If it is okay with you, I think the best thing we can do for Ves right now is to give the Medical some time with him. I will vouch for her." As we moved down the street, she arranged herself at a respectful step behind me. "And I think both of us could use a break. It's either that I help you shop for a Gathering dress, or we go to the Market."

"That's an easy choice."

"Dresses it is," Linah declared with one of her barely perceptible smiles.

"Never that. Never dresses," I smirked in reply. "Lead on, Linah. I don't know the way."

We left the Palisade and headed down Founder's Way, in the direction of the plaza and the SpacePort. "It's past the Port and off the track a bit," Linah instructed, and I almost turned to ask questions. I had never explored beyond the Port on the steep slopes of the mountains. It was only quarries, factories, and the Sideways back there.

We walked leisurely through town instead of riding the transport track. At one point, Linah gently grabbed my arm and pointed to a shimmering, dark blue sari in a Clothing window. Her eyes sparkled at the striking dress. Her fingers hovered just centimeters from the glass. She wanted to touch it, I realized.

"It's gorgeous," she murmured. "I always loved blue. It's not too late to go shopping, you know."

I shrugged, feeling uninspired by a dress that looked like it would get tangled in my feet while I walked.

A hologram advertisement burst awake in front of us. "Nolin Hodgins 7. Legacy by Reform." Another election ad. They were everywhere on our walk down the street. Groups congealed to watch holograms of the candidates proclaim their plans and ideals. Sometimes the viewers seemed angry with one another. Perhaps 'Reform' was getting some attention, although I could not determine if it was good or bad attention. Something turned icy hot inside me.

More Lawmen than I thought necessary patrolled the street. Tensions appeared especially high around the next election, but were things so unstable with this election that we needed Lawmen in the streets? Or was there more? Perhaps it was paranoia, but did their eyes watch every move Linah and I made?

I picked up our pace as we scurried across the street to avoid the Exchange; I did not want anything to do with that building ever again. Its menacing aura leaked into the streets and enveloped anyone standing nearby. To my deep distress, the Lawman guarding the Exchange at that moment was Mudsil. He spotted me and caught my flinch of fear at his awareness.

He stood amongst a group of expensively dressed adults in the middle of an expressive conversation, but he turned all his attention to me in a milli.

"Mx. Bradford!" he boomed and began to cross the street. He left off the 8 in my name, demoting me in the eyes of his listeners. I instinctively stepped further in front of Linah at his approach. All his companions stopped to stare as well, including one with a wicked bruise across the bridge of his nose and his eye sockets. I looked for allies in their midst but knew none of them. I did not see any 7s or 8s; most likely they were 5s or 6s, similar in standing to Mudsil, though Mudsil could be any number. Once a citizen joined the Law, they dropped the generational marker off their name.

I begged myself to find the right words as he approached.

"Mx. Bradford. And your Bound," the Lawman chopped when he approached us. "I had hoped to hear from you, please. That Bondsboy is still missing. Is there anything you want to share?" The Lawman's voice was too loud for the situation. Everyone heard. I did not suspect until later that he did it on purpose.

"Of course not, Lawman. I would have messaged you right away." My voice came out more squeakily than I intended.

Mudsil's eyes narrowed, suspicious always, but he turned back in dismissive disappointment toward his companions. All the men in his group fixed Linah with a hateful glare that made me anxious to get away, but the bruised man inflated with rage at Mudsil's words. Even from across the street, I saw his chest rise and fall with furious breaths.

"We need to go, Linah," I whispered. She noticed the bruise-faced man too, and I felt her go eerily still beside me, as though everything but her brain stopped functioning.

The angry man came toward us like a rockslide, terrifying and inescapable.

Linah sucked in a breath. I secured my stance in front of her, and he was upon us. "You!" the man spat as he talked. Broad for an Attisian, his clothes were cut and tailored to show his powerful build. His tawny eyes flashed with alarming fury. "You! You're that sheking 'log's sister. Shek you. Where is he?" We backed away, but he matched our steps. Mudsil simply watched with one eyebrow quirked in an upward slant.

"Wait. Stop," I insisted. "She didn't do anything. Stop."

"Shut your mouth. Lawman Mudsil thinks she did. Shek both of you. Where is he?" The man attempted to lean around me to reach Linah.

"She doesn't know anything. Leave us alone," I barked at him. Passersby paused to watch our performance.

Linah's silence sent the man over the edge. He shoved me to the side so hard that I lost my footing and slammed into a wall behind us with my hip. He grasped Linah's shoulders and shook her so hard I heard her teeth crash together. "Look at my face, 'log. Look at my face! He did this to me."

"Shek! Let go!" I screamed frantically. "Help!" I tried to force myself back between them, but he boxed me out with very little effort. Lawman Mudsil only squinted at us.

The Tanker boxed me out from Linah. "Too bad you're so pretty. I'm gonna do the same to you, 'log. Shek you. And your sheking brother." His open hand connected with Linah's face and made a bizarre sound. The momentum of his swing toppled Linah to the sidewalk. A liquid hot explosion of anger flared inside me, and I barely had control of my next actions. I certainly did not plan them.

I kicked the man's knee and pushed him as hard as I possibly could "You will stay away from her!" My voice sounded manic, too high, and too loud at the same time.

The man grabbed both of my upper arms to control me. "Watch yourself, citizen. You better keep your little Earthie and yourself in line. She knows something." Before releasing me, he squeezed me so tightly that his fingers left white-hot imprints in my muscles, and I yelped in pain.

He released me with a shove, and I knelt beside Linah. At my touch, her hand left her tunic where I knew she had been grasping one of her knives. I hugged myself with one arm and tried to hug Linah with the other, but she kept her eyes and hands purposefully on the ground, choosing to control herself. For now.

"I want my property back," the man whooped, enraged. Lawman Mudsil sauntered casually closer, finally deciding to getting involved.

From my kneeling position, I saw the flapping of his jaws as he spoke to us again. "Mx. Bradford, this is that fugitive boy's Tasker, please, as I'm sure you've guessed."

"I don't care who he is, and you shouldn't either! He hurt us!" I yelled, my eyes watering. "Do something! That was violence! Right in front of you, Lawman. We don't harm one another. It's right in our creed. 'Abhor acts of violence.' That was violence!"

"Well, Mx. Bradford." He shrugged his shoulders. "He is very angry. He has lost a lot of money. The missing Earthie struck him. Broke his nose even. I am pursuing his vindication, please, as says the Law. This is what happens when Earthies run away. And–" His muddy eyes met my grey ones and narrowed as though he had a message specifically for me. "Societals that aid Law-breaking Bonders in any way have also broken the Law. Makes you a bad citizen. You know that, right, Mx. Bradford? You know there are grave consequences, please?"

"There should be grave consequences for hurting someone, too." I glared at him but did not trust myself to speak more. My rage that he refused to even reprimand the Tasker for striking me, combined with his continued suspicion, justified though it was, filled my whole body with a fluctuating combination of fury and fear.

"What in all the planes of the universes is happening here?" a voice, like a songbird that felt too bored to sing, reached us. My eyes, blurry with pain and adrenaline, focused on my cousin Sarai – shining, dauntless Sarai, who had emerged from the onlookers. The others in the small crowd just gaped at us, completely unprepared to handle the shocking events unfolding around them.

Sarai stood with her hip pushed out, letting the suns nearly blind us as her hood and pants reflected their light. "That is no mere citizen you are harassing, Lawman. Araminta Bradford is an 8. She's almost emancipated. Did you know, Lawman, that she'll have an Advocacy Seat? Stop this. Tsk, tsk. You are all being very poor citizens. Don't make me summon a Lawman to deal with another Lawman," Sarai maintained the tone of a parent disciplining unruly children, disappointed and monotone, as she shifted her weight from hip to hip and toyed with her thick braids. "Stars, that would completely ruin my day. And I can't imagine you are very popular with the other Lawmen already, Mudsil. And you–" She turned her venomous gaze to the Tasker.

The quarryman stepped away from us, clearly surprised at the description of my standing in Society. He flexed his fingers, likely considering what they had just done to my shoulders.

"She – she put her hands on me. She began it!" the tyrant Tasker growled, trying to deflect the blame of harming an 8 as best he could.

Sarai eyed him with disgust, completely unfazed by the brute. She gestured wide, pulling open her ample jacket to reveal the many other layers of clothing beneath. "You've acted like a fool. Get out of here. You've broken more Laws than anyone here, Quarryman."

The Tasker held his ground only millis longer, unable to withstand Sarai's blazing hostility. Instead, he turned to Mudsil, who he had some power over still. "Find my sheking Earthie!" He jabbed Mudsil in the chest to the rhythm of his stomping feet. With a grunt that passed as a snarl, he retreated back to the corner of the Exchange.

"This is unacceptable, Lawman," Sarai reprimanded sharply. "We are more civilized than this."

I looked up at Sarai from beside the track. Only Sarai had stepped in. Sarai, who would eventually have my Advocacy seat if I abdicated it. Sarai, who I had rejected fully in my youth.

The Lawman took his turn to retreat under her cold watchfulness. He said nothing more to anyone. I watched closely until he took up his post once more.

"Do you need anything?" Sarai asked me, but she clearly hoped we did not. She cringed when she looked at us. Not with pity. With judgment. With a different kind of disappointment.

I did not want her to see me cry, so I just shook my head.

"Get up, Araminta," she instructed. "I know you think that being an 8 is the worst thing to happen to a person, but if you are going to be living an 8s life with those grey eyes, you better start acting the part. Stand up for yourself. They don't get to treat you that way." She had nothing to say to Linah, though. "Get up." Sarai turned from us and sauntered back toward the Palisade, signaling the end of her participation.

The rest of the onlookers, still with startled eyes and rigid postures, began to disperse.

"Linah," I whispered, tears still gathered in the corners of my eyes. "Can you walk? Do you want to go home?"

"Yes, to both." A pink swath of skin swelled on Linah's cheek and temple.

"What a jagwad," I declared, using Harkless' word.

To ride the correct transport track, we had to walk past a small crowd of Attisians, now pretending they were not watching us. My indignation spiked as we passed the curious faces who had not intervened. None of these people had stepped in when that man struck Linah, or when he had menaced me. My fellow citizens stood by as Laws were mocked and as violence was perpetrated against another Attisian. I shivered.

Then I glanced up and saw him there, just watching from the entrance of a restaurant across the street. My uncle, Mx. Chi Legree 7. When our eyes met, a flash of shame crossed his face before he could control his features, and he took a step back further inside the doorway. He saw. He saw the assault and did nothing.

My last relative. My guardian.

I burned with anger and abandonment. I thought I had shut off my heart to the power of Uncle Chi's neglect, but I still felt it crack at his blatant demonstration of selfish priorities.

"Chi," I called and pointed at him. My voice wavered, not with fear this time, but with deep sadness. "Is that man your friend? Is he in your little club?" As I spoke my uncle's eyes narrowed. "You just watched while he hurt me." I did not care who heard my accusation as tears flowed down my cheek. "You've made it obvious. You are no family of mine." I tried to put my arm around Linah to lead her away, but pulses of pain prevented me from lifting my arm high enough. Bruises probably already blossomed on my shoulders.

All my doubt was gone. I would not give my uncle anything. I would not agree with his manipulative plans. I certainly would not give him my Advocacy seat.

I snapped my lips into a sharp and calculated smile. "I'll see you on my Entering Day, Chi."

7 MEGAS AGO

Supplemental excerpt from : Making a Way ; the Life and Stories,
Record HAC-3859385738

The girl awoke and remembered the sights and sounds of her injury. As pain pounded through the cavities of her eyes, behind her ears, and down her spine, her memories pulsed along with it. She was herself, but she was also new. Different. There was another presence with her, inside her, and it told her that she was not alone, that she would be all right.

During that time of extreme pain, she practiced communicating with it—listening, probing, exploring. Only once did the presence speak clearly, and it said the same thing as before: "I will show you the way."

When the girl recovered, returned home, and described the presence to her mother, her mother thought for a long time, and then called it God. Called it The First Maker.

The God inside her guided her through the rejection initially offered to her by her people, now that half her head was made of plastic and electricity. Now that she was a strange mutant created by the Taskers, she was no longer trusted by her people.

The blow that would have killed her was wonderfully convenient for an Attisian scientist visiting the Mid-Lats. He had been experimenting with combining bodies with machines. After the blow, the scientist used the Bondgirl's injury to try some new science. Science that no sane citizen would dare to try. Without agreeing to it, the girl became an experiment.

But she was a mostly successful experiment: she had lived. And for that, and sometimes for only that, the girl was grateful.

CHAPTER 21 :
TELL THEM

LINAH AND I HURRIED TO the transport track. The shock from the attack clung to me and squeezed my lungs. The physical and very public cruelty toward Linah and the complete unconcern of the crowd left me hollow and confused. For a Society that shunned violence as barbaric and prehistoric, everyone acted very passively while watching it. I hated the violence. The violence toward Ves and Linah turned my stomach and baffled my mind. I had not known Attisians did such things to Earthens, to anyone. I was repulsed.

"How long, Linah? How long has it been like this? The cruelty is so wrong," I whispered. Linah took a long time before she looked at me. Her gaze was not friendly. It did not comfort me; it judged me.

"Always, Minty. It has always been this way. For me. For all Earthens."

"I thought everyone treated their Earthens like my parents treated you. I'm sorry. The violence is so unfair I can hardly stand it. It's just wrong. How does anyone see it otherwise?"

"More than that is wrong." The conviction in Linah's words was at odds with the soft volume she used. "The whole thing is wrong. Bonding. Being Bound. To own someone is to put them beneath you, Minty, no matter how kindly you treat them. To own someone is to take power that was never meant to be yours. And to own someone is to deny them the right to be human in its true intent. I am human. Ves is human. People on Attis don't understand it. Minty, do you see it?"

I did see it. Of course, I did. At least, I had begun to. A sadness sunk deep into my chest; what Linah said meant that my Society, my own parents, even my own self – we had all been wrong. Horribly wrong. Wrong in a way that hurt others. The magnitude of what that meant for me, for all of Attis, crashed over me.

"Sometimes I get so tired of hoping people will see it." Linah's shoulders fell as she looked off toward the mountainside and took a deep breath. She softly sung The Waymaker's song to herself: Take up now, do not delay. Much may befall, fear shan't allay–

"I do see it, Linah," I managed. "I'm sorry, for all of it. I didn't understand before. How it all was. You are...well, you are my friend, I hope. You are brave and talented and smart. I see that you are a human. I see it, I feel it, I know it." None of my words felt right. They were not nearly enough.

She closed her eyes slowly as I spoke, debating whether to believe me. The sunslight made her bright yellow hair glow where it fell out of her hood. The silence stretched between us.

"If you see it, then you know things have to change," she spoke softly with eyes still shut.

"Yes." And I did know it, though I could not yet grasp what that change was or what my role was to be.

The track continued to pull us up past the edge of town, when Linah turned back toward me and grabbed my wrist. "Come with me, Minty." Her voice still sounded low and flat compared to her normal musical phrasing. I let her lead me without question, mute with the weight of our conversation.

We trekked off-track for what must have been almost a kilometer. The cube-shaped homes we passed suddenly gave way to a manicured garden of grasses and shrubs. On the opposite end of the small park, two deciduous trees struggled their way to adulthood on either side of a beautifully woven bamboo gate. The bamboo still grew from the base of the gate doors. Since settlement, the bamboo was bent and woven upward by artisans in an intricate pattern that now stretched above my head. I knew the gate. Linah brought us to the Memorial.

"Why are we here, Linah?" I asked, stopping short. "Don't you just want to go home?"

"I visit my parents' Memorial on hard days, and on good days too, but this is a hard day, wouldn't you say? A hard cycle. I want to talk to my parents," Linah responded, and some of her voice's regular lilt returned. "Maybe you can do the same." She swung one side of the gate open. I hesitantly followed her inside the Memorial.

A heavy and eerie quiet enveloped us. Rows of polished, evenly spaced rock walls blocked out the brightest light of the suns. On each stacked, rectangular stone brick, chiseled letters formed the names of the Reentered. Since settlement, that was how it had been done. Every name was recorded in the exact same size in the exact same way to make everyone valued equally in their deaths.

The engravings closest to us displayed unfamiliar names, and I struggled to recall the location of my parents' stones. I vaguely remembered their plaques to be at my shoulder height, but it had been more than two megas since their names were etched, and I had never been back.

"My parents are way in the back. So you go ahead and find yours first," Linah told me.

Linah could read, unlike many Earthens, so she would know if I faked it. I walked left, searching for my parents' names in the dark, bespeckled stones. Linah was wrong to bring me. There was no point. I did not want to speak to a rock.

My search through the maze of names only took only a few millis, even though their engravings rested lower than I expected; I had grown taller since I watched them be installed. My father's name, Alden Bradford 1, and my mother's right below his, Emmeline Legree 7. I pointed out the names to Linah and waited. See? Nothing.

"Tell them," Linah said behind me.

"Tell them, what? It's just stone."

"Tell them anything. Everything. Don't tell the rock, Minty. Tell their names. Tell your parents."

I huffed as Linah turned away for my privacy. I had nothing to say to a stone that represented the absence of my parents. For two megas, I ignored the existence of these rocks and all they symbolized.

I wanted to pick a short, true enough thing to appease Linah, and then get back to my Farm and hide away once more. "Um. I miss you," I said just loud enough for Linah to hear. A shiver ran through me when I spoke; something about saying the words out loud softened me, and I touched the engraved letters lightly. "I wish you were still here."

Once I let it out into the air, it became real, which is precisely why I had not wanted to say it. I feared it would break me, make me weak, send me back into the dark places of my grief. But I did not feel broken. I just felt...honest.

"Everything is so messed up here. I don't know what I'm doing. I'm confused. I hope..." An ache in the back of my throat stalled me for a moment. "I hope I'm doing the right thing. I hope you'd be proud. I don't know why you did what you did, but I hope you would feel the same way I do now."

My breath came easier after a while. I still felt angry and lost, but also calmer, unburdened.

"Thanks, Linah."

"I think they'd tell you happy Entering Day at this point." She smiled enough for me to be sure it was there.

"Yes. Probably."

"I am sad they are gone, too," she claimed. "They were unlike most Taskers."

I smiled wistfully then, remembering the unusual existence of my parents amidst our structured Society. "Okay, Linah, let's find your parents now."

I followed her further through the stone maze until the walls ceased completely and the mountainside started to rise under our feet. We went on for several millis until I slipped on the loose gravel of the open hillside.

"I think we missed it, Linah," I groused, annoyed at the bite of rock on my knee.

"Earthens aren't memorialized like 'Posters. Look."

We rounded a rocky outcropping and Linah gestured in front of us. Alone and lonely stood a full-grown tree. I gaped at the gangly growth with its wispy branches arching up from the trunk and draping down in a wide circle. Instead of leaves, beads and colorful scraps of fabric were tied, braided, and woven amongst the branches. Pieces of stone and glass hung from worn ropes. Hundreds, maybe thousands of trinkets decorated the strange tree and created a curtain surrounding the trunk. It dripped with colors.

"What is this?" I breathed quietly, unwilling to interrupt the strange majesty of the place.

"We call it the Cemetree." Linah exhaled. She ran her fingers through the nearest branches, and they made a chorus of tinkles and clinks. "It is a place to remember." She continued around the canopy and even leaned within the branches for a moment. She grasped a trinket attached to a single branch and separated it from the rest. Linah held an intricately braided heart of dried blue and green bamboo leaves.

"I put this here when my parents were sold to the Mid-Lats. They may still be alive, but I'll probably never know. How could I? For Ves and me, they are gone forever." She spoke more to the trinket than to me. She stroked the pattern of braids with her thumbs before clutching it to her chest. She stayed like that for a long time. When she returned to my side, the weight of the day had lifted from her somewhat.

"Now that's done," she said. "I'm going to ask you something, and I need you to be honest." She managed another very slight smile. "The Cemetree is close to the Sideways. If you feel up for it, we could still go to the Market."

"I don't know, Linah. I'm tired. Really angry. And I don't know what's going on in my head. I can't tell if I'm going to explode or implode or just shut down completely. I want to just go back to the Farm and pretend it isn't all true. Just for a little while."

Linah considered me for a moment. "One thing I remember about my parents," she said softly. "They believed that life is sometimes horrible, sometimes sweet, even as Bonders. They told me that if I let the horrible parts ruin the sweet parts, well, then it's all just horrible. Let's fight it, Minty, just for ourselves. I don't want to give that man one more moment than I must. He doesn't get any more from me." Her hand unconsciously drifted toward her knife belt. Her eyes blazed. "Let's go find something sweet today."

Linah, who took the brunt of the abuse in town, now reclaimed herself under the weight of it. I realized that cruel megas had forged her into a girl that, even in the face of her fear, could be composed and purposeful. I admired her. The thought startled me. How much did other Attisians know about their Earthens? Did they see the strength inside?

For megas, Linah and I had worked alongside one another on the Farm, and I never considered her talents or personal life, never asked, never wondered beyond the assumptions my Society provided. I let my suffering turn my whole focus inward. But Linah had been right there, suffering too.

I did not understand how the Earthens gained the reputation that Outposters declared over them, or whether the reputation had been manufactured by Outposters themselves. But, no matter the source, as reputations often did, they had kept me from seeing clearly for so long. And I, as an Attisian 8 who struggled with the Lūnar expectations placed upon me because of my father, should have known better. Earthens, it seemed, were so much more than what I had been told. *Choose well, Minty.*

Even if Linah had not changed my mind with her impassioned declaration, which she had, I would have gone anyway. To support her. To give her anything to help her cope with the unfair world around her.

"Lead the way!" I exclaimed. And we both smiled, genuinely and fully.

CHAPTER 22 :
HUMANITY

FLAVORFUL JUICE DRIPPED DOWN MY my chin, and, unwilling to let any drop escape, I used my finger to wipe it up back into my mouth. "Stars, what is this?" I asked through a mouth full of crispy corn, sautéed protein, and irresistible spices.

Linah smiled. "Tacos."

The Earthen Market in the Sideways bustled with constant motion and noise. It filled me with unfamiliar but welcome energy. Intricately patterned blankets sewn from scraps hung from posts and windows. Vegetables that I had never seen before, imperfect and irregular, shone in bold colors atop market stalls. Second-hand housewares and worn-out tech balanced precariously on tables, ready to be bartered. Vendors called to us in slang I did not always understand. All the artistry that Earthens applied to their skin in tattoos also adorned the handmade signs, shanty walls, and goods for sale at each stall.

The chorus of colors of the market were matched by the colors of the Earthens themselves. Their skin, from richest brown to palest peach, paired with hair of all different textures and colors: black, yellow, white, and even orange. Many had prominent features; others looked delicate. Some were tall and robust; some were petite and agile. Tattoos in incalculable shades, styles, and shapes decorated their bodies. To me, an Attisian used to Attisian forms and figures, they looked equal parts primeval and beautiful.

None of that beauty or vibrancy obscured the poverty of the Earthen establishment. At best, the structures were in disrepair, and at worst they were no more than hovels. Their bodies looked gaunt and in poor nutrition. Their ragged clothing displayed frequent patching and distress from harsh washing, and hardly protected their skin from the harsh suns. Next to them, Linah, fully covered in my mother's radiation cloak, which itself was discolored with use and patched with cuffs for Linah's long arms, looked positively affluent.

I finished my tacos, so Linah put a bowl of steaming broth into my hands. "Pho," she named it. The thick and salty soup went down my throat like the best medicine. I heard Linah laughing and realized I had stopped moving. Pride shone through her eyes as she sipped her own bowl.

"Linah, do they really eat like this? Every day? On Earth?" I queried. We started to walk again, Linah allowing, and being amused by, my consuming wonder and observation.

"Oh gods, no. These vendors are making the recipes of their ancestors, from all different parts of Earth. Pho comes from one culture on Earth, tacos from another." Linah mimed the shape of a planet as she spoke and pointed to opposite sides of the sphere. "An Earthen who grew up eating Pho would never have even heard of tacos. They wouldn't even speak the same language."

"So Earth still has these two groups of people that make different food and speak different languages?"

Linah scoffed, "Two? No, Minty. There are still many Earthen cultures. Hundreds, maybe. I'm not really sure how many. But they all have ancient traditions that go back to before the first wars, so far back that no one knows how they grew. They have their own foods, dances, holidays, and clothing that fit their different environments."

I paused, considering. Hundreds of Earthen cultures? Each with their own food and language? Even after all the wars? It did not fit my understanding of life on Earth.

"My ancestors lived in the cold, where ice came down from the sky for most of the mega and covered the land and waters. They harvested animals from the waters to eat and make into warm clothing. They read colors in the night skies along with the stars. They had boats. At least that is the history my grandparents taught us. It sounds impossible, but it is no more impossible than the tales of other cultures from Earth." Linah gazed upward at the colorless sky. "Minty, what do you think it feels like? To walk through ice that falls from the sky? To be in the cold?"

I only shook my head, unable to fathom such a thing and shocked by the revelation. I thought Earth was nearly barren, nearly dead, with the surviving Earthens fighting one another for the last resources. Earthens were barely more than wild tribes in perpetual conflict. In comparison, Attis' order and relative abundance was a safe harbor for the Bound, an improvement from their strife and violence. But in such an existence, there should not be communities with traditions of food and clothing. I had been wrong once again; Linah was describing entire cultures, whole Societies even, on the planet of Earth.

Earthens did not need Attis after all. They already had homes and communities to which their minds and bodies belonged.

But there in the Sideways, they cobbled together hints and shadows of the Societies that they missed. The Earthens around me found a way to survive on a planet that was strange to them and cruel to them. They lived their culture, history, and knowledge as best as they could. Just as my father missed Lūn, they all must miss their homelands, too.

My father, though, he had chosen his path. He chose to partner with my mother and live with her on Attis. Earthens did not choose this life.

"They have to be very strong, the Earthens," I whispered to Linah. "Thank you for sharing this place with me."

"*I* am Earthen, Minty. What you are learning now, Ves and I have lived our whole lives." She wore a somber expression as she watched me process her words. But then she put on a mischievous grin and added, "I'm glad you get to see it. And I'm glad you are paying for all the food."

"Happy to." I mumbled, and added a smile for her sake. "This place... It's a lot to experience. To take in. Tell me more about it. Are these all free Earthens?" I noticed SubAides glowing blue on many of the Earthens' wrists, but also many horizontal scars, where SubAides once had been. A few of the Earthens had completely bare wrists, without a SubAide or a scar.

SubAides were uncomplicated but effective technology, much simpler than an Aide. Primarily they tracked property and registered ownership. SubAides were designed to be permanent, removable only by the permissions of the Tasker to which the Bonder belonged. Even when a SubAide was removed legally, a scar always remained. But as Ves' destroyed wrist demonstrated, with great effort and pain, SubAides sometimes could be forcibly removed.

"Some of them. Many of the vendors are unbound or have been freed. But most of the shoppers are Bound, like me."

"It's like a city. It's a whole other city right inside of Shamong. How do they get away with this?"

"I don't have an answer. Even those who live and work here aren't sure, but they don't question it." Linah thought hard for a moment. "I have a theory about it. I think Attisians are so obsessed with order and progress, they have built rules for themselves that are less necessary than they believe. I could be wrong. But the ABEs can't be as strict as Attisians think. I've heard that ABEs come through the Market sometimes, observing, measuring. But they've never changed anything. They've never actually Manipulated anything here."

I frowned deeply. Our Outposter lives were so carefully monitored. Why not here in the Sideways? Why did ABEs treat the Earthens differently than the

Attisians they were made to serve? The sole purpose of the ABEs was the survival of the Outpost. So did we misunderstand the intention of the ABEs, or did the Earthens know something we did not? I yearned to ask my parents, especially my father. Did he know a way to get around the monitoring of the ABEs, or did he know that the rules were not as strict as implied? Had he visited the Market himself?

No, my parents would not have dared to shop at the Market and possibly incur more judgment from Society. Choose well, they often said, but they meant it about my own personal well-being. To shop in a place run by Earthens, unsanctioned by the government, unmonitored by the ABEs – they would not risk it. They had already lost so much and fought so hard for any scrap of respect. They could not bear to lose more. Perhaps, I wondered, they could not bear for me to lose any more by their choices.

My thoughts were interrupted by a thin girl–possibly thirteen megas old, with skin somewhat darker than mine–who boldly stepped toward me. She wore a loosely draped yellow tunic that perfectly matched the bundle of enormous and arresting flowers she cradled in one arm. The flowers' long and thick stalks burst wide open at the top in a massive bloom of small yellow petals surrounding a circle of dark seedlings. Something about the impossible and gangly flowers gave me a jolt of joy.

"Sunflower, Mx.?" she queried with a bold but girlish voice.

"Sun flower?" I responded. "These are called sun flowers? I've never heard of them before."

"They are an Earthen breed, Mx. Very hearty. Named because they look like Earth's sun-star. You can eat the seeds with proper preparation too. I just sold out of the seeds, but come by tomorrow again, and I'll have more." She spoke confidently in a way that was just short of haughty. Something about her was familiar.

"Have we met?" I asked. Her tan eyes met my grey ones, and the nagging feeling that I knew her grew. But she shrugged lightly.

"No, Mx. I'm sure I'd remember you. I know all the 'Posters that come through here. Besides, if you've never seen a sunflower before, then you've never seen me either, I expect. I'm always around my sunflowers." Her grasp of Common language was excellent, almost as good as Linah's. Most likely this girl had been born here in Shamong and was raised speaking Common.

"I'll take a sun flower, thank you," I twirled and admired the sanguine flower while the girl transferred payment from my Aide to an old-model device used to complete transactions without the use of an Aide. "Surely, surely Earth's sun isn't this color."

"I don't know from experience, Mx. But wouldn't that be something? A bright yellow sun? And only one of them?" We both grinned at the ridiculous and blinding vision. "Come back again, I hope," she said and receded into the line of vendors. As her oversized tunic slipped down her shoulder, I spotted a colorful sun flower tattoo, as well as an angular symbol rendered in dark blue.

That same angular symbol occurred repeatedly as we strolled down the unpaved pathway. Often drawn or painted in blue, the triangle had lines curved inward and small loops on each point. The symbol decorated flags; it adorned arms as tattoos; walls and windows had them painted in corners. The Earthens applied the symbol anywhere.

"Linah. That shape. The blue triangle. Right there. Does it mean something?" We stood in an uneven clearing, like a courtyard made only by many feet flattening it over time. We ate a greasy and starchy dish that the vendor called "frites," though she corrected herself with a shake of their head, "Well, almost like frites. As close as we can get."

Earthens collected in groups, lounging, eating, or playing unusual musical instruments. The beats of a homemade drum pulsed appealingly and threatened to bob my head against my will. Several Earthens danced freely and feelingly. I had witnessed and participated in plenty of dancing at Gatherings, but never with such open abandon.

A man—tall, broad, and copper-skinned—was lifting a heavy rod draped with fabric while other Earthens scrambled to secure it beneath him, as though the simple structure had fallen and they were attempting to rebuild it. The tall man's smile could be seen all the way across the clearing. While he stood under the weight of their project, others came up to ask him questions or possibly even tease him, as one adolescent pretended to stomp on his foot. The sound of their laughter reached us.

"Oh, yes." Linah surprised me by pulling out the collar of her tunic to show me her shoulder. A tattoo of the symbol decorated her silvery skin, again in blue. The beginnings of other tattoos peeked out from her clothing, and I wondered how many colorful tattoos Linah hid beneath her drab work outfit. "It's the Humanity symbol." She pointed to the topmost point of the triangle, "Earthens." Then she moved her finger to the bottom right point, "Lūnars." The point on the left she described as, "Outposters." She circled all three points. "Together we are all of humanity. We are the ultra-intelligent life in the universe. We are somewhat different from one another, of course, but we are all human. The symbol means unity. Of all human races."

"I like it," I said genuinely. "Where does it come from? Earthens obviously use it. Do Lūnars? Do Outposters?"

"There are rumors that some do." Linah eyed me slyly. "You should ask

Harkless about that."

"Harkless has a tattoo? Of a unity symbol?" I gawked, both highly shocked and highly amused. "His family would shun him. More than they do already, at least. But maybe that's why he did it. Still, kind of risky, isn't it?"

"Not really where he put it." Linah laughed. I studied her. Clearly Linah and Harkless had a longer connection than I knew about. But how? And was it a good connection? Or something more menacing? There was no venom in Linah's voice when she mentioned him.

"Okay, tell me more!"

Linah looked as though she was considering it, until her name was shouted several times.

"Liny! Hey there, Liny!" The towering man was now free of his work with the tent and approached us, crackling with energy. He appeared even taller as he neared, and his smile sparkled even brighter. He wrapped his arms around Linah and swayed in a bouncy dance. His face was lean and undeniably kind. He had experienced quite a few more megas than me, but his pearly teeth shone from an enormous grin accented by his deep brown skin. Grey hairs bespeckled his beard and hairline.

"Don't be rude, Beecher!" Linah laughed. "I brought a guest today." Her tone was scolding, but she smiled. Beecher turned his extravagant smile toward me.

"Oh, of course, ya! Forgive a silly old man excited to see little Linah. You're Mx. Araminta Bradford 8. I'm glad to meet ya. Not many 8s make their way through here. I hope you are having a nice experience." He held his hand forward and outward in my direction. His Common Language, though not as crisp and fluid as Linah's, was easily comprehensible.

Linah gestured. "Minty, this is Beecher. Ves and I have known him a long time. He's mostly wonderful, but beware. He claims to be very witty." Then Linah grabbed my hand and put it behind Beecher's. "Earthens touch the backs of their hands as a greeting," she explained.

Beecher laughed fully from his gut, and his toothy grin did not falter. I discovered a smile on my face in response. I could not help it; it appeared all on its own.

"Beecher is an Elder around here. We call him Elder Beecher. Think of him as an Earthen Advocate or Statesperson," Linah explained.

I eyed the stained shirt that hung on his frame and covered no more than his torso, revealing grizzled muscles on his tattooed arms. His feet were bare. He noticed my gaze and laughed once more.

"I know, ya? I'm not fancy. But around here we try to live like the ancient texts tell us. To lead is to be a servant. Should I lead hungry people if I am not hungry too?" His words startled me with their beauty, but he did not allow me any time to think too hard about them. "Speaking of being a servant, Mx. Araminta Bradford 8, thank ya for what ya did for...our friend. That took guts. And some kinda love. And we respect that around here, guts and love. I do miss that kid. The boys' house is just a little bit too quiet now that he's away. They've been feeling a bit bored without his jokes and troublemaking." As he spoke, his unending smile somehow expressed sadness and affection. He drew Linah into a bear hug and patted her head. "How you doing, Liny? Really."

Linah sighed. "Not now, Beecher, okay? Soon, maybe."

"Whatever ya' need, ya' know that, right?"

"Of course. Beech, we had a bad experience in town. So right now, we are just trying to have a little fun. Minty is a farmer, so she's excited to see the Market for the very first time." Then her voice dropped to a nearly inaudible whisper. "Has there been word? Do you know when he can run?"

"No, child. Not yet. But be patient. The Waymaker is as fierce as a rockslide but much more reliable." He tried to tilt his head to look at Linah's face as he said, "Now, what about this experience in town?" Instead of explaining, Linah just squeezed into his hug tighter to keep him from seeing the early blush of a bruise on her face. Beecher shook his head, compassion in his eyes, strong arms providing a protective embrace.

I started to feel awkward as their hug continued, which Beecher must have noticed because he reached out and pulled me right into their hug. He was tall enough that we fit nicely beneath each arm. Tucked in by hands that seemed as big as plates, and pulled up close to his broad chest, Linah and I were practically nose-to-nose. It was the first hug I had gotten in a very, very long time. Tears gathered in my eyes, but I fought them away.

How bizarre my life had become. I stood in the middle of an Earthen market, staring at my yellow-haired Earthen sort-of friend, being hugged by a huge Earthen elder, because of a little Bound boy hidden away at my Farm. How in the stars did it come to be? I let a strangled laugh escape.

Linah caught my eye and winked. Even her winks were graceful. Perhaps she understood my thoughts, at least partially. I gave myself into the hug, maneuvering slightly to not crush my beautiful sun flower. I heard the rumble of a chuckle in Beecher's chest as I let my head relax toward him.

"Ya," he mused. "Hope always comes when you don't expect it. You just never can tell with hope. It's always been that way, and I suspect it always will be."

But, even there, the small sweetness Beecher helped us to find was to end. There was nowhere to go in Attis unshadowed by suspicion and megas of power unbalanced.

CHAPTER 23 :
DIG UP

AT FIRST, I MISSED THE shift. Warnings sounded in my subconscious, breaking through the pleasantness of Beecher's hug. When I acknowledged them and searched for the source, I found it, across the little clearing. One musician had ceased drumming; he stared at us. Distrust. Anger. Hatred. No, not at us–at me.

The hug broke apart. I fought to keep an aching cry from leaving my lips; my skin and my heart asked for more hugs, more safety, however imagined. I inspected the rest of the Earthen crowd around us. Few of them glared at me with the drummer's venom, but several faces betrayed flashes of anger or contempt. More acted skittish or uncomfortable. I sensed Beecher tensing beside me as he noticed the same.

"Ah," Beecher whispered. "Today is a hard day. There were Stalkers here." Linah's features transformed into a twist of anxiety. Her pale eyebrows lifted high while sparks crackled through her blue eyes, and her hands clasped near her heart.

"Did they take anyone?" she croaked.

"No, no' this time. We had enough warning. They were looking for a man called Wei and his wife, but you know they've got a list of hundreds of fugitives. They made a mess of a few stalls. I could offer the families a small amount of relief, but it's happening more and more often. It's gotten harder t' offer any real help."

Beecher offered me the apologetic version of his smile. Linah, in a low voice, described yet another facet of their Earthen life to me. "The Advocacy passed a law last mega. Attisians have to send fugitives back to their Taskers, no matter how long they have been living free or where they are discovered...even in the Bond-free zones. The Stalkers come through, seeking fugitives for reward money. They take Earthens that they suspect to be runaways and drag them back to their Taskers. No questions, no trial and judgment, no recourse."

Beecher shook his head, the muscles of his neck bulging with the movement. "They are nothing but bounty hunters, and they know no borders. They like t' search here in Shamong; with a SpacePort, many fugitives end up here, or at least passing through here." There was deep compassion in his eyes as he scanned the faces around him. "My Earthens 're angry. No, no, scared mostly, then angry."

Yet another reason for the Earthens to be scared. Another way my Society imposed different and much crueler rules upon them. I thought of the documents, signed by my parents, that listed Linah in my holdings and as my property. Being bound was just another way to say "owned." The skin around my Aide felt hot with shame, along with my cheeks.

Menacing glares from Earthens, who had just been stalked, might be expected. I was unwelcome there as an Attisian, as a representative of those making them afraid. The ambiance continued to worsen in the little park; the music dwindled, and more and more turned to watch me.

"This wasn't a good day to come," Linah mumbled and grabbed my elbow. "I'm sorry, Minty. Another time." Disappointment filled her tone. "We're leaving," she declared loudly enough to be overheard. My cheeks grew hot with injustice and self-consciousness. Their anger felt unfair. They did not know me or what I had done.

Unfair. The word seemed to be everywhere these days.

As we turned back toward the way we came, I cast my eyes downward and hoped to avoid a conflict. Beecher's weight shifted beside me, and I chanced a glance back at the clearing. All was silent, bated. The drummer stood, his posture menacing and his expression ferocious.

"A Societal!" he sneered. His voice sounded older than his looks, and it projected across the eerie stillness. Scratchy. Pained. "And an original from the looks of her. You an 8? Pure Society? And just one of you? Feeling so confident, eh? Just go where you want, when you want?"

"Damon, dig up," Beecher responded. "Ya going to make something bad even worse. She's shopping. Spending money. That's a good thing. Don't keep diggin' the holes, Damon. Hate jus' digs the holes deeper."

"I'll not have your spouts of wisdom, Elder. Not today. Hey, Society." The man ignored Beecher and drew two steps closer. "This is my house. You'll get no welcome from me."

The tension in the little clearing inflated to a breaking point, barely contained, and I wondered what might burst the meager membrane desperately holding the peace together. I held my body completely still, making sure I was not the one to cause the explosion.

Only one thing moved. A small figure, her gait confident, hip popped to one side casually, yellow tunic flowing, appeared beside me. Sun Flower Girl slid her slight arm through mine and beamed at me with oblivious camaraderie. She pulled me along as though we were old friends. "I'd love to show you the sunflower fields sometime. You have to try their seeds. Especially with salt. I can get salt now and then. Yum, salt..." Her chatter continued as we recrossed the plaza. Beecher stayed behind, planting himself between the drummer and me.

"Dig up," I heard him growl once more.

Whether Sun Flower Girl's innocence, reputation, or subtle humane action diffused the situation, I could not tell. But it was enough. Light flooded back into the situation with her affectation. The energy in the space thawed enough for me to unclench my fists. Even the drummer, though with a huff, returned to his instrument.

"Thank you," I whispered to her.

"You're welcome!" she exclaimed too loudly for my preference. "People are so upset. They have a lot of pain, right?" She twirled a few blooms as she spoke. "I hope you'll come back for some more flowers soon. Now that you've seen them, you'll definitely want more."

She walked with us back through the Sideways. At the outer edge of the market streets, Sun Flower Girl beamed at me then practically pranced off, now officially my glowing pixie of a savior. "There are bad people everywhere. But there are good people everywhere too. Bye, Linah! Bye, Minty!"

It did not occur to me until the transport track climbed high up the hillside that I had never told her my name.

CHAPTER 24 :
A LITTLE FURTHER ALONG

BACK IN THE RELATIVE SAFETY of my Farm, I turned to the face of the sunflower on my bedside table and held out the holodoc that had me so frustrated.

"Stars, this is so confusing!" I exclaimed. "Do you get it?"

My sunflower did not respond.

"It's okay. I bought you because you're pretty. Not because you have to solve all my problems."

Linah and I had all but vowed to never visit Shamong again. As soon as we returned, we threw ourselves back into our mundane tasks with revived contentment and purpose. My grey Farm felt like a haven of peace after that wild day.

Dinner came and went; Linah lost herself in the preparation of a salad and spicy dressing, and I cleaned the dishes after licking every last morsel of flavor off my bowl. Afterward, I rested alone in my bedroom. It seemed like a good time to educate myself about all things Shamong, as a soon-to-be-adult ought to do, but the moment I got started, my frustration was hard to work through.

According to recent Information articles and data-blasts, no one seemed satisfied with the state of things in Attis: glass production, ABE progress, our political relationship with Lūn, the Bonder industry. Every side took issue, and every issue took sides. The entire upcoming election for First Statesman hinged around long-term plans for the Bonder institution. Each candidate had different ideas and different versions of truth. All claimed their plan would make the planet strong and more stable. Even candidate Nolin Hodgins 7, Reform.

As destabilizing as those revelations were, I felt mildly relieved. I lay there, in my Outpost settlement, surrounded by Outpost citizens, but I finally knew that somewhere, other Outposters doubted the perfection of our Society, like me. Entire zones doubted. My swirling discomfort with it all no longer seemed quite so traitorous.

As a girl, I had little patience for Laws and Advocacies. On the Farm, they were far removed from my daily life. But after my upcoming Entering Day and my Oath, I would be required to vote with no exceptions.

I projected a map of Attis that displayed all the Zones, moons, and StarStations of the settlement. The map swirled above me, coming in to focus wherever my eyes tracked. I wondered where Ves might eventually find his safety. In Nyx, the ice moon? In the bond-free northern zone of Fortmose? As a crew member in a StarStation?

With Stalkers creeping about, could he ever be safe, anywhere? And how could I help him have the best shot?

My mind spun and experimented with its new knowledge, trying to fit all the pieces together. Trying, and failing, but getting a little further along from time to time. A rumble of relief and conviction twirled and twisted inside me, still uncertain how to express itself.

The map projection was hanging above me like a second sky when I heard the buzz of the door alarm and felt the ping on my Aide. I shot to my feet, at first terrified that Mudsil had returned. But the sun flower that I almost toppled reminded me that Linah expected an Earthen to be delivering supplies for Ves. She had arranged it during the enjoyable part of our Market visit. Please, oh stars, please let it only be a secret Earthens meeting at my front door! My standards had dropped greatly this cycle.

Linah waited for me in the Day Room, eyes kinetic, but posture composed. She used both hands in a calming gesture to me as she noticed my slightly crazed expression. I took a long slow breath. She flashed a sight of the knives on her belt before covering them again under her tunic. She was made of ice. I willed myself to be the same as I opened the door to the night.

Beecher. His contagious smile. His enormous frame. His tattered ensemble that passed as clothing. In his arms, he held a bundle of soft things. "Mx. Bradford 8!" he bellowed. "We meet again. I have a few things for Liny."

I eyed the hillside behind him, fear slow to leave me.

"I'm decent at this type of thing by now, ya?" he teased when he noticed my glance. "You are the one new to this. New baby sneaker. Sneaky baby." He laughed aloud but tried to school his face into earnestness to tell me, "You are just as safe as you were before I showed up."

"Right. Hi, Beecher. Come in." And he did, still smiling. Beecher owned one of those smiles that you never doubted was genuine, no matter how frequently he used it.

Beecher and Linah hugged once again, her smile bigger and brighter than it often was on the Farm. "Can I see him?" Beecher asked her.

"He would want nothing more than that."

"I brought him a set a' clothes. Assumed you didn't have much in his size up here. And shouldn't be buying any." His voice and presence filled the space and made it feel cozier. Linah guided him, after raising her eyebrows at me to ask permission, which I nodded back to her. "Oh, and for you, Mx. Bradford 8. Something from a friend."

He tossed me a dingy fabric pouch, tied at the top with rough bamboo fibers. I caught it easily in one hand. "Um, please just call me Araminta. Or Minty even." He nodded, clearly pleased at our budding connection. The two Earthens went back together to visit Ves.

I tugged open the pouch. Inside tumbled tiny brown seeds, and I could tell they had been roasted by their scent. Speckles of granular salt clung to their oily surface. Sunflower seeds.

CHAPTER 25 :
A VOICE IN THE DARKNESS

BEECHER VISITED OFTEN AFTER THAT, but only at strange times. He helped Ves walk around the rooms, laughed far too loudly at Ves' jokes, and brought a smattering of supplies. He often enjoyed Linah's cooking, as I did, and occasionally accepted some algae bars or treats from me for his own children. I felt both comforted and unnerved by his frequent visits.

Beecher was warm and friendly toward me, but he did not trust me and my Outposter ancestry. Beecher and Linah spoke quietly together in corners when they thought I was busy. And though I knew it was not quite fair, I felt disappointed when they did.

Ves' fever completely disappeared with the medicine. His sparkle came back with a welcome vengeance, but with his renewed energy, he got antsy to move around more. Subsequently, he pestered Linah, and they both grew cranky in waves. They exhausted each other through the day but fell asleep snuggled close, despite their annoyances.

I checked on them before returning to my bedroom every night. The days felt almost normal now, with three Earthens woven into the atmosphere of my Farm. But when all was quiet, and I was the only one left awake, my mind tumbled and twisted. Two things occupied most of my thoughts.

How did I want to live when I became an adult in just a few more days? And when Ves left with The Waymaker, would I be happy or sad?

Both questions held a thousand nuances, and I fell asleep every night sorting through them. Sleep...

My heart began screaming and straining for Ves before my brain fully woke up. My mind raised me out of bed and pumped me full of adrenaline. The sound of a fist slamming against the front door echoed through the whole house.

Oh no, Ves! I panicked. *It's over. Shek, they've come for him...*

I stumbled toward the hall, knocking over my sunflower and spilling water on my glass floor. I slipped as the knocking boomed again, the sound slicing through the night's stillness. Linah and I, eyes still bleary from sleep, hair splayed in every direction, reached the Day Room simultaneously. Linah's light blue eyes looked as big as moons.

"Get him out, Linah," I whispered as loud as I dared. "Through the wall in his room. Get him out!" The last words barely made it through my throat because of a lump of fear that suddenly grew there.

Showing clarity through her terror, she grabbed a jar of drinking water and a box of algae bars and ran back to Ves. I cringed, uncertain as to whether Ves could walk very far by himself. I dared to count to twenty-five while the ferocity of the vehement knocks increased. *Please, please, please,* I begged the Universe or the stars or anyone that would listen. I willed my fear to turn to anger, resolve, cleverness, or anything else less incriminating.

Bang, bang, bang.

Whoever was out there chose not to use the door alert; my Aide remained silent. Unusual.

Bang, bang, bang, pause, *bang, bang.*

"Araminta!" I heard my muffled name. The cold panel of the door stung my overheated fingers, and my ragged breath bounced back to me as I swore against whoever was out there. "Araminta!" The voice shouted once more. I warily resolved to meet my fate.

I slid the door open a crack and barely saw the dark mountains against the stars. And Harkless. Again Harkless, his forehead dripping with sweat and cheeks flushed rosy pink, stood in the night, illuminated only by the dim glow of the Farm's tech.

"I can't believe this," I sputtered. "What?"

"I hope we're right about you, Araminta," he said with a candor incongruous to my perception of him. "I hope you are a friend to the Bonders. Or at least to Linah."

I tried to focus on Harkless, to make sense of his words and his presence, but Ves' face consumed my thoughts. Had Linah and Ves made it out? The Waymaker would arrive any day. We were just so close. We had to be. And now, another visit from Harkless.

Whatever this strange encounter meant, I determined to give Ves the best possible chance at escape. Harkless would learn nothing from me even during a late-night ambush. I had to pull it together, for Ves. "Why would I be? Are you, Harkless Stille 8, son of Calhoun Stille 7, importer of Bonders and weathiest of Attisians... Are you a friend to Bonders?"

He squinted, no trace of the usual joy or banter in his flickering eyes. "It may surprise you to know the answer to that, Minty. Tell me now, and tell me the truth. Are you sympathetic to the Bonders?"

Unfortunately, I could not even answer that question for myself. I disagreed with the cruelty of Ves' treatment, and I knew that Binding someone was unjust, but I still had so much to learn. If I cast my lot publicly with the Bound, what did that mean for my life? For my future? My Farm? And how in the stars did Harkless end up being the one to ask me that question?

Unable to comprehend his motives, doubt and fear kept me silent. That intense Harkless alarmed me as much as the lackadaisical version I knew. I leaned much too close to him, hoping my feigned confidence would deflect some of his earnestness, but his eyes stayed focused on mine. The heat of his exertion reached my skin; he smelled musty and a little bit like wet soil. Streaks of grey dust distorted his perfect face.

I studied him as he studied me, and I detected no deception in his face. I suddenly wanted to tell him, to admit it all, and to hope for understanding. For help, even. The words formed in my throat, but they were not my words to tell. Just as Linah held me at a distance, I did the same to Harkless. Not yet. Not until Ves was safe. So Harkless and I continued to stare at each other.

"Ha! Too long!" he exclaimed, and his smirk, along with a habitual ruffling of his hair, brought the familiar Harkless back to life in front of me. "No answer is just as good as the answer I hoped to hear. By the way, we need to work on your acting, you little groundhog." Without waiting for a response from me, which ideally would have been compellingly caustic, he continued, "Yes, to answer you, I am a friend of the Bonders. At least I try to be, within the capacity I have. Don't tell anyone, yeah? It's a bit of a game, you know. Are you surprised? I hope you are–that's the idea, of course. And so! You are sympathetic to the Bonders too– although I am not shocked at this point. Whew! Now that it's all out in the open, there are so many things that I could tell you, really interesting things–"

"Harkless!" I spat at him. The boy kept rambling. And none of it explained anything. "Stop."

He grinned roguishly. He was so handsome I had to look away. *Shek him.* I sensed him take a breath to continue his monologue, but instead of more energetic commentary from Harkless, I heard a deep, congenial, and full-bodied laugh crash through the darkness behind him.

My eyes shot open in shock. Harkless. Was not. Alone. This other hearty voice burst forth again but startlingly closer. "He sure do talk lots and often," the voice boomed. I had reached my maximum to cope with unwelcome surprises; I slammed the door.

Harkless' boot prevented my success.

"Minty. Calm down. We are all friends here." He turned behind him and spoke to the phantom voice. "She's good, I'm sure. She's a little new to, well, just about everything, right now. But she's right." Then he turned forward again because my aggressive attempts to get the door shut continued. "Stars. Minty. Go get Linah. She'll sort you out, okay? You have an important guest."

I knew that Harkless' superior bulk and strength would not allow me to close the door; only my pride kept me trying. *All right, wits instead.*

"I don't consider you an important guest, Harkless." I released the door in time to let it crack against his forehead. He fumed. Before the look he gave me then, I did not know anyone could fume and grin at the same time. With one hand, he held his head, and with the other, he pushed open the door completely, letting the mild light of the room spill into the depths of the night.

It illuminated six gaunt Earthen faces. The five in back were creased with weariness, their eyes weighted with exhaustion. The sixth, slightly in front of the others, with skin so dark she blended into the shadows, watched me steadily, unabashed, almost amused. Her whole countenance promoted unassuming assurance, even while her clothing barely passed for rags. She stood a whole head shorter than Harkless. Her lips creaked into a brazen smile and the light bounced off her bright teeth, except for where she was missing two. This woman spoke to me, and I knew she owned the dauntless voice and bold laugh.

"Hello, young one." She stepped closer to me, and I felt instantly drawn to her, fascinated. Something instinctual inside of me whispered that I should listen, that she was worthy of my full attention. "They call me The Waymaker. Will you help us this night?"

CHAPTER 26 :

STRANGE TIMES, STRANGE PLACES

IMPOSSIBLE. THAT TINY WOMAN WAS the great Waymaker that the Earthens revered so wholly? The homely, short, and completely inconspicuous woman appeared unremarkable except for her plastic head-parts. Yes, The Waymaker was bionic. The upper left portion of her forehead and skull no longer grew dark, smooth skin like the right portion. Instead, it gleamed with pale plastic plates and rivets. Two opaque cables protruded where her left ear should be and wound behind her head, disappearing in a large mass of coarse black hair. Occasionally her mechanisms emitted a subtle whir or click.

During the early settlement of Attis, when space travel was longer, and when existence was more difficult, there were tales of the ABEs preserving lives by creating bionic colonists. And even in the present, grave injuries in an Outpost certainly could be treated with medical plastics; the ABEs were more machine than man after all. But I had never known an Earthen to be provided with the service. And on such a significant organ: the brain.

Of the hundred things that surprised me about The Waymaker, the worst was that she was in my Farm. The legend, the outlaw, the queen of fugitives, nonchalantly strode through my Day Room. She wrapped blankets, barked instructions, and administered rations to her people.

In the dark, I heard Harkless bang his knee on something and swear colorfully. Linah, who had cautiously returned to the Farm after Harkless tracked her and Ves on the hillside, obeyed The Waymaker's words as swiftly as any robot or Aide program. Her instant adoration and complete trust of The Waymaker was obvious. The room buzzed with their activity. To me, the noise was utterly deafening.

I retreated away from them toward the edge of the room. The kitchen alcove offered me some imagined security. The counter top separated me from the Earthens.

My hand rested unconsciously on my Aide as I watched them. The Law could be here before anyone knew I had even sent out an alert. They would never know it was me because they were already being chased. Hiding a single abused boy was one thing, but harboring a famous criminal and her five fugitive Bonders elevated my transgressions to supergiant status.

Shek it. This secret carried severe punishments, I was sure. I could lose everything. I felt my head shaking and my sweat gathering. But they could lose everything too. Linah and Harkless, the two people that had offered me kindness and respect recently, were counting on me. Trusting me.

"Young one, I see your doubts. I see your fear." I jumped and knocked my hip hard against the speckled glass countertop. The Waymaker stood beside me, close enough that only I could hear her words. She leaned toward me, on the edge of action, but still searching, hoping, offering me a chance. I stepped away from her, but she matched my step and said, "Many who learn a truth feel fear at first."

"What truth?" I whispered hoarsely and tried to back away further into my kitchen. "My truth? Your truth? Earthens' truth? Attisians' truth? Everyone feels differently about truth!" My inner turmoil made the words combative.

"No," she responded firmly. "Beliefs vary, yes, very much. Opinions too. Those you get to choose." She stepped even closer to me and held up a single finger between us. Her slight figure did not make her presence any more inescapable, and her piercing gaze left nowhere to hide. "There is only one truth: that's the nature of truth. It can be very hard to find. But, once you find it, truth is solid as stone. You can stand upon it."

I let out a sigh that was almost a cry. "What truth are you talking about? Please," my voice cracked, "no riddles."

"Oh, I don't enjoy riddles. They are far too indirect. And some are just dishonest." The Waymaker's gaze had softened somewhat, and she came no closer. "You know more now than you used to. You understand more; it frightens you."

"Of course it does. This cycle has changed everything."

"Our world has been this way for a long time. The world has not changed: you have."

Tears pooled in my eyes. Who was this stranger doling out proverbs in my Farm? This stranger in my safe place that was no longer safe? I suddenly ached for my simple life disconnected from the pain of the world around me. But, *shek it,* I knew The Waymaker was right; I knew too much to go back to my normal. Not after growing to care about two Earthens. Not after considering the stories they told. Not after seeing the Exchange and Ves' injuries.

The question pounded in my head, the same question that had haunted me since Ves arrived. Linah's question: *what was I willing to do?* I brought my hands to my head and tried to push back the ache growing there. My mothers words came to me: *choose well, Minty.* But, instead of her voice, the words sounded like my own.

"Promise me, young one," The Waymaker spoke again as she began to back out of the kitchen. "Do not make decisions based on fear. Fear can be a liar." She smiled as though something in our exchange had changed her opinion of me.

"Then how? How should I make decisions?" I released a shaky breath. My sense of right and wrong jumbled and tumbled into a messy blob of uncertainty.

"Ah, now that is a worthy question." She did not intend to answer the question for me. Instead, she simply asked, "Do you have any more food?"

Her calm confidence easily overmatched my lack of resolve, and I passed The Waymaker an algae bar from my stash in the kitchen. She thanked me and immediately gave it to a young man close by who reached out with a bloody wrist, wrapped in dirty scraps, where his SubAide once connected him to his Tasker. I looked at the wrists of all the Earthens, and saw the same: bloody wrists, barely wrapped. They each chose the pain of removing their SubAides illegally in order to flee.

I gave The Waymaker another algae bar, and she handed it off to a greying man whose dirty shirt only partially covered intense blue and black tattoos that crept up his neck and out toward his fingers. I gave her another algae bar, and the results were the same.

"Waymaker." Everyone in the party called her this; her real name remained a mystery. "Don't you need to eat?"

"I have plenty, child, I have plenty. These others though, they don't." She left me to comfort her companions. But it was not comfort that she had given me. Doubt? Wisdom?

In my periphery, Harkless' loud conversations and encouragements were balanced by Linah's gentle administrations. The strange Earthens that decorated my Day Room all seemed haunted, or perhaps hunted. Their postures stooped as though they barely had the energy to sit upright. They all followed The Waymaker with their eyes. She was their hope. Their lifeline.

"Fine. This is a mess. This is completely insane." Though I spoke to myself, the nearest Earthen nodded his agreement. At least we shared that sentiment.

"Strange times, strange places," he gruffly croaked. We made eye contact for a moment before he dropped his gaze.

"What is your name?" I asked the old man. His skin, deeply wrinkled by too much radiation, reorganized itself as his mouth shaped each word.

"I am Grizz. I speak the best Common. But we all speak some. This is Lile, Beetie, Ho, and Glee."

"Hello," I managed. "I'm Araminta."

"Please, Mx., your full name?"

"Araminta Bradford 8. But just Araminta is fine." They all cringed when they heard my 8 designation. Grizz snapped his rickety head around with fresh attention.

"We wouldn't dare, Mx. Please, Mx. Bradford 8. Will you tell the Law that we are here? Will you report us? We are so tired, but we promise to be gone soon. Mx. Stille 8 brought us here for safety. You will bless us so if you do not tell."

Though it was cool on the Farm, their piercing gazes, full of both distrust and longing, condensed sweat on the bridge of my nose and forehead. I took in their taxed and desperate faces. It suddenly felt like choosing between my future and theirs. It was.

Grizz stood laboriously. Joint after joint cracked before he managed to be fully upright. His tone, likely perfected through many megas of addressing his Taskers, humbly pleaded with me, completely inoffensive although he was begging for his own life as a freeperson. "If you will tell, then we must leave now. Please, give us a chance. We've traveled so far. Will you report us?" He reminded me of Linah, pleading with me to keep Ves a secret just cycles ago.

I suppose I never really wanted to turn them in, but settling the matter felt heavy and final. Dooming. They saw me like all the other 8s who had made them miserable, whom they served, whom they were fleeing. It created something defiant in my chest; I refused to be like those other 8s.

The words tumbled out. "You can rest here. I don't want to hurt you. Just… don't go outside. Don't turn anything on. Don't make any noise. If you hear anything, there's a room through the back of the Farm. Hide there. Just…" As I spoke, I also clumsily side-stepped toward the back door. I threw it open and gulped in the oxygen of the atmosphere. "You will be safe here," I spurted, and then left the room to panic in private.

I threw myself down onto the thin ground, the manufactured soil so sparse that the rocks beneath stabbed my thighs. I welcomed the pricks of pain as distractions. The door clicked closed behind me, only to be opened a few seconds later. Grizz poked out and saw me just sitting there.

"Just checking," and he disappeared inside once more.

CHAPTER 27 :
DESTINED FOR IT

MY SHALLOW BREATHS INFORMED ME that I could be dangerously close to a full-on meltdown. I slowed them and thought purposeful thoughts. Hours passed as I sat there, reflecting on my choices and desperately scanning for Lawmen or any unusual activity. A benefit of my Farm's remote location was the barren landscape. Nowhere to hide, nowhere to spy. I could see for kilometers up and down the hillside.

All remained still, watchful. None of the noise and light of the city reached this far up. At one time, when it differentiated me from my peers, I did not like the distance, but now it felt like my only hope of security. Lonely. Grey. Quiet. Slowly, the chaos of my feelings settled into mild resolve. After all, this group, along with The Waymaker, would escort Ves to his new freedom. After Ves left my care, he would be in theirs.

Everything outside the Farm remained undisturbed, normal. I started to shiver before I knew I felt cold; my mind was so occupied. Sometime before dawn, the back door opened again, and a rustling figure emerged behind me. A blanket fell onto my shoulders and was soon joined by the weight of an arm draped across my back. The hand attached to that arm patted me haltingly as it felt my shivering.

I identified Linah by the way the moonlight glinted off her bright hair.

"You don't need to take care of me, Linah."

"I know. Everyone inside is asleep. Even Harkless," she replied, shifting her gaze upward. "Although, most of them seem to be having nightmares." I offered her half of the blanket, and she wrapped herself in it beside me.

Linah breathed out a long sigh. "Harkless says that their Watchtower was compromised. They had nowhere else to go. And they are so weak, hungry. He had to go search for them up above the Boundary after they ran away from the Watchtower."

"Watchtower?"

"I think it's like a safe house. The BackTrack must call them Watchtowers. Homes, businesses, meeting places... Anywhere that fugitives hide or retrieve supplies on their journey." Now that there were fugitives in my home, and my allegiance had been forcibly demonstrated, Linah was finally divulging some rumors. "Beecher says there are several Watchtowers here in Shamong that the Captain utilizes, but the Watchtower this group should have gone to was compromised. The Waymaker sensed it, somehow; they needed somewhere else to go in a pinch."

I abruptly held up a hand to stop her and tried to understand. "Captain? BackTrack?"

Despite the chill and the anxiety, Linah's features sparkled with something–pride maybe, or fascination. "The BackTracks are trails through the Outpost, paths out of bonding–to freedom. The BackTrack uses established ways with trusted friends, hidden in plain sight sometimes. It's secret, mysterious. Shamong, being a SpacePort, is very active with the BackTrack. There are often rumors and whispers here. And Beecher has confirmed more for me recently, since Ves' incident." By the time she paused to gauge my reaction, I knew my eyes were wide and lips slightly parted.

"And the Captain?" I queried begrudgingly.

"Right. There are many people who operate the BackTrack. Mostly free Earthens, some sympathetic Attisians, all over the planet they coordinate the movements of fugitives in their cities and zones. But there's a special one here in Shamong. Beecher and Harkless just call him the Captain. It's a code name, like The Waymaker. Our Captain directs all the movement of the BackTrack here in this city. Since Shamong is a sort of hub, a jumping-off point for many fugitives leaving the planet, I guess it needs that sort of thing. No one knows who it is. Harkless may know since he takes his cues from the Captain, but he won't give anything away. Whoever the Captain is, the BackTrack wouldn't be the same around here without him. Or her."

"Watchtowers. BackTrack. The Captain. I guess I have it?" I said flatly and blew air through pursed lips. "It's like an adventure story."

Linah smiled but then sobered quickly. "But with real lives."

"Including ours."

Linah nodded without looking at me. "Many, many lives."

The weight of it all wrapped around my heart and weighed it downward. I felt...defeated. We–me and Linah, and even Harkless–were too young, too unqualified, and too inexperienced to be in the middle of such heavy matters. And yet, we were.

"I know I'm selfish to think about myself when there are so many lives involved, Linah, but I can't stop my world from spinning. How did this happen? How did I get here all of a sudden?"

Linah tilted her head upward toward the light of the stars, considering. Her bright eyes captured their rays, played with them, then shot them back out into the skies. "Perhaps you are destined for it."

It was a very Earthen thing to say, full of mystery and unknowables and great powers beyond our human perceptions. Destiny.

Our few museums and brief history classes informed us that some Earthens descended from races based entirely upon religion. They believed in various gods and various interactions with those gods, and, if I remembered correctly, most of the time our ancestors had never even seen their gods. As Linah and I stared at the stars, I tried to imagine a god-being out there, orchestrating it all. Taking, giving, directing without anyone else's understanding, altering my destiny, choosing me for anything. I huffed, but Linah went on.

"Really, think about it. With all those problems to solve on the Farm through the megas, you have learned to think on your feet, be creative. You are quick and decisive in a bad situation. And then this lonely Farm is all yours. No one watching, no one meddling." She held up a finger with each point she made. "Then think of all those megas you were teased for being half Lūnar. It gave you compassion for different people." Linah glanced at me to gauge my reaction. "Maybe it has all been leading you here." She saw my disbelief, but instead of being angry, she smiled lightly.

"Even me. Even Ves. Did you know, Minty, when your parents bought me, they walked by my line of Taskers at least ten times? Mostly I kept my head down and only saw everyone's feet. But then I wanted to know who was wearing the simple shoes. I dared to look up, and it was your mother, beautiful and simple. It felt as though she recognized me, or something about me. Your parents bought me immediately and brought me here." Linah made sure she looked right into my eyes. "I think it was destiny. It's all swirled around and mixed and brought us to now." She glittered in the starlight, confident in her belief. "You have a powerful choice now...because of all that."

"Doesn't feel like much of a choice," I grumbled. Her memory of my mother's simple shoes among the pretentious masses called tears to my eyes, and to interrupt them, I looked at Linah. I sniffed and suddenly the tears dried in front of the guilt I felt at ignoring the interesting, wise, and strong girl under my roof for so long. I wished it was not true, but I had neglected an associate, a companion, even a potential friend, because she was Earthen, and I had never given it much of a thought. "All those megas, you watched, you paid attention. It never even crossed my mind to ask you anything. I'm...really, really sorry."

Linah looked into the distance as light glinted off the liquid texture of her hair. "A good Bonder learns to watch and to sense things; sometimes it averts trouble. But I never watched your parents out of fear after those first cycles. I grew to accept my lot in life. I hated the gratitude I felt though, the gratitude that they weren't cruel. Others have had it so much worse than me." She paused and shrugged. "When your parents were reentered, I understood your pain. I began to think of us as similar in some ways. We have both lost the people meant to care for us. We have both had to pave our own ways. Our lives together have been peaceful enough, and I'm grateful for that. I am sorry that Ves suddenly brought all of this here now, but I believe in... I don't know. I just believe. In this. In more for me. And more for you too. You get to choose now. You have to."

Her undeserved kindness overwhelmed me. For the first time in a long time, I wanted to be someone's friend. I wanted to be Linah's friend. "That settles it, Linah," I managed. "You are the superior human living at this house."

For the remainder of the night's darkness, wrapped loosely under the same blanket, we tossed her throwing knives–Linah skillfully and me precariously–conversed occasionally, and watched for anything and everything. But the transport track never buzzed to life, no steps crunched on the gravel, no drones buzzed in the air. Before much longer, the suns snuck above the mountain peaks across the valley, and their rays inched toward us almost fast enough to perceive. Right before their warmth could comfort us, Harkless' head popped through the door.

"There you are!" His jubilant demeanor hid any trace of stress from the night's activity. His cocky smile went to war with our contemplative frowns. "Holy Trinity, did you two sleep at all? Too late now, it's time to plot and plan. I've just heard from the Captain." My mind and heart were in such chaos that I did not question how Harkless had heard from the Captain while resting in my Day Room.

Linah and I shuffled back inside my home, even though it was a home I hardly recognized. So many humans, so many conversations, so many movements. The Earthens, now confident that I had kept them secret, smiled at me timidly and deferentially gave me extra space as I walked by. The Waymaker knelt in the middle of the room, eyes closed, her dark gray hood still obscuring all but her nose and chin, body unmoving. I heard that strange whir and click.

"Is she all right?" I asked. "What is she doing?"

"It's called praying," Harkless said. "She's listening for her God Voice. She does it at the least convenient times. Did you know God was so inconvenient?" Harkless laughed and headed into the fray, but I turned to Linah, completely bewildered once again, for a concise explanation.

"I should have mentioned that," Linah said quietly with a sideways glance.

"The Waymaker practices a religion. Many Earthens do. But Harkless says she also hears a voice. It's a voice that gives her instructions, tells her when to go and when to stop, when danger is near, who to trust. It's like an extra sense. She says it is the voice of The First Maker." A thick pause hung in the air as I considered that this legendary Waymaker took her cues from a voice in her head.

"Isn't that crazy?" I finally blurted. "Is she crazy?"

"Probably..." Linah conceded. "But does that matter? It's the reason she has freed so many Bonders."

Grizz piped up from a stack of containers he used as a chair. "I think it's true. She almost knocked on the door last night, at our first Watchtower, but she froze like she heard something no one else did. Something that made her afraid. Right away she demanded that we hide. Believe me, it was the last thing we wanted to do, so close to rest and a meal, but we did it. Sure enough, a whole group of Societals came walking where we had just been standing, just a few moments after we got off the track. She was right! She saved us. Or her Maker did. I didn't really go in for The First Maker stories until now. I think I might start."

Another Earthen, a male with golden skin and droplet eyes, spoke up. "Sorry to interrupt, but if you don't mind my speaking." His fear of offending an 8 made him overly polite. "She did it when I first joined her too. We waited for three hours to cross a huge transport track field. There were eight, maybe nine tracks running there, each busy. Every time we started to make a run for it, she'd pull me back, just in time to avoid being seen by someone in one of the transports. I even saw a Lawman in one of the windows. We were wet, cold, miserable. I thought I would give up right there and die, but she made me wait. Finally, we ran across the tracks, and no one saw us, and 10 millis later, more transports zoomed past. She said she just had to listen."

"Listening is prayer. Prayer is listening," The Waymaker's bold voice rang from the floor. Apparently, praying did not preclude her from hearing the conversation around her. "Most people think praying is asking, but I say it's listening."

Grizz helped The Waymaker to her feet. "Did he say anything to you? The First Maker? What do we do next?"

"No! It said nothing." Grizz stared at her, wide-eyed and disappointed. "But I think the talking boy has a plan." She pointed to Harkless, who had only recently realized no one was listening to him anymore.

With mock annoyance, he gestured for us to draw close. "Attention, friends...Of course. I always have a plan."

CHAPTER 28 :
IT'S A PROMISE

LINAH AND HARKLESS, WHO HAD ventured out together around midday to gather supplies for the travelers, finally returned to the Farm. They carried tightly-rolled blankets along with some medical supplies for Ves. Sweat glistened on their foreheads from the long hike down and up the mountain, since they did not dare to use the transport track and leave a record of its activation.

I barely contained my panic during the time they were gone. Being the only Attisian in a house full of fugitive Earthens made me crazy. I did not know what to fear most: what was inside my house or what might come from outside. But the day passed with no surprises; the Earthens kept to themselves, sleeping mostly, all of them crammed into my father's workshop. I farmed sloppily, making several minor errors that I knew would annoy me when I had some spare emotions.

Linah and I, with even a little help from Harkless, worked on general farm chores, and before long, nothing remained of my normal daily routines. The shadows grew, and so did the restlessness of the Earthens. Their time of rest and food had rebuilt their hope. They stood taller than when they had tumbled into my Day Room. They spoke more. Ves even had them laughing occasionally. It was as though the Earthens had reentered their own bodies.

The Earthens organized their pitifully few belongings in preparation to depart. I offered them clothes and shoes from my parents' abandoned closet, making sure to keep anything with distinctive embroidery or notable color. The seams of the garments stretched tightly over their broad Earthen frames. Most put the new clothes on right over their old ones, unwilling to part with any scrap of fabric. Their eyes flashed with eager gratitude as I dropped seeds and malformed produce into their pockets.

Ves. The time had come to say goodbye to Ves. I barely held my tears back.

I wanted to feel relieved for myself and happy for him, and I did feel those things when I considered it long enough, but mostly I felt sad. I dreaded the impending quiet and wondered how I would learn any new jokes or care for the orange tomatoes without him.

"I'm going to miss having Ves here," I admitted while Linah and I washed dishes in the kitchen together. She cautiously looked at me out of the corner of her eyes. I found it odd how little she was unaffected by her own feelings of losing Ves. She took a deep breath, blinked, prepared to say something to me, and stood there with her mouth open. A surge of apprehension hit me as her silence stretched on.

Whatever she wanted to say, she did not do it fast enough. The Waymaker interrupted. She had no smile of bright white teeth now to expose the location of her mouth under her oversized hood. "Ah, young one," she directed toward Linah. She gestured at the length of the shadows and the preparedness of the travelers. "I must speak before we depart. To you. And I suppose to you as well." She rested one hand each on our shoulders and gripped firmly.

"Young ones," The Waymaker spoke clearly. "The boy cannot come."

There was gentleness in The Waymaker's voice, but no doubt. "I have watched him today. His body is still too broken. He cannot walk well. He cannot keep up. He needs more than I can give. He will endanger all the others. He cannot come."

Linah staggered backward into me. Her body and the shock of The Waymaker's declaration both pushed the air from my lungs. We stood, stunned, for just a moment before Linah began to beg. "No, no. Please, you must! He needs to be away from here. I'll do anything."

"There is nothing to be done, but let him heal, as you have been."

Linah and I wore matching expressions of dismay. The whole point, the whole reason for this escapade, crumbled before us. "Waymaker," I interjected. "Please, he's just a boy, and he isn't safe here. I will pay you for his passage. Soon I can pay you much more. Take him with you, please. Please."

"Outposter," she reprimanded, "there are problems that money cannot solve. He will endanger the others. He cannot come."

Linah pulled her tunic open roughly to display her knives, glinting conspiratorially in the artificial light. A stormy tension brewed in her features. "You will take him."

The Waymaker raised her eyebrows ever so slightly, but nothing else changed in her demeanor under Linah's threat. She shook her head like a disappointed parent, and calm confidence swelled her words. "I will not take him. Put your weapons away. It is not your way." Instead of backing away from the flashing knives, The Waymaker leaned forward and put her hands on Linah's neck and shoulders. Her hood tilted upward to meet Linah's gaze. "Do not let it be your way. I will not risk taking the boy. You are angry, you are scared, but you must also understand."

The women stared at each other until Linah's anger transformed into panic. It was me that she turned to. "Minty, what will we do? Tell her. Tell her Ves has to go with her." I wanted to. I really did. But I heard the unflappability in The Waymaker's voice from the moment she showed up on my doorstep, and I heard her uncomplicated resolve now. I knew there was no more to say. I took hold of Linah's hand and squeezed it tight.

"We'll figure it out. We will. I don't think we'll be able to change The Waymaker's mind. We'll figure it out. We can do it. Another way." Linah's clammy hand shook in mine. Tears pooled in her eyes, and even though the conflict still raged inside of her, she covered her knives.

The Waymaker crossed her arms, and the hood allowed me a view of her chin, smooth and softly round. "Now," she began, once again equally gentle and firm. "The talking boy–"

"Excuse me! Enough of this boy nonsense. Man, you mean. Talking man," Harkless interjected from the Day Room and joined us.

The Waymaker continued, "Young one, you are a boy to me. The talking boy and the..." She turned toward Harkless. "What do you call it?"

"The Captain," Harkless replied.

"Yes. The talking boy and the Captain of this city will find another way for your injured brother."

Harkless appeared completely unsurprised at the change of plans.

"You knew," I accused. "You knew she wouldn't take Ves."

Harkless casually zipped up a travel bag. Then he shrugged and met my gaze. "This particular trip hasn't gone to plan in any category, you know. And I've been doing this a while. I know the physical requirements of a journey on the BackTrack. So, no, I didn't know, but I'm not surprised." He looked between Linah and me. Instead of laughing like usual, he half-heartedly tried to make us feel better. "It'll be all right, somehow."

When I realized that Linah still gripped my hand, I squeezed it. "You are not very encouraging, Harkless."

"Holy stars, try to relax at least enough to think straight. Really, it will. You are working with the good guys now. The Captain always comes up with something." Harkless, deciding there was no more to be said or done, continued with his preparations.

The suns set shortly after. Linah and I, still stunned that Ves would not be leaving for safety that day, watched from the periphery. When the Earthens assembled at the rear door, a single tear glimmered on its journey down Linah's pale cheek. She breathed in and out purposefully.

The Waymaker clapped once and moved toward the front of the group as they solemnly parted for her. Mid-stride, however, framed by her people, she whipped around to face us again on the threshold. Her head cocked to one side; she considered us for much too long. I wondered what she could possibly be doing. It was just Linah and me, standing together, hands still grasped, confused, alarmed, exhausted. Her cloak shifted as her body went rigid and her head tilted back the other direction. *Whir, click,* went that strange sound.

Whir, click. Whir, click. A loud and boisterous laugh burst abruptly from her mouth, cutting through the solemnity of the room. "Look at you two!" she exclaimed. "Very interesting. Yes, oh yes. We will meet again, soon. I think I will return for the boy. Yes, it's a promise. After these dear creatures are delivered, I will come back." She laughed once again. "Oh, there is so much to come." Then she left the Farm.

Linah and I exchanged a puzzled glance.

Following Harkless, the Earthens filed out of the door and into the young night. Grizz, the last to exit, looked at me and touched the back of his hand to mine in their ancient gesture.

"You've done more than you can understand. We will all remember you. Gratefully," he rasped.

Their dull clothes sunk them into the colors of the night, and they had all but disappeared down the hill when The Waymaker's call reached back to us. "If you feel sad, if you feel scared, if you feel angry, pray! Pray for yourselves! Pray for us!" She paused, and then further away once more we heard, "I'll be back for the boy!"

"Shhhhh!" I urged her, fearful of watchful eyes and ears lower on the transport track. I soothed myself with the truth that it was kilometers to the nearest unfriendly Attisian soul.

And then, as suddenly as they had arrived, they were gone.

My Farm sat eerily once again on the hillside, watching, wondering. The stars glimmered in a subtle dance on the glass and camouflaged the structure with the rocks of the hillside. The effect was otherworldly, somewhat spooky, but it was home. Linah and I stood, peering at the darkness.

The Earthens faced a daunting task. To sneak through the vast zones of Attis, evade the Law in each city, and then board a StarShip without detection required more skill and luck than I thought possible. They would need a lot of help along the way. Who would help them?

I pictured the humans along the BackTrack that would shelter them, feed them, and guide them. I barely knew the fugitives that had just left, but soon Ves would undertake the same journey. The hiding, the hunger, the hunting, and the risk would be his too. My anxiety for him soared. I hoped that Ves and the fugitives who had just left my Farm would find people on their journey who were kind and generous. I hoped that those same people would be clever, wise, and brave, that they would have strength and conviction, and that they would act selflessly. I hoped so hard that it felt like The Waymaker's praying.

Whether The Waymaker's First Maker spoke to me, or whether the roaring emotions of the last cycle finally settled inside me as a new idea, I do not know. But, at that moment, I realized that I could be the person for whom I had just hoped. Those fugitives were beyond my help now, and someday Ves would be too, but there were others like them. Other humans traveled disadvantaged and alone, escaping cruel Taskers and oppressed lives. I knew that I could help them. I knew I should. I knew I wanted to.

The rush of newly found purpose tingled. But did I dare?

5 MEGAS AGO

Supplemental excerpt from : Making a Way ; the Life and Stories,
Record HAC-3859385738

She knew she was too young to get partnered, even for an Earthen.   But that boy with curly hair and broad shoulders was her dream come true. He didn't seem to mind her plastic brain, or the oddity of her God Voice, which seemed to be growing louder as she practiced talking to it. The boy didn't mind at all. In fact, she saw the most of him when she did her check-ins with Attisian doctors and scientists who still gathered data about her surgery. The boy always accompanied her and supported her through those visits, every cycle.

The boy had hopes. He had goals. He loved science. He wanted to be wealthy and famous: the first Earthen this and that on Attis.

She loved the boy. And they would be partnered. The joy of it brought a flush to her cheek and radiance to her expression that hadn't been there before. Her friends all noticed it. But so did her Tasker.

At first, the Tasker's attentions were so slight that she believed she had imagined them. A question might be directed to her instead of the group she stood with. An unnecessary brush of his hand might graze her arm.

But soon there was no doubt. He squeezed her hip and laughed as she startled and moved away. He instructed her how to reach his private offices, sometimes in the earshot of others, but she never went.

She grew more afraid and told her young lover about it. Instead of the protection she expected, he was disgusted. He looked at her criticly and with fear. When pressed, he said that he "would not risk his reputation confronting a Tasker."

He broke her heart, and only her God Voice brought her comfort. During the next days, she looked carefully at her life. Cruel Taskers, physical harm, and the fear of loss and pain weighed down every moment. Now her bright spot, her love, had rejected her, had put his future ahead of caring for her.

"I made you on purpose," the God Voice reminded her in words that were more like a feeling. It stirred inside her. The value and care she heard from her God Voice contrasted sharply with her reality on the bamboo homestead. Her discontentment with that contrast grew to almost unbearable levels. But as her anger grew, so did the love and hope from her God Voice. She had all three in large measure: anger, love, and hope.

She tried to avoid the problematic Tasker, but one afternoon he found her alone as she tied perfectly cut bundles of bamboo together in a shed. He pressed into her from behind and whispered into her ear. He was going away, but when he returned, he was finished with their games. He would have her. He ran his hands over her once before disappearing from the shed.

The girl couldn't move except for a quake of fear. Her emotions fluctuated and stormed until she dropped to her knees to pray, as she had seen many of her elders do. She asked her God Voice, "What do I do?"

"The time has come." It said, "I will show you the way."

CHAPTER 29 :

UNBELIEVABLE, AS USUAL

THOUGH MY PERSPECTIVES AND BELIEFS were still forming and solidifying, the feelings were there, pushing themselves into becoming actions. Helping the Earthens in their distress felt right, and once the idea lodged in my heart, I thought about it all the time. I organized Ves' room in ways that might better accommodate multiple midnight visitors. I began a stash of non-perishable food items and water jars. I peppered Linah with questions that she could rarely answer.

But that was all I could do. I could not shout from the hilltop for fugitives to come inside. I could not walk Ves right up to the SpacePort and put him on the first ship out. I could not vote yet or ping The Waymaker or even Beecher. All I had was Harkless. I had no other safe connections. *Shek, me,* Harkless was it. He was the only one who might be able to answer my questions or get me involved.

I messaged him cryptically, but he responded only with teasing and jokes and without any acknowledgment. Then he completely ignored me. He stopped responding to my pings. Harkless brought Earthen fugitives into my home, asked me to belong in the world differently, and then left me to figure it all out alone.

Nothing changed. Days passed.

So I did the only things I was really good at: Farm chores, crop deliveries, and helping Ves walk and sit. The days were too busy to be called monotonous, but they became routine. We just existed together.

The day came for my final meeting with Uncle Chi, and I groaned my way out of bed, already dreading it. Linah and Ves normally distracted me from my feelings of unease, but I did not see either Linah nor Ves during my chores that morning. As I washed my hands of soil in the kitchen, I resolved to find them in the tomato room.

But Ves surprised me first with an exaggerated hug. He entered the room, upright all on his own, and seemed confident in his stability and movement, and grabbed me ungracefully around my waist. Though his deep bruises remained, and some of his worst cuts still cracked with scabs, most of his wounds closed into a lattice of pale scars. Two fresh bandages, one on his forearm and one on his neck, blocked slow leaks of blood from his movements of the day.

"Steady now, Ves. That was a nice hug." He walked me to the cushions in the middle of the Day Room and gestured to a bowl of our orange tomatoes and fried dough, placed neatly in bowls atop the table. "What's this?"

He smiled impishly at me. "Happy Entering Day! I helped Linah this morning. We did almost all the rest of the chores while you were up in the Farm. She's finishing up. You can have the rest of the day off, Minty!" His grin widened with every word.

I smiled, but I groaned inwardly that Linah had mentioned my Entering Day. I had complicated feelings about turning seventeen megas, and I did not want extra attention, or extra free time, that day. The day brought adulthood for me, according to the Law, and official freedom from my unfortunate relative: also political, social, and financial responsibilities. After some unpleasant negotiations with Chi, which I planned to undertake that very night, I could choose my course. My way. Petrifying.

Still, I did not want to dampen Ves' spirits. "Thank you! I can't believe you helped with the chores! How do you feel?"

"Better and better. Moving around helps now, I think. Hey, Minty."

"Yes?"

"What is the moon's favorite bagel?"

"I don't know–"

"Cinna-moon raisin!"

"Ves, what's a bagel?" I blinked at him; he blinked at me. "Ves, what's a cinna?"

I laughed, but Ves clearly felt disappointed by my lack of comprehension. "Try another one, Ves. I'm sure I'll get one of them eventually."

"How do you get clean in outer space?"

"I don't know. Tell me."

"You take a meteor shower!"

"Ha! Yes. I like that one."

"Finally."

We chatted lightly for a while, and I ended up enjoying our time together well enough thanks to Ves' intense enthusiasm and obvious efforts to brighten my Entering Day. But when Linah came in, and I thanked her for the extra effort, I snuck away to my room.

Adulthood. Independence. Responsibility. The words were good words, by themselves, but my stomach churned to think of them in my own life. The simplest option was to accept the financial strategy that Chi so thoughtfully and selfishly provided, and I was still tempted, but I had to say no. I wanted my own money; I wanted my own control. It would be hard, and I was so scared that it would be too hard.

I still had not made up my mind about taking back the Advocacy seat. I thought of it as a peacemaking tool for when I rejected the remaining proposal. I did not want to represent my settlement, but I also did not want Chi to do it. Advocates argued for hours on end in the presence of the First Statesman and their cabinet, as well as the ABEs, regarding whatever decisions had to be made for the Outpost. All change on Attis began with the Advocacy. It took time, energy, and honestly, gumption – three things already in high demand in my life.

I called up a mirror in the glass panel beside my bed and looked at the girl—well, woman technically as of that morning–in the reflection. I tried to see an adult there. An Advocate.

All my soft parts had rearranged during the dark days when I cut myself off from the rest of the world. When I was not paying attention. Was hardly eating. Was just making it through. My baby cheeks and soft middle had melted away as my hips and breasts appeared. I knew I would always be slight in stature, no longer growing upward, but the gangliness had gone. All of the shy uncertainty that used to hunch my posture and dip my chin had disappeared.

I tilted my jaw, studying the angles of my adult face. Its ovular shape was far from perfect, with eyes too wide and forehead too tall, but I saw my mother in those features and in my brunette hair, with its unpredictable texture. My father's crisp grey eyes, with a ring of dark grey that might almost be blue at the outer edge of my irises, were the one Lūnar concession staring at me from the glass. In my adult body, I was an obvious summation of their parts.

Stars, I missed them. Ever since Linah practically forced me to acknowledge it back at the Memorial, I felt it often. Nestled like a singularity in my chest, I missed them. I wanted them to tell me what to do. But…would they have agreed with me now? My parents believed that I, even as part Lūnar, had equal dignity within our Society. They hated the discriminatory treatment shown to all of us after their partnership. I knew they believed in goodness, kindness, fairness. And always choosing well. Yet they had not considered the plight of the Earthen humans around them, at the mercy of their Society, as worthy of their exertion. They knew that as Lūnars and Outposters, we were equal. Why not Earthens?

I looked once more into my own reflected eyes. I thought the same; barely more than two cycles ago, I had not considered the plight of the human

Earthens on my planet either. Whatever cautions or concerns my parents might have expressed about my recent choices, I had changed. Choosing well meant something different for me than it had for them.

So what was I going to do? And with Harkless unresponsive, how was I going to do it?

I closed the mirror and threw myself back onto my bed, using my elbow to shade my eyes from the sunsrays spilling through my windows. The sunflower once again arched on my bedside after I had rescued it from the floor, but a few of the petals drooped and some rested by the bottom of the vase as the flower aged.

It really was beautiful. I planned to buy more if I ever dared to go back to the Market. At least I had made up my mind about that. The visceral memory of the Market distracted me until Linah knocked on my door. I grunted an acknowledgment, and she leaned in, her long locks of bright hair refracted the light almost like a prism.

"Are you doing all right, Minty?" Linah asked. I groaned, loud and exaggerated. "Worried about tonight?" she asked again. I let a comical whimper escape me.

"I'm glad to see that becoming an adult has grown your maturity." She pressed her lips together to prevent a smile. "And your communication skills."

I rose to a sitting position, making sure every movement was accompanied by a wildly unnecessary noise of discomfort. I heard a muffled snort from Linah, and when I inspected her, she stopped holding it in and laughed. I managed a mild smile.

"Well, then, oh most functional adult, get up." She snapped her fingers with the rhythm of her words. "It's almost time for you to leave if you want to get to Chi's on time. Come on, I'll help you get ready."

Linah did my hair in a five-stranded braid and wove a strip of silvery fabric through it. I rarely wore anything but my utilitarian work clothes, all stain-resistant radiation fabric and pockets, even to visit Chi, but this occasion required a little more formality, according to Linah at least. I chose a soft, flowing tunic in a color that had no certain name, maybe taupe or stone or beige. It fell from my shoulders to my knees in a cloud of shapeless comfort. Linah shook her head distastefully.

"What?" I queried.

"I have an idea. Be right back." She disappeared long enough for me to study the tunic in the mirror. Granted, I looked a little bit like a pleated boulder, but I felt at ease, and it was a huge improvement over my normal look.

Linah returned with an item from my mother's closet. I vaguely remembered the fabric, charcoal grey shot through with something that made you believe it shimmered when you were not looking directly at it. "This," she said firmly.

I put on the new outfit. Stars. If my reflection reminded me of my mother earlier, the resemblance was almost alarming in her old clothes. The rich tunic fitted more like a tailored jacket, with strong shoulder lines that continued down my collar bone and met at my sternum. It allowed for my chest, hugged my ribs, then flared out at my hips, high in the front and low in the back. The simple sleeves formed supplely to the length of my arms and down my fingers, forming gloves that only freed the tips of my fingers. A generous hood hung down my back, ready to use in the sinister atmosphere. My sensible leggings, now on full display with the shorter tunic, looked embarrassingly apathetic, so I changed into a black pair from megas ago that had a textural stripe down the outside of each leg. The leggings were too small now, but my tall boots covered their shortcomings at my ankles.

"Well, there you are. Now you look like an Attisian adult." Linah paused, and I could almost feel her internal debate about how much to press me. "What are you going to say to your uncle?" she finally asked as she clasped my mother's moon rock necklace around my neck.

The grey moon rock, a love gift from my father, all but disappeared against the dark tunic. It was a special rock, a Lūnar treasure. When my mother sung the right note at the right frequency, only then would the rock glow with a pale internal light. I had not tried it since her reentering.

Linah and I both looked in the mirror carefully, digesting the person reflected there.

"I'm not sure how to say it all to him yet. I am ready to be done with him."

"Only to be done with him?" Linah adjusted one strand of hair and pulled my thick braid over my shoulder so that it fell across my neck and chest. "What about being ready for what comes next? Ready to make your own life?"

"Yes. Those things too." I blanched and started to feel a little nauseous.

She nodded then hustled me toward the door. "Those are good things. No use prolonging it. You'll find the words. You are ready!" And I tried to believe her.

The long transport ride down the mountain and through town delivered me to the gates of the Palisade once again. Solar lights illuminated the bustling shoppers and diners as they ended their day with some city pleasures. Holograms ads glowed from storefronts; mechanical music and boisterous conversations burst into the streets from open doors as I passed.

I trudged through the familiar street toward my uncle's office. No nostalgia revealed itself, perhaps gone forever. The Palisade was not my home. The Palisade was not my aspiration. That solid conviction gave me the confidence to complete the last turn down his street, but my feet stalled beneath me at the sight of a tall figure leaning against Chi's door. I froze for a moment, deciding whether to continue forward or feign disinterest and do an extra lap around the block.

"It's just me, Minty. I knew you'd be by soon," said Harkless.

I froze. Unsure whether I was glad or upset to see him. "Again? How did you know I'd be here tonight?"

"Why don't we just agree to assume that I know absolutely everything?" He pushed himself away from the door, and I recognized his posture of casual swagger as he approached me.

"Look, Minty, you have got to stop pinging messages about how you want to help. I know you thought you were all sneaky and mysterious in them, but you weren't. Really, not at all. So, stop. Had to tell you in person, so I could deny understanding the messages. Did you know that the ABEs have access to all our Aide interactions? The Law can get to it, too, when needed. We can't use our Aides to communicate about any BackTrack stuff."

Harkless' suit looked almost like the masculine version of my own outfit; dark and sparkling fabric cut across his shoulders and dipped low on his chest. His hair swooped to one side with a heavy application of paste. And he seemed truly displeased with me.

"Shek you, Harkless." Frustration filled me at the edge in his voice. "I am only trying to do the right thing here. Why won't you help me?" I flushed, annoyed and embarrassed. The stress of the last cycles flared up inside me, and all I had to focus on was Harkless. "If it's really just so horrible that I want to help, after meeting Ves and The Waymaker and all those traumatized Earthens, you could have found a way to tell me earlier how stupid I am."

Harkless clenched his fists and raised his eyebrows. "I don't think you are stupid. I also don't think you understand the complexity of keeping this all secret. I even had to make up an excuse to be here 'randomly' to tell you in secret to keep a secret you insist on pinging me about. I'm telling you now; message received. I know you want to help. Now quit it."

I raged. It was not fair that he was angry with me. Because of Harkless, I found myself in the middle of a game that I did not know the rules of, but he expected me to play by them anyway. I felt like yelling at him. Blaming him for all of it. He was my one hope for a friend in this mess, but he wanted me to "quit it."

He must have sensed my anger shifting to something he felt less prepared for–despair or hurt–because he became still and frowned slightly. "Minty, there is just no room for carelessness. Everything has to be precise and perfectly planned." Harkless raked his hand through his hair several times, scattering his dark brown strands in every direction. "Shek, I want you safe, Minty. I don't know how to manage it yet. I'm responsible for...I... Look, it's for safety. Safety! Yours, mine. But theirs too..."

He planned to say more, but Chi's door behind him opened and interrupted him. Sarai, her hair in a thousand small braids that danced as she moved, stepped out of the building toward us. She wore no tunic at all; instead, her figure barely fit inside a green bodysuit that covered every inch from her boots to the edge of her jawline. Over the bodysuit, an oversized hood and jacket spread out around her like a pleated cone, but the fabric was completely clear and looked like flexible glass. I had never seen anything like it. Clear fabric did nothing to block radiation and was therefore completely gratuitous. Stacks of glowing bracelets decorated her wrists. I could not be sure, but it appeared that her lips glowed too.

"Hello again, Minty," she intoned. "Chi is expecting you."

I had to swallow several times to control my tone.

"Yes, we have a meeting planned." So it was Sarai that had clued Harkless in to my meeting with Chi; her father had told her, and she had told Harkless.

Sarai eyed me for a while, probably curious as to what I planned to tell Chi, sensing my deep emotion, or perhaps just judging my general existence as usual. I should thank her for her intervention with the Lawman earlier that cycle, but under the unfriendly fierceness of her gaze, the words escaped me.

"Obviously. Bye, Minty. Good luck with your Oath, and happy Entering Day. I won't have to scold any more Lawmen, now that you are Entered? Now you can scold them yourself, I hope." She focused away from me and wrapped her arm closely inside Harkless' elbow. "I was so happy to get your ping, Harkless. I'm looking forward to our night out."

Harkless ran a hand through his hair once more, slowly this time, trying to relax from our heated conversation. "Sarai, gorgeous, I'm glad you were able to take a night off from your relentless pursuit of my brother." At this, Sarai swatted him but acted otherwise unbothered. "You look unbelievable, as usual. No one will be able to take their eyes off you. Not even to look at me, which is saying something." Sarai laughed lightly and all but led him away. Dissatisfaction with the whole interaction twisted in my stomach.

As the two of them headed toward the activity of the Palisade's nightlife, Harkless looked back and grimaced. At first, I thought it was his frustration with me, but there was a playfulness in his eyes, a softness. I realized that perhaps Sarai's bizarre attire had not made the impression on Harkless that she had intended, and that maybe Harkless did not want to be angry with me anymore than I wanted to be with him. I could accept his point and trust him for a little longer. He knew how to keep us safe, at least better than I did, and the stakes were terrifyingly high. I would be smarter, more careful, no more pings. But I would not stop asking. I let a small smile accompany my wave goodbye. Maybe it would be okay between me and Harkless.

Good luck tonight, Harkless. You are going to need it. I turned back to face my uncle's door. We both were.

CHAPTER 30

A BUSINESS DEAL

CHI SAT AT HIS DESK, arms crossed, three glasses and a bottle of liquor set formally in front of him. His eyebrows shot up, surprised at my state of appropriately formal attire.

"Chi." I felt my hands clench and unclench on repeat. The mere sight of him reactivated my anger toward him.

"Araminta. My niece. Sit." I sank into the molded bamboo chair across from him as he poured generous portions of the sharp-smelling liquor into the glasses and handed one to me. "Araminta. Let me be clear. I did not intervene in your incident with that foul quarry master earlier this cycle because I was not there in time to do so. I only heard the details later, after inquiring about the situation." He managed to meet my gaze for a moment but then blushed and looked down. I let the silence hang; he lied horribly.

Disgust with my uncle and his pretense turned down the corners of my mouth. "I don't believe you. I think you didn't intervene because it would embarrass you to stand up for an Earthen and for your niece. Your shameful, farming niece who doesn't act the way you want me to. Whose mother screwed up, but only in your eyes. You were too embarrassed to keep someone from hurting me." I only paused to take a breath. "And now you expect me to sign documents that practically give you everything. My money. My seat."

Chi huffed. He grew indignant along with me. "No. The family's money. Built and accumulated by your ancestors. Money that I have tended these megas. I've made it grow. I've protected it. And I will continue to do so. We don't get along. We never will. These new arrangements mean we don't have to. You are unfit to handle matters of state and finance. You are about to take an Oath for which you are unprepared and unqualified. I had hoped to toast to the end of our attachment and celebrate the beginning of something new and better. But you don't seem in the mood to act like an adult. I have tried to create a reasonable solution, one that will minimize damage to our family and certainly avoid you sitting in the Advocacy seat, where you know nothing about what decisions must be made there. I need to be in that seat."

I used to squirm and fret when I sat in front of Chi, but I fought the urge and focused on my anger. "What are you so worried about, Uncle Chi? What horrible thing will happen to Society if you aren't Advocating? If I don't pass my familial role over to you?"

"Araminta, these are exceptionally challenging times. There are those in our own Society who desire unjustifiable changes that will rock the settlement's very foundations. We must preserve, we must persevere, we must see ourselves on to stability and even to greatness." I raised my eyebrows at him before he continued. "I will list a few points. Trade agreements with Lūnar are increasingly complex. There is a dance of power unlike anything we have dealt with before as we grow in strength. Some want firmer alliances, and some want more independence. Then there are those campaigning to decrease the rights of the ancient families, to add elected Advocates of the lesser generations. It is an ungrateful insult to our sacrifice and progress. And in this election, there are even those that seek to alter or even outlaw the Bonding institution." He spit the words. At the mention of the Bonding institution, he glared at me with piercing suspicion. "The very institution that has allowed our Society to prosper, to finally get ahead economically, to gain the respect of our Lūnar rivals. To terminate Bonding is to risk everything we have built." Chi's face flushed from red to purple during his impassioned speech. "Amongst a hundred other points. Most Advocates gain their seat after they have been prepared their whole life by their predecessors, and when those predecessors have passed into great age. And you, Araminta, are the daughter of a Lūnar 1, a farmer, recluse, fundamentally a child; you are incapable of fulfilling your Oath. Will you go to battle for these things, these consequential things, as an Advocate?"

"Battle? Do you hear yourself? Battle is a word of violence! No," I declared, surprising even myself with the firmness in my tone. "No, I will not Advocate for the Bonding industry, not for economic good, not for anything." Linah and Ves filled my thoughts, Beecher too. I could not ever Advocate for more people to be subjected to their fates: the pain and powerlessness. "They are humans, Chi. The Earthens are humans. Like me. Like you."

Chi slammed his hands onto his desk, and the glasses rattled together. "This is exactly what I fear. People like you will ruin us. Whatever sentimental morality you are standing upon is short-sighted. Whatever perceived difficulty you believe the Bound face is nothing compared to their lives on their home planet, or even the lives of free Earthens in the Outposts. By maintaining Bonding, we preserve all our futures, even theirs! You are too naive and stupid to understand this. You cannot be an Advocate!" Chi snapped his teeth together before adding, "think of your duty to Society. Think of the legacy of our family."

I shook my head, scared, but unconvinced. If I gave Chi my seat, Chi and others like him would continue to campaign for Bonding, for preserving their power at the expense of the Earthens. If I stayed silent, maybe nothing would change. If I took the seat…well, who knew what might happen.

"I know that I am young for an Advocate. I have a lot to learn. I know this. I do. But you forfeited any family connection with my mother long ago. And you did the same thing with me that day in town. You are no family of mine. I will take the family legacy. I will fullfil my duty, as best I can, in the way that I believe is right." Chi's gaping mouth flattened into a thin line and his lips pressed so tightly they began to whiten. "I will pay you a fee for the time you managed my money and a percentage of whatever you gained. I don't know what the normal rates are for stuff like that, but I'll find out. It's a business deal then, fair and square, and nothing more." I paused to gulp air that I had forgotten. "I'm 17 megas now, and no longer your concern. I'll hire a representative, and they will contact you soon for all the arrangements. I want to take my Oath now."

"I won't allow it!" Chi bellowed. "You are not capable."

"You have to. I'm 17."

When Chi did not move a muscle, only glared at me from behind his desk, I raised my Aide, activated it, and spoke the command. "Araminta Bradford 8, Citizens' Oath." Between Chi and me, the Oath appeared with the first word highlighted. I knew what to do; I had been instructed in the process long ago. In our Society, Entering was simple but profound. Most families threw small Entering Day parties for their 17-mega-olds to speak the Oath amongst their loved ones. Not me.

> I, Araminta Bradford 8,
> Born of the Attisian Outpost in the Pictor System,
> Declare my loyalty
> To the goodness, wholeness, and health
> Of my settlement.
> I will pursue its welfare
> And the welfare of its citizens,
> Uphold the law,
> And esteem the tenants

Of our new Society
Above all.
I will vote
And otherwise serve my settlement
As a citizen of Attis.
I declare my intent to do so,
And accept all responsibility therein
Now and always.

The highlight followed my reading, indicating each word as I was meant to speak it. My Aide recorded my voice, even as it shook during the last stanzas of my Oath. The words meant something much more complicated to me at that moment than when I had first learned them. Accept all responsibility therein. Traditionally, all other citizens present for the Oath echoed the last line, now and always. But I did not expect Chi to speak.

Uncle Chi watched me with blazing eyes. His coiffed hair had fallen to one side during his outburst and looked like an empty water pouch. His Aide beeped, then beeped again, waiting for his thumb to acknowledge the Oath of his ward. As my guardian by Law, he was supposed to indicate that he had heard me speak it. Another beep. He only glared at me.

"You have to do it Chi." For a moment, I feared that he would refuse, but my Oath was taken, it was valid. "It would be embarrassing, wouldn't it, if I had to get confirmation somewhere else?" I watched him consider all his options and reach the same conclusion. He raised his thumb and swiped his Aide. The beeping ceased.

On my wrist, the eight glowing dots of my Aide turned a bright white hue, where once they had been subtly golden. It was done: the money, and the Advocacy, and all that went with it. I was Entered.

Chi picked up one of the glasses and threw it against the wall. His coif flipped to the other side of his head. "Get out."

After a moment of electric silence between us, I grabbed my glass of liquor and downed it for effect. I gasped at the earthy burn of the distilled mash. I should not have done it, but I felt as charged as a bubble drive. The megas of resentment and desperate aloneness flooded my senses and poured into the space around me. "I will go. But not before I say this: I lost the only people who loved me, Chi. I was just a kid, but you made it all worse. Well, I'm figuring it out anyway. I don't need you. I guess I never did." Holding my inflamed throat, I stomped to the door. I looked into the opulent office one last time and saw my uncle flushed purple with his outrage, fists clenched as he threw another glass against the wall.

"I'll give your regards to the First Statesman!" I screeched before I slammed the door and was free.

A strange kind of adrenaline raised my fists to the sky and brought a smile to my face. The adrenaline was not from danger but elation. From standing up for myself. From choosing for myself. I even jogged the short distance back to the transport track. *Okay, Araminta,* I thought as the tips of my fingers started to tingle and a weird warmth spread from my stomach. *Tomorrow you need to hire a representative that will not mind standing up to Chi. And learn some financial things. And find out how much money you have and where. And look up the Advocacy schedule. And try to get Ves to safety.* It was an awful lot, but I felt stunningly optimistic.

Happy Entering Day to me.

Nighttime arrived before I made it home, but the warm lights glowing from the panels at the Farm felt welcoming and celebratory. The large shot of liquor made my inexperienced body feel unusual.

"Linah! I think I feel drunk," I laughed as I walked through the door. I was giddy to share my news with her. "Not on alcohol, of course. On power! Just a tiny bit on alcohol. I can't wait to tell you what I said. I'm in trouble again, but for once it's a good kind. I think. Hard to think…"

I stopped long enough to look around the Day Room. I had to squint through my inability to focus. How much liquor did I put in my body? Is this how everyone felt while drinking alcohol? There…Linah stood by the kitchen, something blue and intricately decorated sitting on a plate beside her, with an expression of amused surprise. In the middle of the Day Room, lounging on pillows, sat Ves. He grinned at me and gave me a big thumbs up. I could see the slight daze of pain medication in his eyes. Bigger surprises came next.

"Beecher?!" I exclaimed. The large man sat beside Ves. He crunched on something puffy and white from a bowl he held protectively. His smile filled the whole room with kindness.

"Heyo! Little Araminta! Happy Entering Day, girl!"

"What are you doing here? And thanks! And hi!" Alcohol made me enthusiastic, apparently.

"Brought up some supplies for our Ves, and Linah said I could stay for the party." We smiled goofily at one another.

"What!? Linah. A party?" I turned back to her. My euphoria dimmed for a few moments when the lighting accented the dark bruise still on her cheekbone.

"Of course, Minty! An Entering Day party. As a thank you. For all you've done." Linah held out the blue thing in both hands toward me. She had put on an intricately woven, sleeveless cardigan that draped to the floor, and the fibers that formed the lines and loops of the pattern reminded me of the Cemetree; the weave was made of multiple colors of bamboo fabric pulled tightly into thin cords, muted blues and greys and greens. The variance made it beautiful. I was sure she had made it for herself. The outfit suited her in a nearly magical way, making her blue eyes shine and accenting her graceful movements.

"Let's eat the cake, Liny! Let's eat!" Both Ves and Beecher called out raucously. The fancy blue creation on the plate was a sweet cake. Something happy inside me made my eyes leak tears.

"For me?" I barely even remembered my Entering Day for megas, let alone celebrated it. I went to hug Linah but tripped on something. Maybe my own foot?

That was when I heard the guffaws from the hallway. Someone was laughing hysterically.

"Did anyone guess that tipsy Araminta Bradford 8 would be happy and clumsy?" The voice wheezed. "This is the best thing I've ever seen. She turns into her own opposite." Harkless could hardly stand from laughing at me.

"You!" I pointed at him.

"You!" He pointed back, handsomeness projecting across the room.

"Where is Sarai?"

"She found someone else to spend the evening with. She's easy to ditch when she's in a predatory mood."

The five of us sat in a circle on the floor cushions, chatting about our recent adventures and eating the softest cake I had ever tasted. The salty, creamy middle sprang back when touched and perfectly complimented the tangy, luscious frosting that covered it. Blue swirls of frosting danced around a decorative "M" in the center. I had never seen a more beautiful dessert. The food mixed with the liquor in my stomach and cooled the warmth in my chest and cheeks, and I slowly returned to my normal self.

"I think the Captain is a businessperson. Probably a 7. They have to be incredibly well connected," Linah added to our ongoing discussion about the identity of the mysterious Captain of Shamong.

"Agreed! T' have that kind of access..." Beecher mumbled through a mouthful of cake. Ves hung on Beecher's every word and mimicked his style of expression.

"The Captain is an Outposter? Not an Earthen?" I exclaimed. "And none of you know who he or she is?" Everyone shook their heads no.

"That is so sugar," interjected Ves. He glanced at Beecher as if hoping for his approval.

"How do you contact the Captain? How does it all happen? Aides are off-limits you said, so how?"

Linah and Ves shrugged. The men did not respond, but I knew from their faces that I had stumbled upon another secret they might elect not to tell me. Beecher's considering brows raised suddenly above a huge, tension-altering smile.

"Great question! You're smart!"

Harkless decided to explain. "Shamongians on the BackTrack have a clever way to communicate. Anyone with a role in protecting the travelers has a pager." He reached into a pocket and pulled out a rectangular box of technology. Other than a few manual buttons and a sunken screen, the little opaque box shone with a simple glass finish. Very plain.

"A what?" I leaned in with curiosity.

"A pay-ger," Harkless enunciated. "Very ancient tech. In the Outposts, we use starnets and bubble drives, but a long time ago on Earth, they used radio waves to communicate…very analog. The Captain sends messages to these pagers using radio waves. There are some drawbacks. The data transfers are incredibly small. Only a sentence or so can go through at a time. And our pagers can only send messages back to the Captain, not to each other. But it's also reliably secure. The Outposts have all but forgotten about radio waves. Even Earthens haven't used them for hundreds and hundreds of megas. As far as we know, the only radio tech left in space is right here, in Shamong, with our Captain."

"Sugar!" Ves said again.

"Yeah, sugar," I added.

Harkless produced a second pager and held it toward Linah. "As a matter of fact, this one is for you, temporarily. The Waymaker made it clear she plans to return soon for Ves, and so you need to be ready to act in a moment's notice, but…" He paused and shook his head. "The Farm is too far to send runners with messages over and over again. And I can only show up unannounced on your doorstep so many times. The message would change by the time it arrived here." He laughed softly. "So for now, you get a pager. The Captain will send you instructions as needed. You can only send and receive from the Captain, and it's the same for all of us. Keep it secret."

Linah grasped the pager and turned it over in her hands.

"So you, Beecher and Harkless, work together on the BackTrack and hear from the Captain on one of these pieces of ancient tech and save lots of fugitive Earthens all the time?" I asked in awe.

Harkless laughed. "I do. I am a tool in the Captain's belt. But not really Beecher here. He is more like King of the Earthens, so the Captain needs to communicate with him sometimes, too. He doesn't even have a code name. He's just Beecher, to friend and foe alike."

My eyes widened with new understanding of the two men in my Day Room, even Harkless, whose real life had turned out so differently from my assumptions.

Late into the night, the faces around me laughed and caroused, somehow joyful together despite their different complexions and histories. The liquor still warmed my feelings and relaxed my fears. It slowly occurred to me, like uncoiling a rope, that perhaps my loneliness had not begun with the sickness that took my parents. Perhaps it began when my parents married and incurred the wrath of my mother's family. Or maybe it began with the teasing about my Lūnar ancestry. Or maybe it had been fueled by the growing distrust amongst the various factions of humanity for megas. Maybe that affected all of us and made everyone lonely sometimes.

But at that moment, in that pleasant time together, I recognized that my parents' sickness had eventually given me more than heartache: self-sufficiency, my Farm, and these new people. Friends? Beecher laughed heartily at something Ves said. Linah pulled Ves into a reluctant kiss on the temple. Harkless caught my gaze and smiled dazzlingly, but it was not flirtatious or manipulative. It felt warm and uncomplicated.

Yes, maybe I had friends. Real ones. Ones I was not pretending for or hiding from.

Our Outposter Society boasted about being the most civilized beings of all human history, but true civility, true superiority, would not exclude the people around me. I grinned back shyly to Harkless, and a tiny flicker of concern in his eyes vanished. He rejoined the conversation as I reached for a second piece of cake.

CHAPTER 31 :
WHO WE MUST BECOME

VES GREW SLEEPY, AND HE asked Beecher to walk him to his room. Admiration glowed in his eyes as Beecher agreed to help him get settled. They disappeared through the door, Beecher listening to Ves' jokes while gently supporting him under one elbow.

"Beecher is the closest thing Ves has to a father," Linah explained to me. "Beecher is the face of the free Earthens here in Shamong. My people listen to him, respect him, and Ves has always admired him, almost worships him. But Beecher is always in danger, always plotting, planning, working. I worry Ves admires that part of him too much... At least for a boy his age. Ves thinks that he's ready to fight too."

Harkless teased, "Well, he also has a knife-wielding sister!" She shot him a blazing look. I set my mind to watching Linah and Harkless interact more carefully, but I noticed no more than a few extra glances between them, mostly initiated by Harkless.

Linah's distress about Ves turned something in my stomach; I wanted her to feel better, to stop having to worry for just a few moments. "Look Linah, Ves might admire Beecher, but he loves you. You give him all the love he could ever need. He sees your kindness, your wisdom. He'll sort it all out."

Linah's expression toward me held gratitude. "I hope. But his outburst at the quarry... And Harkless is right. Danger is all around Ves. I want him to be strong and brave. But I also want him to have some happiness. More than just survive. I worry so much about him." We sat silently and somberly for a moment before Linah took a shuttering breath. "I'd better make Ves let Beecher go. Beech has children of his own waiting for him."

Then only Harkless and I stood in the dim kitchen drinking bamboo tea.

"You sure I can't spike your tea? I kinda want to hang out with a tipsy groundhog again," he teased.

"Absolutely not. Never again." I shook my head, embarrassed.

"Well, as of tonight, you have become an adult and a true contributing member of Society. And a seat of the Advocacy. And an ally of the BackTrack. And a drunk, too." His list of my new responsibilities drained the blood from my face, and I had to steady myself on the counter.

"Harkless, I don't know how to be any of those things."

"Welcome to the club, Minty. None of us do." He smiled and gave me a playful punch on the shoulder. When the weight of it hit my bruises from the morning in town, I flinched, and Harkless' permanent smirk turned into a legitimate frown. I had never seen Harkless frown so deeply; he looked like his father, and for a moment, it made me scared of him again.

"That pain from something Fitzhugh did to you?"

"If Fitzhugh is a thug that owns a quarry, then yes."

"I heard all about that. Show me."

I had not looked much at the bruise myself, so with curiosity, I pulled out the neck of my tunic and peered at my shoulder. Even after a cycle, spots of brown bloomed where the man had gripped me, and in places, bars of yellowish bruises marked the pressure of his fingers. I shivered at the sight.

"Shek." Harkless' features darkened further. "Shek him."

"It's fine." I wrapped both arms around myself and rubbed the tender spots. I tried to lighten the mood. "Fitzhugh looked worse. At least I can hide my bruises instead of wearing them across my face."

Harkless had his lips pressed tightly, and his attempted smile only affected half his mouth. When his silence stretched on, and dark Harkless continued to disquiet me, I redirected. "It's just a bruise, Harkless. So did Ves really do that to his Tasker's face? Fitzhugh's nose looked nasty."

Harkless blew air forcibly out of his pressed lips. "Oh, yes. What a remarkable little kid Ves is. He hasn't told you the story?"

"No. I haven't asked. I don't even know if Linah has asked."

"Linah knows. From what I've heard, it was quite the incident." Harkless paused to eye me and moved as though he was contemplating grabbing my hand. He decided not to, and I felt a flutter of disappointment. "Are you sure you want to know? It's very...hard to hear." I remembered the red welts that covered Ves from head to toe that first night when Linah brought him home: his pain so great that he could not stay conscious, Linah's panic and desperation. No, I did not want to know, but I should. I nodded to Harkless, and he continued.

"Ves was an apprentice to the mechanists at Fitzhugh's silicon quarries.

Ves has a brain for machines. They also kept a medical Bonder there for all the quarry injuries, and that Bonder had an apprentice as well. A girl, an orphan, older than Vesey by a few megas, named Ritta. Rumor has it that she is a gorgeous thing and sweet as sugar. Unfortunately, she took a lot of harassment from the men there, Outposter and Bonder alike. But Ves had a special friendship with her. They ate together and helped each other out when they could." I nodded. It did not surprise me that Ves had befriended a lonely girl. He had a knack for it, if I was any evidence.

"Last cycle, a bond trader came up from Capron, looking for specialists, and heard that the quarry had a medical apprentice. When he saw Ritta... Well, let's just say it would have been better if she was ugly. He bought her right there, in the workroom. Ves made a ruckus, but for a while, his friends held him back." Harkless took a deep breath. "Unfortunately, as soon as the transaction was done, the Capronian slapped her around a little. Ves went wild. He broke away from his friends and made it across the room to the trader. Punched him. Wrestled him to the ground and got in a few good hits on the Capronian and Fitzhugh when he intervened."

My eyes could not bulge any wider. Ves, little Ves, had fought for his friend against a Tasker while everyone watched. I flinched. Fitzhugh was a cruel Tasker yes, but was a cruel Tasker so different from a kind one, when they held all the power?

And I was a Tasker. The word seemed sour and bitter to me now. I, too, had held all the power over Ves when he arrived at my Farm. I had the power to send him back to torture. I had the power to separate Linah and Ves forever. I controlled the future of their bodies, their family, their lives, all because of where I was born, and the choices of those who had come before me.

It was a power that I did not deserve and never should have had in the first place.

Harkless continued the story. "They stopped the fight quickly, but Ves' Tasker was furious. He–he taught Ves a lesson." Harkless stumbled on the words and his hand raked through his hair again and again. "The Capronion left with Ritta. Lawmen arrived, including our old friend, Mudsil. Under his instructions, Ves was left there, on the floor, dead or dying, while the rest of the Earthens had to finish the day's work around him."

Sobs erupted from me. Harkless grabbed my hand after all. His grip was steady and firm, holding my body in place while my emotions heaved.

"I know." He took another deep breath to encourage me and possibly himself. "Late at night, Ves' friends snuck in and grabbed his body. Found out he was still breathing. They brought him to Beecher, and then the Captain got him up here, to Linah, and you know the rest."

I tried to control myself, but it was the worst story I had ever heard. Not just because of the violence, which I had always abhorred, but because that violence was done to someone I cared for, someone who told jokes, who protected his friends, who was proud of his sister, and who gave me birthday surprises. Someone I–loved, even. My heart ached for Ves to the point of cracking open. I loved an Earthen boy, and his sister too. They had completely rearranged me.

"I wish I could say that it was an isolated incident." Harkless looked at me then toward the hallway where Linah had reappeared with Beecher. "Hey, Liny, Beech, I'm going to head off."

Linah nodded though clearly confused at my profuse tears. She walked the two men to the door, and they talked in low voices. Beecher gestured casually toward me in farewell and went into the night. Through my tear–blurred vision, I saw Harkless lightly touch the discolored part of Linah's face, but she shrunk back delicately. She watched for a while at the door when he had gone.

I met her in the center of the Day Room and wrapped her up in a big hug. Even though my bruises throbbed, I pulled her as close as I could. My mind traveled back to the first night with Ves, when the mildest touch with Linah felt strange and awkward. But now, the biggest hug I was capable of seemed like the least I could offer. I cried for her and for Ves. "I'm in, Linah," I spoke through her yellow hair. "I meant it before, but now, I guess I mean it more. I want you to know that. I'm all in. We are going to get Ves to safety."

She took a deep, shaky breath and lightly returned my hug.

"How do you do it, Linah? How do you survive with the hate? Given to you? In you? Around you? I hate the man that hurt Ves. I hate the way things are for him, for you, for your people."

"Beech says hate never gives, never heals, never resolves. It only takes. Destroys." She faltered. "But I suppose that sometimes we are what we have to be. We become who we must."

CHAPTER 31 :
THE ENEMY LURKS

LINAH SOFTLY SANG A LULLABY as she braided my hair, as if she did not even realize she was singing.

Cruel winds, cold nights, they are hardships to get through,
When winter comes, I'll walk with you, la-loo, la-loo.

Warm rain, fresh life, a chance to begin anew,
When spring comes, I'll walk with you, la-loo, la-loo.

Bright sun, great yield, things display their brightest hues,
When summer comes, I'll walk with you, la-loo, la-loo.

Cool breeze, toil done, rest our spirits now pursue.
When autumn comes, I'll walk with, you la-loo, la-loo.

Linah and I were both nervous, but her song, dulcet and full of mysterious words, managed to calm me somewhat. We had two things to worry about.

The first began earlier that morning when Linah screamed and dropped a mug of hot Keff, her new favorite way to start the morning, all over the kitchen floor.

"What, Linah, what?" I shouted.

"It moved!" she shouted back.

"What moved?"

"The thing! The thing from Harkless. From the Captain!" A knife had appeared in her fingers. "It moved in my pocket!"

"Well, get it out, Linah! Don't stab it!" I yelled, grateful that the Captain of Shamong did not witness our first efforts with the Pager. To our credit, after only dropping it once more, we settled enough to look at the tiny screen together. The letters were formed strangely, as though unable to curve in the normal ways.

From The Captain : Take up now and don't delay

Right there on the Pager was The Waymaker's code. The Captain–the actual BackTrack Captain–sent it to us. Linah met my grey eyes with her blue ones. "She's coming back." The bright light of joy lit Linah's expression. I tried to mimic it, but there was a sudden sadness in me. The Waymaker's return meant goodbyes; The Waymaker's arrival was Ves' departure.

But it was also Gathering Day, and I did not want to go.

Linah and I spent that day in a complicated, messy bundle of nerves. Linah ended her lullaby and pulled me from my thoughts. She turned my shoulders to face the mirror.

She had selected a sky-grey tunic to compliment my eyes. Asymmetrical panels of iridescent, structured fabric alternated with creamy, matte panels of the same color. The panels intersected and terminated in strategic ways to accentuate my form, and an enormous hood of the soft fabric draped behind me like a cape when it was not in use. Coordinating leggings and boots perfectly blended into the pattern of the outfit. The contrast in textures made it difficult to say whether the dress beckoned you closer or was armor to keep you away.

"Alluring," Linah called it.

The garment gave the illusion of austerity, but the complexity and perfection of the cut revealed its extravagance. At least twenty braids of various widths and lengths secured themselves to my head so successfully that I made Linah swear to me that she had not glued them to my skin. Linah brushed my face lightly with pigments that she claimed Attisians and Earthens alike used to accentuate their features.

I clasped my mother's necklace and watched as the plain moon stone settled near my clavicle. Understated and unpolished, it was the only part of my ensemble that made me feel like myself. Linah, in her best efforts to glamorize me for the event, encouraged me to wear something sparklier, but my heart was set. My mother had worn her moon stone to Gatherings, and I would too. As a compromise, I followed Linah's guidance on absolutely everything else.

"You look..." Linah began with lively eyes. "You look like an 8." I raised my eyebrows and made a gagging noise. We laughed, and it felt so good that I kept doing it until a hysterical edge crept into the sound.

"I'm sorry, Linah. I'm incredibly nervous right now."

"Of course. But, Minty, even as an 8, you look very beautiful." Linah hooked a sparkling spiral of glass to the top of my ear that dangled toward my neck in decoration. A streak of blue swam in the middle of clear glass and only revealed itself as I moved my head. "I'm concerned people might not recognize you, though."

I made myself smile in response, but secretly I would not have minded the anonymity. "Linah, how will I do this? I won't function in a room full of Societals. I have nothing to say. They don't care about me."

Linah looked thoughtful for a while. "Maybe you don't need to pretend nearly as much as you think," she replied. "After all, the BackTrack is funded by many Attisians sponsors. There will be Watchtowers there probably. We just don't know who they are. Even the Captain is going to be there."

The possibility had not crossed my mind. "You think the Captain goes to Gatherings?"

"Harkless says he has no doubt that the Captain is an Outposter. Don't all Outposters go to the Gatherings? So the Captain will too. See if you can discover who it is!" Linah suggested sneakily. "Make it a game."

"I suppose playing a game with myself is a good idea since no one will want to talk to me. I'm pretty sure my rejection of Chi's ridiculous recommendations hasn't made me any more popular. Chi probably issued formal orders to ignore me into submission." I gathered my nerves and tried to shed the bad feelings I had about the event. "But I know it's the right thing. At least, I know it's the best thing. For all of us."

Many times throughout the day, Harkless offered to escort me to town, but I refused. As distracting as Harkless might be to my feelings of anxiety, I planned to preserve every ounce of interpersonal energy I possessed for the party.

"This is it!" I exclaimed while I gave Linah a grateful hug. "Thanks for putting my look together."

"It was easy," she said, but her grin held no small amount of pride. "Tell me all about it when you get home. Especially the tunics and saris." It occurred to me that Linah knew about fashion because she liked fashion.

"Every detail!" I confirmed. Linah and I walked through the Day Room as I prepared to leave. "Be safe up here. If The Waymaker arrives before I get back, tell her hello. I'm...excited to see her again. Kinda."

"I will. And, um, I'm sorry, Minty." I did not understand her apology until Linah swung the front door open to reveal Harkless lounging against my door frame. He looked as good as ever, and maybe even better, wearing an ostentatious tunic with flowing swaths and braided ropes hanging from his shoulders and showing off shockingly blue boots. "He insisted that it was a good idea," Linah whispered in my ear.

"Minty!" Harkless pointed from my hair to my toes then back up again. "You wear 8 well. And Linah! I know you are the mastermind; your work is superb. My compliments to both of you." I rolled my eyes. Annoyance seemed to be a Harkless specialty, but this time self-consciousness and warmth mixed with the annoyance inside me.

"Harkless, exactly how many times can I expect you to show up unannounced like this?" I groaned. "I need to know for my health and well-being."

"If I told you, it would no longer be unannounced. There is no way to possibly answer that question, therefore. You'll just have to wait and see. Besides, it's fun. It's our special thing now." Harkless grabbed my hand and pulled me outside. "Come on, groundhog. Let's go to a party." He saluted Linah before the door shut.

I resigned myself to the situation as best I could. "So..." I began, always eloquent. "We got word that The Waymaker is coming back for Ves. On the pager. It worked!"

"Waymaker, Waymaker, Waymaker," he chided. "Now that you know the most spectacular Earthen in all the 'Posts, it's all you talk about. Sure, sure, she's changing lives, rescuing souls. But I feel like you don't even notice me. I am interesting. I introduced you to her after all. Couldn't I share some of your attention? I'm admirable!"

"Admirable? You want me to compare and contrast you and The Waymaker? Really?" I dared as we walked toward my transport track.

"Stars, no. That would be embarrassing."

"To you, it would be." We grinned at one another.

"Listen, no more BackTrack talk for now. The enemy lurks."

"Ha," I forced, convinced that he was merely encouraging me to relax, but his sudden diagonal gaze and furrowed brow made me suspicious. I scanned the hillside and discovered the reason for his caution. At the beginning of my transport track stood a tall figure, this one dressed in a jacket and pants set of the darkest green over a tightly wrapped, pure white shirt that exposed two pronounced collar bones. He had two hands in two pockets, and his head was tilted all the way backward in an expression of utter annoyance.

As if one Stille was not more than enough, Harkless' older brother, Rankin Stille 8, had come to my Farm.

CHAPTER 33 :
LIKE A SCHOOL BOY

MX. RANKIN STILLE 8 WAS groomed his whole life to inherit his family's gigantic shipping company and Advocacy seat. His reputably diabolical father kept him in close confidence, and I assumed Ran possessed the family secrets as well as the family savagery. If I believed everything I heard, Outposters and Bonders alike suffered under the Stilles' administration. Ran and his father worshiped wealth and status, and pursued them even above the welfare of the Outpost–a sin that was only forgiven because of their excessive wealth and influence.

In addition to those formidable facts, Ran's general demeanor promoted his intimidating reputation. Always more reserved than his brother, his high intelligence came across as inordinate focus. He was Harkless' opposite. The brothers had been more similar in childhood. Back then, they had been more alike in personality, but time, circumstances, or perhaps beliefs had chiseled them into very distinct individuals.

They did resemble one another still in color and attractiveness. Ran stood taller than Harkless, but his frame was not as robust. His eyes, unlike his brother's perfect Attisianal tan eyes, were very dark brown and hard to decipher. Their deep tone made his gaze solemn, calculating, and mysterious. Even megas ago in school, I suspected his eyes of saying something different than his mouth.

And this menacing stalwart of Outpost success tactlessly studied me as we approached. In his simple but perfectly tailored tunic, Rankin looked very, very bored.

"Ran!" Harkless bellowed. "Don't stare, you jag. You remember Groundhog Bradford 8? Oh, I mean Araminta Bradford 8?" The three of us stood awkwardly together. Well, I stood awkwardly. The brothers stood perfectly naturally.

"I remember her differently than this," Rankin responded coolly.

"I told you! She grew up nicely since her disappearing act, don't you think? And now it's our honor to escort her to the first Gathering she's attended in megas."

"She'll have a time of it." I thought I saw a flash of amusement in his enigmatic eyes, but his face remained placid and inattentive. "Let's get on with it. It takes forever to transport up here."

Harkless started as soon as we stepped onto the transport track. "You are as bad as she is. Stars, both of you! Just try to have fun for at least five milis tonight, please? My sole purpose will be to inundate you with fun. You won't be able to escape. I know you'll try, but I won't have you sitting idly in corners all night. Notice I said corners and not corner. I know you'd be in separate corners. All alone. Sulking. Shek, you both need to relax. Good thing you have me. How lucky for you."

Then Rankin shoved Harkless right off the track.

Harkless landed with a thump on the sparse dirt, swearing, while Rankin and I continued smoothly to our destination. Rankin pretended nothing had happened. He met my expression of surprise with the tiniest raise of one eyebrow. My heart pumped, suddenly alarmed at being alone with such an indecipherable person. I looked back to where Harkless fell and prepared to hop off the track myself, when I saw him with a finger to his mouth, already upright and sprinting toward us. Still facing forward, Ran swung his elbow backward at the precise moment Harkless' gut should have been there. But Harkless went low and buckled Ran to the ground by tackling the backs of his knees. I abruptly found myself alone, gliding peacefully along the track as the boys wrestled in the thin dirt behind me. After considering for a moment, I stepped off the track to wait for them.

"Is that taken care of?" I asked a bit later as we all shuffled back onto the track. Their shenanigans made me feel equal enough to the task of traveling in their presence, however pleasingly aesthetic and influential they might be. Harkless laughed incessantly. Ran grouched and kept turning away from me. Their expensive clothes showed wrinkles and smears of soil. I watched as they tried to straighten themselves out and noted that the rough, disheveled look suited them more than the pristine perfection they had originally displayed. Although, I thought jealously, what wouldn't suit people who look like that?

"Okay, fix me," Harkless sobered with effort and addressed me.

"That's not possible," I shot back. I really did feel much more relaxed with their display of ridiculousness.

"You are funny tonight. But really. Fix me. And hurry, we're almost there. I look like a schoolboy."

"And you act like one too," I chimed. Ran coughed and turned away again.

"Listen, groundhog. I like this sassy thing you are doing, but cut us some slack. We said we'd escort you. We didn't say we'd be good at it. Just help me get the dirt off my back. I don't trust that sheking jagwad right now. And fix my hair. Make me sexy again." I rolled my eyes but helped him brush off the backs of his arms and shoulders. "Now my hair." He sounded genuinely anxious. I wanted to tease his vanity, but I studied the tousled look he had accidentally achieved and answered honestly.

"You should leave it that way." He paused briefly before flashing the roguish grin that unnerved me. This time, after the brothers' less-than-perfect behavior, I found myself feeling bold enough to return his gaze. Maybe the tight braids were preventing blood from getting to my cortex.

A few of those same braids swished over my shoulder as I purposefully turned away from the brothers and faced our destination. I sensed an intense stare from Rankin, but I ignored it as best I could.

I rode my wave of confidence right up until we stepped off the transport in the center of town, at which time any boldness I had mustered evaporated in an attack of apprehension. The whole street was transformed since my last visit. Bright, decorative lanterns hung from every pole and roof, colorful fabric swags stretched overhead, and music blared. Gone was the usual tone of purpose and economy; instead, voices laughed from all the citizens who were prepared to feast, dance, and carouse the night away.

Even in my youth, I did not share my friends' ongoing enthusiasm for Gatherings. I already tended toward shyness back then, but most Attisians loved Gatherings; they were our only public holidays.

School taught us that our ancient ancestors celebrated hundreds of holidays, and that sometimes different regions and religions celebrated completely different holidays from one another. It was highly confusing and highly wasteful. At the beginning of settlement on Attis, to promote unity, exemplify efficiency, and minimize waste of all kinds, the first Advocacy developed Gatherings: one celebration for everything and anyone. And since Gatherings occurred only twice every megacycle, my Outpost was ready to party.

The two Stille brothers and I joined crowds of Shamong's boisterous citizens as they filed up massive stairs that led to the largest building in our whole city, named after its only function, the Gathering House. Warm artificial light shone outward through the structure's huge glass panel walls and made the building glow brighter even than the daylight of our atmosphere.

At the grand entrance, on the pillars on both sides, two huge plaques of dark grey glass displayed the creed of Attisian Society as written by our original First Statesmen. As each citizen passed by them to enter the Gathering House, they held four fingers out toward the words.

The words, permanently molded into the folds of my brain from daily repetitions at school, were noble to me, even as I walked beneath them. I found myself proud of the words, but as Society currently lived, only Attisians received the protection of the creed and, even then, imperfectly. I wondered how such a virtuous beginning had devolved into such a discouraging application.

I lifted my hand in the traditional gesture, as did Harkless and Rankin.

Then we were inside. After two and a half megas, I was at a Gathering once again.

CHAPTER 34 :

IT'S A GATHERING

EVERYTHING LOOKED JUST AS I remembered. Bright. Loud. Exuberant. Indulgent. The Gathering House practically glittered in glass polished to perfection. Every panel, column, and etching reflected the glow of the lights suspended from the soaring ceiling. Under the perfect geometry of the faceted structure, a long buffet of gorgeous foods lined one wall, tables for games or conversation filled the opposite space, and a sunken area in the center was designated for dancing.

Harkless pulled me inward by my hand, whispering for me to act naturally. I noticed a physical shift as the crowd reacted to the Stille brothers. Their status and good looks drew people's curiosity. But I also I sensed some confusion, and even suspicion, as they observed my hand in Harkless'.

We buried ourselves thoroughly in the crowd, and Harkless tried coaxing me to relax. He offered me a swill from an intricate glass flask hidden beneath the decor of his tunic, but I refused. Just the memory of Chi's bamboo liquor made my stomach roil. He gulped down a few mouthfuls easily, however, and moments later something loose and wily lit his eyes. He invited me to dance, but the flash of disgusted terror in my expression told him all he needed to know.

"Holy stars, Minty. Give me some effort. I'm really trying here. You're a statue. A groundhog statue with big, terrified, Lūnar-grey eyes. Even an angry reaction would be better than this nothingness. I bet if Lawman Mudsil were here, you'd have something to say..." he mused.

"I'm sure I would," I agreed. "He's the worst."

"Worse than me?" Harkless grinned.

"Barely, but yes."

Harkless eyed me speculatively. He raised the timber and volume of his voice and dropped his chin to connect it to his neck. "It's a Gathering, Mx.

Bradford 8. It's supposed to be fun, please. We will all tell your uncle that you're being weird, please."

When I laughed aloud at his excellent impression of Lawman Mudsil, he shouted triumphantly and dragged us to a cluster of Attisians around our age that included my cousin Sarai. I tried to catch her eye, but she skillfully avoided my gaze. Her gauzy tunic, long enough to brush the floor, left me wondering whether or not it was transparent. The seams of the tunic housed tiny lights that twinkled near her neck and shoulders. I looked around to see if other attendees wore light-studded dresses. None. She had taken ostentatious to a new level that was all her own.

Too loudly, Harkless addressed the group, "I told every single one of you. I told you." With a flourish, he directed everyone's attention to me. *Shek you, Harkless.*

"Told us what, Harks darling?" Sarai asked while the lights in her tunic sparkled hypnotically.

"I told you that apprenticing with the Lawman was an excellent life choice." Groans and eye rolls issued from the group. "Everyone can rest easy now. My game is done. You may continue with your bland, Mudsil-free lives. I have bravely gone to where you would not and returned triumphantly to amuse you all. My impression is perfected; even Araminta likes it. Behold, she smiles."

I doubted that a smile still hung on my lips, but upon checking, it was true. I flattened my expression and, to avoid blushing quipped quickly, "but am I amused by the impression, Harkless, or the attempts at the impression?" The group, except for Rankin whose disinterested look remained, laughed tepidly.

Harkless jumped back in immediately. "Look at that. Minty found her sense of humor. But now my favorite song is playing. I guess we'll never know, Minty! No time to talk when there is dancing to do. Onward, onward, everyone. You can't listen to Minty, you know; she's a groundhog." Harkless gulped a shot of bamboo liquor before the Bonder carrying them on a tray could protest, and hustled the group away while winking at me, and everyone else, repetitively. He grabbed Sarai's hand saying, "Dance with me. If I've said it once, I've said it a thousand times: I love a girl who is also a lantern."

I watched my peers flutter to the middle of the room, pair off, and begin to dance. The music, compared to the drummed rhythms in the Market, felt formulaic to my ears, but everyone seemed sufficiently enamored.

"Groundhog–" With a start, I realized that Rankin had elected to avoid the dance and loomed behind me. Just us. Rankin and me. Me and Rankin. "–a small mammal native to northern Grand America that hibernates in an underground burrow for several months each mega as well as during times of duress or threat. Ranked level 395 in Manipulation priority. Introduction planned for

Phase 175." Rankin's Aide projected an informational hologram between us. In a monochromatic picture, the pointed nose of a fat, furry animal with clawed feet emerged from a dark hole in the wet ground. I wrinkled my nose at the image. The creature was not cute. Ran eyed me, probably thinking something similar.

"And so why does Harkless call you a groundhog?" My anxiety at speaking alone with Rankin slowed my words, so he proceeded without input from me. "Harks has nicknames for everyone. You're the first 'groundhog,' though."

I gulped, chiding myself for being so intimidated. "I suppose that...he teases me about disappearing for a couple of megas. After my parents, um... He jokes that I am reemerging. Like a groundhog, you know, after it hibernates, or something like that."

Rankin gave a half-nod of acknowledgement. "Is that what you are doing? You decided it's time to reemerge? Just in time to take your inheritance and Advocacy seat?" I shrugged and brainstormed ways to escape, but he did not give me long enough. "Interesting. And? What is it like to disappear from Shamong, all your schooling, duties, social obligations, et cetera, and then return so abruptly?"

The question could be merely small talk from any other person, but his piercing eyes and intensity made him demanding and presumptuous. Some of the rage I had cultivated recently boiled up, unbidden, and overcame my fright. Instead, I felt angry. I felt angry at Rankin. Condescending, unaffected, and enjoying all the power of his wealth and status, he suddenly represented all the worst of Attis to me. I pressed my lips together as my ideas threatened to reveal themselves. I met his gaze with fiery belligerence, and he returned it with unperturbed expectation.

With limited self-control, I only managed, "It's been somewhat difficult, to say the very least." Our stare-down continued for a few moments. He waited for more, but I decided I did not owe him any more.

Suddenly glitter and gusto forced itself between us. Sarai, her face barely recognizable when highlighted and shadowed by her personal light source, inserted herself into our interaction. She fluttered her eyes at Rankin before blatantly analyzing my entire look.

"Araminta, you are here, for once. And I keep finding you around the Stilles. Someone did a wonderful job on your braids." Sarai's hair was artificially straightened and perfectly smooth, falling long down her back and accented with strings of glittering lights that coordinated with her dress. "I decided against braids for tonight, just for something a little more contemporary."

Having said the minimum to me, she shifted to Rankin. "Ran, darling, I see our fathers engaged in an intense conversation. Dad is fixated on your Starships as best explanation as to how fugitive Earthens can just disappear so completely and mysteriously. I bet that is what he's talking to Calhoun about! It's getting animated over there, and I thought you might want to join the fun with me."

Ran analyzed her eagerly, whether due to her bizarre dress or the exciting topic she introduced, I could not judge. He spared a single glance back to me, deciding. But Sarai continued, coaxing and intimate, "Come with me." They headed off, Sarai pulling Ran close and whispering in his ear. She looked back at me, coyly, as if in some unspoken game of triumphs and failures. She took in everything about my appearance in a long gaze down and up again.

"It's good to see you making an effort again, Araminta." She returned her attention once more to Rankin, and they both disappeared in the crowd. It seemed the secret to Sarai's approval was a perfectly tailored and fashionable ensemble orchestrated by Linah. That could have been helpful to my feelings when I was 12.

Sarai was my lawful cousin, due to her father's partnership with my Uncle Chi. But despite this semi-familial connection, she had just made it very clear that I was not invited to listen to what might have been an informative debate for my newly adopted cause. I needed a break anyway after almost losing my temper with Rankin.

As the Gathering progressed, I purposefully avoided the room's corners since it kept Harkless' attention away, but I tried to be alone as much as possible. Occasionally I felt the attention of semi-strangers' eyes, and infrequently an old acquaintance would attempt to converse with me. I grew weary of platitudes about my parents and questions about my last megas alone on the Farm. I eventually discovered that if I moved slowly but confidently around the massive space, I could avoid most of the interactions. Uncle Chi did not try to speak with me, nor I with him, although I passed within several meters of him often enough. Each time I felt the fire of his angry gaze.

Not much had changed since my last Gathering several megas ago. Attisian children roamed and frolicked together. Full of treats and adrenaline and freedoms not normally allowed, they darted between tables and only found their adults after injuries and squabbles. Some of the littlest were likely 9s. The older kids stood in clusters that occasionally dispersed or traded members. Every one of them looked on the verge of either laughing, hitting, hugging, or crying. I remembered the confusion of that age too well.

My peers, the older teens and young adults, vacillated between glad-handing important grown-ups and amusing each other at game tables, dancing, or sneaking kisses in private moments. Then the adults, mostly sticking together with their generational contemporaries, did all of the above but added experience, strategy, power, and alcohol. And finally, the ancient and elderly attendees reclined proudly in the most comfortable chairs as though the party's joviality was a gift given directly out of their benevolence.

I remembered similar performances from long ago, but as I watched the festivities, I saw much more than an Outposter celebration. I noticed the other participants: Bonders unpretentiously filled glasses, took orders, and cleaned messes. They made order out of the gaiety while wearing borrowed uniforms and ill-fitting shoes, ignored at best and berated at worst by everyone that they served. They practically disappeared if you were not looking for them. After the Gathering, they would all clean and wash and barely sleep before being expected to start their normal workday the next morning. The Bonders did not do it for money; they did not do it to provide for their families or to edify a proud Society. They did it because they had to, because their time and energy belonged to a Tasker.

How could Harkless revel so completely when he surely saw all of that and so much more? He must pretend, or forget. Or just play the game well.

The thought of Harkless inspired me to attempt to shake off my gravity. I sampled the luscious foods and make mental notes about the glamorous apparel for Linah. While Attis honored economy and conservation, as our wealth grew, so did the subtle expression of it. The room twirled with colored fabrics, mostly in the inexpensive neutral shades available at every retailer, but the wealthier citizens imported fabrics from Lūn. Those garments were bold, colorful, and expertly tailored.

My gaze landed on Harkless' mother, Mx. Mariella Stille 7, partner of the notorious Calhoun Stille 7, who, based on the family wealth and her striking beauty, could not avoid setting trends. Her warm yellow tunic reminded me of the sunflower's petals. While the bright outfit appeared simple in the front, the back plunged in a low, swooping cut, decorated with intricate golden braids and beads. She was timelessly gorgeous, a perfect Attisian 7. I laughed because, in between her exquisite smiles, I thought she looked almost as frustrated to be there as me.

Beside Mariella Stille 7, her partner stood grand and proud, undeniably impressive and imperious. Mx. Calhoun Stille 7 was handsome, but his features had become so sharp with age that they discouraged admiration. His tunic was pitch black, long and fitted, with accents of iridescence at every seam. He nodded and spoke often but never smiled.

As I watched the Stilles, a man, who seemed bland and innocuous next to them, interrupted their conversations. Calhoun Stille 7 appeared irate at the intrusion, but the two men spoke animatedly, and his frustration shifted to fervor. Mariella tossed her hands up in exasperation and left the discussion. I wondered what topic could inspire such passionate interactions in the middle of a Gathering.

From my removed vantage point, I discerned a similar change spreading across the entire room. The atmosphere filled with a new energy. Excitement replaced gaiety. Eagerness replaced geniality. Every single dancer left the floor in favor of discussing this new diversion.

Most curiously, the mood of the Bonders also changed. Their postures, previously resigned to their tasks, now seemed tight and tense. Glances full of meaning flashed between them. I might have been the only Outposter to notice.

Alarm lodged in my stomach. I tried to breathe it away, but something highly unusual was unfolding. I could only think of Linah. Ves. The Waymaker. Their names spun in my head.

They could be in trouble, and I was away, unable to help, at a ridiculous Gathering. My heart thumped to get back to them as I considered how to leave the Gathering House inconspicuously. I only made it a few steps away from my spot on the wall before a message pinged from my Aide.

Message from Harkless Stille 8 : Don't do stupid things. I'm by the Jax tables. Come find me. Now.

5 MEGAS AGO

*Supplemental excerpt from : Making a Way ; the Life and Stories,
Record HAC-3859385738*

She heard the rumors everywhere. The Taskers whispered stories of Earthens escaping to freedom or to death. Just cycles ago, a local girl had cried for days when her partner fled without her, then cried again when he was caught and beaten so badly no one thought he would survive.

The girl with the God Voice felt terrified, but she had grown to trust the Voice, and the goal of freedom stirred something inside her that she could not ignore. She understood that her life was unfair. She was mistreated. She was devalued. The rage grew and grew within. Enough. Done. She would take freedom, or she would take death.

She told no one that she planned to escape. On the evening before resting day, she assembled the few supplies she had been able to gather. A sack, a few starchy tubers, scrap fabric.

The girl keenly watched the faces of her family. Her father was not there. He had been lent to another homestead and would not return for days, so only her mother and little brother, who was not so little now, settled into bed that night. She thought that they might notice something strange about her demeanor, that they might grow suspicious of her pounding heart, but then she remembered that not everyone had a God Voice, and that limited their perception.

"Sing please, Mama," she asked, and her sadness almost prevented the words from coming out correctly. Her mother obliged as they lay down. Her lullaby that night was slow and swinging, one of the girl's favorites.

Away, away.
What you are, let it stay.
Become with me,
Take a new way.

Harvest is done,
The past has gone,
Choose now what is old and new,
Come on, come on.

Away, away.
What you've been, you may betray,
What now awaits,
I cannot say.

A hope forgone,
Naught thereupon,
Awake! and decide anew,
Get on, get on.

Away, away.
Take up now, do not delay.
Much may befall,
Fear shan't allay–

Tears flowed down the girl's cheeks. It was the permission she needed from her unknowing mother.

"Thanks, Mama," she breathed.

Her half-sleeping mama replied, "Goodnight, Hettie."

CHAPTER 35 :

FAR FROM THE NORM

I GROUND MY TEETH; I just wanted to leave. But Harkless' concern about me doing stupid things rankled me. What was stupid? How was I to know?

Even though he annoyed me, Harkless knew more about the inner workings of Shamong. After a brief internal debate, that fact alone convinced me to seek Harkless instead of retreating immediately to the Farm. I had no idea which tables hosted the Jax games that evening, but I soon found Harkless standing in a limited circle of well-dressed and similarly youthful members of Society. Rankin and Sarai were not with him.

Vexation was my main accessory by the time I tapped Harkless on the back. He gave me a pointed look and then schooled his features back into his famous aloofness. He guided me into the circle with an arm around my shoulders. My barely contained unease contrasted sharply with the relatively nonplussed demeanors in the small group.

Was Ves still safe? Had The Waymaker been discovered?

"So, what do you think, Minty?" Harkless asked as he fixedly squeezed my upper arm. I frowned.

"About what?" The nonchalant tones of my voice sounded completely fake. They were.

"Stars, Minty. You have the same Aide as the rest of us. Do you even use your Aide?" Harkless seemed genuinely frustrated with me again. The feeling was mutual of course, but he did a better job of hiding it from the group.

"I didn't get anything–" I started. Harkless grabbed my wrist and my thumb to activate my Aide. I allowed him to use my finger to press prompt after prompt, but not without fixing him with menacing glares that he could not miss.

"You have your Aide set to silent except for personal messages and schedule alerts?! No news, no starcasts, not even your community or emergency settings were on," he finally said. "Your emergency setting was on silent, Araminta."

"So what?" I retorted. "I read them when I have the time. Most alerts are totally irrelevant out on the Farm anyway." He and the others gawked at me with their cultured tan and honey eyes. The truth was I hated the constant ping or buzz of the alerts. They reminded me of a world where I did not really belong, where I felt unwelcome. They made me tired. Besides, I read through my alerts every so often, and I had never missed anything really important. At least, as far as I knew. Perhaps it was a little bit irresponsible of me. My cheeks flushed.

Harkless growled at me. "I can't believe you have even survived this long. At least your privacy settings seem pretty tight."

He hit a few more prompts then tilted my wrist so that I could read a Community Information feed. The largest and first headline, with multiple sub-posts after, flashed the title *Local Freeman Unmasked as Runaway Bondsman – Held for Deportation.*

"Oh. That's...well, that's too bad." I hardly knew what words babbled out of my mouth. My relief was so intense. This was not about The Waymaker, Linah, or Ves, after all.

"That's too bad? For who now?" A male with dominant eyebrows laughed. "It's great news for the Tasker. Great news for the Lawmen trying to get a hold of these fugitive Bonders. So many Earthies are escaping these days. Good to show those 'logs the consequences that accompany their selfishness. Seems like a net win for us all if you ask me." His arm wrapped around a tiny female beside him. Some heads nodded with him.

The girl supporting the weight of his arm interjected, "It's bad news for the Bonder, Gav. The feed says he's been here for megas. He has a whole life here that he's about to lose. A job, friends, maybe a family. I'm sure they'll give him trouble; they won't be lenient with him."

Gav continued, "He's just getting what he deserves. He stole from his Tasker. He's a thief. Stealing is highly selfish and highly illegal and has negative consequences in Society."

The girl shook loose from their physical touch and countered, "He stole *himself* from his Tasker."

"Come on, Chiara, it's the same thing. His owner paid for him and owns the outcomes and value of his labor. It's just economics. It's fair." He flipped his palms up.

Chiara's nostrils flared. "You may be accurate in your financial assessment, Gav, but a human life is more than just economics." The girl received several considering looks from the onlookers.

Gav's voice nearly whined. "A human life? It's an Earthen life. They just don't function the way we do, Chia. They destroyed their planet and got themselves into all kinds of trouble. They've been devolving for centuries, so far removed from us. 'Logs need our order, our control, our guidance; all the advancements of a mature and civilized Society. Bonding is the best for everyone. Most Earthens are just too selfish, or too dumb, to understand that."

"It's, it's..." Chiara stuttered in her strong feelings. "It is not fair. We can't just choose who the rules apply to. We can't be so civilized and so barbarous at the same time. Humans are humans." When Gav stifled a laugh at her, she proclaimed, "I can't talk to you about this." Chiara, pink-cheeked, dashed her hands down her side and made fists before stalking away.

"Chiara!" The boy chased her. "Come on. You know I'm right on this. Our economy would crumble without the labor that Bondship supplies. It's very anti-Society for you to say those things. You should be careful..." Then they were too far to hear more. My eyebrows were raised wide, and my mouth open slightly at their exchange. Chiara and I shared some feelings, and she had been bold enough to share them around her peers.

I became aware that Harkless was squeezing my arm too tightly. Somehow, he had listened to the whole conversation without a single comment. I found it comforting to know Harkless could control his babble, but I wondered whether wisdom, anger, or fear kept him quiet. The remaining group stood uncomfortably for a time in silence. Perhaps they were all suspicious of each other's beliefs in comparison to their own on the topic introduced by the fighting couple.

One of the other males, a boy I remembered a little bit from school, possibly named Sashka, ended the lull with an anemic chuckle. "Seems like we just witnessed the beginning of the end of that relationship. Shek it all. It's going to be a very interesting election this mega with all this Bondship discussion. Wild. Some candidates for First Statesman lean pretty far from the norm."

Someone else added, "The First Statesman represents the people of the Outpost. So really, the election is wild because Outposters themselves are leaning pretty far from the norm."

"Only some of them. And stars, we don't change well as a Society, not when the 6s and 7s are in charge." A teasing tone had crept into the discussion and slight smiles were shared.

"How will we ever survive the mega?" another joked, but the comment doomed them to silence once again. The group displayed introspective expressions, masking what I could only assume was some level of collective anxiety. They were scared of the upcoming election but did not want one another to know. What would it all mean for our Outpost? For our lives?

Harkless suddenly breathed out loudly with flapping lips, and his hand relaxed on my arm. "This is a Gathering, all. Sash, Bastia, Moko… You are all very serious tonight. Let's lighten it up, okay? Clearly Minty needs an entire overhaul of her social life and her tech. Please send her your tips and tricks about living life as a normal 8. Send those messages right to Araminta Bradford 8." I slapped him hard in the arm, piqued. "As you can see, she is so looking forward to your advice, don't hold anything back. Minty, hand over your Aide control. I'll take you home now, but only if you let me reset your Aide settings to something more…beneficial."

The temporary sacrifice of my Aide was a small price to pay to get away from the Gathering in a socially appropriate way, so I set it to allow Harkless remote access.

"So," Sashka spoke to me as we prepared to leave. "You are Chi's niece, right? The farmer? Are you two together?"

"No!" I exclaimed. "I mean, yes, I am Chi's niece. Yes, on the Farm. Um, hi, I'm Araminta. But no, we aren't together. No."

I heard Harkless laughing beside me. "Apparently, she'd never have me. I'm more of her life coach." He gave waves to his friends, and we headed toward the exit.

The open air tasted like a lifeline. Just making it outside of the House curbed some of my anxiety. But for the entire transport ride up the hillside, Harkless uncharacteristically said nothing. It could have been his focus on my Aide, but I sensed it was more. Whatever relief I felt from leaving the Gathering congealed into a pit of worry in my gut. A quiet Harkless was very unnerving.

At my door, I took a breath to confront him about it, but he beat me to it. "Your Aide is all set now, groundhog. It will keep you informed enough to do what you plan on doing here. You know, dignity to Earthens stuff."

He returned control of my Aide with a tight smile. "That Gathering was something! Hopefully, the first one will be the worst one for you. I'll, well, I'm sure I'll see you soon. Okay. Good night!" He paused strangely between each sentence like he was trying very hard to edit himself.

Harkless disappeared down the track, leaving me confused. I sat on the steps, gulping the cooler evening air, hoping to decompress. My party tunic squeezed my ribs uncomfortably in a seated position. Before I could take more than a handful of calming breaths, I received two messages on my Aide.

Message from Sashka Rosova 8 : My advice to you: Stay away from Harkless. He seems fun, but he's trouble. I am just as fun, but without the trouble. Ping me next time you are in Shamong.

Though I completely agreed that trouble followed Harkless around, by his own invitation, I had no extra space for Sashka Rosova 8 in my life. I deleted the message from Sashka and moved on to the next.

Message from TheHottestMan OnAttis 1000 : I am not an idiot. It doesn't take me a whole transport up the hill to adjust an Aide. I just didn't want you to read about what's going on until you got home. You still have a horrible game face; I couldn't risk it. I'd wish you a good night, but I doubt you'll have one. All the same, I look forward to our next adventures. Love, Your Life Coach

The latest message, obviously from Harkless, detonated that pit of worry in my gut into an explosion of fear. I ran right inside the Farm without any more delay.

The dark grey of the Day Room at night seemed deeper and more pensive than usual, like a cave that repelled all the light and sound around it. I paused, feeling the stillness of the room with all my senses: not the stillness of peace, but the stillness of apprehension. I did not see Linah until a subtle light bounced off her bright hair. She sat cross-legged in the middle of the room, sunken within a cushion, one hand bracing her head, the other clutching the Pager from Harkless. Ves was nowhere to be seen, probably asleep for the night.

Linah did not even raise her head when I sat beside her. The hair hanging beneath her chin dripped with tears. My heart did not let me ask her about the scene at the Gathering or Harkless' cryptic message. All I managed was, "Linah? Are you okay?"

She offered only silence until I repeated her name and gently pulled her shoulders around toward me.

Finally, her shaky voice crackled through the room, "I can't lose anyone, else, Minty."

My blood turned to ice. Was this about Ves after all? "What happened? What is it?"

"They caught him. His Tasker from the Mid-Lats caught him. His half-brother, Minty… It's been megas, but he still recognized him; they look like each other. That's how he knew who he was. It's, it's…it's horrible." What started as a sob morphed into a growl by the end of her statement.

"What, Linah? Who?" My grip had tightened unbidden, and she suddenly jerked away from my painful grasp. Her pale eyes flashed with sadness and anger.

"Beecher. They arrested Beecher."

CHAPTER 36 :
ONE THINGS

TOGETHER LINAH AND I READ every post and article that appeared in the feeds on my Aide. Some Information described Beecher as a wily fugitive, unworthy of the life he lived in Shamong. His Tasker from the Mid-Lats triumphed at discovering him, claiming justice and resolution. Other Information presented opinions that more closely represented my own: removing Beecher was unjust and showcased a planet-wide problem.

After reading everything available to us, we just waited in the dark. For news. For instructions. For something to do.

I reassured Linah that the Captain had a plan; the Captain could save Beecher. From all we had been told, the Captain must value the work Beecher did for the BackTrack and the role he played for the Earthen communities in Shamong.

But. Nothing. Happened. It was tense and almost painful. I always hated waiting, but that night, waiting felt like electric currents firing under my skin.

Deep into the secret hours of night, the stream of Information and pings on my Aide dwindled to silence as most of Attis slept. But on my Farm, Linah and I sat on the same cushion together in the Day Room, clutching the Pager with barely managed stress. Still waiting.

Buzz. My neck snapped forward out of a light doze that had finally overtaken me. Linah sat close by in the darkness, unmoving except for her rhythmic breaths. The sky lightened where the suns would soon erupt from the horizon. *Buzz.* The pager finally spoke, and I devoured the message with blurry eyes.

From the Captain: Abort Plan A. Go Plan B.

I shook Linah awake. "Linah. Linah. What does this mean?"

Alertness came upon her faster than a gravity bubble. "Is it a code?" I asked. "Do you know what Plan A and B are? What do we do?"

"I-I don't know," she admitted. Linah and I roused ourselves into full wakefulness. We made hot cups of Keff and managed a few sips before another message arrived.

From the Captain : Abort Plan B. Go Plan C.

Adrenaline tingled in my toes. The Captain was definitely up to something, but it did not seem to be working. We debated the possibilities and decided that, most likely, the Captain had created multiple plans involving various agents of the BackTrack. When one plan failed, the next was instigated. A to B, B to C. The BackTrackers involved in those various plans must know their roles; we just were not involved.

The suspense tightened something in my throat that I felt compelled to swallow again and again. I wanted to do something. Abruptly, the first rays of the suns sliced into the grey room.

Message from Captain : Abort Plan C. Stand by.

"It's not working," Linah wailed. "The Captain can't do it. Beecher is too well-known, too involved. His Tasker will take him away; they will hurt him." Her breath came in hiccups that punctuated her sentence in the wrong places.

"No, no." I held her hands in mine, clammy and warm. "It can't be over yet. Beecher is still here in Shamong. It's not over." But the same fear gripped me. Were Linah and Ves going to lose Beecher? I pictured his radiantly smiling face at the Market. I imagined the press of his giant hugs and the care he showed to everyone.

"What's going on?" A voice thick with sleep made me whip around to the hallway. "Something...Beecher?"

Ves stood, braced on the wall, and only a slight twist of his posture remained to indicate his ongoing recovery. His blue eyes brightened as the sleep left him. When we did not reply, he asked again, "Beecher?"

I pressed my lips shut, unprepared to tell Ves the fate of his hero. Ves looked back and forth between us, then directed a cold focus on Linah. He took a careful step forward that displayed his commitment to hearing her answer. A shaky breath went into Linah's chest, and then the words tumbled out in a rush.

"Yes, my darling. Beecher has been arrested by a Stalker. Back from the Mid-Lats. He will be...taken away." Linah rose from the floor and squared up to

Ves. Her hands stretched slightly in front of her, palms down, rising and falling gently, placating, as though she meant to pat Ves' feelings down into calmness. "Shh," she almost begged. "Ves, talk to me. I know it is awful. Shhh."

I looked over to Ves. And there, instead of the sweet Ves I knew from his days at the Farm, I saw the Ves who had to be restrained by other Earthens. I saw the Ves who had attacked a Tasker. I saw the broken Ves with too much rage and confusion to fit into his young heart and mind. Anger clenched his fingers and ground his teeth. His eyes blazed, and he looked ten megas older in an instant.

"Shh, shh," Linah repeated. "Come sit here by me."

Ves did not move. "We have to do something," he spit. "It's Beecher."

"Ves, there is nothing to be done. Not by us. The Captain–the same Captain who has guided many Bonders to freedom here in Shamong–is working on it. The Captain knows Beecher. The Captain knows Shamong. It will work, but it will not be done by us."

Ves's short breaths came under his control as Linah gently spoke a mantra on repeat, "I love you, breathe. Don't let the anger be your master. I love you, breathe. Don't let the anger be your master…" and I wondered how many times Linah had guided him away from the edge this way. When he no longer looked like he might throw something, Linah spared a glance in my direction. There was embarrassment in her eyes, but also something else. Now you see, she said without words, what it has all done to him.

Ves walked over to the hand I extended in his direction. He let me drape an arm around him, squeeze him in a light hug, and lead him to a seat. His body was not pliable; the rage still stiffened him. I moved the half-empty bowl of orange tomatoes to the center of the little circle we made together. We tried to eat them, but even the sweet tang of the wild tomatoes tasted like powder.

"We have to do something!" Ves growled again under his breath. Linah and I had nothing to offer in response.

The suns, fully risen, allowed the possibilities of the day to unfold, and the Information outlets wasted no time with a new outpouring of news. New posts circulated on the feeds. I read headline after headline aloud. Some brought comfort, some fear. But we gathered an understanding of what Shamong had in store for Beecher.

Beecher, after being held in the Lawmen's office overnight, would be escorted to the SpacePort where his Tasker planned to fly him to his bamboo homestead in the Mid-Lats. Already, Earthens, in protest of Beecher's removal, gathered at the SpacePort gates. And in turn, the Attisians gathered there to watch.

I understood the picture the headlines painted, but I could hardly believe it. The moving parts and the lack of control frightened me more than I knew how to express. A singularity of dread formed in my guts. No one knew what would happen next. No one could predict anything because nothing like this had happened in Shamong before. Possibly never in all of Attis.

    From the Captain : All hold.

Ves punched a pillow, frustrated tears shimmering in his eyes. The quick motion made him flinch in added pain. "I'm going to pick some tomatoes," he croaked. When Linah and I did not protest, he pushed himself upright and walked to his room. Two tears dripped from his chin before he disappeared.

Linah, no longer required to play her sisterly role, released her own emotions. Her tears flowed immediately. "Beecher means so much to my people here. And what will I do about Ves? You see him, Minty? Beecher steadied him, helped me guide him. Ves listens to Beecher more than me. What will I do? What will we all do?"

"He's still here. It's not over yet," was all I could whisper, but my hope leaked away. Dispirited, we tried to discuss a few topics, but then the Farm grew quiet.

Then the Farm grew eerily quiet. Something about the utter stillness felt wrong, or right, it was hard to tell. Purposeful, meaningful. Linah's tears dried as she too felt the stillness.

"Vesey." Linah's whisper boomed through the silence. I saw her rise and race to Ves' room, my comprehension slow. When she shouted his name once, twice, again, louder each time, I understood. I rose and raced to the front door.

The view of the hillside revealed nothing but an empty transport track in the dull daylight. A rustle of fabric and sharp breath told me Linah had come back into the Day Room. "He's gone, Minty."

She presented a mangled plant, ripped from the soil at its roots, flatted in places by stomping feet, and cleared to the vine in other places by ripping hands. A few destroyed fruits dripped their tangy juice like blood. My father's orange tomato plant. Somehow, I first felt grief for the uprooted plant, the last living piece of my father. Then pain. Ves loved those tomatoes. I believed he loved the Farm and even me, in the way a 10-mega-old might, and yet he had done this. He had lost himself to his anger. My big rebellion against Society had just destroyed the last remnant of my father's little rebellion.

Perhaps the time had come to stop equating the two. My father's secret had been about his own curiosities and intellect. It was his way of existing in a culture that did not accept him. My secret was about the survival of a friend and the very soul of my Society. It was the difference between plants and people. Hobbies and hearts. Leisure and lives.

"Minty, he's gone," Linah babbled. "He left. I have to find him. Foolish, foolish Ves. God, please help me, help him. I have to find him!" Her luminous eyes darted manically. I grasped her two wrists in my hands and held them tightly between us. She let me. I squeezed my eyes shut and tried to breathe steadily for both of us, trying to guide her the way she did Ves.

My brain spun once again with the question Linah asked me so many days ago. *What was I willing to do?* There was only one possibility.

If Ves was discovered, he would be punished. If Ves was discovered, Linah would suffer. And if Ves was discovered, my Farm, along with other parts of the BackTrack, could be exposed. Everything and everyone I cared about needed one thing. Finally, some simplicity.

"No, Linah, *we* have to find him."

CHAPTER 37 :

TOO MANY PEOPLE

I QUICKLY ABANDONED MY FANCY Gathering tunic in favor of a basic undershirt and dark radiation cloak. I handed a second cloak to Linah, who secured her bright hair beneath the floppy hood. I tucked the pager into my leggings pocket as Linah secured her knives in their wraps. Everything I could need for motivation was on full display in Linah's earnest, glowing eyes. With one mind, we left the Farm and ran down the hillside, with no patience for the steady pace of the transport track, hoping to overtake Ves.

What could he possibly plan to do? I scanned every view but saw no trace of him on the hillside. Linah's longer legs and Earthen physique meant that she could outrun me if she chose to, but she held my pace. I thought it was strategic, rather than kind: two sets of eyes, two sets of hands, two brains. We needed every advantage. We were more effective together.

As the patchy prairie grasses gave way to pavement and modest structures, a strange sensation jerked my attention ahead instead of around. It took me a moment, but I soon realized that our rapid breathing was the only sound to be heard. The unnatural silence and stillness of a normally active neighborhood sent my nerves crawling. We traveled forward more cautiously, darting across open intersections and peeking into dark store windows.

Then a perplexing noise, like an undulating buzz, reached me from far away. It grew louder with every step toward the heart of the city, and at last, I saw the backs of many citizens, all facing away from us in the same direction. Too many people. Holy stars, I thought, repeating Harkless' favorite phrase of disbelief. The incessant buzz was shouting, talking, jeering, calling–a blend of all the voices in the streets.

Surprisingly, my body was still capable of producing more adrenaline; I felt it charging through my veins yet again. Linah and I tried haltingly to progress toward the SpacePort, sometimes taking dark alleys, sometimes shouldering our way through a group of gossipers, always scanning for Ves. We had to intercept him before he carried out whatever ill-informed plan he had made.

At the end of Founder's Way, past the Exchange, at the far side of a round plaza, the SpacePort appeared. The plaza was so densely packed with citizen onlookers that we could no longer move forward. *Think,* I urged myself, *think.* I aimed our progress laterally, toward a bench near the track somewhere to our left. After enough effort to make me sweat profusely, and plenty of apologies to annoyed citizens, I found the bench by tripping onto it. I climbed up before the pain in my shins registered and, clutching a solar light pole, leaned over the heads of the humans swirling around me. Linah climbed up beside me.

"Sheking stars," I said aloud, adding to the turbulent noise.

Attis was a disciplined planet. We valued duteous, reliable, and predictable citizens. We built our world under the moderation of the ABEs and survived by our robust planning and efficient routines. Our celebrations were moderated, our disagreements were addressed privately, and our elections were formal and absolute. The scene in front of me did not belong in my structured world.

Thousands of citizens filled the plaza. Some Attisians, avoiding the action but curious nonetheless, even watched from windows, balconies, and rooftops of the other buildings nearby.

I sensed a rowdiness in the words and gestures of my fellow 'Posters, but still, dutifully, we remained behind a short, semi-circle barricade that kept the crowd away from the SpacePort's enormous bamboo plank gate. The barricade, which must have been erected by Lawmen sometime in the night, kept the citizens back fifty meters from the grand entrance to the SpacePort.

The barricade left a half-circle on the plaza that should have been empty. But a second gathering of people ignored the barrier and collected themselves in the clearing. A hundred bedraggled Earthens stood within. The Earthens spread themselves out between the walls of the SpacePort gate, effectively creating a human blockade that spanned the width of the entire entrance.

The Earthens, as diverse as they had been that day in the market, now donned matching expressions of gritty grimness. They faced out to the street and waited, some with silent tears, some with clenched fists, some with arms linked together. I frowned, disbelieving. Did they plan to resist? To confront the Law? Were they–it took my mind a long time to find the antiquated word from my history classes–rebelling, right there in the light of day?

I sucked in a breath and shielded my face as Calhoun Stille 7 and Rankin Stille 8, along with a team of uniformed employees, appeared atop the wall surrounding the SpacePort. Hostility burned in Calhoun's expression as he beheld the scene below him, but Rankin just watched disdainfully. Lawmen appeared behind the patterned trellis of the closed gate. I could just see them through the gaps in the bamboo ornamentation. I tried to count them all and scowled; Shamong did not employ this many Lawmen. They must have shipped in overnight. The dread grew deeper and wider in my gut.

Almost simultaneously, chatter swelled from the 'Posters near the rear of the crowd, so I leaned and focused my eyes back toward the city. Down the center of the road, where we had just hustled moments ago, came Beecher, tall and broad enough to distinguish easily. He stumbled forward, encircled by four Lawmen who corralled him with prods and shoves. His hands were bound and his eyebrow bled.

My anxious study of Beecher made me oblivious to his escorts at first, but as they all drew closer, the truth was unavoidable. The disproportionate head and the unwarranted sneer were unfortunately familiar: leading the way was Lawman Mudsil.

CHAPTER 38 :
ACCORDING TO THE LAW

THE CROWD OF RILED ATTISIANS parted automatically for the Lawmen and their charge, and Beecher passed through with them unhindered. His Lawmen guards removed a piece of the barricade and guided Beecher into the vacant space between the two crowds. Beecher raised his head and observed the Earthens ahead of him, blocking his progress to the SpacePort. Even from my distance, I saw sadness settle upon him. His gaze moved slowly from one edge of the crowd to the other as he recognized every single Earthen there.

The Earthens stood utterly still, looking back at him. They were soon joined in their silence by the Attisians. The whole city held its breath.

Haltingly, Mudsil separated himself from Beecher, swung his stomach forward, and moved into the empty area. He looked nervous, and for that only, I could not blame him. So many eyes watched him. Mudsil mopped sweat from his forehead and chin and under his ears. He squared himself to the SpacePort gate, gave a twisted smile, and pulled out a stick from a pocket on his reflective uniform. No, a club. A weapon.

A weapon?! My shock mirrored the rest of the crowd's; the Attisians recoiled with gasps and exclamations. Lawmen did not carry weapons. No one in Society did. We were too civilized to require authoritarian violence. Our very Law prohibited it and abhorred it as devolved behavior. The Earthens seemed unsurprised. They had a very different understanding of how civilized we Attisians were.

Mudsil pointed his club toward the Earthens. Despite the slight shaking of his hands, his voice projected into the square. "Descendants of Earth," he addressed them, "you have two choices, please: leave immediately, or let us pass through to the SpacePort peacefully. I speak for the Law, and our honored Society, when I say that nothing else will be tolerated." Perhaps only cycles ago, this speech might have seemed reasonable enough, but now I rolled my eyes angrily. Weren't all of us descendants of Earth?

He continued with a gesture backward toward Beecher. "This prisoner is a criminal against our Outpost and our way of life. He will be treated like one, according to our Law. If you do not let us pass, you also will be treated as criminals, please." He paused. His verbal tick for a moment made him seem as though he were begging. But the rest of the Lawmen chose that moment to draw out matching weapons, and the illusion dissolved.

An unidentifiable voice from the Earthen blockage shouted back, "You already treat us like criminals!" Another collective gasp sounded from the Attisian observers. I reminded myself to breathe.

The pager's buzz at my hip startled me enough to lose my balance. The noise of my scramble to stay upright on the bench only turned a few heads; the crowd's attention remained locked firmly on Beecher, Mudsil, and the collection of brazen Earthens. Linah, the radiation cloak mostly concealing her brilliant hair, steadied me at my elbow and peered at the pager when I drew it unobtrusively from my pocket.

`Message from the Captain : All agents HOLD. HOLD.`

When I looked back up from the pager, nothing had moved except Mudsil. He experimented with several steps forward then gestured to his counterparts. "Let's go."

A Lawman shoved Beecher, and the group began to cross the open space through the plaza. I strained to watch the Earthens and their reactions. *Leave*, I begged, *please just leave.* I did not want violence. I also did not want Beecher in the SpacePort. I wanted too much.

The tension grew tangible, viscous, like I could have scooped it right out of the air. They drew closer, closer, closer to the Earthens and the SpacePort gate.

The Earthens did not leave. They did not disperse. They did not make way.

CHAPTER 39 :
THE WORLD WE MADE

FROM MY ELEVATED VIEW ON the bench, I watched the world we made so carefully begin to change. If I had not seen it with my own eyes, I would not have believed the Information reports that circled the next day through my home planet. The war really began that day. We started it, right there in Shamong.

At first, when the group of Lawmen moved into the line of Earthens, they were stalled only by firmly placed bodies. The Earthens pressed around them, asking, begging for Beecher's freedom, refusing to allow them passage by simply being in their way. But then shouting, a shove. Both sides increased in agitation. Their words blurred into a roar of fury. Reports said that an Earthen threw the first punch, but I really could not tell.

The Lawmen's clubs began their work. The Earthens fought with fists. Fists and clubs, up and down. My eyes, horrified, darted between blows and injuries until my sight became blurry, and I had to wipe away tears. I yelled Beecher's name, beginning to experience some of the crowd's hysteria myself.

In a storm of reaction, the Attisian citizens around me broke the barricade and ran into the fray. Riot. The word made me quake from my spine to my fingertips. No, please, no. This is not our way. I thought this was not our way.

Linah grabbed my shoulders and leaned in, mouth right at my ear to be heard, as bodies pressed forward around us. "Do you see him?" Linah called me back to our true goal. Find Ves. But I did not see him, and I shook my head in response. Could we be wrong? Surely Beecher was his destination.

Slowly, slowly, violently, violently, Beecher was forced deeper into the chaos toward the SpacePort.

The SpacePort gate groaned bitterly under the unusual pressure of bodies pushing at perpendicular angles to its hinges. As Mudsil reached the gate, Calhoun signaled, and the gate inched open, complaining, only wide enough for a few people at once. Mudsil disappeared inside, then Beecher, but almost simultaneously, the gate gave up. Its hinges cracked; its tracks bent. The left side of the gate fell, awkwardly influenced in its direction as humans poured through the wide opening and into the flat, immaculate launch bay of the SpacePort. Outposters and Earthens surrounded the hangar buildings and the sleeping StarShips.

The bodies of the riot effectively grounded all the StarShips in the field, including the one set to take Beecher away. No Ships could launch without slaughtering the citizens that now surrounded the machines.

A smarter Lawman than Mudsil must have recognized this, because promptly the group surrounding Beecher redirected their movements toward the hangar building. I saw Mudsil, face sweaty and hot pink, as his friends cleared a path to the door, and Calhoun shouted instructions from the turret. The Lawmen gained the hangar door, the frenzy peaked, and then a ripple surprise spread through the crowd.

Fingers pointed to the rooftops as the pandemonium paused, and, with the sound of my ragged breath suddenly audible in my ears, I scanned the scene and spotted them: the ABEs had arrived. I counted five ABEs on top of the surrounding roofs. Five! I did not even know five still existed. The dull sunslight shone on their metal housings. No visual evidence of their partial humanity could be seen through their robotic parts. They just looked like machines to me. My stomach churned. My panic turned to nausea. What were they doing?

The five ABEs watched us. As the executors of the settlement's purpose and success, they must have judged the danger great enough to intervene, which meant they thought our Society was at risk. *Yes*, I thought. *I agree, actually.* But I still feared them. As still as statues, they observed the scene in the plaza and SpacePort. The hairs on my arm rose. Bile hit my throat. *They cannot reenter all of us,* I reasoned, and yet my instincts whispered to hide from them. The rest of the Attisians and Earthens must have been feeling similarly, because there was stillness now. The presence of the ABEs had startled or motivated the crowd into a temporary peace.

From my view on the bench, a movement near the hangar drew my gaze, and I saw that, shockingly, Lawman Mudsil recovered the earliest from the presence of the ABEs. He used the lull in the fighting to throw Beecher, battered and weak, forward through the hangar door. Only one figure, small and bright, awoke enough to battle him, and I could not breathe at the sight.

The shock of bright yellow hair that flashed in the sunslight told me all I needed to know. It was Ves, right there in the middle of it all. Mudsil slammed the door behind Beecher and turned to face his assailant.

He turned to face Ves.

CHAPTER 40 :

I DID IT FOR VES

THE SLAM OF THE HANGAR door brought the rest of the crowd's attention back from the ABEs, who had done nothing but remind us of their presence. Pressed closely together in the SpacePort, with anger and fear overpowering their reason, the Earthens and the Attisians could not separate from each other and disperse. Instead, the violence began again. The sound of it made me sick—crazed voices shouting barbarous words, the thuds and smacks of injuries being inflicted, the humans around acting like unthinking beasts, the complete chaos.

I grabbed Linah's shoulder to pull her off the bench. "I saw him!" I shouted, and we willingly pressed into the thick of the fray.

Amidst the bodies, most of which were taller than me, I could see very little but the motion of limbs in the flashes of light that they allowed. We dropped low and darted into whatever gap appeared in the direction we thought to be correct. It took too long for us to even reach the hangar gate, and I despaired of finding Ves. We could hardly see past the few bodies surrounding around us.

A blow caught me in the chin. I reeled, my hearing dulled, and I would have toppled over but for Linah catching me before I hit the ground. Onward.

Arms. Fists. Feet. Knees. Shouts. Grunts.

The closer we got to the SpacePort, the wilder the participants behaved. *Stars.* I alternated swearing and sobbing between every labored breath.

We found him. Ves, with sweat from his forehead mixing with blood from his nose, latched himself to the back of a different Lawman that I did not know. Ves snuck his arms around the Lawman's shoulders, pulling hard, and tried to prevent him from defending himself against the blows of another Earthen. I wished I could not see it.

And then Linah moved. She shoved her hands between Ves' chest and the

Lawman's back like a blade and put her lips right on Ves' ear. The words she spoke to him did not reach me in the pandemonium. She began to separate her hands and pry Ves away. He shook his head but Linah had her adult strength, and Ves did not. Her strength of body and will slowly pulled him away. Something she said to him struck his heart. He cried out, frustrated and sad.

"Help me!" Linah looked at me. "Take him!" I hardly heard the words, but her mouth made the right shapes, and I understood.

With another roar, Ves released the Lawman and fell back. I caught him and wrapped my arms around his shoulders and head, cradling him. He let me. I tried to shield him from the bodies around us, to conceal his distinguishable hair with my cloak. Linah shoved the untangled Lawman forward toward the Earthen already engaged with him. She hustled back to us, grabbed my shirt with both her hands, and pulled us around.

"Let's go." Now that we had Ves with us, Linah took the lead, moved by frantic energy. Ves followed my guidance, my arms wrapped around him, my body and my cloak still shielding him. We headed toward the plaza and the dark alleys beyond, and I made it three steps.

Then Ves was ripped from my arms.

He disappeared. My arms flopped from where they had been upheld by his shoulders. My cloak blew in the breeze of his departure. First, I only felt surprise as I yelped and looked around me. Then other feelings came. Horror. Rage.

Lawman Mudsil held Ves. He held Ves by the neck with him facing me so that I could see the red growing in Ves' cheeks and his eyes beginning to bulge. Too tight. Mudsil held him too tight! But of course, he meant to.

Ves clawed and struggled. His eyes, when they focused, looked at me and begged for help, for air.

The Lawman's eyes also focused on me. The expression on his reptilian face told me too much. He knew what I had done. He was disgusted. He was triumphant. He raised his other hand, and a finger of accusation pointed at my chest.

"You sheking 'log lover! You thought you could fool me, please." Everywhere Mudsil had extra body–his chin, his belly, the tops of his arms–rolled and vibrated with his impassioned words. "Araminta. Bradford. 8. You Lūnar trash. Sheltering a violent Earthen. Lying to me. To me, please." Ves' lips went purple as Mudsil's lips spat. "The Law has so much in store for both of you."

I choked on tears. I could not think of a solution. Every path my brain followed ended the same way. No options. Whatever fueled my emergency stores of adrenaline suddenly gave up or had been depleted to nothing. My fear turned icy cold, so deep and jarring that I put my hands to my gut to try to tame it. I stood there with nothing to do but watch all my worst fears come true. Even if I could break Ves free somehow, Mudsil knew that Linah and I were involved in his disappearance. It was the end. Of my Farm. Of my fortune. Of my life as I knew it. I had lost the game: this ugly, twisted game with impossibly unfair stakes, this game I did not even know the rules of.

Mudsil saw defeat in my posture and expression, and he laughed at me.

He laughed until a flash of movement passed behind him. Whatever it was, it bumped him slightly, and strangled his laugh into a stunned silence. The hand that was pointed at me moved to clutch his throat. The eyes that already popped from his floppy face now looked as though they wanted to explode from their sockets. His eyes showed disbelief, then anger, then terror. Mudsil released Ves, who took a few faltering, falling steps forward for me to grab him. For a sickening moment, in my view, Ves and Mudsil both clutched their necks so similarly that I thought Mudsil was mimicking him.

But Mudsil no longer had any attention for Ves. He focused on a nondescript spot in the distance, his eyes searching, sometimes unfocused. I waited to see what he would do or say.

Dark red slipped through the cracks between his fingers that clutched his neck, at first just colorful lines decorating his pale fingers. Extra pale. Deadly pale. The red dripped, then flowed, covering the white of his fingers completely and making trails down his silvery, impermeable uniform.

I clutched Ves to my chest and still did not understand. Blood. Blood all over Mudsil.

Mudsil's lips pressed together, and when they opened again, more blood flowed out of them. "...Please," he managed through the puddle in his throat. Then he collapsed in and down. He landed next to another unconscious person on the ground, just another injured body in the crowd. But his injury...

Linah appeared in my periphery and yanked me so hard that my shoulder popped in its socket. She spun me and Ves around and dragged us back, back, away from Mudsil's unmoving form. My mind did not work correctly. Everything around me blurred into swathes of bland colors and confusing shapes. Had I taken a breath recently? I should try to do that. Were my feet moving? I should make sure.

In the chaos of bodies, it was Linah who managed to keep us together. She guided us with fierce intent, and we made it out of the worst of the conflict. We found the first space between buildings to hide, and the sudden quiet of the dark, glass alley felt like a bath of ice water. But instead of relieving me, it illuminated and amplified everything I had just seen. I fought back a panic that I knew would immobilize me.

Linah leaned against the wall and heaved a huge and desperate breath. She clutched her heart with one hand, then started to tremble. Every part of her shook. Next came sobs, not the sobs of sadness or grief, but manic sobs of losing control. I helped Ves lean against the wall next to her and placed my hands lightly on her shoulders. I felt her muscles spasm in the regular rhythm of shivers, but it was not cold out.

"Linah! Are you hurt? Where does it hurt?" Linah squeezed her eyes shut and wailed between gasping breaths.

"I'm sorry. I'm so sorry," she spoke to the air, not really to me. "Sorry!"

"For what?" I felt around the back of her head, feeling for injuries, down her arms, but found no blood, no wounds. I ran my hands down both her arms until I reached her hands. I easily pulled her right hand from her chest and flipped it over to inspect, but her left hand she held firmly at her side. I yanked up the black folds of fabric and saw what she was hiding. Her pale and trembling fingers clutched one of her throwing knives. The blade dripped, dirtied with red blood.

My body turned to stone. I felt each heartbeat reverberate through my bones. When I tried to meet Linah's gaze, her eyes confused me. In their blue, the same Linah stared at me, wise, compassionate, unassuming, and capable, the Linah who had treated me with patience I did not deserve. But now, Linah was also a murderer. Right in front of me, she had killed Lawman Mudsil. I could not make her fit together. There was utter panic in her immobilized stare. I did not mean to recoil, but pure instincts controlled me as I jerked away.

"He was killing Ves. Minty, he was killing him. I did it for Ves," she whispered. "For you," and she shivered so badly the words barely made it through her lips.

Even at that moment, through the density of all my feelings, I knew she had saved me. Mudsil's destruction had saved me. And Ves. And other operatives on the BackTrack. But revulsion rolled in, each wave more intense. I saw Mudsil's blood seeping through his fingers, saw the terror in his eyes. His very last expression. The color of his blood was hauntingly dark. It was not the bright, promising red of the tomatoes I grew; it was the wrathful, mysterious red that I had only seen once before, on the night Ves bled in Linah's bed. The same red.

On the opposite side of the alley, I threw up.

I heaved three or four times, and the discomfort cleared my head enough to know that we were in more danger than ever. I would have to sort this all out, if that was even possible, in another place and another time.

I straightened and tried to spit out the acrid taste in my mouth. Linah clutched Ves and ran a hand down his head over and over. Linah watched me, eyes confused. Shocked. Incapacitated. Oh stars, oh stars, oh stars. We looked at each other for a few seconds. I did not know what there was to say. Linah just killed a Lawman. I could not absolve her from this. Nor could I condemn her.

I had nothing to say.

I willed myself to focus and peered around the edge of the building to scan the square. Through the gaping gateway of the SpacePort, the conflict still raged. I wiped my eyes, wiped my nose, and commanded myself to keep going. But I noticed him.

Rankin Stille 8, poised and unaffected, turned my way from the top of the gate. He did not avert his gaze as I found it. I withdrew with a start from his line of view. I told myself that surely he did not recognize me from that distance, in the mass of bodies and covered in a radiation cloak hood. But there was something in his posture.

Did he know it was me? How much had he seen? And most importantly, what would he do next?

Fear crashed down upon me and almost knocked me to my knees. I was hiding in an alley surrounded by unglued Attisians, Lawmen, and seemingly apathetic ABEs, trying to save myself, a fugitive, and a murderer. And Rankin Stille 8 had possibly seen me doing it. Whether he recognized me or not, we had to leave. Immediately.

5 MEGAS AGO

Supplemental excerpt from : Making a Way ; the Life and Stories,
Record HAC-3859385738

Hettie had known hunger before, but not like this. She struggled to get her limbs to obey her; they groaned in weakness as her stomach shouted in agony. For five days, she went north. Through bamboo forests, over peaks of rocky mountains. North. Always north.

She dug her raw and dirty fingers into the shallow soil and found the tiny tubes of the irrigation grid. Shakily she unscrewed one connection and let the water drops fall into her mouth, slowly, slowly, slowly.

When it was time to continue, her body at first refused to move. Hettie scolded her muscles and got them going again. It was a process she was used to now; her body grew weak, but her mind stayed strong. An unyielding resolve had settled inside of her the moment she had snuck away from her homestead. She knew there was no point in giving up. Only going on.

She crested a hill and lost her footing in the dark. Down she tumbled to the other side. She tried to protect her face and mechanisms as she rolled, but she passed into unconsciousness.

Hours later, in the dawn, she woke again. Her back pressed against something hard and tall. Everything ached, especially her head. She turned slowly and saw the structure that had interrupted her fall—a rough bamboo shed. Bone by bone, muscle by muscle, she peeked around the corner and saw a deep, vast cut in the mountainside. The excavation dropped down further than she could see, and its edges were dotted with terrible machines, currently unmoving and casting eerie shadows in the angled morning light.

Hettie's breath caught as she heard voices. They seemed far in the distance, but as the light grew, so did the volume of the speakers. She scurried inside the shed to hide, thinking that if she could just conceal herself through the day, she could travel again during the night.

The shed held shovels, axes, and many things that Hettie did not understand. She discovered that, unfortunately, it did not hold any food. She squirmed into a dark corner and prayed.

Later, a shirtless man opened the shed door and saw her. Their eyes met. Desperation caused tears to stream down Hettie's face during the silence that stretched between them.

Eventually, the man, an Earthen, picked up a tool. He held one finger to his lips. "Shhh," and then he left.

For the next hours, Hettie prepared herself for arrest and other unknown horrors. She heard many voices from outside the shed, mostly male, sometimes close, sometimes far. No one came for her.

When the suns once again disappeared, and all the voices faded, Hettie dared to stand. By now she was delirious with hunger, dizzy, and sore. "Get up," said her God Voice, and it gave her the confidence to try.

Her first steps out of the shed were so painful that they consumed all her focus, and she did not see the hulking man standing nearby and watching her. It was the same man who had entered the shed earlier that morning.

"How long you been running?" he whispered. She fell to her knees, unable to answer for weakness and fear. "Oh, young one," the man said. "I know it's been so hard." He handed her water and a dried algae bar, both of which she consumed, this time weeping with relief. "I can help you," he said. "But you have t' trust me. Just a little."

She stared at the large, old man with a smile that reflected the starlight. She could not trust anyone, even a fellow Earthen who showed a little kindness, but her God Voice boomed through her brain, almost jovial and excited. "Go with him. This is only the beginning."

She nodded to the stranger who helped her stand and began to guide her down the mountain. "You've done it," he said. "You've found the BackTrack." She didn't understand, but he continued, "I will help you find your way. What's your name?"

Hettie shook her head, unwilling to leave any evidence of her presence.

"That's all right," the man said, compassion etched in his features. "I don't need your name, but you can call me Beecher."

<h1 style="text-align:center">CHAPTER 41 :</h1>

FRIENDS WITH DIFFERENT SKINS

STILL UNABLE TO FIND WORDS, I motioned Linah back further into the alley. Every click of our shoes, every brush of our clothes, every scrape of our ragged breath, ricocheted off the glass walls around us and announced our flight.

"Hey!" a voice called from where we had first entered the alley. "Stop!"

Immediately I found my words again. "Faster. Faster, Linah, faster, Ves." We scurried. Light in the streets we crossed, dark in the alleys, light, dark, light, dark. Then the buildings were further apart, and everything blurred to shades of grey, punctuated only by the black of our cloaks and the radiance of Ves' uncovered hair. Our feet crunched into the gravel at the edge of the city, and we kept going. We scrambled over small crests and strange valleys until Ves wailed that he could go no further. In the shadow of an outcropping, we collapsed, sucking in air and feeling our hearts beat through our ribs.

Through the spots in my vision, I saw a cutting ravine in the slope before us. Huge machines leaned over the edge and decorated the striated walls. Ves coughed beside me. "A quarry," he groaned. A vast quarry stretched out and down, the source of Shamong's most prolific mineral, silica. Because of our abundant silica, Attis was mostly made of glass. Glass buildings. Glass transport tracks. Glass Keff mugs.

Long ago I visited a quarry on a trip with school, but not the one before us. Perhaps twenty quarries surrounded Shamong in the mountains, and I was thankful, unendingly thankful, that the one we stumbled into stood quiet. The machines, the sheds, the transport tracks...all was still.

Eventually, I believed in the silence around us. No footfalls. No shouts. No pursuit.

"What now?" Ves fit between two intakes of air. Linah and I looked at each other with similar expressions of dismay, although I felt as though something was missing from hers. Some vitality, some energy that normally lit her eyes had ceased to glow. I leaned my head back against the stone and let tears slide down my dirty cheeks.

"I have no idea," I answered.

Creak.

My heart stuttered at the deliberate sound. Before I could even leap to my feet, Linah crouched before us, arms spread protectively, a knife in each hand, though she sobbed again at the feel of them in her fingers. A shed nearby, a dilapidated structure barely held together with cord and nails, had a rickety door, a door which slid open ominously. A very small human figure shuffled into the light from the shed's depths, hooded in a way that concealed its features.

"Ah," it said. "I might have guessed it would be you: the friends with different skins. And you already have your broken boy with you. No need to fetch him." The voice, too loud in the eerie quarry, shot electricity through my senses and explained everything and nothing. I would recognize the magic in that voice anywhere, ever since it had shown up on my doorstep in the middle of the night.

The slight figure in front of us was The Waymaker.

CHAPTER 42 :
SOMETHING NEW

MY BRAIN WAS NO BETTER than sludge. Linah collapsed to her knees and her shoulders draped forward in a posture that resembled a bow.

"Waymaker," Linah whispered, "how did you find us?" as her knives clattered onto the rocks, dropped with disgust.

The Waymaker, now close enough to reveal some of her dark features beneath the hood, took in Linah's posture and expression. "Young one, I did not find you. The First Maker told me to come back to that shed, and I did. I had no idea what might turn up, but it was you. Does that comfort you? That The First Maker sent me here for you? You have done nothing that deters his long plan of freedom for you. So, stand up. You are not destroyed. There is more to be done."

Linah shook her head minutely, but when The Waymaker refused to say another word, she obeyed. "But Waymaker, something in me *is* destroyed. Something. I've done something horrible..."

The Waymaker, almost a whole head shorter than Linah, drew close enough to stare right up into her face. "Then so be it. You have done something horrible. You must decide what to do with that. It will not be quick. It will not be easy. Yes, something in you is destroyed. But *you* are not. Now you are something different. And if you breathe, that means there is more for you in this life."

Abruptly The Waymaker turned to me and examined me in the same intense way. Only the direction of her hood and the shadow cast by her nose told me where she was looking. Right into me. *Whir, click.*

"And you? Are you something new too?"

I lifted my eyes to where hers likely were in the depths of her cloak. "I've been a thousand new things this cycle, Waymaker, if we are going to think of it that way," I replied, and then her teeth were reflecting the sunslight. A smile did not belong here in this ugly situation, so it took a moment for me to even recognize it as a smile.

"Indeed, oh New-Thing-with-the-Grey-Eyes. So be it. There is more for you in this life as well. What do we do next?"

I balked and frowned the deepest frown I could muster. The Waymaker should know, not me. Her strange God Voice should give her instructions, not me. She saw my angry confusion.

With a shake of her head, she explained, "I'll hear from it when we need to. But I hear nothing. Why would that be?"

"Well, I'm sure that I don't know!" I yelled through gritted teeth. The Waymaker acted as though she still expected an answer from me, so I walked away from them and fought down my panic.

She allowed me to leave without interruption. I saw nothing but grey rock in my view and under my feet. My brain spun and sputtered; I struggled to think rationally. My emotions and exhaustion kept my better abilities from working at their maximum, and I could think of nowhere to go.

If Rankin recognized me, my Farm no longer offered us safety, and I did not have many other connections to exploit. I kicked a rock, and its momentum knocked loose a shower of smaller stones down the slope. I had no idea what to do without the guidance of Harkless or the Captain.

A spasm of optimism roused me. Of course, the Captain. I lifted the folds of my cloak to find my pockets. After a short search, I breathed in relief. The pager felt light and insignificant in my hand, but perhaps it was going to save us.

```
To the Captain : Help. Can't return home. At a quarry
with L and V and Waymaker.
```

I stared at the manufactured square in my hand, willing it to buzz with a response. I counted the time by the pulse of blood through my veins. Just as I planned to send a second, even more desperate message, the pager shook. I nearly dropped it in my eagerness to read it.

```
From the Captain :  Cemetree. Don't be seen.
```

My heart sank. Based on the direction we had fled and the location of the Cemetree back through the heart of town and up the other hillside, I thought it would be impossible. There was not enough luck, or enough of The Waymaker's magic, to make us invisible for so long.

"The Captain wants us to make it to the Cemetree." I raised my voice so everyone could hear me while I took a few steps closer to them once more.

Linah looked as dubious as I felt. "Why there?"

"I don't know. But we can't go home now." With my words, Linah flinched, the blue of her eyes still lackluster and vacant.

"It's a long walk through town to the Cemetree," Linah bemoaned softly, as though the words pained her.

"Young ones," The Waymaker's voice challenged, "why would you go through town to get to the Cemetree at a time like this?"

"You know the Cemetree, Waymaker?"

"Indeed. It is my favorite part of your city. What a holy place. And quite close to the Boundary. Of course we will not go through town and up to the Cemetree. We will go along the Boundary and down to the Cemetree."

"I don't know the way, Waymaker."

"Ah. But I do."

CHAPTER 43 :
THE IMPORTANT WAYS

THE WAYMAKER LECTURED VES AND demanded that he obey her every command. "No young tempers or untrained hands of justice in my wards," she insisted. "I will lead you, but only if I can trust you to do what you are told, how you are told, and when you are told."

He looked pale and sheepish at being singled out so obviously, but then she grabbed his hand in hers and pulled him to standing. She led him toward a steep slope and began to scramble out of the quarry pit.

"Do I even deserve freedom now, Minty?" Linah barely whispered from a boulder where she sat. "I killed him. A human." She did not stand to follow The Waymaker. "I don't... I didn't want to. But I killed him anyway."

I lowered myself in front of her, appreciating her goodness even now, that she would be so devastated by murdering a man that would have done the same to her with far less objection.

"I don't know, Linah. Maybe we all do bad things, and no one deserves freedom. Maybe we all do bad things, and everyone still deserves freedom. Either way, you need to get up. Ves needs you." I took her face, pale as cream, between my dusty hands.

A dull ache of sadness hit me. I knew what Ves' freedom meant for me. I had been thinking about it all cycle: what I was willing to do. What I had to do. Linah told me at the Cemetree that things had to change, and only recently had I allowed myself to truly understand what that mean for me. For her. This was the beginning of the end.

"Up." I charged Linah, and she listened. We climbed together, slipping on gravel, choking on dust, and getting lost in deep wells of complex feelings.

The four of us reached the elevation of the Boundary. The irrigation grid ceased. The atmosphere changed. The rock morphed from rough and broken debris to the sharp edges of massive boulders.

I had never been so high on the mountainside. The air was desperately thin where The Waymaker led us. Only the stray tendrils of artificial atmosphere that escaped the Boundary sustained us. Stars swam before my eyes at times, demanding that I put my head between my knees. The going was slow and uncomfortable under the radiation of the suns, but The Waymaker led us onward with assurance. She found occasional shade from unusual, curved outcroppings, striated with grey, black, bespeckled, and almost crystalline layers of geology. The Waymaker allowed us brief dips back toward the Boundary to fill our lungs, but only in areas she knew to be uninhabited and shielded from the view of the town far below.

Half a day later, with our heads pounding for oxygen and our throats screaming for water, The Waymaker turned us downhill, the city of Shamong like a dream far below us. We behaved more cautiously. Using crevices and boulders to hide behind, we got further down the mountainside and closer to civilization. I had no room for more fear though; the joy of my lungs filled with satisfying, manufactured oxygen pushed out every other feeling.

One last scramble brought us to the Cemetree, this time from above, the opposite direction that Linah had taken me from the Attisian Memorial. The plethora of color almost hurt my eyes after so long in a landscape of utter greyness. We parted the rainbow fronds and snuck within and collapsed to the hard-packed ground. I willed my heaving breaths to slow and rubbed the aches and cuts from a hundred stumbles on the rocks of the hillside.

At the Cemetree, all was still and secret. The thousands of colorful scraps and trinkets that hung from the branches separated us, sight and sound, from the rest of the world, and cast luminous colorful reflections on our skin. It felt like a sacred place. Or maybe a tomb.

At the base of the Cemetree, a black bamboo cloth bag slouched. The fabric showed no signs of dirt or even dust, which convinced me that it had been left recently. Perhaps on purpose.

I untied it quickly and let out a cry of delight. Water. I threw pouches of water to each of my companions and gulped down one of my own. It tasted sweeter than any sugar. As I felt the water traveling through my body, I examined the rest of the bag. Inside were piles of Food Bars, more pouches of Amplified H2O, Algae Crackers, a few other foodstuffs, a brand-new sub-aide, radiation cloaks, and outfits of various sizes. We could binge on the supplies but still have an excess. Enough supplies remained for another ten people easily. Why? Were we supposed to stay here for days and days?

Ves had forgotten to breathe while he drank his water, and I heard him intake a few aggressive gulps of air. All at once, right before my eyes, Ves' anger overtook him once more. "I failed," he accused. "We failed."

Linah just looked at him with sad eyes and offered no comfort this time; her will was shaken beyond her ability to comfort Ves.

The Waymaker asked, "At what, child?"

"At saving Beecher!" I heard the wild edge in his voice.

"Oh, young one." Her words were strong but gentle, as though she understood his feelings but nevertheless would not accommodate them. "I learned long ago, it's not up to me to judge the outcome. I just try. If I try, truly try, then I have done my part." Her simple faith met my fear head-on and overcame it. I slumped over to cry. I knew that if my tears were flowing, the worst of the emergency must have passed. I took some comfort in that.

My emotional display startled Ves into a less combative mood. He came and sat next to me and leaned on my shoulder, deciding to offer me comfort instead of expressing rage for himself. "Sorry, Minty," he whispered. "I probably messed up. Don't cry. Sorry."

"Who's to say?" The Waymaker then submitted with her deliberate voice, embellished with the accent of some other language. "Perhaps we did not fail in the most important ways; ways that we cannot understand. Not yet. Maybe never." Shades of colored reflections moved over her face as she spoke, highlighting her strong jawline, wide nose, intense eyes, and plastic head parts with different hues. She looked more like a mosaic statue than a human. I knew that I would always remember her exactly like that.

"People are moving. People are changing. Hoping. Learning. Things are different today than in days past. No, we did not fail in the important ways. We stand for goodness, young ones. We stand against selfishness and ignorant misunderstanding. We are enacting the heart of The First Maker. And you must know, The First Maker's love story is long. We are a short moment in an eternal story."

Her gaze shifted to me. She saw that I remained doubtful and defeated. "Not only that! Beecher is still here, alive. And, you. You are here, doing things I'm sure you never imagined doing."

I could not argue with that part. I was there. I was doing things I never imagined doing. But it did not help me feel any better. We lapsed into silence once more. Only the whir and click of The Waymaker's mechanisms broke the spell. I wanted to send a message to Harkless, but his warnings about pings being tracked or hacked held me back. I refused to risk betraying our position.

Instead, I scanned the Information reports on my Aide. There were plenty of posts about the riot, but the details were confusing and conflicting. Lawman Mudsil's murder topped the headlines. While the articles made me relive those awful moments, I read every single one to make sure we were not suspected. My name never appeared. Perhaps Rankin had not recognized me after all.

I tried to rest, but when my eyes closed, I saw only fists and clubs as they smashed down onto shoulders, arms, and heads. My body complained about my lack of sleep and the hits from earlier that day. Thoughts of the Farm, Linah, and Beecher flowed through me so fast they made my feet twitchy. With no instructions from the Captain forthcoming, I took it upon myself to ask.

```
To the Captain : Advice?!


From the Captain : Hold.
```

Nothing more came through for a few millis. I watched my pager with wide eyes and willed some instructions or encouragement to arrive. I exhausted my limited patience quickly.

```
Message to the Captain : ????


Message from The Captain : Instructions soon, A. Just
hold on.
```

That felt a little personal. Something fluttered in my stomach. Suspicion at the Captain's identity rose from my gut like an instinct, and my brain tried to sort out the input.

I narrowed my eyes at the pager. Who was on the other end? Who did I, and so many others, trust so completely to organize and coordinate the BackTrack here in Shamong? To save so many lives? At the beginning, I believed it had to be some wise, elderly, well-connected Attisian within the swirling powers of politics and business. Someone I had never met.

But suddenly, despite our circumstances, I could not shake the uncanny feeling that the Captain knew me.

CHAPTER 44 :
A PRAYER

With short and simple statements, the Captain outlined their plan, one step at a time. I read each one, resignation and fear battling inside. The Captain figured it all out; the plan was creative but shockingly precise, and daring too. Unfortunately, the very logical plan fell short of being foolproof. Where the Captain was telling us to go, there would be no help for us. But if the plan went flawlessly, at the end, Ves would finally be safe.

Ves rested his head in my lap. I looked down and ran my finger lightly over his hair. A lump of tears rose in my throat. I would miss Ves, but there was even more to lose, and the dread of it stole my breath away. I knew what I needed to do, but it still felt raw and incomplete, and now it needed to happen that very night. Tears leaked out of my eyes, and I let them quietly flow.

Linah noticed, but she said nothing. She had her own internal battles to fight while we all waited for darkness. The Waymaker brimmed with anticipation and sang her ancient songs. Ves entertained us with jokes and exuberant musings on his future life as a free Earthen. He hoped to earn enough money to buy what he called a sports ball.

I did my best to appreciate our last hours together, but the danger of the task at hand was never far from my mind. Each milli that passed made my heart beat that much faster and harder.

I measured the passing of time by a large blue reflection that traveled across the ground of our hiding place. We packed and repacked the bag, tightened our boots, adjusted our black radiation cloaks. Linah fiddled with her throwing knives. Then, all of a sudden, the suns set.

"Get ready everyone." Linah's voice had an ethereal purpose behind it when she spoke the heavy words into the atmosphere. "Do exactly as I do, Ves. No speaking unless you see something dangerous. Follow me, not The Waymaker, and whatever you do, don't follow Minty. She has special things to do tonight." Linah looked like she was trying to rub the instructions into his face as she caressed him and pushed strands of bright hair behind his ears. As Linah took his hand, Ves reached for me with his other.

"Young ones," The Waymaker stalled us. "A moment. A prayer." She connected our circle of hands and then closed her eyes and bowed her head slightly in a humble posture. Linah and Ves did the same, but I chose to watch the faces of my dearest people. Their bodies relaxed and the shadows of the early night moved around their features. I treasured them up in the calm before the storm. What an old-fashioned saying that was. Storms could not have been all that bad, at least not as bad as what was ahead of us.

The Waymaker's indomitable voice filled the sanctuary of the Cemetree. "God of Stars, First Maker of all humans. Guide us tonight. Lay the path before our feet, and let us not stumble upon it. Write a new story through us, a story of love, light, and wholeness for all humankind. Give us the courage to accept our role in this story."

"May it be so," they all said together. Signs of tears glistened in Linah's eyes, and she met my gaze at the same moment that the pager buzzed once more.

`From the Captain :` Go. Now.

Yes, First Maker, I entreated. *If you are out there, give me the courage to accept my role in this story.*

CHAPTER 45 :
ONWARD

ALL REPORTS CLAIMED THAT BEECHER remained in the hangar building where the mob had chased him and the Lawmen. Preparations continued to force him back to the Mid-Lats the following morning. Arrests were made. The whole city decried the death of Lawman Mudsil, scarcely believing such a horror, but still unable to muster many kind words about the man himself. Many Earthens were relegated to the quarries as punishment. The SpacePort still crawled with extra Lawmen, including the reinforcements from nearby cities, but if we wanted to get Ves out of Shamong, the SpacePort was exactly where we needed to go.

First, however, the Captain's brilliant but terrifying plan required a detour. When we left the Cemetree, we did not head back toward the plaza. Instead, we snuck, dressed in dark colors, shadow by shadow, into the residential neighborhoods of Shamong. The square plots of manufactured earth were uniform and equal, the houses on top of them almost identical. Before long, block after block of square homes on square plots had me completely disoriented. But not The Waymaker.

When I was completely lost, she stood stock still, palms upwards, for the space of two whirs and clicks of her mechanisms, and then instructed us in which direction to proceed. Once I felt her hand grasp me hard and yank me to an alleyway. Two Lawmen sauntered past soon after. No sound, no sight had alerted her. She just felt it, she explained. Perhaps we all could if we practiced, she insisted.

"Perhaps we all could if we all had plastic brains," I retorted under my breath.

To my embarrassment, she overheard but laughed heartily. "Perhaps you all could if you let The First Maker be louder, and everything else, softer."

She found the home that we sought although it looked exactly like the rest. The four of us darted behind the structure and knocked on an unlit back door with a thick, blue, corded knot decoration. I stood closest when the door opened a crack.

"Code?" a scratchy, low voice whispered from the blackness. I could not make out the figure inside, so I addressed the door itself.

"Right, of course, a code. Just a moment..." I began and gestured behind my back for Linah, but the door began to shut on me.

"Take up now and don't delay!" I blurted. "The Waymaker! I know the Captain and Hark–"

"Hush," the occupant snapped in a vaguely accented voice. An Earthen then. "Wait."

The door closed quietly for just a moment, before a very short person emerged, covered so completely in a dark tunic and hood that nothing about them was identifiable. The haunting figure gestured with a gloved hand for us to follow.

Our guide led us further away from the road, and I felt the ground beneath me slant upward. The rising slope meant that we had crossed town and arrived at the hillside. The same hillside that, in the opposite direction, rose to my Farm. But here, before we had traveled very high, a startlingly lofty wall of murky glass panels blocked our progress. We reached the fortification that surrounded the Palisade.

"Where are we?" I questioned from the back of the line as I ran my fingers across the cool glass.

"The back of Savorgnan Park, near the Southern wall," whispered our guide. "You cannot go through the front gate tonight."

Once again, I had to find a way to fit into the Palisade. Not only that, but the Captain's plan required that I fit in at perhaps the most ridiculous home within the entire Palisade. I let out a long breath and rehearsed some cultured and mature lines of conversation. I practiced straightening my posture and pursing my lips in the fashion of polite Attisian Society. I shook my head and knew I was distinctly under-practiced.

At a deeply dark location, our enigmatic guide paused and focused at a spot on the wall. I heard gloves brush across the surface of the glass, searching. With a scrape, our guide slid two blocky glass panels from the construction of the wall, and an inlet to the opulence of the Palisade appeared. Warm light glittered through the opening, turning us all a shade of dark gold. Linah unzipped the tote, told me to remove my radiation cloak, and tossed me a luscious tunic. The golden tone of the fabric looked too vibrant in the monotony of the night.

Was the tunic even mine? Surrounded by my friends, I struggled to put it on modestly, but once my arms and head found all the right spaces, I could feel the tunic's tailored fit and unctuous material. "Where did this come from?" I queried as I caressed the fabric on my forearms.

"It was in the bag of supplies. I figure it's for this part of the Captain's plan. It's your size, and you can't go walking through the Palisade looking no better than a common Bound." Linah shrugged. "Unless you think I should wear it?" She smiled, letting her envy show freely.

"You can have it when this is all over. But who bought it?" Linah's smile flickered once again. Even though it was still strained and lacking some vitality, I was so relieved to see her smile.

"I suppose it's a gift from the Captain." She then draped far too many sparkling necklaces to count over my neck. My favorite moon rock necklace disappeared beneath the faceted glass beads and chains. "The Captain must have bought these too."

The Captain thought of everything, but Linah thought of more. She pulled my hair into a simple but organized braid, and I could only assume that I looked my part. The others put on new grey radiation cloaks from the pack. They were inexpensive and worn, perfectly innocuous attire for a busy city Bonder. The three of them fell into line abjectly behind me. We all looked our parts.

Once inside the Palisade, if we acted as though we belonged, no one should suspect our scheme. I was just another Attisian, walking the streets of the Palisade with my three Earthen attendants.

I pulled The Waymaker's hood lower over her mechanisms. Ves and Linah followed suit. It was a disadvantage to sneak through the Palisade with two Earthens who had practically glowing yellow hair and one Earthen with a head made of plastic.

And yet that was what must be done. The Waymaker waved me forward, and I nodded to my companions.

"Onward."

CHAPTER 46 :
MAKE THE FARMER
DO IT

THE MOMENT WE STEPPED THROUGH the hidden door and into the park, the panels were replaced by our guide. No goodbyes were spoken.

"Mx. Friendly back there," I jested, but only Ves laughed.

We beheld our surroundings. We had emerged within some kind of meditation or leisure park. Shrubs, flowers, and even the occasional trees were tastefully dispersed between paths of glass tiles and native rock boulders. To normal Attisian eyes, the park would be beautiful: organized, purposeful, efficient. But with my new taste for wild tomatoes and sunflowers, it felt sterile.

We observed the palatial homes in the distance, lit by colorful spotlights, and we directed ourselves toward them. More Attisians appeared as we neared the entrance of the park. They walked leisurely in small groups, flirting, conversing, exercising. I felt ostentatious in my expensive tunic and sparkling necklaces, and I sensed many glances in my direction, some analytical, some jealous, some admiring. Their attention made me cringe, but I knew that as long as they were looking at me, or more accurately, at my notable fashion, they were not looking at my friends.

To exit the park, we passed beneath an especially bright solar lamp. It alarmed me by taking away any sense of secrecy the nighttime lent us, but what alarmed me more was Ves' small voice ringing out behind me. "Wow! You look so fancy!"

The lamp allowed him to see my braid, tunic, and jewelry clearly for the first time. He'd never seen me in more than my work clothes, and he responded as the sweet boy he was whenever rage was not his master. But Ves' enthusiastic comment attracted critical glares from the surrounding citizens. No matter how kind the words, Bonders did not initiate unnecessary conversation with their

Taskers, especially in public.

I froze in their suspicion. Their eyes went to mine, waiting, wondering. I plastered a frown onto my features and whirled around to face Ves. "Child!" I nearly yelled. His confusion at my anger almost melted my resolve. I could not let my last moments with him be full of fake, hurtful words. Instead, with my face hidden from our observers, I made ridiculous expressions at Ves while acting out a rant. I pushed my nose up.

"You do not, under any circumstances, speak to me without my permission. You will skip your meal tonight." Under Linah's arm, Ves watched me carefully, trying to put together the truth of what was happening. I crossed my eyes. "Don't ever do that again, or I'll sell you to Mid-Lats." I stuck out my tongue. Thank the stars, a sparkle lit Ves' eyes, but he said nothing more. Good boy. Sweet boy.

A man, wearing long braids that wrapped up over his head and dangled in loops around his ears, spoke conspiratorially to me. "Sheking 'logs. Those Earthies will never learn." His female companion, with an identical hairstyle, nodded furiously, while her eyes watched the man for additional cues. I managed a bleak smile and clasped my hands to hide their shaking.

We passed between two lampposts and out of the park. I led them parallel to the main street of the Palisade and did my best to orient myself. As we walked, the nighttime colors and lights of the Palisade dazzled all of us. I heard Linah gently reminding Ves to keep moving and not to gawk.

Instead of the simple, square houses outside the Palisade, around us loomed multi-faceted glass structures with terraces, gardens, and artfully crafted ornamentation. Every surface glowed with colored solar lights. I wanted to admire it but knew I was supposed to look unconcerned and unimpressed, accustomed to the magnificence. I kept us moving along as best as I could and hoped that none of the other evening revelers would take notice of us.

I chose to turn right and head higher up the hill where the homes only got larger. Unfortunately, I guessed the wrong street the first time. As confidently as possible, I led my group back to the main street to try again. My nerves peaked as I paused to think. If I could not find the right house, our mission would be over before it started.

I dug deep down in my memories and found one where Sarai and I, along with a few other schoolchildren, sat eating ice bars and trying to look more grown-up than we were. We wet our lips and sat at exaggerated angles.

"He lives right up the street," Sarai sneered as her tunic fell low off one shoulder. We all admired her beauty, and it gave her power over us. "Let's go say hello." We had giggled and squirmed, but she convinced us to climb higher up the hill and stop in front of the grandest and most fortified house I had ever beheld.

Sarai stood brazenly, feet apart, chin and chest pressed out, and we clustered behind her. "Make the farmer do it. She's the closest thing we have to a Bonder."

She turned to me with just enough of a smile to make me think she was trying to be funny, but the words stung, as they always did. Under the unkind supervision of the group, I rang the doorbell. The speaker buzzed to life, but then there was an extended pause. I felt that I was being judged through the video function of the security system.

"Well. State your business," an annoyed voice finally crackled.

"Umm..." I wavered. I heard laughter from a place further away than I expected, and I turned to see my friends running down the street, abandoning me. "Nothing. Sorry," I murmured and followed them, my cheeks burning with embarrassment.

The memory was uncomfortable, but it provided me with the information that I needed. I followed the path from that memory, and I found our first destination: that same grand house where a young, ice-bar-covered Minty had behaved so foolishly. The home was just as spectacular as I remembered it, and I felt nearly as intimidated. At least this time, I was expected.

Buzz. Buzz. I rang the door alert in front of the sturdy gate. The lattice displayed perfect lines and geometry, complicated and austere. Money! Prestige! Ancestry! it practically shouted at us. Quickly this time a voice crackled into the night from the Aide system.

"Welcome, Mx. Araminta Bradford 8. Master Harkless Stille 8 is expecting you."

I stifled a snort. I could not help it. "Thank you," I choked out. "Please tell Master Harkless that it's ridiculous you have to call him that." I should not have said it, but my filter regarding Harkless never worked well.

"Yes, Mx. Bradford 8. He, he said you might say something like that." I could detect a hint of exasperation in the Bonder's voice even through the mechanisms of the intercom. The lock clicked its release, and the gate began to separate in a surprising pattern, not down the middle as I expected, but separating angles and panels to the left and right of the center. We entered a formal courtyard, and a few steps later, the gate closed behind us once again.

Here's where things get interesting, I told myself. Linah, Ves, The Waymaker, and I were locked inside the Stilles' mansion.

4 MEGAS AGO

*Supplemental excerpt from : Making a Way ; the Life and Stories,
Record HAC-3859385738*

Hettie's new life was difficult but better. After meeting Beecher, and under his guidance, she traveled between stops on the BackTrack, a network of free Earthens and some sympathetic or justice-minded Attisians. Each stop on the BackTrack was different, but often there was food and shelter, and always instructions on where and how to travel next. Once she buried herself beneath bolts of fabric to avoid the attention of some Stalkers. Hettie took in every detail of her journey; every landmark, every road, every place to hide. She drew a map in her mind.

Where she finally settled, in a tiny town on the outskirts of Fortmose, Hettie cleaned and cooked and farmed and did whatever job she could find. She went home every night to a small rented room, generously offered to her by a large family of unbound Earthens. Though her body always felt tired, and sometimes she still didn't have enough to eat, she controlled her time and made her own choices. There was no fear of abuse, no condemning words. She was free.

Her adoration for that new freedom eventually convicted her as well. She couldn't keep this gift to herself. She imagined her family and every other Earthen still languishing on the homesteads. Helpless and degraded. Always afraid. At the whims of their Taskers.

She sensed the pleasure of her God Voice as she started to save money and form a plan. She met a few friends that provided her with extra funds and supplies in support of her goal.

She could go back. She could help them get out. She could show them the way.

CHAPTER 47 :

THIS ONE IS DIFFERENT

THE FRONT DOOR OF THE Stille residence, made of a strange dark wood that was not bamboo, spilled out beams of light and guided us forward. A wizened, grey-haired Bonder escorted us into the home.

"Welcome, Mx. Araminta Bradford 8. I will escort you to Master Harkless' quarters. But first, please allow me to fetch someone to show your Bondspeople to the galley."

"Oh. No, no, thank you. You can be informal with us. I can wait here while you take my Earthens, Linah, Ves, and…Emmaline," I used my mother's name for The Waymaker, "to the galley." The Bonder fought to keep his eyes on me. He kept glancing toward the others and wrestled to control his obvious curiosity. Did he know The Waymaker was among them?

"Truly," I pressed. "Perhaps we can be casual tonight. Please take my Earthens to a nice, safe location. I insist."

"Ah. Yes. Yes, of course. Since only Master Mariella and Master Harkless are here tonight, perhaps informality is acceptable. It's lucky for you to visit on such a night. When the other gentlemen are away, it's a much more relaxed experience." His eagerness overcame his fear of breaking the customs of the house. "Follow me, if you please, Linah, Ves, and Emmaline." I felt certain there was an emphasis on The Waymaker's pseudonym. "Mx. Bradford 8, I will return in just a moment."

"Just Araminta, please."

"I wouldn't dare, Mx. Bradford 8." He opened an artfully concealed door to a flight of steps that seemed decrepit compared to the grandeur of the hall surrounding it. My three friends left me with backward glances, and I was alone in the great hall of that great house, doing my best to control my racing thoughts. I had expected Calhoun's absence with all the activity at his SpacePort, but Rankin's absence at the house brought me so much relief that I almost laughed aloud. He was one less person to fool. One less highly observant and indecipherable person to misguide.

The Stilles' perfectly polished, grey and black entry hall contained four doorless thresholds. Beyond each, I saw more grey and black decor, except for the one on the far right, where a flight of stairs, covered in an intricate mosaic of swirling color, rose to a second level.

Down from this rainbow stairway glided Mariella Stille 7, Harkless' dazzling mother. The softest tunic I had ever seen flattered her perfectly; the burgundy fabric clung to the right places and floated in all the others. She wore no braids, her chestnut hair falling onto her shoulders however it pleased. She looked both unattainably glamorous and completely comfortable.

"Darling Araminta! Has our Biko left you here unattended?"

"Oh, hello, Mx. Stille 7. By my instruction, yes." For some reason, I felt like I should bow to her. I barely stopped myself.

"Sweetness, please call me Mariella." My eyes shot up in surprise, and she laughed brightly. "Yes, yes, I know. While you are in this home, call me Mariella. Everywhere else, you should probably stick to convention." I nodded mutely.

"Come to the Day Room, and I will make sure Harks is on his way. You are here to see Harkless? Not Ran? Ran isn't here, currently. All this ruckus at the SpacePort has Ran and his father rather preoccupied." Between her expressions of attentive kindness, there was a sharp curiosity. She gave the distinct impression of the same observant intelligence her oldest son possessed.

"Yes, Harkless invited me."

"Ah. Harkless, then." She smiled and flashed me another inspecting glance. We walked slowly together through one of the doorways into a monochromatic room of leisure. Lush cushions, foggy bulbs of light, and a plush fiber rug surrounded a huge central entertainment hologram that displayed a cylinder of twirling vines and blossoms.

"I'm not surprised to see you. My boys have described you as a force to be reckoned with. We like big personalities around here. I know that after such trauma with your parents, life cannot be easy for you. We should discuss it." Apparently, Mariella was both beautiful and incredibly blunt. "Will you come back again for a casual visit with me? I knew your mother somewhat. I'd be honored to remember her with you."

I opened my mouth to reply, but I could not select any words. She had rendered me speechless.

"I'm sorry, darling. I know I come on very strong. I've been curious about you, and now here you are!" The surprising direction of the conversation and her startling charisma made it difficult for me to keep up. I expected that Mariella Stille 7 did not even know my name, but instead she invited me for a personal meeting.

"You're being very kind, but, um, everything you say is a surprise. I can't believe you have heard of me Mx.–I mean, Mariella."

"Is that so?" she mused, quizzically, but then a coy smile crept into her pink lips. "In that case, perhaps I shouldn't say much more." She glanced back to discover Harkless leaning against the black post of the doorway behind me. "Ah, here's my baby."

"Stars, Mother. I work very hard to achieve this chiseled physique," Harkless gestured with one hand to the muscles on his opposite arm, "and look very much unlike a baby."

"I know you do, my baby." Mariella floated toward the door and brushed his cheek. "Remember, Harks, I've told your father to take me to the holiday house until this madness dies down again. Too many people who know nothing are saying far too much about everything. It's ruining me. I need you to fly me to the 'Port in about twenty millicycles. I'm sorry you'll have to leave your guest so soon after she arrives, but please, Araminta, make yourself at home until he returns. He won't be long. All right then, I'll leave you to yourselves. Don't do anything I wouldn't do."

She paused for another piercing look toward me. "What a negative turn of phrase. It sounds much better to say, 'only do things that I would do'. Your mother would wish the same for you, Araminta. And you know, she would do almost anything." She smiled in a riveting manner. I could only raise my eyebrows in fresh surprise. To Harkless, she whispered loud enough to project through the entire Day Room, "You couldn't have dressed up for an evening with such a lovely companion?"

Harkless did not even blink, let alone blush, at her comment. If anything, he seemed more relaxed. And then Mariella was gone. In her absence, I shivered and tried to process the whirlwind that was Mariella Stille 7. According to Mariella, she knew my mother and seemed to think highly of her. And she wanted me to come back here, to the Stille residence. To talk about my mother. And–

"You do." Harkless brought my attention back into the room.

"What?"

"For what you've been through, you do look lovely."

"Oh."

"And you are great at talking," he said after a few moments of silence.

"I almost bowed to your mom," I blurted, still awestruck.

"Shek…That settles it. We are never going to survive this." He held out his hand to me. "Are you ready?" As cool as his demeanor might be, I could feel a cold sweat on his palm.

"No. Are you ready?" I asked him as he led me upward through his massive family home.

"This one is different. It's more than just sneaking fugitives from watchtower to watchtower or delivering supplies. It's more like a deadly game of chess," he replied. "So no, I don't think there's any way to be ready." He paused while interlacing our fingers. "But now you have an alibi, so we are off to a good start."

The pressure of his hand around mine flustered me; I still felt so unaccustomed to friendly physical contact. I knew he could see the fear and doubt all over my face.

Truly, Harkless did not look much better as he declared, "Come on, groundhog, let's go. The timing has to be perfect."

CHAPTER 48 :
SLEEP WELL, BE BRAVE

"MINTY, TURN OFF YOUR PRIVACY settings and send me something. There will be a record of interaction then; it will look like you've been at my house all night." Harkless instructed me.

"What should I send you?" I asked as I adjusted my settings.

"Get creative!" When I shook my head, and Harkless deemed things to be taking too long, he sent me something instead. A picture of a groundhog, making a twisted and toothy expression, popped up on my Aide. I groaned.

"Now, privacy settings back on, please. And you can wait in my room." Harkless gestured toward a pristine hallway at the top of the translucent stairs. "I'm going to get things rolling around here."

"Your room?" I asked shakily. The intimacy of spending time in Harkless Stille 8's room intimidated me into an uncomfortable sweat. He glanced back at me and laughed aloud at my hesitation.

"It's just a room, Minty. I'm no genius, but I'm smart enough to know that there isn't time for any fun bedroom activities tonight." I desperately tried to keep any color from my cheeks. "Right?" He let the question hang in the air, eyebrows raised with a wicked grin plastered on his face. But when I forced myself to meet his eyes, there was kindness and amusement there. "You know, like, games, reading with hot keff, naps, maybe."

I whipped around and headed toward the first door dismissively. "Bye, Harkless." I grasped the handle and pushed, but the door stayed firmly closed. I pushed again, harder. After one more hard tug, I swirled back to Harkless, hands raised, seeking an explanation. His look of amusement had grown as he watched me struggle with the door.

"That is Ran's room. I would never, ever make you go in there. For your sake.

Mine is the other door." He shot his thumb out and used it to point across the hall from where I stood. I crossed the hallway and opened the other door with ease.

"Ran locks his bedroom door?"

Harkless shrugged. "Ran is weird."

"You are both weird. Bye, Harkless."

"Bye, Minty." I felt his gaze until the door closed behind me.

Harkless' room. I was a stranger in a strange place. Warm and soothing lights popped on automatically as the door latched. The bedroom had the proportions of a suite, vast with multiple spaces created by the arrangement of the furniture. I wondered if Ran and Harkless' rooms took up the entire second story of the family home. Two enormous windows looked out over the downward slope of the Palisade and allowed the lights of the city to dance into the room. The austere grays and blacks of the space matched the rest of the Stille home, but the textures in Harkless' room offered overt comfort. Thick, furry blankets and velvety smooth upholstery made me want to touch everything, which I went ahead and allowed myself to do.

After writing my initial in the ample fuzzy fabric of a stuffed chair, I squatted and ran my hands through the sumptuous rug. My fingers sunk beneath the fluffy strands. Each slow step I took around the room left a print in that grand rug.

There were maps everywhere; most were hologram projections, but some seemed to be made of actual paper. Harkless displayed maps of Shamong, old settlement maps, maps of the planets around our suns, and maps that I could not identify, even after reading their labels: *The Grand Americas Circa 2125, Star Map Sector BA670, Lūnar Ring 2 Section 4x.*

"I see you have a thing for maps, Harkless," I said aloud before stopping at some shelves next to his bed. Hundreds of uploads stood in perfect alphabetical order, ready to be transferred to Harkless' Aide whenever he wanted to read or watch them. It seemed impossible that Harkless could have used them all, especially when I realized that most of them were historical records. And Earthen history at that. The quartz uploads near the front displayed titles like *Technology Before the Age of Gravity, The Last War, Earth's Crazy Creatures, and Ancient Religions of Early Humans.*

They piqued even my interest. We studied history in school, but with my eyes on Harkless' shelves, I realized that we studied Attisian history, with the rare mention of Earth and its current effect on the Outposts. But there, in Harkless' homemade library, there was so much more to learn. Maybe a thousand megas of annuals, records, and accounts of Earth sat there. I did not even know how long people had lived on Earth before they formed the Lūnar Rings and the Outposts.

I snatched a random upload and projected the summary with my Aide.

"In the years following The Last War, destruction of infrastructures and systems could not be overcome. As worldwide civilization deteriorated into tribalism, violence, and other chaos, elite scientists and other experts strategized to save and preserve the society of humankind–" While reading, I backed unthinkingly into Harkless' bed and sat down. Though I immediately sensed the luxury of the the blanket, I only had attention for the changes that my weight triggered.

Two subtle lights popped on above me, while the larger room lights switched back off. A dim clock and alarm appeared on the wall above the opposite pillow, and next to me, a large holoscribe flared to life. I could not guess why Harkless kept such a large scribe right beside his bed.

Hundreds of short paragraphs, sometimes only a sentence, presented themselves as I scrolled through the notes that Harkless had written, and the words were bizarre.

Drowned. Under water, hundreds of bodies. Earthens. They watched me, black, dead eyes. I couldn't breathe and they watched. I think they drowned me.

Havi crying, crying. I can't find her.

Stop hitting me. He laughed and kicked. Blood in my mouth. Ran said, "It's the only way, Harks." He made my legs disappear somehow and turned into an ABE with wings and then threw me into outer space. Just tossed me out right from the ground. He had those dead, black eyes too. Even Ran has the black eyes.

Dinner at home. Food was dead creatures.

They all knew about me. No one said anything. Tried to escape for hours and hours and hours. Had lots of good ideas at least. Thank Zeus I'm so clever.

The black eyes are in my ceiling. I just can't see them with my eyes open..

The holoscribe held a record of Harkless' nightmares, full of half-truths and terrors and lots of dead, black eyes. Tears pooled in the corners of my eyes. Dauntless, enigmatic Harkless had awful nightmares. Hundreds of them. I did not know how it made me feel, exactly, to realize that Harkless was so haunted by what he knew, what he did. I considered him a slightly reckless pusher of boundaries, but now it seemed he was just as scared as me.

The room lights popped back on a milli before I heard, "Snoop much?" from the doorway. Harkless watched me with one eyebrow raised.

"Oh stars, sorry. So sorry. I didn't mean to..."

"Didn't mean to read my diary of horrors? I can't leave you anywhere."

"I'm sorry. And I'm sorry about the nightmares... It's nothing to be embarrassed about."

Harkless blinked twice at me, then gave a resigned smile. "I'm not embarrassed. Just not sure I was ready for you to know how messy it is around here." He pointed at his forehead.

I considered the boy in front of me and let out a long, dramatic sigh. "Actually, makes me feel better about how messy it is around here." I pointed to my own forehead.

He nodded. "Right then, we are both exemplary messes, but we also both have a mission. Sitting here delving into our darknesses won't help Ves. Everything is ready. Let's go."

"Okay, darkness delving another time."

"Hm. Sounds like my kind of fun..." And he was out of the room.
I scrambled to my feet with a roll of my eyes, but paused before I left his bedside. Quickly, I typed in the blank space at the bottom of his holoscribe:

Messy just makes you human, I think. Sleep well, be brave. – A

I left the room and shuddered. If things went poorly with the Captain's plans that night, those words could be the last I ever scribed, my last thought preserved in the universe.

Embarrassing. I could do much better. But it was too late. Harkless beckoned me toward him.

CHAPTER 49 :

COMPLICATED THINGS

THE STILLES OWNED A PERSONAL StarShip called a Helicraft. Helicraft primarily functioned for planetary travel, but they could get to the moons and StarStations when properly fueled. Very few families owned one; most Outposters just rented Helicraft as needed from the SpacePort.

Of course, the Stilles' model seemed especially luxurious where it sat in a perfectly proportioned launch bay on their roof. The lines of the design undulated gracefully, and the seams of the metal and glass practically disappeared. My stomach dropped. Except for a few class field trips megas ago, I had never flown, and I had certainly never flown in something as tiny as a Helicraft.

Harkless, unusually quiet and once again holding my hand, guided me around the bay and to the back of the Heli. He pressed an invisible button that opened a hatch, then gestured for me to climb inside. There, already seated snuggly inside a rear storage compartment, hunched my three Earthen companions. Ves' teeth reflected the lights of the colorful city as he smiled, but everything else was hints and shadows.

Ves fidgeted. "Minty! Can you believe it? We are really doing it!" Linah had her work cut out for her with Ves. She would have to work hard to channel his anger productively and to heal in whatever way they could.

I climbed in tightly beside them after putting my dirty radiation cloak back on over my fancy outfit. I shifted and squirmed into a position that seemed like my best shot at comfort. An opening near my left eye granted me a tiny view of the Heli's control panel. The position put me practically back-to-back with the pilot.

Harkless reached to close the hatch. He looked grim, and that above anything else made me realize the gravity of our situation. "My mom thinks Minty is at my house, security and our Aides have a record of it, so Minty has an alibi. If things take a turn, let's agree to help her stay out of this. From now on, no one makes a sound. No one makes a move. This is where things really start to get dangerous."

He scanned the group, lingering on Linah. Then abruptly he flashed a huge, toothy, totally fake smile, "And hey, have a great flight!" He closed the hatch, and complete darkness concealed us.

"I've never seen him so serious," Linah whispered to me while we waited.

"He's scared about this one. I suppose it's personal for him. His house, his Heli, his family business," I replied.

"His friends," The Waymaker interjected. Ves leaned his head against my shoulder, and the quiet millis dragged on. The Waymaker began a song in a low, confident voice. My mind raced, and at first, I did not listen, but my attention caught on some familiar words within the lyrics. The Waymaker was singing her siren song, the song that called her people to her. I tried to appreciate the song and all it meant, sung in the rich, bold voice of The Waymaker herself. There was a power to it that I did not understand and that kept us anchored to hope in our desperate endeavor.

But then, "Shhhh," her song trailed off into a gentle urge for us to be silent. Soon I heard the faint sound of voices outside, one male and one female, but their words slurred through the hull of the Helicraft. I could not tell who spoke until they climbed into the driver and passenger seats. The tonal, unapologetic voice belonged to Mariella. Harkless sat next to her in the pilot chair, and my tiny view allowed me a sight of his hands pressing buttons on the controls. I imagined his hands scribing descriptions of his nightmares during the blackest of nights.

We took off, the hull vibrating subtly beneath us. The Stilles said nothing for a time. We hardly dared to breathe.

"Harks, you seem as nervous as your brother," Mariella eventually chimed, and it caused me to start. No one else moved around me, and I realized, thanks to the opening by my cheek, only I could hear their conversation distinctly.

"I'll never be as nervous as Ran, mother. I would implode, I expect. I'll never be as smart either, but that's the trade-off, isn't it? He gets the brains and the anxiety. I get the stupidity and the ease."

"Hush," Marcella replied. "I'd encourage you, but I know your ego doesn't need it. I just don't like you putting yourself down, even for a laugh."

"I'm afraid I won't be able to stop doing that, mom."

"How about just around me?"

"Fine, I'll do my best."

"Is it the girl? Causing your nerves?" There was a long pause.

"I suppose so." Harkless finally sighed. "I'm not sure she'll be there when

I get back."

"Well then go find her. If she is important, she is worth finding."

"Very idyllic, mother. Unfortunately, it's complicated." A gentle change in the rhythm of the engine buzzed my eardrums.

"It always is, baby. Don't underestimate my comprehension of complicated things." There was a pause between them. Then I heard Harkless chuckle gently.

"You are the master of complicated things, mom."

"Complication is a part of our time. We must face it or be destroyed by it. I love you, Harks. And I love your brother. Let's go find him, so I can tell him so. Oh, and your father too. I was almost able to forget about him."

Harkless chuckled slightly again. His hands moved confidently over the controls. A slight bump rattled the Heli and then the engines cut out completely. I heard every breath taken by my three companions as we waited, crushed together in a storage compartment.

It was a short trip across the settlement; we had already landed on the roof of the SpacePort.

And so began the next phase of the Captain's plan.

CHAPTER 50 :
A MATTER OF TIMING

THE SPACEPORT: CURRENTLY THE HUB of all awful things in Shamong. The plan suddenly felt much too big. For me. For my friends. For anyone. My heartbeat grew in pace and strength. Sweat gathered across the bridge of my nose. The hatch door had not even opened yet, and I was breaths away from panicking. *Save Ves,* I told myself again and again. A calloused hand suddenly grabbed mine and squeezed. I squeezed back, clinging to the small comfort the contact provided.

The door hissed. Harkless' bleak grin appeared from the opening of the hatch. Everything was starslight; no artificial lights shone to betray us. The hand in mine was not Linah's as I had thought, but The Waymaker's.

"Peace, young one. I hear your fear. Walk boldly in your choices." Her voice ricocheted off the hard surfaces of the Heli as I untangled my hand.

"Welcome," Harkless intoned, "to where none of us actually want to be. We're at the SpacePort, hub of planetary and intraspace travel on Attis, source of my family legacy, home to yesterday's riot and tonight's mission. This roof isn't made for take-offs, but a Heli this size does fine. Only my family uses it. Dad makes sure of that." He helped each of us out as he spoke. "Take some time to stretch, pray, whatever. Talking to you, with the direct line to your First Maker, Waymaker. The trip will take the rest of the night, so you'll have to get comfortable. I'll be back in no less than 15 millis. Everyone has to be loaded in by then."

His eyes bounced between me and Linah. "Everyone. Do we all understand?" I nodded.

He curled his fingers in my direction. "In that case, groundhog, you're up." Harkless and I left the roof together through a basic door leading to a bare staircase. In the dimness of the hall, he passed me a badge and a workperson's simple grey radiation hat with a wide brim that hid most of my face when tilted the right way.

He paused while I battled my braid and frizz up beneath the hat. It was not much, but combined with my dark radiation cloak, the disguise made me unremarkable. Harkless glanced back toward the roof again several times while I tightened my collar to hide the beautiful shirt and now extraneous necklaces underneath.

"You know, Harks," I said slyly. "There's still time."

"Time for what? And I like when you call me Harks."

"Time to go back and say something you haven't yet." His eyes snapped to mine, and he thought for an extended moment, barely frowning.

Then he smiled warmly. "Aren't you a perceptive little groundhog? I always say everything I want to though. Don't you worry about that." He wrapped an arm around my shoulders and turned us both to face down the stairs. "And it's not a matter of time, perhaps. Just timing."

He began the descent, pulling me along beside him. "Although time is tight, now that we're talking about it. Time to shut our mouths and do this outlandish thing."

The hallway brightened at the bottom of the staircase. We stepped cautiously into an austere, perfectly pristine hallway of uniformly pale panels punctuated with bars of precise illumination. I gulped. Nothing could hide in these empty, sterile hallways.

"Remember this stairwell. If you get back to here, you've practically made it." Harkless drew me into a huge hug, and I felt completely hidden inside his large frame and strong arms. Still unaccustomed to our fledgling friendship, I forgot to hug back until he was letting go and walking away from me.

"I'm going to go get my own alibi. Check that pager! And whatever you do, do not change your privacy settings." When he was nearly out of sight around a corner, his gait shifted back into the casual swagger that he most often offered the world. Barely a moment later, the pager buzzed in my pocket.

`From the Captain :` Proceed with extreme caution. Right.

How did the Captain do that? Perfectly timed. I searched the hallway for cameras but saw none. A bit dumbfounded, I stared from the pager to where Harkless had just disappeared.   I started to wonder...

`From the Captain :` And act naturally.

Right. No time for anything but the plan. I turned right. I tried to walk at a regular, inconspicuous pace, but I knew I looked more like a skittish animal. I wondered what predators hunted groundhogs. *Breathe,* I told myself. *Breathe.*

I followed the Captain's instructions further into the depths of the building. I took in every detail in hope of an easy retreat, but soon the hallways blurred into a nondescript landscape of light and glass. I wished the Captain could turn off some of those lights with all that foresight. I felt totally exposed.

Shek, voices! I threw myself against the wall and frantically scanned for a hiding place. No doors, no nooks. Just blaring lights. The voices were closing in faster than I could get back to my last turn and conceal myself.

The truth punched me in the gut and fried every nerve that I had not already destroyed with overuse: the owners of those voices were about to see me, no matter what. What exactly they saw, was up to me.

CHAPTER 51

STATUS

"SHEKING, SHEK, SHEK," I WHISPERED aloud. Near the floor, I spotted the only interruption to empty walls: a vent installed precisely between the smooth panels. I kicked it as hard as I possibly could and begged the First Maker to muffle the noise. Another kick. Three of the vent prongs broke apart and revealed electrical wires of various colors. My toe throbbed from the kicks, but I had an idea.

I whispered some urgent instructions to my Aide and called up a manual for my Farm irrigation system. I already had it downloaded, so my rigid privacy settings stayed intact. The projection glowed in front of me. I scrolled down to the middle of the schematics to obscure any obvious titles, crouched down with a hand on the vent, made sure my eight Aide dots were covered, and then waited, using every sense to prepare for whoever was coming around the corner.

It was a close thing. Two men appeared just a milli later.

I spoke too loudly into my Aide. "Contact Mx. Li 5 about broken wall, um, vent...at the primary SpacePort hangar on floor..." I glanced up offhandedly toward my visitors and prayed that they would not notice the sweat coalescing on the bridge of my nose.

The men, Attisians, wearing the same worker's cap that I did, stopped when they saw me. Confusion and surprise marked both faces. "On floor..." I said again in a leading tone. I tried to channel Sarai's overt confidence as I flashed them a smile and inclined my head toward the vent. "Either of you know what floor this is? I'm hardly ever in this building." I wondered if they could hear my heart beating since I could barely hear anything else.

The older of the two furrowed his brow, but the younger spoke readily. I estimated him to be just a few megas older than me, though we had never encountered one another before. He had likely not attended the same school in the Palisade that I had, since I saw only four bright pinpoints of light glowing from his Aide. "Floor G2. Mostly just Offices on G2. Some Parts storage too." He returned my bold smile.

"Thank you," I replied, trying to mimic his level of enthusiasm and eye contact. Was this flirting? Hopefully. It took a lot of effort.

"You're a little young to have a work assignment, aren't you?" the other man spoke, unaffected by my unpracticed charm.

"Ha!" I laughed lightly and pretended to read the manual on my Aide. "You're too kind. People always think I'm younger than I am."

"You know this building is on lockdown, right?" the older man continued. I wondered at his generational marker because he looked perfectly Attisian, even if a little unkempt.

"I know," I lied. "I happened to be inside already when that all went down. I have some of those special permits. You know the Stilles, never wasting time or money." His eyes remained narrowed and suspicious, but he also nodded slightly at my apt description.

"You must be good at your job," the young man said with an easy grin.

"I try!" My enthusiasm sounded overdone. I scrolled on my Aide again. "Well, thanks for your help!" I ignored them and waited for them to leave. My acting reserves were completely tapped. Into my Aide, I spoke, "Floor G2," to continue the charade.

I allowed myself a full breath of relief as I listened to the sound of the pair moving past me and further down the hallway. My shaking hands wiped a creeping drop of sweat on my nose, but then I heard a shuffle and squeak. Someone was coming back. *Oh, shek.*

I whirled around to find the younger one just a meter from me. His brazen smile gained a twist of shyness. My crazed expression took him aback, and he held up his hands peacefully.

"Oh, sorry to, um, to scare you," he stammered.

"Oh, that's...that's no problem." I forced a grin somehow. "I get too focused sometimes. I, uh, like my work."

His ease returned. "I like that. Hey, so, I obviously have no idea if you are partnered up with anyone, but I'm not, and I was wondering if I could buy you dinner next cycle."

I blinked. And blinked again. Of all the things I feared on this mission, navigating an invitation for a dinner out never even crossed my mind. He read the shock on my face easily enough. I could not believe the boy had been so bold as to invite me out with him. A four would have to be as brazen as Sarai or as feckless as Harkless to pursue an 8, but then I remembered the costume I wore. We were as good as equals as far as he could tell.

And then I felt deep shame for the thought. We were equals, in all the ways that matter. Generational markers should not matter. My own father was a 1. It was all so arbitrary, who got what and why. Even after everything, those discriminating thoughts came to mind so unthinkingly. I wanted them out. I would have to work hard to get them out.

"You don't have to answer now. Here's my Personal. My name is Abdu." He used his Aide to send me his contact information, unaware that my settings blocked the transfer. "Think about it, and let me know. Hope it works out!" He smiled warmly and returned to his companion. The older man tapped his foot impatiently but gave him a pat on the back when they proceeded down the hall together and disappeared.

From the Captain : Status?

To the Captain : Delayed. Turning down last hallway now.

I felt flustered. The delay could not have been more than two millis, but I worried it was long enough to ruin everything. My brain spun, and I had to recount the doors several times to make sure I found the third, as the Captain had instructed, in a long line of identical doors.

After my fifth count, I felt reasonably confident. I pushed the third door open, cautiously. With the door's movement, a light clicked on in a dark space. Someone released a low groan.

Sitting on the only piece of furniture in the room, on a stool much too small for the person using it, sat a dark man. Drops of blood fell from his square chin as he lifted his head. Both eyes, swollen almost shut with bruises, squinted even further closed to focus on me.

"Ahh." He breathed out and dropped his head again. "It's good t' see you. So the Captain recruited you after all?"

I tried to choke down the sounds of my distress, but inside me, anger and grief battled for supremacy. Seeing him–face beaten, arms and legs bound–I was completely ashamed. My people had done this. Outposters. In my oh–so–civilized Society, humans were treated with cruelty, people were penalized because of where or when they were born, and my friends just kept getting hit. Hit bad.

"Hi, Beecher." My voice echoed in the bare room. I looked at him, almost broken by violence, while a new, crashing anger caused bravery to bloom in my chest. "We are going to get you out of here."

Yes, but how? I pondered as I drew nearer. Not only did Beecher outweigh me by fifty kilos at least, but he also looked in horrible shape. Both his eyebrow and lip bled, and more blood dripped from his hands tied behind him. I sliced through the bamboo cords with one of Linah's throwing knives, and Beecher growled as his hands came free.

"Thanks, young one." He massaged his shoulders and wrists while I cut the cords around his ankles. "Freedom always hurts at first, I've noticed." He flashed a smile, but it served to widen the gash on his lip. New blood ran down his chin.

"In your case, it seems like it hurts a lot. How are your legs? Can you walk?"

"I took a bad kick to the knee, but I will crawl if I have to." Slowly, laboriously, he stood. I saw him battle the pain in his powerful body, the force of his spirit overcoming the agony. "Don't cry, little one," he spoke again. "I'm going to get another chance. That is good news."

Beecher had noticed my tears before me. I wiped blood from his chin and wrists with my cloak, but the fabric resisted the moisture and only smeared burgundy arcs over his skin. I lifted my cloak and used the luxurious fabric of my tunic instead. The blood left a dark blotch on the golden garment.

From the Captain : 5 millicycles. Status?

I responded with a short update to the Captain and then said aloud, "Let's go, Beecher. We are running out of time." Thankfully, with an arm over my shoulder and supported by my hand around his waist, Beecher walked. "Great job!" I said, incredibly relieved.

He tried to smile without bleeding. "Thank you, Mx. I'm very proud to know how to walk." Even with Beecher more mobile than I feared, our progress was slow, and reversing the Captain's directions took careful thought. Every left became a right, every down became an up, and I could not get it wrong.

From the Captain : 4 millicycles.

We climbed a staircase between floors, one painful step at a time, both of us sweating with effort and the fear of being discovered. The pressure of the clock kept building, but I heard more echoing voices down the hall.

"Back, back!" I whispered. We hid in the shadows of the staircase as the voices grew louder and then stalled just meters from where we hid. Beecher and I held our breath. Keep moving, keep moving, I begged, but the voices did not acquiesce. The workpeople casually chatted about their partners and the Gathering and effectively blocked our path.

An immediate response came in from the Captain : Confirmed.

The response felt devastatingly unhelpful, but I had begun to trust the Captain's ability to organize a situation. Even so, every moment felt like an entire cycle, and I fully expected the workers to smell the desperation in the air. I calculated the possibility of running for it.

Ping. Ping. Ping. I checked my Aide with a jolt of terror, but it was not mine: the workpeople's Aides pinged repetitively. "Stars," one of them grumbled. "Those Earthies are at it again. They're tenacious about this one."

"My partner says he's one of those political ones. He gives speeches and stuff. Kinda organizes things for the 'Logs. He's a ringleader, a real troublemaker. If you ask me, it will be good to get him outta here; things are getting kinda crazy around Shamong these days. Doesn't feel like it used to." A short pause.

"Looks like the boss wants us all down there in case it gets wild. I think our closest door is 1G3. Let's go." They left at a jog back the direction they had approached.

"Come on, ringleader," I whispered and supported Beecher once again. He had too much pain, or anxiety, to respond.

With a bang of a door and a gulp of the air, we finally made it. The night tasted sweeter than ever before. I could tell Beecher felt the same and more. It was his turn to shed some tears.

As soon as we threw the roof door open, Linah and The Waymaker were there, taking Beecher's weight off my shoulders and his own feet. As a team, we escorted the depleted Beecher to the hatch, and he climbed in gratefully. His skin blended into the shadows. I could hear his voice, but he had disappeared.

"Goodbye, for now, Mx. Araminta Bradford 8." Beecher grunted. "That number of yours–keep doing good with it."

The Waymaker placed a hand on my cheek before she joined Beecher in the guts of the Heli. "See? We can never really understand the whole story. It's a good thing, a good thing you are here. Look what The First Maker has done through you. Tonight, to Beecher, you are the hands of The First Maker." She climbed in.

The words punched me in the chest to the rhythm of the sentence. Time. To. Go. Three punches. I faced Ves and Linah. This was going to be the worst part of all.

CHAPTER 52 :
YOU CHANGED EVERYTHING

VES SQUEEZED ME IN A fierce hug. "I'll miss you, Minty. I'm really, really sorry about Orangey." He used the name of the wild tomato plant in his room, which he had once lovingly bestowed upon it: Orangey. "And running away. And all the rest. Sorry." The look in his blue eyes nearly broke my heart, but in a good way. It broke my heart because I believed his words. He would miss me. I would miss him.

"I love you," I discovered myself saying. The words felt like hugs and hits, ripping away and sewing back together, power and weakness, all at the same time. "Be so strong. Be smart. Ves, whatever happens, choose well." I used the same words to leave Ves as my mother had used to leave me.

He accepted a hand from The Waymaker into the Helicraft. With a heart cracking open, I turned to Linah to do what must be done. I had decided it would come to this, but the words always stuck in my chest and never made it to my throat and out my mouth. I had been a coward about it. And now, at my last chance, it was no different. I still did not want to say the words. But if Ves and Linah were going to have a family, I had to lose what remained of mine.

Something tumultuous boiled in Linah's expression. One of her feet pointed forward toward me, the other pointed toward the Heli and her brother. I had to do it. Now. If I was going to adopt a new way of understanding my world, I would have to live by it too. All the way. Even if it hurt me.

"Linah. Go. Go with them. Go right now." I began to turn her toward the hatch. "I want you to be with your brother. Be with family. You don't belong to me...or anyone but yourself. You are free. You should have always been. I'm sorry I didn't do it before. I filed the transaction the day after my Entering Day. It's all official. You are free. This is it. Go right now, with Ves." I knew my leaking eyes made my demands unconvincing, so I kept physically guiding her away from me.

Linah forcefully stalled my movements and made me look right at her; I would never be a physical match for her. She placed her hands around my face and held it still. Her gaze was proud and concerned. I blinked away tears to look at her pale features. Even if I could not say the words, I hoped she could read them in my eyes.

"I deactivated your SubAide. It is basically just a bracelet now. No tracking. I can take it off it you want. But it's your choice." I pulled her arm toward me and held my Aide at the ready.

Linah looked at me, only debating for a moment. "Off." She declared. "I want it off."

"It will hurt." I grimaced.

"Off," she confirmed.

"You will have a scar. You won't trick anyone that you are Bound."

Linah shook her head at me. "Minty, I've been dreaming of taking off my SubAide as long as I can remember. I know. I want it off. I'll be proud to show my scar. To tell all the stories about it, including the story of who took it off."

She thrust her wrist up to touch mine. I nodded and gave the command. With a click, a mechanism in the SubAide loosened and released its hold on Linah. She gasped as the device pulled away from her wrist and brought some skin with it. As gently as I could, I slid the SubAide open wider and removed it completely. An angry band of red remained on Linah's skin, and blood ran from several wounds at even intervals.

"I'm sorry," I whispered as Linah wrapped her injury with her other hand. We looked at one another for a breath, and then she smiled, ever so slightly.

"Don't be sorry. Not about this," she whispered back.

"Goodbye," I finally managed the word I had been dreading.

"Come with us, Minty," Linah said. "Come with us." Her suggestion brought a wave of longing. The part of me that felt strong, the part of me that had only woken up a few cycles ago, the part of me that I was most proud of, desperately wanted to get on that ship with Linah and Ves. But I knew I could not leave. I should not. I was an Advocate, I had my parents' Farm.

Maybe, just maybe, I could help somehow. There was work that only I could do. I was useful in Shamong.

Linah already knew my decision; I could tell because she began her goodbyes without waiting for an answer. "We will think of you every day. You changed everything for us."

"You changed everything for me," I said. "I will miss you, so much. Here, take these, take them all." I pulled the gorgeous, beaded necklaces from around my neck and pushed them into Linah's reluctant hands. "Sell them. I meant to give you more, but this isn't how I expected to say goodbye. Use them to start something new."

An absent glaze veiled Linah's eyes. "Minty – I can't believe I did that to that Lawman." She began to shake again. "I'm so sorry. He was awful but, but, I'm so sorry." Linah trailed off.

I took her shoulders in turn and gripped as firmly as I dared. "Look at me, Linah. You saved Ves. You rescued me. You rescued my whole life from him. And now I'm going to sheking save others. Remember that. You saved me and everyone after me."

"But I never wanted it to come to that. I wanted…a world where it doesn't come down to one life or another," she whispered. "I just want us…to be better."

"Me, too," I whispered back. Linah clutched the sparkling necklaces. The delicate clinks they made sounded like my heart slowly cracking open.

"We will see each other again," she declared to the universe with a weak nod. "After this is all over. When it ends, we will see each other again."

We let each other go, and Linah backed toward the Heli. Sick with sadness, her words replayed in my brain: When it ends.

Would all this turmoil settle into something different? Were we part of something new? Better? I had never realized it before, but of course, that was the whole point.

"The end…" I asked her, "How will it end, Linah?"

"I don't know," she replied right as the hatch buzzed shut and hid them all from me.

CHAPTER 53 :
EVEN MORE THIS TIME

THEY WERE GONE. THE WAYMAKER, gone. Beecher, gone. Ves, gone. Linah, gone. A hull of metal and technology separated me from them, and soon so would hundreds of kilometers and the vacuum of space.

The abrupt, unfriendly quiet of the night froze my blood, and I shuffled my way, alone, to a hiding place on the roof. I bit my hand to stifle my raspy breathing when I heard the voices of all four Stilles as they walked out from the same staircase that Beecher and I had just used.

"Honestly, Mariella. You pick the worst of times," a calculated voice said.

"Honestly, Calhoun, I am not the inconvenient person in this partnership. You will be working like a madman for the next cycle at least, and we never do well together during those times. Treat me like the expensive match that I was and allow me to get out of your way." Mariella's voice held no traces of intimidation while addressing her partner. She might have been the only person in Shamong that was not afraid of Mx. Calhoun Stille 7.

To her sons, Mariella sang, "Goodbye, my sweets. I love you always."

"Rankin!" Calhoun's voice roared. "Shutting down the 'Port today cost a lot of money. And we'll be catching up on things for cycles. It's ridiculous. Ping me regularly about the progress with the Earthen disturbance at the gate and the preparations to begin launching again. I hold you responsible for my awareness while I am escorting your mother to the Dinlas house. I'll be back tomorrow morning."

"I know," Rankin's flat voice answered.

"Harkless," Calhoun said, much more coolly.

"Dad," came Harkless' equally cool reply.

The Helicraft soon whirred to life, and I heard the brothers leave the roof. All around me, the noise of the Heli engine echoed off the glass, growing louder as it prepared to launch. I covered my ears. I could not bear to listen to them flying away from me.

Even in my hiding place, the Heli's engines blew my hair and clothes in every direction as it zipped up and off into the night. Calhoun Stille 7 was unknowingly flying fugitives to their escape. Even if he discovered them, he would conceal the news from the public; he abhorred a scandal; especially an embarrassing one. I smiled ruefully. Stars, the Captain was very clever.

My smile faded as soon as the quiet of night returned.

It was done. I had completed my original mission: Ves was on his way to freedom, away from his abusive Tasker. I tried to experience some satisfaction, but instead, all I felt was loss. Deep sadness swirled in my chest, and when I acknowledged its presence, it tried to climb up to my brain and completely overtake me.

My breathing was not working correctly. I stumbled across the roof to the regular indentations that functioned as a safety ladder down the back of the building. With each step down, I felt more alone and more unable to control my feelings. My faulty breathing turned into sobs that forced themselves out of me. I reached the glass pavers below and ran, scared that my noisy descent might have given me away. Someone spotted me sprinting between shadows, but my momentum was too great for them to overtake me. For a kilometer or so, I heard their shouts of protest, but I lost them in the alleys and dark by-ways of the city.

My steps beat a rhythm in the silence of the sleeping settlement. The glass tiles soon disappeared beneath my feet, and each step sunk into the developing soil. Sweat soaked my tunic as I ran up the hillside to my Farm. The first sight of it, a dark building in the dark night, pulled me up short. It looked desolate and devoid of the warmth of my recent life inside. The empty rooms mocked me: *Alone again?*

"No," I insisted. "No!" The sadness caught up with me and squeezed my heart, hard.

Even more alone this time, the dark rooms sneered. *Even Linah is gone.*

I turned and ran off again in another direction, unwilling or unable to walk into the Farm by myself. I ran up past the Boundary where the air was so thin, I could only choke breaths spasmodically. I ran into rocky crevices still uncovered by the new soil and irrigation systems of the ABEs. I ran down into a silicon quarry and scrambled back up to the other side.

My knees eventually gave up in utter fatigue. I collapsed and allowed my lungs to suck in air. Everything hurt now. My body. My heart.

White spots cleared from my eyes, and I saw where my legs had brought me. I was back at the Cemetree. A weathered blue strand of rope swayed under the influence of my heavy breaths. On my hands and knees, I crawled beneath the canopy of branches and back into the little copse of solitude I had shared earlier that day with Linah, Ves and The Waymaker.

"Fine," I gasped aloud and sniffed. This was where people mourned their Earthens. This was where they said goodbye.

It was exactly where I should be.

CHAPTER 54 :

VERY ADVANTAGEOUS

I WOKE TO THE SUNSLIGHT gleaming through the rainbow of the Cemetree. But the sadness in my heart had spread to my limbs while I slept and made me heavy and indifferent, so I pulled the blanket up around my shoulders and went back to sleep.

Wait, what blanket?

My eyes flew open again with a start. Hours had passed. The dark of night once again covered the hillsides. Under the Cemetree, I had lain for too long, and now a blanket tangled my legs. A pillow cushioned my head. A Harkless sat nearby.

I startled into a crouch, but he held very still. His demeanor was completely nonplussed, but also more solemn than usual, as he watched me closely. Neither of us spoke while I slowly relaxed. I braced my head in my hands, and to my undying horror, I cried some more.

Harkless Stille 8, the most verbose person on the planet, sat quietly and let me cry. When my sniffles slowed, he tossed me an algae bar.

"You know what I think?" Harkless began. "We need a brain doctor. One for all of us on the BackTrack. None of us know how to deal with all this. I should send a smart Earthie to school on Nyx. What do you think? Do you know any genius Earthens that could learn to help us out?" I ate the algae bar and felt less ill, but still had trouble caring about anything.

"My genius Earthen just left." I stared vacantly at an irrelevant spot on the ground.

"So…" he trailed eventually. "Why did you stay?"

"What?" I croaked back.

"I know Linah asked you to go with them," he continued while handing me a flask of water. "Why did you stay?"

I thought for a long moment as I gulped the water. I missed Linah and Ves, and I was afraid of continuing without them. They were such a part of what I had become, and now I felt lost. Lost, lonely, and afraid. All over again. Even so, I knew the answer to Harkless' question. I stayed because I was angry with the things I had learned. I could help. I could make things more...right.

"I'm just trying to do the right thing," I finally answered him with a gushing breath that I had been holding. "I'm scared of being alone again. It was so hard when my parents were Reentered. I don't like what it did to me, and I don't want to feel that way again. But...I stayed to help. I know I can help."

"Okay." He stood up and held out a hand to me. "Then get up, and let's go do it. Let's go help."

I plodded back toward my Farm, following Harkless. My big toe, where I had kicked the grate in the SpacePort, roared like fire. Without being flooded with adrenaline, I felt its protests fully. My limp made the process even slower. For once, I wished Harkless would talk more to distract me from my stormy thoughts. I dreaded reaching my lonely Farm in the dark once again. I would see it, and he would see it too, all empty and lonely, and I might cry again. Maybe I could ask him to sleep in the Day Room, just for one night, just to have some company. Probably a bad idea. Stars, I was a wreck.

"Harkless, are they safe?" I ventured through gritted teeth as it occurred to me that I had slept through most of my Earthen friends' journey. "Did they make it?" Even as I said it, I felt no fear of the answer. I already trusted the Captain that much. I knew they had made it.

Harkless smiled and, though the shape of his face was correct, it looked a little wrong. He seemed weary and sad too. "They sure did! A Tracker got them out of the ship, nice and sneaky. Dinlas is just a day's hike to a Bond-free settlement. Everyone is on their way. I suspect Linah's farming and cooking capabilities will help them settle in quickly, either at that settlement or wherever they choose to go after. For you, newbie, a Tracker is short for BackTracker. As in, one who works on the BackTrack."

Once again, Harkless was fully informed. Curious suspicion swirled inside me. Perhaps Harkless caught the gleam of it in my gaze because he averted his eyes. I would have asked more questions, but I tripped and fell, cursing my possibly broken toe.

Harkless grinned, more genuinely this time, while helping me up. "Eat another one of these," he passed me another algae bar.

"No thanks," I said. "I'm behind on harvest now. I'll have a bunch of surplus produce to eat. And even if I don't have Linah to cook it anymore, I don't really ever want to eat an algae bar again."

"You won't be behind on harvest," Harkless said offhandedly.

I fixed my attention toward him again. What a strange thing to say. "I've been gone for two days, right? I'm sure the whole town is a little off because of the riot, but the Farm is absolutely going to need some attention. And now, without Linah, I'm going to have to do all her work until I can find some more help." My mind flashed to that young, black-haired girl from the Exchange cycles ago. Perhaps I could find and purchase her away from her Tasker. I wondered if she'd let me call her Linah.

Not really, of course.

"It's so precious how much you love that Farm," Harkless teased. "But really, it's going to be fine."

"Very optimistic of you, Harkless. But thinking positively doesn't change the way you run a Farm. I know the facts, you don't." Arguing with Harkless made me feel better than anything else so far. I had lost a lot, but not my Farm, my newfound sense of purpose, or my arguing with Harkless. I would have to make do with that.

"Oh, groundhog, like most times, I know everything," and he gestured forward. We had arrived home. Instead of the looming desolateness that I had expected, all the solar lights shone out into the night, and I saw the shadows of a form moving within. Two produce crates were halfway loaded on the transport track. I stared in shock.

"...I don't understand. What is happening?"

"Let's just say that the Captain didn't want anything to point to your involvement: he covered for you. If you do want to become a Watchtower someday, you would be the only one so close to the Boundary, you know. Very advantageous."

"I did not know. Of course I did not know." I still could not decide how to feel about what was going on at the Farm. Actually, I still could not decide what was happening at the Farm.

"Everything is proceeding as normal, as best as they could figure out at least. The Farm needed to be preserved for you in a way that averted any suspicion involving your recent, ah, subversive activities."

"Harkless." My deep tone forced him to look at me. It was a lot to process, but the Captain once again had managed to think of everything. And once again, Harkless knew all about it. In addition, only a very few people knew about my recent proclivity for inhabiting the Cemetree.

I had to ask. "How did you know to look for me at the Cemetree?" He shrugged. "Did the Captain tell you?"

"...Yes," he stated after a long pause.

"Harkless, are you the Captain?" Silence hung there for a long moment.

Finally, he grinned, hugely and naturally in his truest Harkless way. "I thought you'd never ask."

CHAPTER 55 :
FROM GREY

"BUT NO," HE DECLARED.

"Wait, no?" He was such a jagwad. "You are not the Captain?"

"No, I'm not, thank one-hundred Earthen gods. I am so incredibly flattered though that you think me capable of such a feat. Maybe I should try. I should be a rival Captain! I'll start another BackTrack in direct competition. The ForthTrack. Get it? But maybe people could call me Sultan, Emperor, or something else better. Competition drives invention, you know. It would be for the good of the whole endeavor. Stars, you've given me a lot to think about, Minty."

I just gaped at him, and he laughed.

"Between me and you, the Captain is...impressed with you. You've handled a lot in a very short amount of time."

I struggled to keep track of what was real and what was Harkless' tireless wit. "Now that we have that out of the way, let's go inside and see how it's all going."

"You are...kind of a jag," I stammered.

"Indeed. But I am the kind of jag you are glad to have around, right?"

"I suppose so," I said begrudgingly but with a smile. He smiled back and took my hand. His hand was starting to feel familiar.

"In we go."

My Day Room smelled different. Amazing, but different. Instead of the warm and hearty smells of Linah's cooking, a boiling pot on the stove emitted a fresh and spicy scent. The whole room looked different too. Every dish, cushion, and kitchen utensil rested perfectly in their correct places. Everything appeared spotlessly clean, much cleaner than Linah or I had been able to maintain since Ves arrived.

"It looks–" I started just before a young girl bounded out of the hallway and barreled toward Harkless.

"You found her!" her energetic voice rang before being muffled in a hug from Harkless. "I knew you would!" I could just barely hear her voice from the folds of Harkless' perfectly tailored tunic. "When you didn't come back, I figured you must have found her!"

Harkless spun the small figure around a couple of times. Setting her down, he crouched slightly to be on her level. "Status report, please, Sunshine."

The girl giggled. "Of course! Things are amazing here! I moved into Linah's room and explored the Farm. I cleaned and harvested what the Farm system told me to. I'll have a lot to learn, but oh, I am so excited to work with all the plants." She turned to me. "Hi, Minty!"

"You will have to call her Mx. Bradford 8. You remember that, right?" Harkless asked the girl.

"She doesn't want me to call her that!" the girl insisted. "At least not when we are here. Right, Minty?"

I knew this girl. Sunshine was the perfect nickname for her. "Sunflower Girl, hi, again," I said. "Um, yes, calling me Minty is just fine."

She smiled. Something about her smile startled me into looking more closely at her. She continued, lightly, "Lovely! My name is Havi, short for Haviland. But you call me Havi. Or Sunflower Girl is fine, too. I like that. Or, as you just heard, Harkless calls me Sunshine. Hey, Minty. Where can I plant my sunflowers? There is just so much space up here! Nothing for kilometers and kilometers. I've never been up this high before. Did you know that sunflowers require very little depth of soil? I'd love to get a field going. Don't worry, I'll only work on that when the Farm is completely in tip-top shape and ready for anything. And you know what I mean by anything, right? I mean BackTrack stuff. Oooo, I am so excited. I can't wait to meet The Waymaker."

"Slow down, there, Sunshine," Harkless began. "There is no BackTrack stuff going on here, and even if there was, you wouldn't be involved. I went over a lot with you, but we should have talked about giving Minty a little time to adjust..." He continued on and on, and she responded on and on. They both talked over each other and to each other until it hit me in a flash.

"Excuse me! Please, stop talking." They looked at me with their faces identically full of amused interest. One was perfectly Attisian, and one was full of Earthen pigments. Even so, I felt confident. "You are related. Tell me you are related. You must be!"

They laughed delightedly. "Well, I wasn't going to tell you because I thought you'd act negatively to living with a Stille, but yes, you've got it. Havi's birth is what got us started on this whole thing, you know. She's my half-sister." They were smiling, clearly affectionate with one another. I did some quick math and figured that Harkless must have been just a boy when Havi was born.

"Wait, who is 'us'?" I queried.

"Hmmm?" Harkless asked as a veil of secrecy shadowed his eyes. "You said that Havi 'got us started.' Who is 'us'? You and…?" Even though Harkless denied being the Captain, he remained incredibly informed about the ins and outs of the BackTrack. The mystery of it all was beginning to drive me crazy.

"Oh!" Harkless frowned slyly at me. "Well, me and Havi, naturally. Got us connected with Beecher. Got us started. My father… well, he impregnated a Bondswoman. One of our house staff. Calhoun is…not a good man if you hadn't noticed." He colored. I had never seen Harkless embarrassed before, but his father's horrid abuse of his power deserved it. "The woman didn't tell anyone, but then after she was born, Havi very obviously was not the child of the woman's partner. My dad found out, followed shortly by my mom. Personally, I learned of it via the yelling and screaming occurring daily at our house. Calhoun sold and shipped Havi's mom off to who knows where, the devil he is, and buried the truth of it all, but we made sure Havi was all right. She's grown up in the Market where you first met her. She even lived in a youth house with Ves."

This was mind boggling news, though it explained the familiarity between Linah and Harkless.

"You did it again!" I said. "You said 'we.'"

"Yes, like I said. Me, Havi, and Beecher," was all he replied with a diabolical grin.

Sunflower Girl, or Sunshine, or Havi asked me so many questions about tending the Farm, some very relevant, some driven by pure curiosity. The number of questions she asked about my mushrooms and lettuce leaves showed me that, if indeed she was to be my new live-in help, I would never again worry about a lonely silence. Instead, the opposite. I might worry about my ability to sleep through all the chatter.

"Havi, there a lot to learn—" I began. The sparkle in her eyes made me confident she was ready for it. "And lots to show you, including a secret room where you can grow all the sun flowers you want. But I think, as far as running the Farm, we'll start with everything there is to know about tomatoes. And we'll start tomorrow."

I did not say much more as Harkless filled bowls of a fragrant stew for each of us. As I raised the first spoonful toward my lips, I wondered if it would taste of dust and gravel, the same way all food tasted after my parents were gone. But no. It tasted of heat and pepper and sweetness, and it stung the tissues of my mouth a little as I swallowed it.

I brought my hand to my ribs, and pressed the softness there, the softness that proclaimed my predilection for Linah's cooking and other delicious flavors. The softness that proved I had learned how to live in the grief of losing my parents. It was a softness that I would not let slip away this time.

My parents were gone, Linah was gone, but I was still there. And I was going to choose well. Choose even better than my parents.

My companions discussed everything energetically during our delicious dinner. Harkless occasionally cast a concerned look in my direction. Each time I was able to meet it with a mild but genuine smile. My gratitude for eating dinner with friends that night overcame my darker feelings; I missed Linah and Ves, and I would continue to do so, but this new arrangement was much better than I feared. Yes, I felt very grateful.

Before we all went to bed, Havi asked me if I wanted to approve of everything they had done, including how she had settled Linah's room.

"No," I said. "Make it yours. Do what you want."

She practically pranced away to her new room. I smiled to think of the next days. Tomatoes, then possibly chia…I created a mental list of Linah's daily tasks Havi should learn, until an important realization came to me.

"Harkless–" I began, sorting the thoughts in my mind. "I freed Linah today. I don't believe in owning another person anymore. Isn't that the whole point of the BackTrack? To free Bonders and treat them the same as all humans? I can't just have another Bound."

Harkless had considered this. "Havi is willing to be here, to help you. She knows I'm a Tracker and that you are an ally. She wants to take part. And anyway, it would help with appearances…Make you less suspicious."

"If I'm going to be an Advocate, my votes will speak for my opinion eventually anyway. I can't own anyone now."

"Then pay her," Harkless said. "Employ her, in a real sense." I nodded at the simple, reasonable idea. We walked together to the door.

"Thanks, Harkless, really, thanks. And thank the Captain for me."

"Thank the Captain yourself," he retorted. "Send a message. You get to keep the pager."

I looked at him quizzically. "I know you know who the Captain is. And I'm going to figure it out."

"Good for you," he said, and then he paused a long time. "You're going to be all right, Minty."

"I think I will, too. Somehow. I'll miss them so much, but…they've made me stronger. When my parents were Reentered, I barely made it through. I shut down, broke down. But this is different. There is more to my life now," I said, convincing myself that it was true. Linah and Ves had given me enough to sustain me even in their absence: purpose and friends. "We can make Linah proud here, don't you think? And we'll see her again someday."

Through a sad and doubtful smile, he just said, "I sure hope so." Understanding the ways of the world was quite a burden; even Harkless struggled to maintain his spirit under such a weight. He shook his head and his bronze hair messed into another successful disarray.

"Goodnight, Minty. Good luck with your Captain investigations, but first maybe get some sleep. I'm sure tomorrow will bring a new adventure."

I said goodbye to Harkless and went to my room for the first time in days. I collapsed into bed, grateful for the soft and clean mattress. Despite my comfort, my mind stayed alert and active.

The pager that rested carefully on my table buzzed. Adrenaline shot through me as I picked it up, but the message was not alarming.

    From the Captain : Glad that all worked out, Grey.

    To the Captain : Grey????

    From the Captain : I give all my BackTrack operatives
    pseudonyms.

    From the Captain : The title is yours if you want to be
    a Tracker. After all that, you've proven trustworthy.
    More to come.

I smiled, grimly but broadly. A Tracker. With a code name: Grey. Grey like the rocks of my home planet. Grey like the glass of my Farm. Grey like my Lūnar eyes. I felt known. I felt strong.

I pondered whose fingers had typed that message, whose mind had picked my new code name. What does a freshly minted Tracker say to her Captain for the first time? I had no idea, so I stared at the ceiling from my pillow.

    From the Captain : Tracker Grey, confirm?

The despair at losing Linah and Ves found me again, but it clung to me in a survivable way. It became a blanket of sadness, wrapping me in my love for them, but it did not crush me. There were too many other things to think about: training Havi, running the Farm, planning travel to my first Advocacy meeting, becoming a Tracker, and discovering the identity of the Captain all captured my imagination in turn.

Harkless had spoken the truth. Tomorrow was a new day, and it would be full of its own adventures.

       To the Captain : Thank you. Confirmed. Put me to work.
       From, Grey

4 MEGAS AGO

*Supplemental excerpt from : Making a Way ; the Life and Stories,
Record HAC-3859385738*

Her brother had grown, in height but also in grimness, when Hettie saw him again working the bamboo fields. She crouched, hidden in the weeds, after a grueling journey back to her original homestead. She would not risk revealing herself during the day. Instead, she sang her mother's lullaby. Many Bonders passed the day with song, but she knew the moment her brother heard hers. His shoulders squared, knuckles tightened, but with Taskers nearby, he didn't dare look for her.

She finished the song, "...take up now and don't delay," and snuck away, hoping it was enough.

That night, she found her brother waiting for her behind their family hut. He hugged her desperately before admonishing her for coming back at all.

She explained that she was going to take them, him and their mother, on their journey to freedom. She knew the way, she promised. Her brother thought for a long time, then told her to come back the following night.

She did. And waiting there were her brother, her mother, and another boy who dared to take the journey. Hettie at first didn't want to bring him along; he was still young, and she only had meager supplies for her mother and brother. She looked into his eyes, told him how hard things would be. When she saw strength and resolve reflected there, she allowed him to join.

Days later, they made it back to Beecher's town, half-starved. Beecher provided extra supplies and then sent them a different way, with different stops than Hettie's first journey, to other places that he called Watchtowers. Hettie memorized every detail of her trip once again.

She believed that her family's freedom would be enough to let her heart and mind rest. But it was not so. The souls of her fellow Earthens haunted her. Not with fear, but with love.

She knew the way. She had her God Voice. And now, she had practice. The God Voice whispered to her, "Love your brothers, love your sisters."

So when her family had settled into Fortmose, and she received a message from Beecher containing the location of some Earthens about to be sold away from their families, she was ready. "Will you help them make their way?" Beecher asked.

Hettie went back again.

END OF BOOK 1

ACKNOWLEDGMENTS

When one works on a side-project for more than seven years, one experiences many things: the first stirrings of inspiration, discouragement, eagerness, doubt, elation, and occasionally a complete hopelessness that the project will ever, ever, ever be real.

But now, it is. Real! This reality is due to so many people, and I want to express all the gratitude.

Back at the beginning, my sister Kiki read one disconnected chapter at a time. Her hype and willingness to enter the fun made me feel like my idea was not out of reach. My mom, who believed only as a mom could, reminded me that I have always told stories, and that maybe writing a novel was not as much of a departure as I feared it was. My dad dove in willingly, and he asked all the right questions about the timeline and the science. My sister Neen has a future in editing; her suggestions started to make a collection of events into a single story. My brother JoeJoe made me speak boldly about my project and even bet me money to keep me going. And my other brother, ButterJohns, lent his support by surpassing me in historical nerdery when he joined the family mid-way. My mother-in-law is a great proofreader and always ready to step up and in. My whole family contributed in overt and subtle ways to the project, my well-being, and my perspective.

My team of book-loving friends read early drafts and offered encouragement and critique. They let me blush and gush while talking about the characters aloud, and they were gentle enough with me on those early drafts that I didn't give up. They never stopped listening, and they lovingly responded to my desperate pleas for help. That's you: Jen, CathCath, Mal, LaLa, Amyham, and Karen.

My editor! Oh, yes, my editor. Isabella Betita is a word wizard, and if you found my book from a blurb or any marketing writing, that's all thanks to her. She helped me dig down to the heart of the story and the hearts of my characters. She was able to see all the ingredients, then helped me bake the story into something better. Work with her!

My proofreader, Jennifer Hunter, delights in color-coded edits enough to make me enthused as well. She made FROM GREY cohesive and professional in a way that is beyond my capacities and may always be. Work with her!

My spouse, CJ, always seemed to understand how important this project was to me, and never pressured the time I had to invest to accomplish it. He listened to all the brainstorming and decision-making, even after bedtimes and on date nights. He has been supportive with time and energy, and I am so grateful. And for a man new to fiction, he has had ingenious insights into the characters and plot. I like him a lot, even after all the years.

I have two wonderfully unique and delightful children, whom I also love and like thoroughly. In their futures, I hope they are so full of love that they can be confident and unshakable in spreading love around them, even when there is darkness or hatred. May they read FROM GREY some day and feel brave enough.

FROM GREY is inspired by real life events and heroes. Without giving too much away about the next book in the Outpost War series, I want to honor the men and women of the Underground Railroad. It was hard to write this story sometimes; to look directly and honestly at the history and to imagine who I might have been during that time. It was hard, because that time in history was hard. Real people lived real lives that were unimaginably hard. Unsettled. Violent. Wrong. The bravery, the sacrifice, and the fortitude that the heroes of the Underground Railroad displayed moves my heart. As their American descendants, we remember what they did, and are grateful. Please view the Appendix for excellent resources about the Underground Railroad.

Humans, all humans, no matter what planet they come from, are valuable. I believe that value comes directly from a creator God, and part of our job, in our short time, is to do our best to build a world that reflects that value.

As Minty says, "Our work is not done."

APPENDIX

While a completely fictional story, FROM GREY was inspired by research into the very real stories of the American Underground Railroad. The Underground Railroad existed from the 1780s until 1863 when slavery was finally outlawed in the United States by the Emancipation Proclamation.

The Underground Railroad (UR) was a secret network of routes and safehouses that enslaved people could use to reach freedom from enslavement. Some estimate that more than 100,000 individuals used the UR during its operation.

My city, Cincinnati, Ohio, was an active location on the UR because of its southern Ohio location. Kentucky, just to the south, allowed the practice of slavery, while Ohio did not. Once an individual crossed the wide and wild Ohio river into Cincinnati and the surrounding rural areas, enslaved people became free (unless a slave patrol found them).

The Cincinnati area is rich with former UR safehouses, well-worn UR trails, and a history of purposeful action in the face of oppression. The following literature and locations are a few of my favorite sources for information about the Underground Railroad. You may get some hints about the plot and characters in FROM GREY with your own researvh. I plan to provide additional sources after the second book in the series, INTO BLUE, is published.

Harriet, the Moses of her People

Bradford, Sarah H, Susan B Anthony, and Susan B. Anthony Collection. *Harriet, the Moses of her people.* New York, Printed by J.J. Little & Co, 1901. Pdf. https://www.loc.gov/item/16007872/

The Underground Railroad. A record of facts...

Still, William. *The underground railroad. A record of facts, authentic narratives, letters &c., narrating the hardships, hair-breadth escapes and death struggles of the slaves in their efforts for freedom.* [Philadelphia, Pa., Cincinnati, Ohio etc. People's publishing company, 1879] Pdf. https://www.loc.gov/item/31024984/

Harriet Tubman : The Road to Freedom

Clinton, Catherine, 1952-. *Harriet Tubman: The Road to Freedom* Boston, Mass.: Little, Brown, 2004

National Underground Railroad Freedom Center

50 East Freedom Way Cincinnati, OH 45202
Phone: (513) 333-7500 https://freedomcenter.org/

ABOUT THE AUTHOR

LISA ARCONA IS A GRAPHIC design practitioner and professor in Cincinnati, Ohio, where she has immersed herself in the local histories of the Underground Railroad. Because of a life-long obsession with both science fiction and Harriet Tubman, FROM GREY was somewhat of an inevitability.

When not designing, writing, or researching, Lisa might be found with her husband and two kids, most likely traveling, hiking, or planning theme parties.

www.ingramcontent.com/pod-product-compliance
Lightning Source LLC
Chambersburg PA
CBHW040902010826
48978CB00013BB/1114